THE HIGH FLYER

Nicholas Shakespeare is the author of *Snowleg*, which was longlisted for the Man Booker Prize 2004, *The Vision of Elena Silves*, winner of the Somerset Maugham and Betty Trask awards, and *The Dancer Upstairs*, selected by the American Libraries Association as the best novel of 1997 and adapted for the film of the same title directed by John Malkovich. He is also the author of an acclaimed biography of Bruce Chatwin.

Nicholas Shakespeare

THE HIGH FLYER

VINTAGE

Published by Vintage 2004

2 4 6 8 10 9 7 5 3 1

First published in Great Britain in 1993 by
The Harvill Press

Vintage
Random House, 20 Vauxhall Bridge Road,
London SW1V 2SA

Random House Australia (Pty) Limited
20 Alfred Street, Milsons Point, Sydney
New South Wales 2061, Australia

Random House New Zealand Limited
18 Poland Road, Glenfield,
Auckland 10, New Zealand

Random House (Pty) Limited
Endulini, 5A Jubilee Road, Parktown 2193,
South Africa

The Random House Group Limited Reg. No. 954009
www.randomhouse.co.uk/vintage

A CIP catalogue record for this book
is available from the British Library

ISBN 0 09 946618 X

Papers used by Random House are natural, recyclable
products made from wood grown in sustainable forests.
The manufacturing processes conform to the environ-
mental regulations of the country of origin

Printed and bound in Great Britain by
Bookmarque Ltd, Croydon, Surrey

To Barbara, with love

Author's Note

All the characters and events in this novel are fictitious. I am nevertheless grateful to Eric Shaw and John Fa in Gibraltar, particularly for their insights into the barbary macaque, to the management of Euro-Tunnel, the Trustees of Hawthornden Castle, to Natasha Spender and to my editor Christopher MacLehose.

Despite its position as the "the navel of the world", there is scant literature on the southern Pillar of Hercules, but I would like to pay tribute to *The Track* by Arturo Barea (Faber, 1943); *Morocco that Was* by Walter Harris (Eland, 1983); *The Other Russia: the Experience of Exile* edited by Michael Glenny and Norman Stone (Faber, 1990) and *Ceuta: Historia, Presente y Futuro* by José García Cosió (Godino, 1977).

There is no going back in the matter of sensation.

Ernest Hemingway: *Death in the Afternoon*, 1932

PART ONE

Chapter One

ONE AFTERNOON IN the African War a rogue mortar bomb spiralled into the bell tower of Santa Maria, damaging the clock. The bell continued to announce the time casually, after a pattern of its own. It was faithful to the quarter hour and often enthusiastic about Mass; otherwise, it might strike two at six o'clock, six at one o'clock or midnight at half past seven.

An engineer was once sent for from across the Straits. He was told how both the bell and the clock had been prised from a Jesuit chapel in the jungle of another continent. He returned to the mainland after less than a week, defeated by the unfamiliar system of springs and pulleys.

Over the years Abylans had learned to ignore the hours sounded out by Santa Maria de Africa. The chimes were a reminder, nothing more, for them to consult their watches. This was the reason many in Abyla knew the precise moment they became aware of the accident at sea. A thick cloud of smoke blotted out the sun as the clock struck five. It was shortly before midday.

The smoke unfurled off the sea, masking the city. It had an acrid, tarry, spiteful smell. Captain Panteco smelled it in Las Rosales as he worked on the file of the drug-smuggler known as El Callado. He was entering the name "Joseph Silkleigh" under the heading "Suspects", when a thought occurred to him. The Basques in D-wing had set fire to the prison! He covered his face with a lilac handkerchief and charged out of his office.

Joseph Silkleigh smelled it as he sat on his usual stool in the Café Ulises. He was staring into an open notebook. The pages

11

were blank except for the words "Chapter One" above which he had written and crossed out *A Man of Promise*. "The words are not leading me by the hand, Mohamed," he told the man behind the bar. He was reaching for his glass when his nose filled with what he knew at once were diesel fumes.

Dolores caught the same smell and wondered if it might not be something to do with the books, possibly those in the Local History shelves. She locked up the library in a hurry. It was Friday and early closing and she was meeting Rosita for lunch. Rosita wanted to discuss Silkleigh. She wanted to discuss Panteco. Depending on how long lunch lasted, they would end up talking about Ernesto, the conductor.

At that moment the conductor's widow was contemplating the cluttered drawing room of her apartment in Calle Zamora. What a revolting smell! thought Genia Ortiz, and she hurried to open the windows. The smell liberated several memories she had imprisoned in the green trunk under her bed: the empty lake-lamps in Balnasharki, the snuffed-out candles after dinner, her arrival in Abyla sixty-eight years before, aboard a ship wreathed in black flies. More disturbingly, it reminded her of Ernesto, whose memory she had made strenuous efforts to fumigate from her life.

In the dining room of the red house opposite, Senator Teodoro Zamora de Avellaneda Mancheño y Centurión, was eating lunch. It was a while before he realised the smell had nothing to do with the soup which his Portuguese cook had splattered over his purple cardigan as she summarised the plot of last night's soap.

Senator Zamora sat and nodded. But his mind was promiscuously elsewhere: on the Governor's letter, unfolded beside his bread plate, inviting him to be President of the Bullfight; on this afternoon's drive with his grandson, Pablo, to visit the rock formation known as the Footstep of Hercules; on the tunnel.

"Give that to me, señor." Señora Criado, concluding her synopsis, had noticed the soup spot on Senator Zamora's cardigan. Before he could protest she was undoing the buttons.

"Thank you, Señora Criado," he said, allowing her to peel

the cardigan off him. She held out a hand and he passed her the bowl. He gave his cook an erudite smile. "A day without soup is a day without sun!"

If it wasn't the soup, could the smell be in some way connected to his next course?

To Marie Amaral, closing her flowerstall for the day and catching sight of the rancid drift above the Club de Pensiones, the smell brought back such a terrible and unexpected memory that she dropped the yellow begonia she was bringing inside and her lungs filled with an Algerian night, a night of burning hair and animal screams and mad klaxons and flames of every colour twisting through the trees. Think of something else, she told herself. Anything but that, Marie Amaral. Anything. Her left arm had been weakened by a tetanus booster and she pulled off her gloves with her teeth. She needed the sanity of her flowers, but their sanity deserted her. She bent to gather up the pieces of shattered terracotta, the spilled earth, the plant. "Where shall I put you?" she said aloud to hear a voice.

She disliked begonias, but Marie Amaral could never throw flowers away. She would give them away, to the Café Ulises, to the asylum on Calle Silvestre or to old ladies passing through the Plaza de los Reyes, although not to Genia Ortiz who took offence. "That's very kind of you, Marie Amaral, but I only like white."

If there was no one passing through the square, she would leave the flowers in a bucket by the fountain. As an offering. By the time she unlocked her stall in the morning they were always gone.

"Who do you think takes them?" Senator Zamora's grandson, Pablo, would want to know.

"The spirits of the square."

"I don't believe you."

Marie Amaral scanned the shelves. No empty pots. She opened the cupboard beneath the till. She curved her hand behind her scissors, her envelopes for messages, her sulphur dust, searching for a spare pot, and her fingers met a hard object on its side.

13

She drew out a teapot by the spout. David's!

And here I am, not wanting to think of you.

She opened the silver lid. Why not? she thought. She put in the begonia, packing the earth not too firmly about the stem. She pricked the surface and sprinkled it with hydrated lime. Come now, she told herself, brushing her eyes with the back of a hand. Good eyes are not afraid of smoke.

According to *El Faro* it was "a smoke from which there was no escape, not even if you dived to the bottom of the sea". Hardly anyone in Abyla escaped it, but one of these was the driver at the shaft head of the Straits Tunnel. Not until the following shift, four hours later, was he to learn how the ship carrying replacement blades for his boring-machine had collided with a fishing boat off Punta Benzú.

Chapter Two

I

FOURTEEN MILES ACROSS the Straits, a senior British diplomat on his way to lunch paused before a telescope. His name was Thomas Wavery. He was a tall, silver-haired man, in his late fifties. An intelligent man, distinguished even, you would have thought, meeting him on the road to the belvedere – a contented don, or a financier to be trusted. And had he stood perfectly still, you might have added, observing his clothes and the way he held himself, a successful man. But when he walked, his shoulders and the cast of his face betrayed him.

He had flown into Gibraltar an hour before. He had taken the cable car to the summit from where he walked north down Middle Hill. The road inclined steeply towards the bay and was scattered with gravel. When a military Land-Rover overtook him, he slipped, but kept his balance by pressing his hand into a bank beside the road. He noticed Aaron's rod and Rock crocus and sawfly orchids, all flowers he had planned to plant with Penny in his retirement garden.

A drop of sweat salted his eye. He removed his overcoat and afterwards his jacket, folding it into his yellow duty-free bag. The bag contained his wallet, his passport and a box of chocolates for his sister-in-law, the Governor's wife.

He walked on, rubbing earth from his palm. The road widened into the belvedere. There was a telescope and, set into the low wall, a slab of Portland stone. "At this spot Her Majesty Queen Elizabeth II and HRH the Duke of Edinburgh stood and looked over Gibraltar. 10 May 1954." Across the slab had been sprayed FUCK IS GOOD.

Wavery stood and looked. Below and to the right of him was the reclamation project where deposits from the Straits Tunnel had soaked up the sea. An empty lorry moved towards Europa point, disappearing into the rock mouth. From that mouth the tunnel began its fourteen-mile journey to the African coastline.

Wavery placed his plastic bag on the wall and he searched for the city across the Straits. It was to be home for a year. Not for a moment had he dreamed he would be taking up this appointment without his wife. Nor had it crossed his mind that it would be located on the southern coast of the Mediterranean. He was anxious to have one glimpse of his last post.

"You'll remember the Yeats poem," Cullis had said, when informing Wavery of the appointment. The Permanent Under Secretary quoted in a Scottish accent, "The heron-billed pale cattle-birds that ... cross the narrow straits". He couldn't remember the title.

While not knowing the poem, Wavery was, nevertheless, familiar with the stretch of water below. He wanted to suppress his knowledge, but a dozen classical and historical allusions bobbed into his head. The channel had been dug by Hercules for his Tenth Labour. After separating the continents, the god had erected two pillars, one on either side. Where Wavery stood had been the edge of the world, beyond which *orbis terrarum* crumbled into the Green Sea of Darkness. These Straits were the key to the association of the Old World and the New. The Phoenicians had sailed through them, as had St Ursula, and Columbus, too, who had nearly drowned when his boat was attacked by pirates. He had reached land clinging to a plank. Wavery thought, I used to make love with Penny on that shore, outside a pleasant town called Lagoa. But he couldn't help seeing a man in the water, clinging to the small spar the Foreign Office had tossed to him.

Wavery fumbled with a coin. Like Columbus, he had travelled the world. He had lived in seven of its countries. Now he was

16

destined, in his final days, to be chained to a rock. From that rock, the southern pillar of Hercules, the Moors had invaded Europe, Count Julian sending Tarik's men to avenge his daughter's rape by the King of Spain. Wavery fed the coin into the telescope and swivelled the lens towards where he calculated Abyla must be. The lens would open for two minutes. He pressed his right eye to the glass. He had looked back long enough, he told himself. Now, in late middle age, he must look to the future.

In the channel there was a band of thick fog. A trail of dark smoke coiled out of the fog, transforming the horizon into one absolute and dreary blankness. In the smoke Wavery thought he deciphered the contour of a hull. When he looked again the shape had vanished.

2

The ape climbed urgently through the wild olives, the five fingers of fear on his back. At the base of the low wall shoring the road to Upper Battery, he sat and rested. His heart beat fast. He did not hear the herring gulls in the updraught, nor the lorries, only his booming heart.

The sea was in the wind. He could taste the spray. The wind blurted that his reign was over. It blew against his cheeks and unbalanced the haughty gulls. He listened to its argument. It blew through his beard, over his arms and stomach, blowing coldness onto cracked teeth and fingers knobbly with arthritis, patterning its current on the grey winter fur where his body had lost its slenderness and his hunger was audible.

A gall wasp circled his nose. He batted the wasp away and the sun burst from the silver case in his hand. He held it against his face. The surface was curved and it smelled of dry tobacco. An inscription read LAWRENCE – FROM EDWINA, WITH LOVE and there was a date. Mesmerised, he inspected the outcrop of limestone over his shoulder, the military pylons above him, the slopes of Middle Hill spotted with corn poppies. He rotated the silver and in the net of fine scratches he caught his own features.

He was contemplating the wound on his neck where Philip had bitten to the bone, when there was a movement in the reflection. He sprang about. Twenty yards to the left of him, the wild olives shifted and Charles' head appeared.

Until last night, Charles had been his sentry. But last night Philip had challenged him. Afterwards, Charles had blocked his path. They faced each other, listening to sounds in the leaves. They were the sounds of his children's heads being ripped from their shoulders.

Charles' appearance meant Philip was not far away. If Philip was near, so were Marlene, Catriona, Germaine.

There was a shriek of alarm and Charles disappeared in a blur of light fur. Futilely, he hurled the case after him. He was alone in the darkness of his fear. Desire also resounded in that darkness. He felt the buffets of his desire, his fear. Hungry, frustrated, angry and lonely, he climbed the wall.

The shutter closed on the telescope. Wavery's time was up and he had not seen Abyla. He raised his head and, hearing a scuffle, looked down into a pair of fierce brown eyes. Had he reacted by gathering up his bag and retreating he might have avoided the embarrassment of what happened next. As it was, his attention remained elsewhere. He continued staring, with the result that the ape bared its chipped teeth and let out such a growl of distress that Wavery was compelled to step back – and so abandon the plastic bag he last saw as a yellow flash tumbling down the hillside between clumps of lavender borago.

3

At the Convent, Sir Lawrence's ADC was massively aloof. He conveyed to Wavery the Governor's profound regret he could not after all make the lunch arranged a fortnight before. Something requiring his immediate attention had unexpectedly cropped up.

Wavery, who had been bracing himself for this lunch, said: "Could I speak to Lady Tredwell?"

He was led through a courtyard planted with bog primulas into a pale green room in the middle of which stood a round table. On it were two packs of playing cards and a history of the Royal Fleet Air Arm without its dust jacket. After a while he heard the hard stab of heels on the tiles. Edwina Tredwell appeared. She accepted his hand.

"Thomas, how nice to see you," she said glacially. "I'm so sorry about lunch. Lawrence's golfing, as you know."

"I didn't, as a matter of fact."

"I thought he left a message."

Wavery understood her remoteness. For three weeks since the announcement she would have had to endure her husband's contempt for the Foreign Office. Wavery and he had never got on. "They've sent him here to annoy me. He divorces my sister and they send him *here* – when they had the whole world to choose from."

"Darling, it can't possibly have been intended personally."

"Edwina, you have no idea of that miraculous organisation. I disliked him from our very first meeting. I knew from the start he would treat Penny like that."

"His message must have come after I left," said Wavery.

"I could offer you a sandwich," said Lady Tredwell tentatively.

"As a matter of fact, Weena, I've come about something else."

"Penny?"

"No, not Penny."

"I was sorry to hear about that. Both of us were."

"That is kind of you. But actually it's not about Penny."

She said, "We'd better sit down."

They took up positions in a pair of high-backed orange chairs. She crossed her legs and stretched out her hands one above the other on her left knee. "Well?"

"I've had a slight mishap," began Wavery and he described the irrational, furry mad thing which had swiped his identity. "There were some chocolates for you," he added.

"Oh, Tom!" Lady Tredwell's voice was a whisper. Her behaviour had altered. "Then it's the same one."

"Sorry, Weena. What are you talking about?"

"I *know* it is. It must be." And she explained.

It had happened two hours before, when she went to clear the breakfast tray. She recalled the crystal tentacles tinkling overhead and how she had murmured, "What a breeze." She was thinking that when the British took Gibraltar they brought their weather with them. She bent to pick up the tray and she screamed. Sitting among the breakfast crumbs on their unmade bed and bleeding into the eiderdown was a large Barbary macaque.

"It made off with Lawrence's cigarette case. That's what distresses me."

"Can Lawrence not do anything?"

"He's unreachable. I've been trying to contact him all morning, but he was so determined to miss you."

"I know what he must feel, Weena."

"When it comes to family, he can't see beyond. Are you sure you won't have a sandwich? We could eat it in the garden. You still like gardens, don't you?" she asked, as if that too might have ceased to be a certainty.

"Listen, Weena. I need a passport."

"A passport?"

"It was in the bag, with your chocolates. Without a passport I can't get to Abyla."

"When are you expected?"

"There's someone meeting me this afternoon."

"Oh dear," she said, and she had to prevent her heart going out to him. "Then it's not Lawrence you need. It's his deputy, Giles Hoyter."

The Deputy Governor's office in Convent Place was reached through a side entrance opposite a funeral parlour offering competitive terms for a repayment plan.

It was a grey building, in the Palladian style and newly fitted throughout in caramel linoleum. It had been used variously by the Board of Sanitary Commissioners, the city council and as a school administered by Loreto nuns.

Three flights up the staircase, behind a formica desk and beneath the gaze of his twenty-five-year-old sovereign, imperial, beneficent, velvet-robed and rather pretty, Giles Hoyter swivelled in the black plastic chair negotiated from a downstairs office and said, "Who the hell's Wavery?"

He listened, running a hand behind his ears through a skirmish of ginger hair. "Can't you deal – Oh, all right," he said, "send him up, then."

He had been occupied with the collision at sea. At four-twenty that morning, the Lloyd's signal station had picked up the *Admiral Grau*'s distress call. The Spanish-registered container ship had swung to port into the Straits at the correct latitude, but at the wrong angle. She was sailing two degrees closer to the African coast than the captain was aware.

The captain must have seen the fishing boat at the last moment.

In the panic and confusion, he failed to notice what had happened to his cargo. One of the crates had stove a hole in the hull. Another had upset a crate of turpentine. At some point the liquid had caught fire.

. Eight hours later the *Grau* was still burning. She had been holed above and beneath water line and had lost six thousand tons of fuel oil. Two crewmen were dead and four wounded. Royal Navy helicopters continued their search for survivors from the fishing boat. Meanwhile, the Merchant Marine office in Madrid had requested fire-fighting tugs to contain the slick. Hoyter was considering their request when the Governor's wife interrupted him with the first of three hysterical telephone calls.

As he listened to Lady Edwina, the Deputy Governor looked ahead with longing to the occasion, four months from now, when he would assume his position as Number Two in Tegucigalpa. Were there apes in Honduras? Probably not, he decided eventually.

Hoyter was a Foreign Office appointment. While not in any

21

way lacking the qualities demanded of officers from the E-stream, he was described in the report supplied by Personnel Department as not a high flyer. As the Governor's deputy, he did not need to be. His work was methodical, with a particular reverence for the password. The report determined that he was not an unpleasant man, though he might give this impression. Women generally disliked him.

"It was there, Giles, in our bed. Imagine!"

"Horrible," he managed, but he failed to calm the Governor's wife. She knew, as women do, what he thought of her husband.

On her behalf, Hoyter had been attempting to reach his governor. The Colonel of the Gibraltar Regiment also wanted to speak with him. He wanted to have the ape put down.

"Technically, of course, I don't need his permission," barked the Colonel who acted as Officer in Charge of Apes. Sharon, the regimental pet, had been named after his daughter – an honour he felt more keenly than his daughter did.

"But I'd be happier if HE knew what we planned." The CO paused. In Colonel Jim's pause – that was another thing about the military, their chumminess – Hoyter heard the unspoken contempt that had been his experience since arriving in Gibraltar: a contempt which spread from the Governor through the disbanding armed forces, to the staff in the Prince of Wales where Linda and Paul were famous for greeting everyone with their warm Welsh welcome, except Giles Hoyter – the contempt the whole of Gibraltar felt for the Diplomatic Service which had negotiated the Straits Tunnel Treaty.

"Jim," said Hoyter sternly. In the absence of his master he assumed easily his master's voice. "I'm in favour. Wholly. As HE will be. But is it *such* a good idea for the Gibraltar Regiment to be putting down its apes at the present time? People can be superstitious, Jim."

But the Colonel was not in superstitious mood. There was a wounded ape running loose through the town, looking for a mate. He thought of Sharon. "Send a car if you like," he said. "If you're so concerned, I'll make Sergeant Rossy available. He'll fill you in."

22

"OK," said Hoyter. He refrained from asking why the Colonel could not himself send Rossy. He knew it was the Colonel's way of implementing to the letter the defence cuts ordained by Hoyter and his ilk. Jim's regiment had witnessed every conflict since the Jacobite rebellion. The contemporary rage for pacificism was achieving what no German or Spaniard had ever accomplished.

"I'll send a car."

Until six months ago, the ape-keeper had been a tough ex-sapper who could stop hockey balls with his padded head and uttered strange sounds which attracted the Middle Hill pack into a silent circle around him. He had known how to swear in their language and he had sworn at them for twenty years until the death of his dog, an Irish setter which had grown up among the apes and presumably supposing itself one of them had leapt for a branch in a gully behind Windmill Hill. The keeper retired the same day. That was in June, since when Sergeant Rossy had been appointed. He had spent a year on an uninhabited island north of the Shetlands investigating the kleptoparasitic interactions of field mice and another year among the macaques of southern India. The author of a paper on promiscuous brood parasites in *Macaca sylvanus*, Rossy was the choice of the regiment's ecological lobby.

From eleven-thirty until twenty minutes past twelve, he outlined those features of the Middle Hill pack which, in his opinion, had contributed to the deposition of their leader. Hoyter took notes, puffing along behind, but still in sight – until a point was reached where Rossy embarked upon the subject of agonistic buffering, whereat Hoyter abandoned the chase and resigned himself to smiling and nodding.

His dissertation at an end, Rossy informed Hoyter he would be using a blowpipe, not a rifle. He would send Johnnie away in as humane a manner as possible.

"Very good, Sergeant," said Hoyter. He smiled. Who did the man think he was – Tarzan? "I take it you can find your own way back."

He was about to dial the Merchant Marine Office when the

telephone rang again. He eyed the receiver. Could it be the Governor's wife?

"Hoyter," he barked.

It was the desk downstairs. There was some gentleman wishing to speak with him.

"Says he's a colleague of yours, sir."

4

They shook hands.

Wavery had asked, "Might it help if you put in a word, Weena?"

"Not in the least. He's one of you. We don't get on at all."

"One minute," said Hoyter, at the same time pointing to a chair which his secretary, a girl with a high forehead, had drawn to the desk.

He was speaking on the telephone. "Darling? I'll be home for lunch. Did you go shopping?"

Wavery sat down. The desk was dominated by a plastic model of a neolithic skull, which Hoyter employed as a paperweight. There was a board on the wall to the right of the desk and pinned to the board a postcard from Paris, the timetable of flights to London and a motto written in green felt-tip: THE SECRECY OF MY JOB PREVENTS ME FROM KNOWING WHAT I AM DOING.

"Yes," said Hoyter. "Just the one of me."

The Deputy Governor replaced the receiver. He crossed his ankles. He checked his moustache. He leaned back in his chair.

"I'm all ears," he said.

In the course of his time with the Service it had frequently irritated Hoyter that the British public perceived Her Majesty's Foreign and Commonwealth Office as existing for the sole purpose of bailing them out of trouble. It was also an inflexible rule among Distressed British Subjects that they should lose their passports on a Friday lunchtime, not a Monday morning.

As Wavery explained the incident on Middle Hill, Hoyter leaned forward and rested a chin on his hand.

"I've never heard of an ape stealing a passport. A dog, yes." Most passports were ruined by children scribbling in them or mothers throwing them with the jeans into the washing machine or the sea pulping them.

"I expect you gave him the stare? I'm told they don't like that. Lucky it wasn't a leopard." He uttered a bitter laugh and telephoned his secretary to ask for two teas and a couple of those biscuits.

"He's called Johnnie. If you're interested."

"Who is?" asked Wavery.

"The ape who stole your bag." Hoyter looked down at his notes. "He was listed as a female until he took over the pack. In those days he answered to Margaret. They're named after VIPs."

"He wasn't with a pack."

"No," said Hoyter patiently. "He's been peripheralised. They don't like the term rogue male here, but that's what he is. He's been kicked out by a younger man. Break up, join up, break up. That's how it goes in these fission-fusion societies." He waited to see if the words had sunk in before returning to his notes. "It's the start of the mating season and his sex life is more or less ruined."

"I see," said Wavery.

"Lucky he didn't bite. They can give you Herpes B."

The girl with the high forehead entered.

"Thanks, Gill," said Hoyter when she had gone. He lifted a stainless steel lid and stirred the contents with his pencil. "You can't hurry tea. Biscuit?"

"Probably not," said Wavery.

"You weren't feeding it, were you? That's illegal, unless you do it at Queen's Gate." According to Sergeant Rossy the Queen's Gate pack were so obese they had stopped breeding. "They just sit on their backsides eating Smarties," said Hoyter, thinking of his Governor. "They say the syndrome is not dissimilar to that of humans who have everything done for them. But

you don't want to hear this," he realised. "You want a passport."
He poured the tea.

Thomas Wavery. A faint bell was tinkling.

"En route to Abyla, you say. I believe that's where the apes
came from originally." Hoyter rapped the skull on his desk.
"Which means us too, I suppose."

"I'm expected today," said Wavery.

"Been there before?" asked Hoyter. He and Mrs Hoyter had
passed through on their way to Morocco and hated every
moment. The dust, the flies, the Arabs themselves. They had
stayed long enough to buy a video recorder – which was discovered afterwards to have a problem with its pause button –
and a piece of amethyst sold to them by a child at the Moroccan
border.

"Put it down to experience," said Mrs Hoyter when the
purple came off on her hands.

Wavery said, "No. I've not been."

"It's a nice place. How long's the posting?"

"Until the Royal Visit."

"Your last post?"

Wavery nodded. "My last post."

Hoyter looked at him over his cup. The tea tasted of pencil.
"Personnel told me nothing of this," he went on cautiously.

"But the Governor must have warned you?"

"I don't suppose the Governor had the least idea you were
coming."

"Mr Hoyter," said Wavery, "Sir Lawrence not only happens
to be my brother-in-law, but I spoke to him two weeks ago."

"Dear sir," flustered Hoyter. "People come in here the whole
time saying they're the Governor's brother-in-law. What was it
you wanted with Sir Lawrence exactly?"

"I had a lunch appointment with him. But he cancelled."

"Cancelled his own brother-in-law?" Hoyter's smile was
almost playful.

"Apparently he's playing golf," said Wavery.

"There's a competition on top of the Rock. The idea is to
see how far you can drive towards Africa. He's been hitting

balls into the sea all morning. I've been wanting to get hold of him myself."

"I think he would vouch for me if he was here."

Hoyter placed his cup on the desk. He said, "I suppose we *could* stamp a temporary passport." In the circumstances there was something impressive, even dignified about the man sitting opposite. He dialled a number. "Gill? Get me Personnel Department, will you?" He exchanged a glance with Wavery. "In case you aren't who you say you are. After all," he said reasonably, "you could be pulling the wool over my eyes. You could be anyone." He issued another bitter little laugh. He recalled the last time he had rung Personnel Department over a matter concerning his own future. They had no idea who he was either.

He opened a drawer from which he produced a white form and, after more ferreting, a book with a torn cover. He opened the book. "Dewsnap ... Pulleyblank ... Queesal ... Wavery ... Here we go. Wavery, Thomas. Deputy Head of Mission, Lima." He wrote down the name. "Place of birth?"

"Mathon, Herefordshire," said Wavery. Hoyter nodded. "Number of passport?"

Wavery could not remember.

"Date and place of issue?"

"London. But I've forgotten the date."

"If it's London I can probably speak to the records unit in Hayes," said Hoyter. "Someone who knows you locally? Let's leave that, shall we. Visible peculiarities?" The pencil hovered. "Mole? Scar? Tattoo?" he added helpfully.

"No."

"Height? Let's say about six foot. Occupation? We know that, I think. Also conditions of loss." He chuckled. His concentration reverted to the Diplomatic Service Handbook. "Might I ask what your other posts were?"

Wavery listed them.

"Lima must have been nice."

"It was horrible."

Trapped in the six lines of Wavery's life, Hoyter had no

alternative but to press on. He reached for the second biscuit. "University?"

"Cambridge."

"Where you read?"

"Classics."

"Your wife's name?"

"Penelope."

"How many children do you have?"

"None."

Hoyter bit into the biscuit. His nod was approving. "And how long have you been married?"

"Thirty-five years. But we're getting divorced."

Suddenly Hoyter knew who it was. It came back to him that the man across the desk might now be serving as Ambassador to Portugal had he not been discovered by the Permanent Under Secretary in the embrace of a woman not his wife.

He closed the book and relaxed. Then he thought of something else. "Of course, this is an HMSO publication. You could have boned up on it –"

The telephone rang.

"Hoyter." He listened. He nodded. He looked across at Wavery and raised his thumb. "Personnel," he whispered, winking. "How do you spell it?" He spelled out Wavery's name. "Has he taken over from someone? Have you? No. He says he hasn't." His eyes returned to the desk. "You want me to describe him . . ." A note of embarrassment crept into Hoyter's voice. "Are you sure?"

His face went hot and red. He squinted at Wavery.

"How old is the photograph?"

Chapter Three

I

THE *BAHIA DE ABYLA* sailed out of Algeciras at five. It was the last ferry of the day. Wavery carried his suitcase to the upper deck. He had removed his tie and the sleeves of his shirt were rolled up. The deck was empty. He lifted his bag onto a seat and walked to the rail. He had forgotten to wash his hands. His fingers tingled with dried earth. Gripping the rail, he inhaled.

The air smelled of grease from the lifeboat cables and engine oil from the funnel. Most of all, it smelled of the bay which rose and fell in the wind, a short fetch between the waves. Over the shuddering deck Wavery heard the waves fizzing into tangled veils of foam. He followed the wake to Gibraltar.

Gibraltar had been everything he hated about England. He hated the Union Jack T-shirts and the early Christmas decorations. He hated the chips and the beer, and he hated Hoyter who was all he had hoped to avoid and a reminder of the man he had become.

He watched the battered hat of rock until the haze claimed it. When he could no longer see Gibraltar, he crossed the deck and looked into the grimy horizon for Africa.

2

"Now I know who you are," Hoyter had said conversationally, accepting Wavery's two specimen signatures. "You were ear-

29

marked for Lisbon, weren't you? Anyway, Abyla's nice."

But Wavery had not requested Abyla on his "Post Preference" form. For nine years he had written down one preference only: the Portuguese capital. In their inimitable, roundabout way Personnel Department had informed him the post would be his.

There was a time when Lisbon had been the least of his ambitions. He might have hoped for Paris or an important governorship. He had been going a long way then. The future held out promise of a knighthood and Wavery Commissions into an assortment of vexed issues. Once upon a time he had been a high flyer.

"I realise I held you back, Tom."

"Darling, please. Not even in jest."

But Penny was right. In the end, it was no good having a wife who was more committed to the German Expressionists than the Queen's Birthday Party. When a choice had to be made, at some indefinable point an enormous number of years ago, he had chosen his wife. He had been faithful for all those years and deserved credit. But he did not deceive himself. If he had left her he would have been sunk anyway.

Penny wanted Lisbon above all. "God, we were so *happy* then. Weren't we?"

They had met in Cambridge thirty-five years before, at a dinner party in Barton Road. It was a time in Wavery's life when the party always seemed elsewhere. He noticed Penny sitting in the corner, on a pile of reddish cushions. She sat with her long legs drawn into her side, tying the lace on a grey boot with severe concentration. She had dark agate eyes, fair hair she had forgotten to brush and a round white face. "That is the girl I am going to marry," he told himself.

He had been looking to make such a statement. He was twenty-three and a virgin. The capacity to love lay heavy inside him and he wished to discharge it full square, with maximum force, at the person with whom he would share his life. When she said goodbye to him that evening he smelled the gunpowder.

She was studying art, the daughter of a Suffolk lawyer. He was a third-year Classicist, the only son of a professional historian –

whose books, concerned with a seven-year period in the eighteenth century, he had never managed to finish.

Wavery was too inexperienced to know how we tell people we love them before we mean it, to create a space for love to move in. He recognised the distance between himself and the pretty art student. But with the confidence of a young Latin scholar he believed he might bridge it. When he realised he could not, he respected the distance – until, finally, it became a matter of acceptance.

At Easter they met in London. Penny was working in a department store on Knightsbridge, behind the ceramics counter. He was studying for finals. One lunch hour they took a picnic to Hyde Park. The pollen was bad that year and she spent most of the lunch sneezing.

She wore a new linen dress, white with narrow shoulder straps, but was unable properly to flaunt it. She sneezed again and held out her hand for support. He gripped it, saying how sad she couldn't see the perfect day around them.

All afternoon his fingers felt the absence of her hand.

When he returned to his aunt's house in Holland Park he wrote to Penny, proposing. He wrote out the letter four times before he was satisfied with it, after which he walked up Ladbroke Grove. At the pillar box, he was arrested by doubts. He paced up and down for half an hour, unable to decide. After half an hour, he placed the envelope in the box. He was on the point of snatching it out when he felt rain on the back of his hand. Rather than allow the rain to blur the ink in which he had written her name and address, he posted the letter.

They were married in August. On returning from honeymoon in the Ardèche, Wavery learned he had been accepted into the Foreign Service. Six months later they arrived in Lisbon, occupying an apartment on the lower half of a palace in Lapa. The apartment's finest feature was a broad, blue-tiled terrace with a matchless view over the Tagus. On this terrace Penny learned to paint in oils.

Their happiness was conventional. Both were delighted to fall into a mould. They were perpetuating a way of life and a class. They saw nothing wrong in their background, beyond the jibes young people make. If their love was not as passionate as love could be, this was because it had never been put to the test. Neither one had been denied the other. Together they were accepted by society. And they were young.

Sometimes after work Wavery would rush home with flowers from a barrow in Estrela, tumbling upon Penny on the terrace where she sat in a thin grey slip, undressing her as she tried to smell the blooms through the tang of paint and turps. They would weekend in the pine trees near Lagoa. At night they made love on the beach among the abandoned beach chairs. "Oh, Basualdo," she breathed, licking his shoulder, calling him by the name of the make-believe lover she had been awarded in her Portuguese class. She kissed him and the sweat on her tongue was gritted with sand.

When after two years Penny had not conceived, she saw a doctor recommended by the Embassy. A preliminary examination found nothing untoward. "He said he'd better check you before going further." But the problem did not lie with Wavery. Three months later Penny made another appointment. Wavery was sitting on the terrace when she returned from the clinic. She had not expected him to be there. He had told her he was having drinks with a friend of theirs at the British Council. She had not prepared herself.

"Michael had to go to Evora," He explained. He waited for her to speak. "Well, darling? What did he say?" But he could see the answer in her face.

In the months afterwards Wavery realised it was not possible to overestimate the misery of childlessness. It became a source of profound insecurity in Penny. He had daily to perform feats of assurance, telling her it made no difference to his feelings. If he saw someone childless he learned never to ask why they didn't have children. But when he did come into contact with children he was accidentally wonderful. Not having experience of them, he treated them like adults – which they adored.

For a while Penny's infertility bound them together, producing in her a fervour of creativity. On the Lisbon terrace she painted Wavery as he was then. Pale, black-haired, so black that others joked he used boot-polish. Intelligent. Efficient. But not vain.

"Penny, am I vain?"

"Totally."

He was proud of his wife, although he could not pretend always to understand her paintings. But he could understand her talent which blossomed on that terrace until it bewildered him. Once coming to wash her brushes, she found him alone, standing before a canvas. "I love it – but I don't see what's going on," he said.

"You don't have to."

"There's something so –" and he said what he had meant to say, "– so *gloomy* there. You're not gloomy are you, darling?"

She touched his cheek with her brush. The paint had dried and the brush was harder than she knew. "Thomas, when will you learn not to confuse me with my work?"

At art school Penny had experimented with gouache and aquatint. Then her most successful paintings had been blurrily delicate landscapes – trees reflected in the Cam near Granchester, cornfields with a patina of frost, studies of Wistman's Wood. In Lisbon she discovered the influences which transformed these landscapes beyond all recognition. She discovered surrealism. The Museu Nacional de Arte Antigua below their terrace housed a "Temptation of St Anthony" by Bosch, a few unrestored canvases by Romney and Reynolds, and a selection from the Portuguese School of the sixteenth century, whose motifs – decapitated saints, mongoloid Christs, fish-shaped Satans – she found pertinent to the twentieth century. Late Picasso she would acknowledge also as an influence; and a teacher whose lessons she attended at the Gulbenkian, who advised her whenever she found herself blocked in the execution of a painting to turn it upside down. Wavery had no such recourse. It was something he envied his wife.

Her favourite Surrealists were women. Their reproductions would decorate her studios: the shrouded figures of Sage, the

33

bird paintings of Tanguy, the uneasy perspectives of Ithell Colquhoun, whose gothic novel *The Goose of Hermogenes* she had discovered in a first edition on a stall in Sintra.

In those early days, she was nervous about showing her oils, but under Wavery's encouragement these made a stealthy advance into the drawing room. They hung alongside the Victorian cattle scenes supplied by the Overseas Estates Department and the signed photographs of sovereigns with vacantly royal expressions, and gradually Wavery's own visions of the Leper King's temple at Angkor or the Devil's Throat at Iguassu or the Benedictine woods behind Buçelas (originally a fond, untroubled memory), were replaced by a fissured surface of staccato colours disturbed by half faces, single eyes and animal horns. At moments of depression, Wavery joked, he felt accurately represented by Penny's portraits of him. But in truth he could not readily distinguish between her portraits and her landscapes.

She gave curious titles to her paintings. Time and again he could not discern a relationship between title and content. In "Danger, Mirror Ahead", painted in tempera, she staged a mournful dialogue between an empty guitar case, a serpent of the underworld and a moustache. "I thought of calling it, 'Melusine on a Saturday'," she told him, folding her arms. He thought she might have been teasing. He searched the canvas for clues but it resisted his participation.

He watched Penny type her preferred title onto a white card, the year in which it was painted, its size in centimetres and the materials used in its execution.

"Lovely, darling."

Many galleries had given her exhibitions. These included the Galeria Lobo in Lisbon, the venue of her first show. When there was a reasonable chance Wavery might return to Lisbon thirty-three years later as Ambassador, Penny was pleased – not merely for herself, intending to keep the owner of the Galeria Lobo to his long-held promise of a retrospective, but also for her husband, she being more ambitious for Wavery than he had become for himself.

Lisbon might also restore something that had gone underground between them.

When first he joined the Diplomatic Service, Wavery had been full of the great anticipations in life. But in Lisbon his ambitions began their guttering out. Asleep, he might dream of sitting again the Foreign Office exam, yet each day greeted him with the miserable pettiness of diplomatic life, until one morning, fumbling with the combination on the bag-room lock in Phnom Penh, the realisation came to him it was no longer Thomas Wavery who occupied the position of Second Secretary with commercial responsibility, but the position which occupied him, a position spent opening letters, answering them without exposing the Embassy to commitment, never ever letting slip what he felt; wax setting in the Service's ways.

After five years abroad, in Lisbon and Phnom Penh, Wavery was posted to London and discovered he represented a country he knew nothing about. He had been living out the middle-class manners of a generation that had vanished from the face of Britain. He had been speaking for a people that no longer existed. Like the boy in *Woyzeck*, he had glimpsed the moon and believed it was friendly. He had flown to the moon only to discover it was made of cheese. He had returned to earth. But the earth wasn't there any more. The earth was an upturned pot and he was quite alone.

Instead he saw its nation states and its cities reduced to counters. Budapest, Buenos Aires, Amman, Lima – not real places inhabited by real people, but each a residence and a large staff who formed a barrier to knowing about the city, or the country beyond it, or the people. They were counters in a game to further a career.

Five years became thirty-five. He rested on his oars. He crossed his fingers behind his back, hoping no one suspected the truth about him, merely playing the role expected of an officer in the Administrative Stream, the part of a responsible, patriotic, intelligent, efficient and above all virtuous career diplomat. And no one did suspect. They might see he lacked the hunger for high office – and the day must have arrived when it was decided he would never be given Paris or Moscow after all – but they thought incredibly well of him, at any rate well enough for Lisbon, which was the only post he coveted anyway.

At fifty-eight, Wavery had a fine haggard look. He was not a handsome man feature for feature, but he exerted a definite presence. He had the aura of a wise man and people deferred to him. If a conversation bored or irritated him he did not let it show. When he looked at you his gaze was always active and direct. That was his gift, a talent for appearing interested. Of himself, he never revealed anything. You never enquired what it was that shamed or hurt or excited Thomas Wavery because whatever it was he had a knack of burying away. He was content to be the kind of quiet Englishman who had attributed to him all sorts of resources and strengths he did not possess. Women found him attractive because he exuded an air of safety, but it did not cross his mind to be unfaithful, as much out of support for Penny as from an incomplete sense of himself. Diplomatic life had been a continuous party at which he could not be himself. After years and years of not being himself he was beginning to believe there was no self to be.

And in that limbo, love had also died.

Encouraged to put down roots, and then to tear them up every three years, Wavery became wary of going too deep. He remembered the hurt it had caused him when he broke off friendships in those early years, in Portugal, Cambodia, Jordan. He learned to protect himself and never to become too intimate. He learned the skill of evading anything which might disturb him.

Without knowing it, he found himself behaving in the same manner towards his wife. They had been married ten years when Penny said, "Whatever happened to your hands?"

"My hands?"

She had been sitting back, contemplating him. "I've just been thinking, you never wave your hands anymore."

"Don't I?"

"You're tired, darling, aren't you?"

She came forward and embraced him. "Tom, I'm sorry," she said, her closed eyes adding, "Sorry for not giving you children. Sorry that I have found a life instead."

Penny's paintings were the children they had never had. She lavished on them what once she had lavished on him and over a period he came to miss the burnish of her attention which he received whenever he sat for her. And Wavery, looking at his wife as she painted him, would think: That palette knife is a scalpel. She is scraping herself into her work. She is giving to her art bits and pieces of herself which can never be retrieved. The better the work, the more its completion leaves her diminished, exhausted, brittle. The more it drives us apart.

When signing the portrait, she wrote P. Tredwell, not her married name. "Penny Wavery – too many y's," she explained making a face, and he thought he understood. He didn't want it to hurt him, but it did.

He grew to be in awe of her art and the people she met through it. She had gone further in life than he had. Some part of himself that in her was satisfied on canvas lay unresolved and combustible inside him. He had his work, but the work you did in an embassy offered no landscape to anyone.

As Penny grew more successful as an artist, Wavery made an effort to create a landscape for himself. To his surprise and delight he discovered he possessed a natural talent for gardening. Luck played a part, and intuition, in particular the way he learned to feed his plants – not too much nor too late, but as they came out of the dormant season. He might have been a childless, unfathering creature, but he was able to bring plants to life.

"Of course, it's very akin to being a painter," Penny would tell visitors, more and more of whom tended to be fellow artists. "He takes everything from his own palette. But instead of putting it into words or pictures, he makes a little curve of lime green or a patch of blue. The only drawback is the place is so full of bees."

He dreamed of the gardens he had been forced to leave behind.

Travel exacerbated the distance between them. Those people who once would have been her friends, she no longer tolerated. She complained that his colleagues treated her simply as a decoration, a leaf of lettuce to brighten up one of those plates in the Ambassador's residence embossed with lions and unicorns. Wavery felt in his heart, on the contrary, he was the useless one.

To himself he argued that his heart was a robust thing. It would fill again like the magic cistern they visited near Petra, where water was a crop that ripened, oozing mysteriously from the rocky walls. But he felt unreplenished until the time came when he told Penny he loved her and she, recognising the tone he employed to appreciate her paintings, said, "No, Thomas. You don't love me. You're just very, very fond of me."

She was right. She had not called him Basualdo for many years. He longed to experience the passion they had lost. He thought, people never tell you about the end of sex. In the silted channels of his desire, he noticed each new hair on her breast, each scratchmark below her eye. He saw all her vulnerable parts and he exaggerated them. He criticised Penny mercilessly to himself. Because he loved her, loved her, loved her, he told himself. But it wasn't that. The sweet words he had used to preface their lovemaking, he now used later – usually following an argument. In this new territory, it became easy to argue, to say the wrong thing, to dip the brush in any number of false colours, to apply another small, indelible mark to the portrait of their life together.

To avoid unpleasant scenes at home, it became natural to employ the distancing platitudes of the office. His words missed their mark deliberately, as wrongly sighted as a fairground rifle, until the moment arrived in the sixteenth year of their marriage when they both felt they understood each other enough and this feeling went hand in hand with the sense that they had nothing more to say, or could risk saying. When questioned by a third party Wavery chose to abdicate responsibility. "Who is my favourite modern author, darling?" "What newspapers do we take on a Sunday in England?" "When is our farewell party?"

Penny knew that by deferring to her he was able to satisfy himself that a dialogue had taken place.

Wavery was content to live with his unfulfilment. Penny was less content. She had been inflamed by his passion, loving things in him even he found repellent. When his passion subsided, fading imperceptibly, she continued to feel the scalds.

So they proceeded in the pantomime horse of their marriage, towards the Lisbon Embassy, followed by compulsory retirement at sixty –"Just when you know what you're talking about!" – in a cottage on the Sintra hills, where he planned to lay out a garden modelled on Monserrate and look at the sea through olive trees.

Then one evening towards the end of his time in Lima, they were invited to supper by the American Chargé d'Affaires.

"It's very informal," said Penny. "He won't be wearing a tie."

Wavery had not wanted to go. The Tennysons' house was lah-di-dah gone mad and party games were promised. But Penny insisted. Rita was one of the few diplomatic wives Penny liked. Attractive to men, Rita reserved her fiercer sympathies for women.

Penny said, "You can't pretend Denver's thrilling, because he isn't. He's a perky bore. But Rita does throw good parties." Besides, Rita was the President of the Damas Diplomaticas. "She's not your type, but she's doing a lot for the young wives."

He returned home late. A bomb had exploded near the Pan-Americana, killing a policeman. The traffic thinned beyond the Gold Museum. Wavery turned right, past an empty playground from where the shouts of children woke him in the morning. He hooted twice at his gate. Antonio reached in to take his attaché case.

He said, "Gin-tonic, Antonio."

He tumbled a week's worth of *Times* onto the sofa.

"Penny?"

He walked towards the bedroom, untying his tie.

"I'm ready." She came into the bedroom from the bathroom. She was over-dressed. She wore her fair hair in curls, a treat she liked to give him. He preferred her hair long and unbrushed, but by the time he had acquired the courage to tell her, it was too late. The curls bobbed against the earrings he had bought in Buenos Aires – her favourites, she claimed, overlooking their tendency to inflame her lobes.

"How was the office?" It was a courtesy question. Out of courtesy he answered that the Ambassador suspected two policemen guarding his residence of involvement in drugs trafficking. "And there's a letter from Lawrence."

"That's nice," and then, "That's the fourth bomb this week." She opened a cupboard, separating some dresses. The hangers grated as they grated every morning when she rose to paint and poked about for something to wear. Once, removing the pillow from his face, Wavery asked, "Why not decide before going to bed?"

"Because I don't know if I'll wake up feeling fat or thin, ugly or pretty."

She drew out a crimson alpaca shawl. "I hate this place."

"Only three weeks now."

"Why haven't we heard. I suppose you still haven't heard?"

Wavery shook his head. "They have other things to think about." There was the Gulf. There was South Africa. There were the French farmers. "Lisbon's not that important. They'll probably tell me in London."

"Did you ring Personnel Department?"

"I left a message. I couldn't get through to Dewsnap."

"*Again?*"

"He'll ring tomorrow, I'm sure."

"Bloody Foreign Office. They send you to the end of the world and then take the phone off the hook."

"It's my bread and butter, Penny."

"But look at the way they treat you." She threw the metal hanger onto the bed and walked to the window. "I look out at this fog and I wish I was in bed with a bear."

He said, "Have I time for a bath?"

"She wants us at eight."

"Not even a small one?" But he didn't insist. He telephoned

Antonio. "Antonio, don't bother with that drink." He changed into a pair of flannel trousers folded on a chair beside her easel. In the cupboard he found a shirt and a jacket.

"You're not serious?" she said. "That shirt. With that jacket?"

He felt stupid. "Why not? The jacket's Harris tweed. And you gave me the shirt."

"I may have bought it, but I didn't expect you to wear it with a jacket like that." She left the room and Wavery dressed. He was not interested in clothes. All his work went into the initial purchase. Once he had made the effort to buy something good, he felt it had to look after itself on him, an attitude which annoyed Penny.

Her unhappiness tonight upset Wavery. He tried to conjure away the moment, hoping it was dust on the needle. But he knew it was more than dust. Long ago Penny had parted company with the young woman he had sat down beside on a Cambridge floor. Wavery was different too. In earlier days he would have had his bath come what may.

Afterwards, Wavery told himself: had he insisted on his bath, they would have left the house in Monterrico fifteen minutes later and the evening would have been no different from a thousand such evenings.

They would have walked through the Tennysons' door, his arm at her back, suspended two inches above her shawl, and they would have greeted Rita, a tall woman with a long neck and sharp elbows, who was telling the Colombian Defense Attaché, a man with crumbs on his face, "It's life, isn't it, and life is people and if you don't invest in people . . .", and Rita, catching sight of Penny would have said, "Remember Tino?" who had grasped the opportunity to vanish in pursuit of a tray, and Penny would say, "Yes, he's frightfully nice," and Rita would say, "Thomas would like him," and stick a piece of paper on their backs with the name of someone famous whom they had to guess by asking ten questions, yes or no answers, no cheating, mind, and why don't you start with Denver, he still doesn't know who he is, no, really he doesn't, and dutifully they would make their way over to Denver, to find a placard on his back with the words

KING KONG, and Denver who was a little hard of hearing so one was obliged to repeat oneself would smile fixedly and ask, "Am I alive?" and tell Wavery that Rita always had such nice friends and this was their very good friend Mr Riding who'd just come from London on business and Wavery would politely have enquired of the good-looking, florid-faced man with CLARK GABLE on his back how long he had been in the wine trade, and the waitress whose shoulders Mr Riding was squeezing would pause long enough for Penny to remove a tomato juice and Wavery would take a gin and tonic and two long swallows and Will you excuse me? cross the room to greet his Ambassador, a man with a whim of steel who had published a monograph on the whiskered tern and kept black-necked geese in the residence garden, and they would talk about the latest bomb in a spiritless way, the Ambassador blinking because he believed himself to be a security risk, and too distracted to ask Wavery a yes, no question, he would say he must go and speak with Denver who had a fairly good ear to the ground, and turning reveal himself as RONALD BIGGS which was perhaps not a clever move on Rita's part, and Wavery feeling very dull would move towards the buffet table where presently Penny would join him escorted by a Peruvian artist, a dirty word in the art world, having overcleaned the treasures of Lima's National Gallery, who was giving her some painterly advice he'd picked up from a most terrible woman, his mother, and Penny would tell him in her most earnest voice, "I believe people who hate their mothers often get on very well in life," and did he know her husband, they were chalk and cheese, which is so much better – if you have things in common, you only fight over them, to which the artist would reply holding Wavery's hand for several seconds longer than necessary, "I have heard proof he is of our species," and very shortly afterwards, to escape the German Cultural Attaché, a narcolept who fell asleep in mid-sentence, to escape the wife of the French Number Two, an attender of poetry readings, "I'm coming to talk to you when I've done my stint with Denver!", to escape the cigarette smoke and the fly-plague of questions, am I dead? am I alive? am I a movie-star?

a politician? no seriously, Jesus Christ?, to escape for a moment this party and its brutal similarity to every other party he attended, Wavery would have walked out of the throbbing light and breathed a sigh of unrestrained relief because Rita's patio was empty, not a soul, just a chair for him to sit and count the shooting-stars, because fifteen minutes before Catharine Riding would have left the room for her hotel in Miraflores, and Wavery's destiny would not have shifted forever.

3

"But he would have done Lisbon so well." This was the general reaction of colleagues when they discovered that Thomas Wavery had not after all been appointed to Portugal. A day or two lapsed before the reason was whispered after him in corridors, and then it depended on who had spoken to whom as to which was the version retailed. On the whole, the mood was pro-Wavery. He had been harshly treated by Cullis.

A month after the Tennysons' party, the Permanent Under Secretary stood in Heathrow waiting to collect his suitcase. He had spent the weekend in Strasbourg and was eager to be back in Berkhamsted. He had collected a trolley and was wheeling it towards the baggage claim when he passed a man and a woman clinging together in an embrace of such intensity he was reminded of his father's departure from Golspie railway station, in the uniform of a fusilier. The young woman was close to tears. Sir Derek's gaze would have discreetly passed over such private grief had he not all of a sudden recognised her companion.

The spectacle of Wavery with a strange woman at Heathrow airport was not an automatic cause for alarm. But there are certain rules you can break only if you are incredibly lucky. Wavery was clasping the woman's hands, kissing the top of them. When he pressed her knuckles to his eyes, it seemed a gesture of utter desperation. She pulled away, distressed. It was at this moment as her knuckles were torn from him that Wavery became aware, over her shoulder, of Sir Derek's astonished gaze.

Sir Derek could not dismiss the expression on Wavery's face in the second before their eyes met. It was devoted to a single object – a person Cullis knew not to be Penny Wavery. Cullis had seen it on that platform in Golspie and once or twice afterwards, and he was familiar with its end. Where the devil could not reach he sent a most attractive woman.

Two days after the incident, Wavery's expression remained fresh on Cullis' mind as he walked through Whitehall and into the Ambassadors' Entrance.

He prepared to show his pass, but the grandiose foyer, suffused with the aroma of Dettol, was empty. Along the corridor, he saw a cleaning lady in an ill-fitting blue coat. She rapped at the open door of Personnel Department. She was shouting, "Is there a Mr Dewsnap?" Cullis did not know whether she acted under specific instructions or whether she considered answering the telephone to be one of her responsibilities. But if she was cleaning an empty office and the telephone rang, she would always pick up the receiver.

He tucked away his pass and mounted the staircase towards Goetze's mural of Britannia Pacificatrix.

Two doors away from his office Cullis came to the Sensitivity Room. Here for £65 a day a handful of former ambassadors sifted through thirty-year-old documents on the eve of their entry into the public domain. The idea had been Cullis' own – a precautionary exercise designed on the face of it to prevent the dissemination of information which might continue to cause embarrassment, but in reality to discourage the Sensitivity Officers, who included a number of untidy individualists, from writing their memoirs. "The sinister censors of the FO," the *Daily Express* had dubbed them.

"Telephone for Mr Dewsnap." The voice climbed the staircase in his wake. The door to the Sensitivity Room was closing as Cullis passed, but not before he had glimpsed Sir Richard Croby, a former envoy to the Gabon judged to have gone native.

"Bloody terrible to forget the name of the man you're having lunch with."

"Does he have a beard?" Cullis recognised the voice of John Pendock, known to have kept a mistress in Peshawar. Pendock's appearances had grown rarer since the introduction of computerised telephone calls.

"Better if he did."

And still the dinning voice. "Mr Dewsnap . . ."

The PUS walked on, reaching his office at nine-thirty according to the Van Cleef and Arpels clock on his mantelpiece, a gift from the French Foreign Minister.

Yes, in the circumstances the Appointments Board under his guidance had arrived at a correct decision on Wavery. Couldn't sack a man because he had betrayed his early promise, but one could post the hell out of him.

In welcoming Wavery to his office that morning Cullis made no mention of their encounter at Heathrow.

"Take a seat, Thomas. Yes, there. I want to hear all about Peru." There followed ten minutes of perfunctory talk while Wavery outlined the political situation after which Cullis said, "I do see you deserve something calmer."

The PUS spoke with a marked Scottish accent. His pleasures were dry-fly fishing and photographing cemeteries and listening to the shipping forecasts before he slept, normally while reading from a zippered Bible. His reports were admired for their perception and their incision. Whatever humour he possessed found an exclusive outlet in verse. As a young man whose evenings were spent alone in a Lambeth rooming-house he had occupied himself with composing limericks. He had not relinquished the habit in office. A marbled folder in his desk contained several hundreds of verses in what had been described by his late landlady as "a gorgeously light vein". This trait was not consistent with the rest of Sir Derek's character. On the few occasions he told a joke, he was terrifying.

Britain's ability to shift matters on the international stage had diminished during Cullis' journey up the corridor. Not so his regard for senior diplomats, whom he continued to treat as direct descendants of Homer's heralds. An ambassador, Cullis believed, was the personification of his embassy. He was not a man in a suit who spoke the language. Quality not quantity was Cullis' watchword and he harboured a grim dislike for those politicians, with their Rayner scrutinies and Plowden reports, who would wish to retrain his officers as accountants in a global chain store. Cullis, too, was in a pragmatic business. His primary interest was not to make friends, but to defend the interests of the United Kingdom. If the morale of the Service was good, he gave credit to his staff. If it was bad, the fault was his.

This morning there lay on his desk two yellow folders. One contained a post report, including a map of North-West Africa. The other contained Wavery's career file, to which had been clipped the recommendation made by the Appointments Board at their monthly meeting.

Cullis opened the first folder. Diplomacy, he reflected, was the science of telling someone to go to hell in a way that would make them look forward to the journey. He primed himself for the task.

He cleared his throat. "It's not Lisbon," he said. "In a number of ways it's more important than Lisbon." With all the solemnity he could manage he said, "We want you to be our eyes and ears in Abyla."

Wavery ran his tongue over his teeth. He had no idea what Cullis was talking about. "Abyla?" he said.

"That's it, Abyla," said Cullis, much as he would have said Paris or Rome. "'The pearl of the Mediterranean'."

He rotated the photocopied map and searched for the Spanish enclave. His finger descended on an area opposite Gibraltar, covering it.

He said, "Abyla's of considerable interest at the moment." The enclave was the southern exit for the tunnel linking Europe with Africa, a dream to exercise the minds of men since Hercules separated the two continents.

"Work on the tunnel should be complete by August next year," said Cullis. There would then be a grand opening cere-

46

mony attended by the monarchs of Britain, Spain and Morocco. This treaty, the fruit of wearisome diplomatic endeavours designed to neutralise centuries of argument, would result in the transformation of Gibraltar and Abyla into International Zones.

There was no need to remind Wavery, Cullis reminded him, of what it meant for an officer to be involved in the preparation of a Royal Visit. Cullis was confident the customary knighthood would offset any disappointment Wavery might feel on not being promoted to Ambassador. In designating Abyla and Gibraltar as free zones, it had been decided to take as model the former International Zone of Tangier: Wavery's appointment, in common with his European colleagues, would enjoy the rank of Consul General.

"I don't think you'll find any problems of an Anglo-Abylan nature. The Moslem community is quite small. It's all in the post report." Cullis closed the folder and launched it with the back of his hand towards Wavery.

"Congratulations," he said warmly.

Wavery accepted the folder. He could not find any words. He squeezed out his most diplomatic smile, that of someone who believed if he smiled in uncomfortable situations it had an effect comparable to squeezing lemon on a fish that had begun to turn. Cullis divined his disappointment. "Listen, Thomas . . ." The PUS despatched his gaze out of the window, through the transparent trees, in the direction of his club where later he would walk to lunch and order, as he ordered every Monday, a dish of cauliflower cheese – "but without the sauce".

His reason for vetoing the Lisbon appointment had nothing to do with the reasons he had advanced yesterday to the board, that Wavery was due to retire in eighteen months' time, that despite a first-class report his heart evidently wasn't in it, that the Foreign Secretary was on Cullis' back to find something for a young high flyer threatening to leave the Service for banking. No, Cullis had vetoed Wavery's appointment because of the expression on his face at the airport; and out of sympathy for Wavery's wife. Did Penny have any inkling of what he had seen?

Cullis had met Penny only once, in Cambodia, during his first tour as a junior inspector. He had been drawn to her. (A small oil decorated an upstairs room in the Wiltshire cottage.) Penny had entertained him beside the pool and late in the afternoon escorted him shopping. A rickshaw led them to a covered market near the palace. She wanted him to meet an old man who wove beautiful silk belts. She encouraged him to buy one for Hilda. Thirty years on, Lady Cullis continued to wear the black and gold belt.

Cullis hoped Penny was spared the knowledge of her husband's infidelity, but he doubted it. Anyway it was none of his business. His business was not to solve problems that had arisen, rather to prevent them from arising in the first place. He thought of Croby in the Gabon. He thought of Pendock in Peshawar. He thought of Dwindell. And Wavery.

Why did so many intelligent men become blithering idiots when it came to matters of the heart? Wavery had been given his chance. Cullis simply couldn't, not and remain true to all he held sacred, have recommended Lisbon in the land of Fatima to a diplomat who had discovered late in life that there were more ways of eating cauliflower than off a plate.

He retrieved his stare from the window. Rain then showers, moderate becoming good, he reckoned. He had forgotten what he had been going to say. "How's Penny?"

"She's well."

"Do give her my love."

"Rather."

Cullis rose to his feet, Wavery too. "Better not forget that, Thomas." Wavery gathered up the post report. The PUS opened the door. "Keep an eye on Morocco, will you. Keep us posted, above all, on what the Berbers are thinking."

Cullis closed the door and walked to the mantelpiece. He warmed his back against an unlit fire. What actually *had* he been going to say? Something to do with the Yeats poem, the title of which had escaped him?

He scratched his leg where it itched between the trouser and the sock. He thought of Penny. He thought of his own two children and the sanctity of family life. If diplomats couldn't promote the British ideal of family they, by God, deserved to be treated as accountants. He was still scratching when his secretary rang.

"Sir Derek, you won't have forgotten your lunch appointment?"

"Remind me."

She reminded him of an inspector who was taking early retirement. "You wanted Personnel Department's list of possible replacements."

4

The post report which Cullis had given Wavery contained the Political Department's potted history of Abyla.

A Spanish possession since 1580, Abyla has long been claimed by Morocco. The southern pillar of Hercules, the enclave is situated on the North African coast fourteen miles across the Straits from its northern pillar, Gibraltar. Officers should refrain from the temptation to find parallels. The Spanish position is that Morocco is not entitled to ask for Abyla's return since Abyla never belonged to Morocco in the first place: it was captured by the Portuguese in 1415, becoming a possession of Spain a century before Morocco united as a kingdom.

Previously occupied by the Phoenicians, the Romans and the Vandals, Abyla enjoys a place in history as the site from which the Arabs launched their invasion of Europe in 711. Invited by Abyla's governor to avenge his daughter's rape at the hands of the King Rodrigo, the Arabs remained in Spain seven hundred years.

The enclave, a former Spanish penal colony, is nineteen and a half square miles, with a population of 60,000, one quarter consisting of immigrants from Morocco. The city remains the Headquarters of the Tercio (the Spanish Legion) and is consecrated to the Virgin of Africa who also acts as the community's perpetual mayoress.

The port is one of the principal thoroughfares into Africa. Because of its duty-free status it is popular with day-trippers. Last year there were 2.3 million visitors, staying an average of three hours. The British Consulate was closed in 1980. No records exist for British resident passport-holders.

The yellow folder also provided background material on the tunnel, and a summary of the meeting held six years before in Marrakesh at which the original decision had been taken to construct a fixed link between Europe and Africa. Four hundred delegates had attended from thirty countries and several options were discussed. In a plan favoured by his King, the Moroccan Minister of Public Works proposed a bridge across the Straits. The Spanish delegate, in a proposal endorsed by the British contingent, argued for a modified version of the Anglo-French Channel Tunnel. A representative of Cuticle USA proposed the laying of a pipeline, eighteen miles in length and wide enough for the transit of two electric trains. The pipeline would be constructed of optic fibre, a material tried and approved by NASA and ten times cheaper than a tunnel, with no risk to navigation.

The Japanese delegation followed the debate with close attention. They wished to know who would bear overall responsibility and who would finance the project. The Chairman of SNED (Société Nationale des Études du Détroit) explained the project would be the joint responsibility of the respective British and Spanish authorities under the authority of the EC, but the finance would be raised from private sources. Here the Moroccan delegate made a formal protest. He reminded the conference that Abyla was regarded as part of Morocco and he requested them to confirm that any project would require the endorsement of his government which was known to welcome closer links with Europe (as was evinced by His Majesty's repeated application for membership of the EC).

On 18 May 1988, the decision was taken to implement the fixed tunnel link, and for a feasibility study to be made with immediate effect into all technical, judicial and ecological aspects of the project, to be known henceforth as the Straits Tunnel.

The breeze flapped his shirt, blowing a strand of grey hair into his eyes and thinning the fog into mist. Wavery searched again for Africa. This time he found what he was looking for. It began as a solitary speck of white, suspended above the sea-line. More specks appeared, the whitewash of walls on a hill, and then the darker, higher watermark of a mountain. Above the mountain a thick black pall of smoke darkened the afternoon sun.

That was Wavery's first sight of Abyla.

The promontory had the shape of a young woman. She was lying on her back, with her head in the water and the mountain was her face. She had the features of a broken god, smashed by a power beyond a god's.

PART TWO

Chapter Four

I

WAVERY STOOD IN the empty house. Asunción had left and he had never felt more isolated. He tried closing the door behind her, but there was something wrong with the lock. When he moved away, the door opened and smoke seeped into the hall. The smoke attacked his eyes and caught the back of his throat so he was unable to breathe without coughing.

"I'll speak to the workmen on Monday," insisted Asunción.

She had been on the quay to greet him. "Asunción Ortiz," she said, not sure whether to shake his hand. She was nervous. Her hair was plaited into a bun and she wore a light-coloured trouser suit. He judged she was in her mid-thirties, although the clothes made her appear older. Her face was open, honest, good. A perfect secretary, he thought.

She drove him in an elderly blue Seat, parking outside a house less than three hundred yards from the port. The house stood on a corner facing the sea and was concealed by scaffolding. What you could see of it was painted yellow, like an old apricot.

He peered through the windscreen. "This is the residence?"

"Señor," she said, holding onto the steering wheel. There was despair in her voice. "They promised me it would be ready for you. They promised – but what can I tell you? It is not ready."

The residence was not only incomplete. It contained nothing but some building materials. Several times on her tour through the rooms Asunción apologised for the absence of furniture. London had told her it would be here in time for the Consul General's arrival. Then, yesterday, London told her another fortnight. She had lent her own furniture for the moment, the pieces in Señor Wavery's bedroom on the third floor.

"There is some food in the fridge. Halima comes in the morning. I wasn't sure if you wanted someone to live in."

"Thank you," said Wavery, "I'll be fine."

She lived with her father in the lane behind the Residence. She wrote down her number. "Till Monday, then."

Now that he was alone, he could explore the house. He had the weekend to pace out his boundaries. Outside in the smoke a bell struck six. He adjusted his watch. He had been on London time, but it was earlier than he thought. He looked about for something to jam the door shut.

2

For three days Abyla lay in her wrapping of bituminous smog. Then on Monday evening, wind. It blew from beyond the bay, whitening the sea, rubbing the stuccoed cheeks of the houses along Calle Zamora, rustling the political posters pasted to the bust of Leopoldo Zamora, quinologist (1822–96), slamming shut the windows in the asylum on Calle Silvestre and disturbing for a moment the concentration of the inmates who sat as they sat every Monday afternoon, reproducing the portrait propped on a chair, their renditions of "Lieutenant Zamora, the Death-Betrothed", to be respectfully disseminated or disposed of as the superintendent thought fit.

"The *levante*!" said Sandra the Rapist, a hand flying to her chest. "The *levante*!" And a shudder ran through the easels. Every sailor feared the *levante*, the mad-bull wind that paced out of sight on a mirror sea. It came at you from nowhere. You saw it shivering awake the waves and you heard its breath, the desperate breath of a creature locked in the cavities of the deep.

The mad bull charged from the east. A mile away, in the

Moorish quarter of El Hadu, lived those who believed you could prevent its charge. They believed the *levante* could be frightened off, in the same way a child might summon it by playing with a sieve. They would truss up a dog and make it howl. They would sprinkle dry blood on a fire, hoping the smoke would blind the wind. But you cannot blind the *levante*. In fact there is little you can do when the *levante* hurls itself from a ring of sky, removing boats, beaches and restaurant roofs on both sides of the Straits.

"Come Sandra, away," said the superintendent, closing the window.

It was not the cruel east wind, he told the artists. It was the *poniente*, a mild westerly which blew from the Atlantic, driving rain and sea mist through Hercules' pillars and winnowing the valleys.

Joseph Silkleigh felt the *poniente* at sea. He was searching for Emilio, the fisherman, beneath a turtle egg of a moon. He had steered from the headland, to where the *Grau* was blazing. The wind bid the waves rise to spray and a current tugged at the wheel of his boat. Silkleigh looked at the *Grau* lolling in the swell. He listened for some cry. But of the fisherman who had been sailing his new boat home when that vast prow towered through the fog, he heard nothing.

Rosita heard the wind in a room above the Café Ulises. It flapped the blue awning with such force that Gallo, the bellboy, who had climbed the stairs to enquire if she was ready, was obliged to knock twice. "Yes, yes, I'm coming."

The wind blasted through the shutters of the library, where Dolores painted her long nails. Tonight the library closed at eight. She was blowing on her varnish, a shade of scarlet that shrilled "I don't work", when the telephone rang. It was Panteco to say he still had business at the prison. He would collect her at nine. As the policeman talked, Dolores put on a large brown coat. This had been Ernesto's coat. It had deep velvet-lined pockets down into which she would plunge her fingers when they were dry. "Feel there, put your hand in," she would challenge a man. Anyone who didn't say immediately, "Yes, it feels wonderful," she didn't trust. It was a primitive test,

57

but the coat was all she had of Ernesto. She would never give it up.

The conductor's widow heard the wind and for the first time in three days unfastened the balcony window. Immediately, a pigeon blew into her room and toppled onto the television a cup of tea she had poured herself and forgotten, and then an empty bottle of White Bear perfume which had belonged to her mother, before settling briefly on a book belonging to her mother's friend Colonel Slava who was forever leaving her bits and pieces from better collections, including the third volume of a priceless history of Kiev, printed in French in 1633, upon which, lifting its tail before flying off, the bird deposited a small grey memory. If vodka were made out of pigeons, Ernesto used to say, there would be no pigeons. Ernesto! Genia Ortiz flinched at his memory. She sat down on a banquette of pink window cushions and breathed in the fresh air. Her eyes smarted from a weekend's confinement. She felt old and fragile. She felt worthy of her grandson's nickname for her, "Age".

Time had not been cruel to Genia Ortiz, but she considered it had been mischievous. From behind, her figure had the shape of a teenage girl.

In only a few places did her eighty-seven years betray themselves. In a line below her nose, which made it seem as if the skin was smiling against itself; in the liver spots on the backs of her hands; and in a stiffness of movement. When she turned, as now, she turned with her whole body.

She faced the small, cluttered room. Through watery eyes she saw her brocatelle curtains, coloured in the blue and yellow of the Free Ukraine; the clock she overwound, its hour hand fashioned as a swinging pierrot; and standing in the centre of a dark blue carpet her oval Viennese desk on which was a framed photograph of her father in the elkskin breeches of a cavalry officer. This was the only photograph in the room. There was no likeness of her husband. Ernesto had been banished to the trunk beneath her bed, where with a feeling it served him right, she had locked away her childhood photographs.

"Your bloody photographs" – these had been the conductor's last words to her, or the last words she recalled with clarity for he probably mumbled something about lunch at the Café Ulises with Periclito. So, as a penance, she forbade herself to look again at the photographs of her father's estate. Ernesto might not have needed Dolores, his last love, or any of his other loves, had she done so earlier. From that day, she refused to think about him. Most of all she refused to think about gypsy-lipped Dolores who worked in the library next to *El Faro* and whose white skin Ernesto would joke was an octave too high for his taste but in whose long white arms on a second-floor room in the Hotel Zamora he had died.

Revived by the air, Genia Ortiz abandoned the window seat. She wondered if they had found Emilio's body. She turned on the television. It was a present from her son, who made soap operas in Madrid and who was always promising to come for Christmas and then cancelling, causing Asunción, the wife from whom he was separated, to say, "See! Now do you understand? He was always impossible. But what do I tell Pablo?" Genia Ortiz could see how impossible Tromso was – "Exactly like his father." The effect of his father's absence on her eight-year-old grandson was too clear. She could only say, "I know, Asunción, I know. But next year, when he's not so busy."

This year again he had promised to come for Christmas. "If you don't, Tromso . . ." But she had nothing to threaten him with.

She was too late for the news. Tromso's soap was playing, for once free of interference. One woman was saying to another, "Every little fish expects to become a whale, Tania." But Genia Ortiz never watched her son's programmes, not in the evenings nor in the mornings when the episodes were repeated. It was another challenge she had set herself, like her refusal to look at the photographs beneath her bed.

Genia Ortiz attended Mass on Sundays, but the smoke from the *Grau* had so affected her she had forgone yesterday's service. Suddenly she felt a desire to sink on her knees before the Virgin of Africa and bother her to be a dear and bring Tromso home this Christmas.

She prepared herself to go out and collected a black wool cape and a shopping bag. In the bag was the only possession of Ernesto's she could bring herself to touch. It was his gold-knobbed baton presented to Ernesto by the Teatro Amazonas, where in 1921 he had conducted seven performances of Ponchi-elli's *La Gioconda*. She used it to tap melons in the market and to smack the hands of pickpockets.

She removed the baton from the bag and opened the door.

Senator Zamora, dressed in his purple cardigan, listened to the bell as he ate dinner. His ancestor, the quinologist, had transported the entire mechanism from a chapel on the banks of the Amazon near Manaus. Possibly it was ringing for Mass. He looked at his watch. It was ten past seven.

Clotilda, the younger of his two daughters, was out. Please God, a date. Asunción had telephoned from the British Consul-ate to say she would be working late. Her son, Pablo, was in disgrace after it was discovered the baby daughter of Porcil, the banker, had been baptised with Seven-Up.

Clearly, Abyla was no place for an energetic fatherless eight-year-old. Which was why at the weekend Senator Zamora had driven him to the promontory west of Tangier to see the rock formation known as the Footstep of Hercules. Hercules consti-tuted one of Senator Zamora's few successes with his grand-child. On the subject of Hercules' labours (not least his tenth labour), Pablo never failed to be enthralled.

Varro had mentioned twenty-four different Hercules. Senator Zamora's hero was the man who first sailed this coast and opened up Africa to trade. At his death, a violent death, the Phoenicians deified him. He became the protecting divinity of navigators, the god of the purple dye, and the patron saint of promontories similar to this one. Nevertheless, he could not be certain of his divinity. Every year, in summer, he had to die. He was resurrected in the spring.

On Friday afternoon, as they drove towards the cave, Senator

Zamora told Pablo how on each of his two pillars Hercules had inscribed a warning not to proceed further westward. Beyond was the Green Sea of Darkness where the ocean boiled and where mountains magnetised the nails from ships at the same time provoking men to laughter.

"They sailed towards the shore grinning and sinking," said Senator Zamora.

Pablo was sceptical. "You mean the mountains made people laugh, even if they didn't want to?"

"That's right."

"And you say these mountains could remove metal from wood up to ten miles away."

"That's what I'm saying," repeated Senator Zamora. They stood in the cave where Hercules had squeezed Antæus to death.

"Who was Antæus?"

"He was a Libyan giant and the son of Neptune. He wished to build Neptune a temple made of skulls, so he killed anyone he met."

"Except Hercules."

"That's right, Pablo."

As they explored the footprint, Pablo's expression grew more disbelieving. Before going to bed, he made a calculation on his computer, last year's Christmas present from his absentee father.

"Grandpa?"

"Yes."

"If that really was Hercules' footprint then he must have been seven thousand, five hundred and fifty-nine metres tall."

This evening, Senator Zamora continued to dwell on the feat accomplished by Pablo's machine. He had reached the age of seventy-five without having anything to do with the technology crowding the shelves of Calle Real. How much – but Señora Criado had entered the room to serve the next course and was speaking.

"But that's wonderful!"

"What is?"

"That you have decided to become President of the Bullfight."

"Yes, señora, yes, I have decided after all." He had decided at Cap Spartel. He wanted to impress his grandchild. "I will tell the Governor tomorrow," he said, contemplating the dish before him. "Señora Criado, what is . . ." His moustache became a broom sweeping down the corners of his mouth. Steady, he told himself, steady, you can't ask orange trees for figs.

She clasped her hands together and with great pride said, "*Bacalhau*."

Salted cod. Jesus Hercules Christ. The hairs stood to attention on his neck. Why hadn't he sacked her? He should have sacked her years ago, but Minerva, his dear wife, had forbidden him. Now it was too late. He achieved a smile. "Thank you, Señora Criado. But isn't it a bit chilly in here?"

Señora Criado closed the window onto Calle Zamora and returned to the kitchen. So her master was to be President of the *Feria* in August! She would tell Don Ramon tomorrow. And Honorio in the market, and Marie Amaral. Perhaps Periclito would come back for it.

She looked back at the Senator through the kitchen. She saw his thin face, his thick moustache, his long grey hair that curled behind his ears whenever he visited the baths below the Club de Pensiones. By what accident of fate had she not been born her employer's grandson, to be spoiled and indulged by him? Every man suspected his wife of desiring an affair with Senator Zamora, but Señora Criado knew he did not have affairs. She knew him for what he was, a gentle, learned man who would eat the sand on Playa Benitez before he was false to his principles.

Senator Zamora picked up a fork and prepared to face his cod. There had been a moment in her third year of service when Señora Criado had set fire to the kitchen. He might have acted then, but she was Portuguese, and were not the Zamoras, Abyla's oldest family who arrived with Henry the Navigator and who boasted among their descendants not only a physician who had cured Sancho the Fat of his obesity but also the great

62

quinologist, Leopoldo Zamora, were not they too originally Portuguese?

"Señora Criado," he said at last. "I forgot to ask on Friday. What is that smell?"

"But Senator Zamora, you have heard the news, surely?"

"What news?"

"The accident."

He had been with Pablo at Cap Spartel. He knew nothing of any accident.

So she told him how the container ship *Admiral Grau*, loaded to the gunwales with equipment vital for the tunnel as well as a cargo of fuel oil, had collided in the *poniente* with a fishing boat. The oil was blazing off La Mujer Muerta and the current drifting it towards Abyla.

"It was Don Emilio's boat!" The boat he had scrimped eight years for, the boat he was sailing from old Mogador, the pride of his life. "And now they can't find him," and her mind filled with Emilio, whose beard could not hide his freckles, so many his mother would say the sun must have kissed him through a sieve.

Senator Zamora stared at the dish before him and silently swore. He pushed away his plate. He wondered if he should make a telephone call to his office. There would be no one there. Anyway, since the beginning of dinner an idea had taken root in his mind. He could not bear to abandon it.

"Delicious, Señora Criado. As always. But probably that will do."

He rose from the table. He opened the door into the hallway, passing from one set of his father's eyes to another. He climbed the staircase to his study. When he emerged he carried a leather file bulging with papers. On the landing he paused to adjust the portrait of his sovereign which for six years he had hung in the same position, upside down, as a mark of his extreme disrespect. He tiptoed up the stairs, past Pablo's bedroom to a room on the top floor. The nursery. Tomorrow he would speak in the Chamber and play *petanque* with Governor Menendez' head. He sat down before Pablo's computer. He opened the manual.

He switched on the screen, watching a green dot explode into a square of green. Tonight he had work to do.

In the Plaza de los Reyes, Marie Amaral felt the *poniente* on her cheeks and thought of another wind, the *chergui*. All weekend she had been gored by memories. Things she didn't want to remember kept coming back. She knew the *Grau* was to blame; but there was the vase she had dropped. The dull shards, glazed on one side, remained in a heap in the corner of the Floresteria Amaral. She had tried to throw them away, but couldn't. She did not see pieces of broken pottery. She saw mirror fragments. She was in Oran again and a turbaned head was bursting through the doorway.

He enters her room in Mers-el-Kebir, kicking open the door. There is a knife in his boots. Nervous hands grip a machine-gun. There have been shots from this building. Some Europeans have fired on the crowd. It is the day after Independence and there are crowds in the streets. Ten people are dead, including a child. Up the stairs comes the oo-oo-oo of women ululating.

It's over. He will shoot us. We'll be free.

But he doesn't move. He sees the mirror, full length on the wall, and in the mirror himself.

Or rape me, she thinks. On the floor beside my son. The Arabs never raped in bed, not the men from the Aurés. His young face came from those mountains.

Still he does not move. He confronts the long mirror, a wedding present from her father. He stands there rooted to the boards, such a look of terror on his face Marie Amaral thinks, Is it possible? Is this the first mirror he has seen? Can he never have seen a mirror before? Does that explain the awful cry as he jerks up his gun and squeezes the trigger on his reflection? His cry is more terrifying than the sound of the women below.

And then, desperate, on all fours, he searches for a body in the glass. He whispers something, noticing her at last. She crouches in the corner. She has urinated and her feet are damp and steamy. In a thin, dreadful voice she says to her maid, Zohra. "What does he say?"

"He says, 'Where is he?'"

He speaks again. His fingers are tipped with blood.

"'Or was it a woman?'"

But Marie Amaral is not listening. She has seen the bed. She has seen her mirror-wounded son.

When a mirror breaks, seven years of misfortune follow. But when a mirror is shot?

Marie Amaral, making a supreme effort, pressed one foot on the bin-pedal and threw away the pot.

And still the *poniente* blew, ruffling the lanky palms along the Marina Española, following the road upwards, past the massive red fortress of San Felipe built by the Portuguese in the fifteenth century and now a Sala de Bingo, past the Multi-Cine Cervantes showing *Persadilla en Elm Street 5*, beyond the Museo de Arqueologia with its empty sarcophogae, where Senator Zamora had spent the past month restoring what he believed was a Moorish prickspur, but had found to be a rowlock, past the catering vans, the terrapin sheds and the compound fence of the tunnel workers and into the decrepit alleyways of El Hadu, no broader than a shoulder.

It blew over the prison, over the lighthouse, over the orchids beginning to flower on the slopes of Monte Hacho, over the protected military beach where a figure crouched stiller than stone and over the mother who walked up and down the shore hallooing again and again and again to the gloating sea.

"Emilio! Emilio! Emilio . . ."

3

"Emeeeeleeeeoooo . . ."

The waves were huge things, but they had not brought him in. For three nights she had faced them and her cry, at first the anguished-angry call of a mother for a truant son, had become irregular and flattened, like a gull's cry.

"Emeeeeleeeeoooo . . ."

She stood on the beach in the dusk. Wavery saw her as he walked home along the Marina Española. Where she stood a group had gathered that morning on the grey sand. They were looking at Emilio's overnight bag, empty and pulpy and pearly with oil.

"Emeeeeleeeeooooo . . ."

Passing a line of concrete apartment blocks, Wavery understood why it was the average visitor took care not to prolong his visit beyond three hours. He thought, "I could have said No." He could have told Cullis, "I'll take early retirement." But for Penny's sake it was kinder he had gone away. Abyla was as adequate an out-of-the-way place as any. It was a place where he knew nobody and no one knew him. He was going to be by himself for the rest of his life. Why not start here?

He had said No to something more important. "That's it," he had promised himself and Catharine. In making the promise he was depriving himself of the one thing he loved. Making it, he discovered the person he had been was shattered into someone impossibly different. It would be months before this person learned to touch and speak intimately with anyone. He had no idea if the ability would come back, whether he would welcome it if it came. But if Catharine was not to join him, he would have to refashion his life. One thing alone would keep him sane in the weeks ahead, until he worked out who he intended to be: the exercise of those muscles which had made him a diplomat in the first place.

On his first day at the Consulate, Wavery had worked late, throwing himself into his duties as Consul General. He waited for the tunnel workers to leave their site before locking the office in Calle Camoes. The streets were deserted. The day-trippers had sailed, the workmen had returned to their compound, the only sounds were the cries from the shore.

The esplanade lay in darkness, except for the beacon of a telephone kiosk three blocks away and opposite the kiosk, the lamps of a café. Wavery had nearly reached the café when a large black dog trotted past him. A lead trailed some feet behind, grazing the tesselated pavement. Before Wavery could alter his step he had trodden on the lead. The dog yelped, twisting. Wavery stepped forward to soothe him but the dog bounded from his reach, padding on strangely webbed feet towards the kiosk light. Inside the kiosk a telephone was ringing.

The dog pressed his nose to the glass, before crossing the road and disappearing into the café.

Wavery's residence was on the corner beyond the café, between a block of flats and the road up the hill to Plaza de los Reyes. The three-storeyed building had been a sweet shop and the words *Tejidos y confecciones* could be read through the scaffolding.

How quickly a corner became familiar.

On the first floor, the room designated as the Royal Suite opened onto a green wrought-iron balcony with a fine view over the Straits. To the right could be seen the bosky gullies of Monte Hacho and the military fortress on its peak. To the left, the harbour, the palms along the Marina Española and, above the roofs of El Hadu, La Mujer Muerta, the dead woman, from whose limestone cliffs every evening the sun rolled into the sea.

Five cranes obscured the view ahead. They rose from the tunnel site. Every day, from seven in the morning until sunset, the houses along the Marina Española were deafened by machinery pecking away at a black hole in the earth.

It was Wavery's experience that the spirit of a place could be caught in the first week, after which your impressions dulled until the moment arrived when you noticed nothing new and then, as sometimes happened, it required the blast of a bomb for you to notice anything at all. Wavery felt he had netted the spirit of Abyla by the time he turned up for work that morning.

He had a clear sense of his isolation after a weekend in the residence. Every room spoke back to him of his disgrace and loneliness. Unable to face their vacancy he had locked the two spare bedrooms sharing his floor. Their keys at least worked. Had there been children, the floors would have been messy with toys. He could not imagine Penny arriving. Was there anyone else he might invite? He made a rapid inventory of his friends in the Foreign Office, but it was in the nature of Foreign Office life that the few friends he had made were in posts thousands of miles away. Who was in Algiers? he wondered. Or Rabat? He knew who was in Gibraltar.

On Saturday he had escaped his prison to buy milk in the grocery behind the house. He had drunk both cartons in the fridge and his mouth was dry. It tasted of smoke from the *Grau* and tunnel dust.

"So far, not a thing," said Don Ramon. The grocer was talking to an elderly and petite woman who tapped the counter with a conductor's white baton. "Patience," she told him. Didn't Don Ramon remember the British ship sinking off Cap Spartel in nineteen twenty something? Abdel Akbar and his *Moros* were in the hills. Don Ramon did not. But his mother, she might have done. "Sixty pesetas," he said, finding the price on the Stallion tea. He removed the pencil from behind his ear.

"Let me see, there was the Duke and Duchess of Fife, the Princess Marie Louise and the Princess Helena." Saved, thank God! Not so their luggage. For several years men strangely caparisoned were seen on the slopes of La Mujer Muerta.

"Berbers," said the woman, her voice lowering. "With diamante buttons!"

"Not possible!" said Don Ramon.

"True. It's true," said Genia Ortiz. She paid for her tea and turned from the counter – only to discover the person with whom she had been sharing the queue. So this was her neighbour! The Consul General de Gran Bretaña! Her eyes played over Wavery, hoping to hook some indication that he might have found her attractive as a younger woman. Because of her squint, it was a moment before Wavery realised her attention was directed at him, not the woman behind him.

She introduced herself. "Possibly you don't know who I am . . ." Hers was the balcony which overlooked his terrace.

"Ah, yes," said Wavery.

"I believe my daughter-in-law has the honour of working for you."

"Asunción?"

"Just so."

"She very kindly met me yesterday off the ferry," said Wavery.

Genia Ortiz, her head at the angle of an alert bird, said: "May I ask where you learned your Spanish?"

"In Peru," Wavery told her.

The smile shrank her eyes. How pleased she was that the Court of St James's had sent this man to Abyla. The *presidio* must be more important than she had supposed. He reminded her of Tromso, only nicer.

"I could tell by your accent," she went on. The purest Spanish was spoken in Peru. How lucky he was to know it! She had always wanted to visit Lima. "The City of Kings," she murmured, remaining by his side as he paid for the milk.

"You must meet the rest of the family. My son, I'm hoping, will be home for Christmas. He's done very well. He's in television. He makes that series – Oh, what's it called? Well, it's the biggest by far. If we talk about something else for a bit, it'll come back."

Wavery, who did not wish to talk about anything else, waited for Don Ramon to return his change.

"And how do you find your house, señor?"

"There's quite a lot to be done."

"Do you feel any *vibrations*?" Her eyes widened and diverged as she mined the last word.

"Not yet," said Wavery. But Asunción had warned him of the earth tremors. On her brisk tour of the house she informed him of her father's opinion that the skeleton discovered in the basement belonged to a camel which had perished in the Lisbon earthquake.

Genia Ortiz gave a fluffy laugh and tapped his chest with her baton. "The General's wife felt them immediately!"

"The General's wife . . . ?"

Asunción hadn't told him? The wife of the general who built the house.

"The General?" said Wavery. He had arrived in Abyla only last night. He knew nothing of any General.

At this point, Don Ramon raised his hands, but he could not stop the conductor's widow. Before he could say: "At least make way for the lady behind," Genia Ortiz was transported back to her first year in Abyla.

Where did she begin? Did she begin as tradition required her to begin with the General's triumphant entry into Abyla bearing the body of Lieutenant Zamora, whose actions had saved the enclave from Abdel Akbar?

She did not. "Ah, the General. What can I say?" she said, one eye fixed on Wavery, the other over his shoulder on the monstrous shape of the man whom she had first seen in Moorish trousers and a corset as he chased a boy up the street – not yet called Calle Zamora – slapping him on the seat of his pleasure with the flat of a sabre.

The General was the first man Gena Ortiz had ever seen in a corset. "He was a ferocious *homosexual*," she said pronouncing a word that had not existed in the vocabulary she carried with her as an eleven-year-old from Balnasharki. In Señor Wavery's house he had entertained his Moroccan lover, who had instructions to light a candle every night on the balcony so that from his quarters on Monte Hacho the General could see someone was thinking kindly of him.

Genia Ortiz had thought no such thing. She had made an enemy of the General since the evening at the Club de Pensiones when she had informed him in French – not yet having mastered Spanish herself – "I'm the only person you will have met socially who has known the Princess Yekaterina and seen her beauty plain." Thereafter whenever he saw her in the street the General would draw himself to his full height, walk up to her until the peak of his cap touched her nose and say, *"Madame, je vous dis bonjour!"*

Oh no, she had no time for him at all. She did not find it amusing as her husband did that for three years in succession he should win the Miss Dainty Ankles competition held each Christmas in the Café Ulises. His perversions were stupendous! He didn't mind who knew, not even Genia Ortiz. Indeed, when he told her, "I've been through the whole of North Africa," the impression was conveyed by a slight movement of the left eye that it was not the geography to which he referred.

"Then something extraordinary happened!" In his late sixties, the General underwent a hormonal hurricane. He became engaged to the daughter of a Belgian nose and throat specialist. They were married in a lavish ceremony in Santa Maria de Africa. After the service he carried his wife along the Marina Española. The door into the house was open. He carried her over the threshold. She was about to slip from his arms to the floor when suddenly! she hesitated. She clutched his arm. "*Mon cher, il y a des vibrations dans cette maison,*" she said and she ordered him to walk back immediately through the door. "Her feet never touched the ground!"

The couple rented an apartment on the Plaza de los Reyes, but the General retained the house. Twice a week while his wife attended Mass, he climbed to the third floor and sat on the terrace surveying the rooftops. He balanced a shotgun on his knee and kept a bottle of whisky beside him. If he saw a cat he shot it.

"Cats reminded him of the *Moros*!"

Wavery paused at his front door. He looked up, to see if Plaisir des Yeux had installed the telephone cables, but the four wires remained strung across the yellow wall beneath the roof.

Two men had been working on the residence for six months. After the General's appointment as Cultural Attaché to Sierra Leone, the house had been sold to an Indian confectioner who stored his sweets on the second floor. The top floor he closed off without noticing an open skylight, so there was damp rot everwhere and also problems with the drains which erupted periodically for no reason anyone could detect, and flooded the ground floor. In view of the Royal Visit, the Overseas Estates Department had authorised a comprehensive redecoration, since when the architect responsible had been given leave to return to Cadiz where he was constructing a casino. He had done his professional duty. Wiring and painting were matters that might be left to local workmen, in the event two Arab builders from El Hadu.

The housekeeper had told Wavery their names, but it was easier to refer to them as she did by the architect's sobriquets of Pas de Problème and Plaisir des Yeux. Of the two, Wavery had only met Plaisir des Yeux. A message delivered to Halima explained in ungrammatical French that his foreman was in Morocco securing building materials.

The hall smelled of plaster and paint. Wavery pressed down a switch, and light flared on the debris of trestles, pots and tiles. Plaisir des Yeux was working on a room to the right of the stairway, a room described by Halima who had seen the architect's plans, as "the banqueting room". The confectioner's sweet counter was recollected in pale lines on the floor boards; the shop entrance by a rectangle of fresh cement. Loose plaster and the paintmarks of feet led from the room and up a carpetless staircase. Wavery climbed to the kitchen, following the white footprints of Plaisir des Yeux. Everything would be ready within three months, he had been assured.

The interior of the residence was made altogether bleak by the absence of furniture. OED had promised Wavery this would be arriving imminently, in the same ship as his belongings.

Halima had left. Wavery's dinner was in the fridge, a small tortilla and a tomato and onion salad. Afterwards he made a pot of tea. He opened a carton and milk spilled onto his suit. "Open other end," he read in Spanish. He carried the tray upstairs.

Wavery's bedroom was the only habitable room in the house. French windows opened onto a roof terrace where the low calcimined walls retained the afternoon heat. The terrace, fifteen feet by twenty, was large enough for a roof garden.

There was a tree the size of a large magnolia overlooking the terrace, growing from the lane below. Wavery recognised the silken-haired leaves of a handkerchief tree. Had the General lived to see it flower? You had to wait twenty years or more for the *Davidia involucrata* to drop its white, handkerchief-shaped bracts.

Wavery opened the French windows, disturbing a grey cat

from the branches. The animal leaped onto the wall and seeing Wavery, lazily raised its tail. "The cat, sometimes known as Ham (!) seems a happy little creature," Asunción had written in the notes she had left him. Ham's stomach was not strong, but she flourished on a diet of horsemeat and water.

"Hello, Ham," said Wavery. He stretched out to caress her tail. She was descended from a line which had survived the General's shotgun. There was hope if Ham had survived. He looked over the wall and into the narrow cobbled lane. The Calle Zamora ran parallel to the Marina Española, spanning the block between Calle Millan Astray and Calle Silvestre. It was a back street, but busy. Pedestrians used it as a short cut and motorists to double park, so that every morning began with furious hooting.

People changed in the Calle Zamora: they felt no one was watching them. So they spoke to themselves. They shook their heads, giggling. They urinated against the cars. Girls with the night's party on their faces sang pop songs; students sat on doorsteps reading texts; the grocer's son thumped his ball into the chalked goalpost Plaisir des Yeux had said he would paint over. Perhaps it was the tall asylum on the corner of Calle Silvestre which made Calle Zamora such a refuge, an escape from the ceaseless tap-tapping of inmates anxious to secure the street's attention.

Apart from Wavery's residence and the red house opposite, the street was composed of nineteenth-century mansion blocks, in the smartest of which lived Genia Ortiz. A narrow gulley five feet across divided her building from his. Her apartment was across this gulley at the same level as Wavery's terrace and had a balcony arrayed with cowrie-pink pelargoniums.

Asunción lived in the red-painted house opposite with her son Pablo, her younger sister Clotilda and her father Senator Zamora. Wavery supposed Senator Zamora to be the figure in the topmost room concentrating on a computer screen. Wavery had been invited for drinks later in the week.

A car bounced into the lane and halted outside the Zamoras' door, its engine turning over. A girl stepped out, her corn-coloured hair in pigtails. She stooped to kiss the driver, then waited for the car – a white Renault with one headlight working – to accelerate away. Clotilda, thought Wavery, finishing his tea.

Back in his bedroom, he switched on a small television set, wiping a layer of dust from the screen. A stout party in a white suit was talking. It was the same man Wavery had called upon this morning, to present his improvised credentials.

When he said to Asunción, "Tell me about the Governor," she said she was not the best person to ask. Her father and Menendez were bitter enemies. She knew how Senator Zamora explained away the Governor. Everything about him boiled down to a single unalterable truth: on the mainland he had been an actor, but as a voice on the radio. Even in those days, what Menendez had aspired to was television. He had not extinguished the hope that one day he would be discovered by a scout. His gestures remained extravagant in consequence. He behaved towards everyone, whether Don Ramon or Dolores, as if they might be plain-clothes emissaries paid by the powers that be in Madrid to uncover genius in Africa.

"He's not a genius," she added. "But I don't think he's evil either."

"Ring me and we'll have lunch," said Governor Menendez, and laughed. He had a laugh that was not hard to provoke, but disappeared quickly. All weekend he had been preoccupied with the accident at sea. He had cut his upper lip shaving and he smelled of his second after-breakfast cigar. When he reached the stub, he held up the object and a man ran to collect it.

"So how do you like our city, Señor Wavery?"

"Lovely," said Wavery. "Really lovely."

"The pearl of the Mediterranean!"

He punched Wavery playfully in the stomach and the accreditation ceremony was over.

On television, Menendez leaned forward buttoning his white jacket in response to a question about the *Grau*. A slick of oil was shown washing ashore beneath La Mujer Muerta. The waves were lifeless humps. A sea gull walked in clogged hops

74

across the black sand. There was no trace of the fisherman.

"I wouldn't use the word panic," he was saying. His fingers strummed his chest. "Or rather I would." But moves were afoot to disperse the oil. The Health and Safety Executive were convening tomorrow in response to this afternoon's emergency debate.

A disembodied voice asked, "Is it true the *Grau* was carrying vital drilling equipment?" A list had reached the network from the office of Abyla Independiente. The cargo was itemised. Neoprene gaskets. Bolted cement segments. Replacement blades for the disc-cutter.

Menendez nodded, his eyes rolling under the load of information passing overhead. A stubby finger plucked at the chain creepering his neck. More blades had been ordered from Seattle, he said.

Could the Governor give his assurance that the loss of the *Grau* would not result in a delay to the opening of the Straits Tunnel?

"Absolutely!"

What about funds? There were rumours the money had run out. Was it true the workmen had not been paid for a fortnight?

Wavery changed channel. "And finally . . ." a man said in English. On screen appeared the fluorescent figure of Sir Lawrence Tredwell, demonstrating the stroke with which he had driven a golf ball two hundred and forty-eight yards towards Africa. Wavery switched back. Menendez had departed and a voice was urging Wavery not to go away because next on Abyla Channel was another instalment of everybody's favourite programme. "Yes, it's time once again for *The Strong Tend to Leave* . . ."

There was an interval for advertisements. "Is your marriage a source of joy or a cause of pain? Talk to Dorita at the Catholic Marriage Guidance Service." The address gave way to a pair of woman's eyes, the rest of her face blacked out as if she might have been wearing a veil. The eyes belonged to Abyla Television's "Whose Eyes?" competition. "Do you recognise this local personality?" pleaded the voice. "The first twenty correct answers will receive rollerball Parkers . . ." Nor was that all. If, at the end of the month, the eyes remäîned unclaimed, then the prize would double!

The eyes remained on the screen, steady and appealing. By the time he sat down on the corner of his bed Wavery was no longer in Abyla. He was escaping a congested room at a party in Lima.

4

He hovered on the steps of the patio. In the corner he registered Queesal. The Commercial Attaché was listening to a tall woman, with shoulder-length black hair. Wavery thought, There's George, wanting to be unlucky again.

Queesal had been drinking. He was speaking in an aggrieved, bellicose voice. "It's not what you see. We're just servants. Any Tom, Dick or Harry feels a right to come out here and be sick over us."

She listened, but she behaved like a woman who is expecting someone else. Queesal must have noticed. She was reaching down for her glass, when, as if to keep her attention, he spluttered, "That drunken, womanising oaf in there, for instance, Clark flaming Gable." He was intending a joke, but aggression roughened his voice. By the way in which she reacted, Wavery immediately knew that Queesal was abusing someone close to her.

Until that moment Wavery had seen her simply as another attractive woman of which the room behind him was full. Her beauty had not impinged on him. He had assumed such a woman could handle the Queesal brand of clumsy rudeness. He assumed she would be bound to have the armoury of most beautiful women, which for him diminished their attractiveness. What he saw was the vulnerability of a child who needed his help.

Her hands moved up to her face. She tried to speak. No words came. She looked about, bewildered, and saw Wavery.

Queesal became aware she was not looking at him. "Tom . . . hello."

Wavery stepped forward. "I've come to interrupt."

Queesal chuckled uncomfortably. "I've been filling Mrs Riding in on our glamorous duties."

Wavery held out a hand, "Thomas Wavery."

She closed her eyes and leaned forward, not having properly heard. Wavery repeated his name and she said in reply, "Catharine Riding." As she straightened up, the light from the doorway fell on her face. Her eyes were darkish green, a shade he had never seen before. They looked through him and beyond him, exploring the contours of his vacuum. They had been seeking protection and now they had found it. But the effect on Wavery was more than the knowledge of a person coming into shelter.

He looked at a paving stone a yard from her feet.

"She's off to Arequipa, but," Queesal went on, "I've been telling her to fear not."

Abruptly, Wavery acted as if Queesal had disturbed them.

"The Ambassador's looking for you, George."

"Where –"

"He's with Denver."

Queesal excused himself.

Wavery said, "I don't know if you've been here before." He waved at the rock garden. "Rita's achieved a miracle. And here of all places. It was nothing. Stones and rubbish, literally."

She unfolded her arms, lifting them to her cheeks. She shook her head as if to clear it. "There," she said. "Thank you."

She was a woman again, in her early thirties. One hand fretted at her hair, as if spinning it. The other moved down her slender face, white, except for a constellation of three moles on her right cheek, and the tip of her nose, which the sun had reddened slightly.

He went on, "But I don't suppose you're interested in gardening."

She gave a small laugh. "It's what I would like to do all the time."

"Really?"

"Oh, yes." She laughed again, with more confidence. She picked up her glass from the table. "I'm one of those dreadful specimens like Rita, an urban gardener. That's probably why we get on."

There was a hand-clap. Their hostess occupied the door. "Have they given you a sorbet? Now does everyone know who they are? Tom, have you looked at Catharine's back to see who she is? Catharine? Tom?" She clapped again. "Remember, Yes or No answers only, girls and boys," she said and passed into the house.

Catharine, half turning, said, "Do you want –"

"Don't worry."

"That's a relief," she said. "I don't believe I could face a party game. You're Bob Hope, by the way." She turned her back towards him. "Who am I?"

Wavery told her.

"Jane Fonda! Rita is ridiculous." She walked to a low brick wall supporting a flower bed. She needed to touch something. She bent back a small bush of orange-scarlet flowers. "Oh, she's got one of these. Now I should remember this but I don't."

He sat down beside her. "*Embothrium coccineum*, could it be?"

"That's exactly what it is. You are clever."

"It's what comes of studying Latin," he said. "About the only thing." But her compliment pleased him. He never wanted people to think him wise or strong. It had been a fearful burden. Drawing the same response out of this charming stranger, he found himself giving in to his own pleasure.

She said, "I'm afraid we can't do Chilean fire bushes in London. Too cold. It would never flower."

"It might, if you found a sheltered spot."

" I wonder if Rita would give me a cutting."

"Of course she would." He felt a rush of generosity towards their hostess. "That's the thing about gardeners, they give things to each other."

"But it's so funny." She was conspiratorial. "Have you

noticed her conscientious objection to yellow? Too assertive, she says."

"Are you good at telling people from their gardens?"

"Oh, yes. Definitely. People who assert in their gardens are all the more delicate in life. I wonder what you would make of mine."

"What *is* it about gardens?" replied Wavery. He was trying to rein in his excitement. "People go on and on about them, but I see why they do." And before he knew it he was speaking to her of his own craving, one day to create a garden in Sintra.

She listened, head down, as he described for her a view of the sea through olive trees. Her hair covered her eyes so he could not see what she was thinking. When he had finished she looked up. Her mouth was an immaculate smile. "But that's a wonderful thing to want to do."

Wavery leaned away. Her reply had undermined him. He was embarrassed. "Are you here alone?" he asked.

"No, I have a husband. I saw you talking to him. Clark Gable."

"Ah, that's him," said Wavery. He remembered the handsome man flirting with the waitress.

They were on a three week visit to Peru. Adam had hopes of selling an auto-vinification plant to the Tacama Wine Company in Ica. They were staying at the Miramar. She was telling him all this when a voice came from the doorway. The wife of the French Number Two was saying, "Tom, I'm coming to talk with you. I have done my penance with Denver."

But Wavery did not move. "Oh," said Madame Palliasse. "Oh," and she retreated inside. "That man had swallowed a rainbow," she later told her husband.

"Oughtn't you to go in?" said Catharine. Again her eyes gusted through him. He knew he should look away, but did not.

"No," said Wavery. "Unless you want to." He heard the emotional edge to his prattle. She made him feel boyish and intense, something he was not aware of having felt in a long time.

"You know you have a spot on your trousers?"

"Where?"

She pointed behind his left knee. "A pen might have run . . ."

She had seen the mark across the room. A crude black circle at the height of his ankle, spreading furry legs into the light brown cotton. That's what she first had noticed about him, she would say at another time of the paint mark from Penny's easel. That's what stopped her leaving. That's what prevented her from collecting her husband and escorting him to their hotel. But none of this she explained in the patio because at that moment a man tottered onto the step.

He held Rita by the waist.

"And I get to take the prettiest one home," said Mr Riding who was slightly drunk.

He detached himself from Rita. Catharine let him arrange his arm like a stole about her shoulder. "Rita, we must go," she said over his limp arm.

"Say goodbye to Denver and I'll see you by the door," said Rita. "I haven't spoken to Tom."

They watched Catharine take her husband away. The woman who a moment before had been so vulnerable in the patio was supporting him. Her support was more than that of a wife helping her drunken husband across the floor.

"I love Catharine," said Rita. She scratched her long neck. "I've only known her for three years. But I love her."

Wavery was silent. She had never said goodbye.

"It's never what you think," Rita continued. "Adam's a highly successful, immensely attractive businessman – and a great flirt. But in private he depends on her I would say one hundred per cent."

"They were both charming, I thought," said Wavery. He was moved to follow inside, but Rita had not finished.

"I don't know why, but it's a fantastic shame."

"What is?" asked Wavery.

"Her sustaining his myth to the world. That's been her role from the beginning. He couldn't be the man he is without her, yet the man he is leaves her with nothing."

*　　*　　*

80

At eight forty-five on the morning after Rita Tennyson's party, Wavery arrived at the Embassy in Plaza Washington and walked out on the eleventh floor instead of the twelfth. The lift doors had closed by the time he realised his mistake. He prodded the button and waited. The lift returned to the lobby. He watched the green light making its halting ascent to the eleventh floor, every stop marked by a pinging bell. The doors shuddered open and he entered. Apart from Catharine Riding the lift was empty.

The doors closed and Wavery gazed at the overhead strip waiting for the button to flash twelve. There was a brass plate on the ceiling. SCHINDLER. 900 KGS. MAX 12 PERS., he read. The bell pinged.

He said, "I know it's a mad idea. But do you have time to see an exceptional garden?"

Afterwards, at lunch, he would say, "Always these things occur to you later, but this time it occurred to me on the spot."

They arranged to meet the following day. At midday she waited for him in the Miramar lobby. Her hair was tied at the back with a black velvet band and she wore a dark-green dress. They shook hands and he apologised. He was five minutes late, and out of breath.

The garden was twenty minutes away in the Barranco district. Wavery had come across it first with Penny. She bought painted trays from a young widow in the same street. She had been telling him about the husband, killed in a police ambush near Chimbote, when he noticed the wrought-iron railings.

"Well? There you are. What do you think?" he asked Catharine. "See what you can do in a simply ghastly climate."

Her hands gripped the ornate gate, fastened by two coils of rusted chain. The garden was planted in a rectangle no more than twenty yards long and thirty wide. In that space, with no sense of overcrowding, were most of the colours under the sun. White clematis climbed over white hydrangea. Double hibiscus grew blue among red japonica, and a path lined with pale pink cherry trees drew their eyes to a squat house, purple-coated in bougainvillea.

She put her hand to her mouth and pointed. "An Australian bottle-brush!"

They identified other shrubs and flowers. He admitted, "I can fall for plants in the way people go on about falling for Mozart concertos."

"What a marvellous place," she said. Her excitement could not be restrained and escaped in a joyful rattling of the gate. It was the excitement of a young girl at the zoo with her father. Wavery too pushed his head through the railings. He wanted to prolong this moment of sharing the one small thing they had in common.

Someone moved behind a window. The door opened and a man in a brown uniform advanced down the path, speaking urgently into a walkie-talkie.

Wavery withdrew his face from between the bars. "I think we'd better go."

He drove her to lunch in a restaurant on a cliff two miles south of Lima. The restaurant, El Salto del Fraile, was named after a friar who leaped into the waves when the woman he loved sailed for Europe. Vicente, a friend in the Senate, once mentioned to Wavery he took his girlfriends to the Friar's Leap.

A waiter drew back the chairs at a table by the window. The day was overcast and a cheerless wind clawed the glass. It was one o'clock but the waiter flicked his cigarette lighter, applying the flame to a candle in a red glass holder. Catharine fiddled with the candle as they spoke, the light darting onto her face and over her bare arms.

Wavery raised his hand for the waiter, who returned with a bottle of Tacama Gran Tinto. It was good, said the man, pouring the wine. He'd had it for breakfast.

Another couple entered the restaurant. The man was corpulent, his fleshy face rammed into a greying beard. The eyes at the bottom of his face were hard and shiny, like buttons in one of the Ambassador's Chesterfields. The girl was younger, with a small nose and overripe hips.

The waiter drew back two chairs at an adjacent table.

82

Wavery said, distracted, "I thought you might like lunch by the sea."

Catharine smiled at the lowering of his voice. When she smiled her smile was fenced in by two small lines at the corner of her mouth.

He said, "Do you want me to ask for another table?" None of the other tables were occupied.

"Don't be silly," she laughed. When she laughed another line appeared, outside the boundary.

"I'm glad I saw you in the lift," he said. "I realised at Rita's I had done all the talking."

"Wasn't it lucky!" she said. Adam wanted some papers collected from Mr Queesal. "To do with the wine company I was telling you about."

" Look –" He tilted the bottle. "We're drinking it."

"He spent all last week in – Ica, is it? It sounds pretty grim, the situation there."

"Then you were alone in Lima?"

She shook her head, her concentration on the candle. "It was a very strange feeling. I'm not used to being alone, not abroad."

"We could have had you to lunch."

But she needed to explain what had happened to her, alone in Lima. "I felt exposed."

"Did you walk through the centre?"

He hadn't understood. "Not exposed to anyone else. Exposed to myself." Alone in Lima she had felt none of the myriad props by which she was encouraged to construct her life at home. "I was forced to be myself."

"Is that such a terrible thing to be?"

She sat back. "Look at me, telling you things like this. You can't be interested."

He was dismayed. "Oh, but I am, I am. Someone who thinks as you do. I can't tell you. It's not –"

"What I've been describing, you must feel it the whole time."

The waiter returned. Wavery was about to tell her that he felt the opposite, but the moment had passed.

They ordered, Wavery recommending the *ceviche mixto.* They

talked and he learned she lived in London, off Kensington High Street. She had been married seven years. She had two daughters and a younger half-sister who worked for a charity for the blind.

To avoid the subject of her husband Wavery asked about her parents.

"My father was a soldier."

"Did he fight ever?"

She mentioned a name, a military operation known to Wavery in childhood. "He led it"

"Did he now?"

She could tell Wavery's admiration.

"Good heavens. So a very great man." He could remember the obituaries. The front pages had been devoted to testimonials of her father's courage, to the horrors he had endured at the hands of an unforgiving enemy, which resulted late in his life with suicide.

"Yes." She dropped her gaze onto the lateen of light in front of her. "It's funny. I hardly ever think about him, but I was thinking about him last week in Lima."

"And your mother?"

"My mother? She was, well, she was a wife."

"Did they discuss his past?"

"Not much. They separated when I was ten. He shot himself shortly after."

But a strange expression had come into her face. It was not the child's expression Wavery had witnessed on Rita's patio in front of Queesal. This face was older, more worn. She looked about, upset. And then, as if it was the most natural thing in the world, she stretched over to the next table where the couple were preparing to eat prawns off a raised plate, and she plucked one.

She began shelling the tail. Wavery, shocked, whispered, "You can't do that."

To emphasise the same point, the bearded man made a performance of offering her the whole plate. A grim smile crept along the young girl's face. The smile said, "This woman may be attractive, but she's mad."

"It looked so tantalising," Catharine said. She smiled at the man. "I'm sorry," she said sweetly and replaced the prawn on the crushed ice where it lay accusing and untouched until the end of the meal.

Her simple gesture had broken a taboo. For a moment Wavery sat opposite another person.

"But why did you do that?"

"I don't know. Might I be hungry? Can we talk about something else?" and they became very serious about a matter neither of them in the least cared about until the waiter arrived with their food.

The tension remained until after lunch when a boy appeared in the restaurant supporting a tray of plastic roses. He made for the bearded man's table. Each rose was planted in a small green tub and adorned by a pair of white-framed sunglasses. The boy set down a tub next to the silver plate. He invited the señorita to sing. When the young girl giggled the plant reacted with a lascivious writhing.

"What an extraordinary thing!" said Wavery. The fat man waved away the boy, who turned to Wavery. He shook his head.

"They're called rock plants," said Catharine. She was laughing.

He was glad. They did not have the luxury of time that allowed them to quarrel. When she laughed like that it was impossible not to laugh with her.

They began to talk again and there was lightness between them. They remembered places both of them knew: the country-side near Cambridge, where she had grown up; the garden at Hidcote; a walled town in Italy; a hotel with a virulent ceiling fresco of Aurora. Drawing Catharine out, Wavery felt he might sit and listen to her for as long as she chose to talk. He thought, This is what happens when people communicate. This is exactly what happens. You are fascinated to know what makes the other person tick. And he was genuinely interested in this lively, alert, intelligent woman. She was someone whose company he cherished in a way he had forgotten.

She in her turn was touched by his reticence, his grace, by

his acceptance of her as a charming companion and someone he would like to spend time with.

"You were *so* interested, Thomas, so amusing, and, I suppose, older. I felt liberated. I felt far funnier, far more intelligent than I'd felt for ages. Because you were a good listener. I could tell you were trained to be like that with everyone."

Something else Catharine admitted to herself in the course of their conversation. Something she had only begun to articulate. She didn't know who Wavery was, beyond the fact he was a diplomat. As a diplomat he was perfect: he couldn't lay a finger on her. She could use him without ever knowing who he was. She saw his apparent strength and kindness and she believed he could do for her what she had not been able to ask of anybody. As the afternoon went on, a voice crept into her head. Look here, said this voice, I think this man can help you in a way no one else can.

"What are you thinking?" asked Wavery over coffee.

"I was thinking about the rock plant," she pretended. "We could have planted it in that marvellous garden."

"How silly," he said. "We should have bought one."

She dipped a finger into her wineglass and retrieved a breadcrumb from the bottom. "What are *you* thinking?"

"Where do you think they make these labels?"

"I don't care."

"I was thinking about your husband."

She said, "Oh, he's fine," as though he had been involved in some accident and was recovering well. She adjusted herself. "He's a very clever man. He's done terribly well with his wine business. People aren't buying a lot in the recession." Wavery could see the effort she was making to describe the man as the world saw him. "He's pulled off the most brilliant coup with Tacama. He's fine . . ." She stopped, acknowledging that what she had said was boring. Her words hung between them both, heated by the candle in the distorting air.

"We ought to go," said Wavery. He raised his hand for the bill. "Where is he?" He looked at her watch and she twisted her wrist for him.

"Two-thirty," she said.

The couple rose from the next table, leaving without a glance. Through the window Wavery saw the man open the passenger door for the girl. The car was parked beside a pillbox. Through the slit in the pillbox could be seen the perforated muzzle of a machine gun

"A gun for a restaurant?" she said.

"Last month the terrorists lobbed a stick of dynamite in here. A month before they forced everyone to the floor and removed their wallets."

"So you suggested it."

"It's the same everywhere."

"Will you be happy to leave?"

"Oh, I think so."

"Do you know where next?"

"Portugal. At least that's what I'm hoping."

"I've never been there."

"For God's sake, you've never been to Lisbon! You have to go. You'll have to come and stay."

But he was thinking how stupid he felt and what was he to do, how was he to stop this gibberish toadhopping from his mouth, how could he crash his fist through the glass and grab the appropriate words, how could he after a lifetime of never ever saying what he felt, say now what he felt?

After he had been thoroughly beckoned at the waiter arrived.

"We're in rather a hurry."

"Si, señor."

She laughed and a boundary line moved. "My sister always irritates me by saying the cemetery is full of hurried men."

The waiter produced the bill on a plate accompanied by two fortune cookies. Wavery's biscuit was stale. The little paper said: "The fun is just beginning. Take it easy." It burned quickly, floating a man's height in the air, then collapsing in a web of ash. Wavery rose to catch it. He sat down and she was talking. There was a dullness to her voice. He folded his napkin. She was talking about the trip she and Adam were about to make to Arequipa. Was Arequipa lovely, as Queesal said?

He folded his napkin again. "Noel Coward wrote a play there." But he was not concentrating. Even logic told him this lunch was coming to an end. When it did, it was inconceivable he could handle the ending.

She bent to get her bag from the floor. Wavery avoided looking at her breasts, her ankles. She sat back and stretched her legs. One leg touched his knee, not moving away. He was unable to fold the napkin anymore. She saw his gaze stray to a mole on the side of her cheek. He was looking, without listening, watching her face, the dart of light on her cheeks, her nose, when she stopped talking. She met his eyes directly.

"What is it, Thomas?"

"I really have to go."

In the bedroom there was a loud buzzing. Wavery switched off the television set. The soap opera was over and already the screen had acquired a fresh layer of dust. He went into the bathroom to clean his teeth. He blinked as he brushed, exercising his eyes. They had grown more short-sighted since Lima. They registered people as indistinct blurs. In the days before he needed to wear glasses, a man in Jordan had told him he had lovely eyes. "I would swap my hotel for your eyes," he said. It hadn't been a particularly nice hotel.

Wavery spat out the toothpaste, rinsing the basin with the cold tap. He closed the windows onto the terrace, lay down on the bed and inspected a finger. A nail needed clipping. Penny kept her clippers in the bedside table. Out of habit, he opened the drawer: a pencil, two reed drink mats and a booklet which Asunción must have left there, entitled *Guidance to Diplomatic Servicemen and other Officers and Wives Posted to Diplomatic Service Missions Overseas: Some Do's and Don'ts*. He read, "Going abroad should be fun," and turned the page. "A single officer may find the evenings very long. Try not to be a moaner. If there is a down period, don't just sit and brood about it. See if there any language courses you can attend, or social clubs you can join. Are singing and amateur dramatics catered for? What about the orienteers?"

He returned the booklet to the drawer.

Outside, a voice stumbled into the night. It carried a grey wisp of song which made Wavery sit up. The song was one his favourite *fados*. He began putting on his clothes again.

5

Night fell as suddenly as the ink that spilled onto Captain Panteco's report on Abdul Hadi, a smuggler of duty-free tobacco. The ink flooded over the report towards the table edge and Panteco leapt to his feet and cried, "Fuck it!"

The ink dripped onto the red linoleum. Panteco reached into his pocket for a handkerchief, but he saw that it was Rosita's.

Rosita had once lived with Captain Panteco, but one day two years ago had ended their affair without explanation and returned to her brother's flat above the Café Ulises. When she told him she was singing tonight in memory of Emilio, and would he come and hear her sing, he said "Of course, *querida*."

"Do you mind if I bring Dolores?" he said, hoping she would mind. Rosita didn't mind. Dolores was her friend too. The only person Rosita minded about these days was the Englishman Silkleigh.

It tormented Panteco. Silkleigh was small, the perfect shape for a diver. Panteco was too tall for a policeman. Everyone saw him coming. He couldn't help his booming voice, so that before they could see they could very often hear.

He pressed the handkerchief to his nose and then mopped his cheeks where his complexion was worst. The doctor had diagnosed his acne as an acute manifestation of Rock Fever, seeing the same people every day, seeing the world through the wrong end of a telescope, believing this *was* the world. "Rock Fever, my arse," said his chief. "You don't wash your ears out." Panteco's problem was that his brain was too small for his body.

Panteco's head rose above the table. He placed the handkerchief in a safe corner.

"The newspaper," suggested Abdul Hadi, sitting handcuffed on the bench.

"You think I haven't thought of that?" said Panteco, feeling ugly. He spread the pages of *El Faro* over the table.

"Let's start again," he said and he waved at the damp, black fists of paper in the wicker basket. "Forget those lies. You're a mouse with only one hole, Mohamed. This time, the truth." He smoothed out a fresh form.

The truth was this. At two in the morning, one mile north-west of La Mujer Muerta, he had apprehended Abdul Hadi in the illegal possession of twelve crates of Winston cigarettes.

"What are you doing, Mohamed?" asked Panteco, steering his crab-boat alongside. He looked at the crates bobbing in the water. This little Mohamed's having a party, he thought. Abdul Hadi, holding himself upright by his carbide lamp, surrounded by a lot of cardboard boxes that wouldn't sink, about eight of them, which was a lot of Winston rubios, but not quite as many as Abdul Hadi would have liked because there were still ten crates on board which in that stretch of water constituted a criminal offence meriting four months in this Holiday Inn, said, "What do you think I'm doing, monsieur? I'm fishing. They're not mine. They're just there."

"I got you fried, Mohamed. Hear that? *Frito*!" Captain Panteco stepped on board. "Do you have any arms, stowaways or animals?"

But Abdul Hadi had only the cigarettes. Panteco knew where the Winstons had come from. They came from Gibraltar, purchased from Stagnetto's in Main Street for £245 a crate and sold to Abdul Hadi for £325. The profit of fifteen thousand pesetas was nothing to what Abdul Hadi would make in Abyla. Each crate contained fifty cartons. They bore no health warnings and were sealed with a United States blue sticker. Inferior Winstons made under licence in Spain were sealed in grey.

Panteco had seen all manner of Mohameds on the Playa Benitez, their trousers rolled, running up the beach with ten thousand fags on each shoulder. There was precious little

90

Panteco could do. Every time he tried to do something, an army of fisherman's wives and children rushed from their houses and blocked his path to Mohamed's lock-up in El Hadu.

Panteco scratched five circles with his pen before the ink flowed.

"Name," he began, but even as he noted it down Panteco was exhausted by a sense of futility.

"Address?" He asked. Abdul Hadi didn't even have a visa. It wasn't like the old days when Panteco's grandfather fired his cannon at six o'clock and the Moors had to leave town for the night. Now they lived here. A plague of them. Coming to work on the tunnel. Coming to enter a Europe without frontiers. Poisoning his patch with their bundles of hash on their way. Crossing on the bridges of their own dead.

Tabacañeros like this Mohamed were harmless. The harm was done by men the other side of La Mujer Muerta. Until five years ago, these men had been content to smuggle the hash they grew between tomatoes in Ketama. But the tunnel had made them greedy. They had set their sights on whiter drugs. If one believed *El Faro* half the Tercio were zombies. Panteco's boss believed it. Panteco believed it too. He saw them in the streets, outside schools, collapsed in church. They left their trail in blood on elevator doors and on the backs of pews. He had only to look into their eyes to see what they had done. They'd look at you, through you, like maniacs.

"The darkest place is always underneath the lamp." That's what Panteco's grandfather, the night watchman, used to say. The biggest maniac was not in Ketama. He was not in Tetouan or Tangier. He was here among them, in Abyla. No one knew who he was, or even what he looked like. No one knew anything – save that he was known to all as El Callado.

"Get the bastard's ass in here, Panteco," said his chief.

"Oh, yes sir, by all means." But how? Panteco had already been five years on the trail, and for five years he had been looking at no El Callado. It was like untying a knot when you're fishing, a maddening, inextricably tangled knot that caused you to sit there picking while the plumpest fish you ever saw swam

91

a slow striptease in the water, gurgling "Panteco, Panteco, Panteco . . ."

Five years on, he believed he had identified El Callado's boat, a Ford-Maclaren which started on gear. It had the power to leave Abyla, make the pick-up off La Mujer Muerte, cross to Atunara and be back in an hour, clean as his whistle. El Callado paid three million pesetas a job, that's what his chief reckoned. Not that El Callado was silly enough to register the boat in his name. It was chartered from some bona fide smart arse in Bermuda and never to the same crew. They were weekend sailors who walked on deck in shoes and tied weird knots to fenders and if the *poniente* blew forgot the springline. If they sailed out of Abyla at night, Panteco would telephone Algeciras. Sometimes Algeciras bothered to send a helicopter and its lights would criss-cross the sea searching for a telltale wake. Or they might send the turbo which could race without fear over the tunny-nets, the trouble being it only raced at 40 knots. El Callado's men sat on Monte Hacho with radio sets and night-goggles and when the coast was clear they flashed their torches into the telescope on the belvedere and just the person at whom the telescope was pointed could see the sign. All this Panteco knew. But in Abyla he didn't have a helicopter. He had no turbo. He had a crab boat suitable for monitoring the rocks – and for catching *tabacañeros* like Mohamed.

Panteco had to admit he had been hoping for a catch bigger than a cigarette smuggler whose propellers had fouled on a bin-liner. He had been hoping to train his searchlights on a row of orange blob buoys. If he found a blob buoy he was likely to find a *palangre* line and the chances were it wouldn't be weighed with grouper fish but another catch which El Callado's men pulled aboard with grappling hooks.

Because a good *palangre* fisherman didn't use blob buoys. He didn't want people to know where he fished.

Emilio had been a good *palangre* fisherman, thought Panteco, jabbing his nib at the desk.

And what would happen to Mohamed, grinning on the bench? Panteco could ask him anything and go on asking from arsehole to kingdom come without hearing one truthful reply. He was right to grin like that. Panteco knew what would happen. After two weeks in Las Rosales, Mohamed would have acquired fifty thousand pesos to pay for his confession. In two weeks' time a man would knock on the prison gates and admit that Mohamed's boat and the twelve crates, half of them soaked, were his.

Panteco leaned forward. "Mohamed?" he said.

"Monsieur?"

"Suppose they're not your cigarettes," he said reasonably.

Abdul Hadi grinned. "No, monsieur."

"Suppose we forget about this morning."

"Yes, monsieur."

"Suppose I need something to help me forget."

"Monsieur?"

"What I want to know, Mohamed, is this. Who is El Callado?"

The Mohamed said nothing, but sat there grinning.

The sight was too much for something in Panteco. He dashed forward and ploughed a fist into his clear, smooth face.

6

Inside the Café Ulises, Mohamed had decided. He was determined to win a biro in Abyla Television's "Whose Eyes?" competition. He entered the kitchen and scrutinised the temporary cook with a look of such intensity she hurled a bread roll at his head.

The kitchen could be glimpsed through two diamond-shaped panels in the swing doors at the rear which, each time they swung open, revealed a number of notes pinned to the inside. The *sopa del dia*; those dishes not available on the menu; the telephone number in Caracas where Periclito Amaral, the café's owner, might be contacted during the next three weeks.

Back, forth, back, forth, back, forth swung the doors until, just when they had closed together with a little shudder, Mohamed burst out of the kitchen and walked balletically across the floor to where Ghanem the Mute sat vacant-faced under the television set.

Mohamed served Ghanem his usual plate of *calamares*. He was in the process of twisting a large pepper grinder, as taught by Periclito, when he yielded to temptation and looked up. Instantly he became lost in admiration for each of the thousand and one faces he saw everywhere reflected on the walls and on the pillars. They were the faces of an Arab in his mid-twenties, with short frizzy hair and an apologetic moustache like a circumflex.

In Periclito's mirrors not only did people see themselves repeated at curious angles and larger than life, but everyone saw everyone else. They saw the banker, Dionisio Porcil, playing dominoes with the chairman of the telephone exchange. They saw Ghanem the Mute watching *The Strong Tend to Leave*. They saw Captain Panteco arriving for a late dinner with the librarian. And if instead of sitting, they stood as Mohamed stood, and leaned against the central pillar, itself a four-sided mirror, beneath the celebrated features of Lieutenant Zamora, they could see the bar against the wall, the guitar on which Gallo, the bell boy, was quietly playing to himself, three chords at a time; and the semi-curtained stage on which a moment before Rosita had completed her first *fado*.

It was Rosita's prerogative, as the owner's sister, to sing whenever she chose. For Mohamed, the sounds she expelled from her throat lacked unambiguously the power to seduce, reminding him rather of her brother's cries as he lunged at the central pillar on those afternoons in the locked café when Periclito practised his *mariposas*, raising Mohamed's black apron behind his back, first one side, then the other, like a butterfly. In his mirrors, Periclito could see himself from every angle, front back and in paunchy profile. In those mirrors, he discarded his limp, and the bull's head he alone could see, eternally ready for Periclito's truth, exposed its neck. That's it, my darling, put your feet together. Hand me the sword – my sword, Mohamed!

"Mohamed!" Panteco was calling. Mohamed nodded. All right, he'd seen him.

"Enough?" But Ghanem was engrossed in *The Strong Tend to Leave*.

Mohamed planted the pepper grinder on the table, then swerved around the pillar to where Panteco stood beside Dolores. The librarian wore a new indigo blouse and gold wind-mill earrings. She scratched her throat, tossing the hair she had half-twisted into a bun and half-permitted to hang down one side of her face so that everyone could see her burnt-sugar eyes. On her arrival the whole café had fallen into a library hush.

Mohamed inspected her closely as he smoothed out a fresh tablecloth and, bowing, announced to the Captain and his pretty companion, as if they did indeed merit the attention of the entire café: "Señores!"

But her eyes were not the eyes featured in the biro compe-tition.

Wavery stood at the bar next to a vase of wild berries and a stand containing hard-boiled eggs. It was lit by the same coloured lights that gaudied the empty stage. Several of the lights were broken, making it the darkest part of the café.

He waited for someone to serve him.

"Señor?" Mohamed appeared at last.

Wavery ordered a cognac.

"Naçional?"

Wavery nodded. Above the bottles, the stuffed head of a bull was repeated in the glass, its horns tossing a battered sombrero.

"Jam de kiam okazis la akcidento li etas malzata."

Beside him a man leaned down, to give a potato crisp to the dog Wavery had seen on the esplanade. The dog's lead was attached to the leg of a barstool. The man sat up and his face came blue, red and yellow into the lights.

He was small, about fifty, with a crease about his eyes as if he might have been wearing a ski-mask. His hair was thinning on top, but elsewhere needed a trim. He was dressed in a long grey T-shirt, and jeans which had been tucked into a pair of cowboy boots stamped with black cartwheels. A gold propelling pencil was clipped to his T-shirt at the throat. On his chest

Wavery read the words VIRGIL IS STILL THE FROG BOY.

"Ever since the accident, he's been hungry."

He spoke English, with the trace of a west country accent. Wavery looked away. Below the bull's head there was an enlarged photograph of a rotund man in matador's uniform. Wavery read: "*Periclito Merimée Amaral, triunfador de la feria de Chinchero, 1987*".

"Esperanto," the Englishman was saying. He addressed the dog at his feet. "Who is the strict gentleman on the chair?" He laughed to himself. The merriment rattled with unhappinesss. "Language of the future," he said. The words rolled out of sight under his chair. "Sounds silly, but there's an element of truth in it. Isn't that so, my angel? I know, you're looking for your master."

He ruffled the dog's ears, then patted the air above the animal's head. It was a curious gesture, as if he were flicking his fingers dry. The dog pulled at the lead. The bar lights flashed on his blue teeth and in his eyes and on the pink foam frothing his gum.

"Now go and lie down like a good dog. If we were underwater and I flicked my fingers like that, you would sparkle. Just like an angel."

He glanced at Wavery. There was an urgent friendliness in the glance. He held out a hand smeared with oil. "Joseph Silkleigh," he said. "And this is Toribio. That's Emilio's seat you're sitting on, old soul."

Silkleigh talked to the fractured strumming of the guitar and Wavery listened. "I run a business. It's not running very fast, either." He sold water-purifying systems to houses, hotels, "any ippety-oy who will buy them – you just plug them under the sink and they take the diseases out as the water flows through. Simple as that."

But what really interested him was the sea. The sea was never dull – ever, ever, ever.

He'd been diving all day for the fisherman, in the shallows off Punta Leone. In the afternoon he had dived to eighty feet where the water fell into night and the air was almost chewable.

He couldn't stay long because of the current and the oil burning on the surface, broken by the *poniente* into several flaming slicks. He had swum ashore below La Mujer Muerta where the beach was noisy with the flap of oil-glued wings and dying sandwich terns and the air smelled of dead seals. There would be a stench in the sand for months.

"The pearl of the Mediterranean," he said. "More like Armageddon."

Only God and the damsel fish knew where Emilio's vessel lay. His new boat had found old stones. There he was one minute, sailing her home from Essaouira, the next watching a great bow slice out of the sea mist. This was one of the most dangerous stretches of water in the world, a ship a minute and then the wind, for which the narrow Straits acted as a funnel, and which came – he clicked his fingers – like that! When the wind got up, it didn't mess about. And once you had negotiated the wind you still had to reckon with the current, the Atlantic rushing in at ten knots, meeting the sill connecting Abyla with Gibraltar, bursting upwards, so if you were crossing by boat you could be rolling backward and forward, starboard to larboard. You could be swimming in sweet innocence at ten feet and a couple of breaths later you could find yourself at a hundred and twenty feet, saying bye bye quickly.

He hadn't found Emilio, nor his boat, the colour of Rifian honey, but as he reached the surface he had seen a green turtle swimming out of the oil towards him. The shape of her mouth was very, very sad, as if she had lost someone and her shell had been eaten away. As she swam, the bio-luminescence in the water made her shine. She sparkled with angel dust. She was looking for somewhere to lay her eggs.

"She was gorgeous."

He twisted his glass. The shadows slurred over the counter. He rolled his tongue round his mouth. Abruptly he sat back so that his feet slipped off the bottom rung of the stool, startling the dog.

"Mohamed!" he called. "I shall have another." He patted Emilio's dog and a tail slapped his leg. "Take Toribio," he said.

"Take nature." The image returned to Silkleigh of Emilio's mother three hours before, her face above him on the quay. Madness had leaped into her eyes as she called for the sea to give back her son, rocking still in the lap of the deep. "If a woman can go mad, why can't the world? No, Mohamed. That's whisky. He's so bloody useless. He's been here five years and he hasn't learned a thing. When Periclito's not here the place goes to pieces. Hear that? There'll be fog again tonight. Poor Emilio. At least his boat will make a beautiful coral reef."

He looked into the mirror, but he didn't see himself. He saw a golden turtle swimming in at high tide, under a full moon. He saw the unscarred sand and the waves lifting her onto the shore. They drain away and return, lifting her higher. She lies with moonlight on her wet shield. She sculls herself up the beach. She scrapes a hole. She lays her eggs, straining and sighing. Afterwards, she covers her eggs with sand. The sand cakes her face, except where the sea-tears gutter it. She begins her slide towards the waves, flippering out the tracks as she moves backwards.

"Some bastards wait for her. They wait and then, when she's laid her eggs, they run towards her. They turn her over. Onto her back. Like that. One hundred and fifty million years turned on her back. So she can't move . . ." said Silkleigh in an awful voice into the television voices, the sounds of dominoes scraping wood, the sounds of the guitarist's three chords.

"I'm writing about it, old soul," said Silkleigh. There was a splinter of determination in his voice. His life as a diver, the turtles, the fish, the things he'd seen. It was quite a life. He was only fifty-four, but a lot of interesting people were dead by fifty-four. Byron, Keats, a poet he'd met in La Linea called Danny Huckin. He'd been wanting to write his life story for years. He wanted to write it so badly, Mr Wavery had no idea. When he wasn't diving he thought about it all day long. But to write. It was hard. It was like walking up La Mujer Muerta backwards. Not that he wasn't prepared for the climb. He'd had a short story published. In the *Gibraltar Chronicle*. Quite a prestigious little publication actually. That's when he first had the idea he might embark on something bigger. A more important book, to show people the terrible things we were doing to the world. Something for all men and women to read. A book to cross all frontiers. Which was the reason, speaking frankly, he had once thought of writing it in Esperanto.

"They say you can get by anywhere in the world if you speak English. Well, that's nonsense."

One thing alone had held him up. "I need a title," he said. It was absurd, very possibly it couldn't be understood by someone who was not a writer. But he found it impossible to write a word, a single word, until he had decided on the title. So far the story of Joseph Silkleigh's fifty-four years was contained in six Lion Brand notebooks which only helped to remind him of the moments when with an absolute certainty and clarity of vision he had decided to call his autobiography *Summoning the Wind* or *The Dust We Play In* or *A Shadow in Love with the Sun* or *Dying in Paradise* or *Sisyphus Happy* or *The Nomad of the Time Streams* or *Stolen Air* or *I Had a Wild Thyme Too* – none of them, he realised a day or so later with the same clarity, any bloody good at all.

"I've got the story, old soul. That's the easy part. Once I've got the title," Silkleigh said, "everything else will flow."

Wavery was on the point of telling him about Penny and the problems she would have with her paintings, but at that moment Silkleigh glanced at the stage. There was alarm in his eye.

"Oh, *no*," he said.

The lights were switched off. The only light in the café came from the stage and from the television set on the opposite wall. Mohamed turned down the volume. The curtain parted and a small woman was revealed standing awkwardly in the silence. Her stomach was cramped into a belt of gold braid and she wore a tight red shirt. Her hair was tied into a bun with black lace and a black shawl draped her shoulders. She adjusted the shawl, making sure. The guitarist offered her a glass of water and she drank. He began playing. She breathed in. Her hands came together, then her dark eyebrows. She stepped forward, her eyes concentrating on the pillar and the portrait of

Lieutenant Zamora. At Silkleigh's feet, Emilio's dog gave out a frightened bark.

"*. . . a minha terra, a minha gente, a saudade e a tristeza que magoa.*" She hurled her song across the room. Her body swayed as she sang, her shoulders lifting, her fingers moving occasionally as if she were releasing something from her clasped hands.

"*Fado,*" whispered Silkleigh. "You can see why it never caught on." When she had sung some more he pinched Wavery's arm.

"'Canoe, take care'," he translated. "'If you're run over by a boat you'll never return to the wharf'." He leaned an elbow on the counter, his heel falling and lifting with her doleful cadences. "It might explain why her brother has za-za'd off to South America."

After a while he translated some more.

"Really, there's no need," said Wavery. "I used to live in Portugal."

"Oh," said Silkleigh. "Right you are, old soul."

They heard Rosita's hoarse, aching voice. She had thrown back her head. Her hand gripped the air as if it were a rope.

"Frightful, isn't it? Poor Rosita. Her talent is for dancing, but she thinks she's a singer. Just because you're ugly doesn't mean you have a beautiful voice."

Silkleigh exhaled and his eyes lingered on Dolores walking confidently through the peacock shadows. She leaned against the bar and asked Mohamed for a packet of Winston rubio.

"Do you know Dolores?" Silkleigh asked Wavery. "She never says a single word of interest, but she's an absolute darling. Hello, dear." He struck a match and offered it. Dolores looked into her bag, ignoring him. "Why do you go with Panteco?" he said, looking at the flame creep towards his fingers.

She shrugged. "Why not?"

She produced a lighter from her bag and Silkleigh blew out his flame, smarting.

"I love you," he said, blowing on his fingers.

She said, "Go pick your nose, Silkleigh." She returned to the Captain's table, shaking her long hair, her cigarette glowing.

"Longing for it," said Silkleigh joylessly. He elevated his glass. "To the love that lies in women's eyes. And lies and lies and lies."

When Wavery ignored the toast he said: "Don't say much, do you, old son? Still, I suppose you're taking it in."

And suddenly the *fado* was over and Rosita was applauding the guitarist. Someone in the crowd called "*Bonito! Bonito!*".

"Must be a Portuguese," said Silkleigh, one hand clapping the counter. He faced the bar and toasted the singer's reflection. She bowed a final time and was lost in the curtain.

"What brings you to Abyla, Thomas?"

Wavery told him.

"Is that so?" Silkleigh nodded to himself. "Hear that, Toribio? A diplomat. That's a chap who says nice doggie while looking for a stone. I knew a diplomat once. Teheran. I never met such an excessively shy halfwit. He spent all his time having dinner with the Bulgarians and knew nothing, nothing, nothing about what people were really feeling. Didn't have a clue the Shah was unpopular."

"A lot of us are like that," Wavery conceded. He asked Mohamed for the bill. He was leaving. He could afford to be more civil than he felt. Joseph Silkleigh had been alive when he talked about the sea.

"So what have you done wrong?" The voice bored on. "We're all here for funny old reasons. What's yours? You've been giving money to the Russians? Cohabiting with a goat? No one gets promoted to Abyla. It's just a rock at the edge of the world. Abyla has one Englishman. Me," and a finger tugged at his right eye.

"My posting has more to do with the tunnel."

"*If* that floperoo is ever completed," said Silkleigh. Not with Menendez hating his right leg to know what his left leg was doing. From his face tonight – Silkleigh nodded at the television which could be heard again – both legs had gone walky-walky.

Mohamed presented Wavery with a bill and Wavery paid.

Again Silkleigh lifted his glass. With his hand he made a curve of the room. "If you're planning to live here, old soul, you're going to have to admit us into your life. Not just me, but *all* of these people. Just like I have."

"Is that so?" said Wavery.

"Ask me anything and I'll tell you about them. I'm good on others. I can size them up, their foibles, their weaknesses, what makes them redeemable. We're all redeemable, for God's sake, even a buff-fucking-foon like Policeman Panteco. Under every carapace there's a turtle egg. That's what I say."

"Yes, I can see that."

"Want to know about that table of Basque dissidents over there? Or Ghanem the Mute? Or Periclito, our absent landlord? Then Joseph Silkleigh's your man."

"Thank you, but not at the moment," said Wavery.

"Any time, *ambasadoro*," said Silkleigh. "All in my notebooks. I tell you, there's thousands of them. All just waiting to be unlocked by that title, by one simple phrase –"

He stopped, looking down at his lap. A large man had propelled himself to the bar, knocking over a glass. The contents dripped from the counter.

"Mohamed!" said Silkleigh, pointing at a cloth.

"Hello, Silkleigh."

"Ah, good evening, Captain. How fares the drugs war?"

"I warn you, Silkleigh. I've got you under the belljar." Panteco spoke in a voice quieter than normal. He did not want to be heard by Dolores, sitting two tables away. He felt her eyes on his back.

"Them's fighting words, Captain."

"Every move you make," said the policeman.

"Go swat some flies, Captain. There's a good chap."

"Every move, Silkleigh. I'm just waiting." He gave Silkleigh a broiling stare. He yearned for Silkleigh to be in some way connected with El Callado. What could Rosita possibly see in him?

"Trouble with you, Captain," said Silkleigh patiently, "is that being head and shoulders above everyone else, you don't see very much."

A second or two elapsed before Panteco realised what he had

heard. The smoke drifted from his nostrils as if his insides were burning.

"You're . . . you're drunk!"

"Not so, sir. Look! How still my hands are." Silkleigh held out his trembling hands.

"Drunk!" Panteco's voice rose to a penetrating treble. Behind him Dolores watched, her hand stroking a long cobra throat.

"Oh, why don't you *tenu la busa fermita*," said Silkleigh.

"Lustrino." The voice belonged to the singer, Rosita. She rose between them, taking Panteco's arm. Her cheeks were patched with rouge, her eyes ringed with masacara. "You're going to fall on your laces."

Panteco gazed down to his black shoes and the laces she had a moment before untied. He kneeled. She leaned on her elbow against the bar, watching him. "Two years can be a long time, Lustrino," she said, with a sigh.

Panteco stood up. Under the lights his blush was green.

"That's Emilio's dog," said Panteco, ignoring her. "That's Toribio. You've no right to take him."

"*Calma, calma*, Captain." Silkleigh's boots squeaked as he slid from his stool. He stood up, releasing the lead. "Take him. He was hungry."

Panteco jerked Toribio towards his table. "Sit," he ordered. The dog slumped to the floor like a coat falling from a hanger. He lay there panting, his eyes half-closed as Dolores plunged a white hand through his warm thick fur.

Rosita's voice was tired. She lacked the ease of a loved woman. "Will you never learn, Silkleigh?"

"Rosita, my passion-killer," said Silkleigh. "Cheer me up. Tell me I'm wonderful."

She turned from him. She stood with her gold-braided back to the room, one hand rubbing her arm below a vaccination scar.

Silkleigh removed a sprig with yellow berries from the vase on the bar. "This is the plant the cattle won't eat. Have a nibble, Rosita," he said. "Tell me why the cattle won't eat it."

"Mohamed," she said. Mohamed poured her a whisky. She was crying.

"Neither in women's tears nor the skies of the mountain should men put their trust," intoned Silkleigh.

She bowed her head.

"Oh God, I can't bear tears. Pass me that cloth again, Mohamed." She shook her head, burying her face in her arm.

"There, there," he said. He made an ineffectual dab at her cheeks. After a while she lifted her head, allowing him to pat the cloth below her eyes.

"This is Mr Wavery," he said tenderly. He rotated her. "The British Consul General who has come to live with us a long way from home."

"How do you do?" said Wavery, embarrassed. She looked at him, not taking him in. "This is Rosita Amaral," Silkleigh whispered, lulling her. "The best *fadista* in Abyla." He held her in his arms. He was a changed man. He was the diver again, the turtle.

"A long way from home . . ." Silkleigh tried out the words. "You know, that's not a bad title," he said. He unclipped the pencil from his T-shirt and wrote down the words on his bill.

"See how it looks in the morning, shall we?"

Chapter Five

I

WAVERY LEARNED TO ignore the unpredictable chimes from the bell tower. Every morning at six-thirty he was woken by the trumpet in the barracks, after which he lay in bed listening to the horns of trapped cars in Calle Zamora. He rose at seven-thirty. At seven-thirty the tunnel opened its mouth on the Marina Española.

At seven-thirty an enormous worm could be first seen and then heard slithering down the hill from El Hadu, its scales composed of dirty yellow helmets. This creature made up of a thousand workers of all creeds and races, of men who had dug below the earth in Holland and Japan and below the English Channel, had a goal. But there was a sense that at any moment the millipede could twist its blind head up an unfamiliar street and separate into a thousand segments.

For half an hour in the morning and for half an hour in the evening the Marina Española became a place to avoid. Conversations ebbed away, watches were looked at, meetings remembered. Everything possible was done to remove oneself from the tide of men flowing into the dark heart of the earth.

The men were known by Abylans as *ratas*. Thanks to the efforts of Senator Zamora and Abyla Independiente, the *ratas* were confined to their prefabricated village, and to the tunnel mouth which swallowed them.

The tunnel was never silent. From shortly after sunrise until sunset you heard hammering, shovelling, drilling, welding, scraping, revving, shouting, clanging, clashing, squealing, roaring. At night these sounds were replaced by a subdued churning. Everywhere you went in Abyla, you felt this churning, as the tunnelling machine nosed its subterranean passage towards Europe.

Abyla presented her back to Africa. No one was the least bit interested to know what happened beyond La Mujer Muerta. In Abyla, everything looked to Europe and the sea, even the trees. Everything strained to escape the grimy coverlet of noise and dust which all day hung above the city, only disappearing at night, blown away by the *poniente*. Then, for a short time, Abyla smelled the orange trees in Calle Camoes.

That was at night. By day, it was different. Everywhere the same thick chaotic dust, whirling off the muck-lorries, whirling off the spoil lagoon inside the new sea wall. Everywhere the same short streets making their dash like muddy children to the sea. Everywhere the noise.

At eight-fifteen each morning, half an hour before his builders arrived, Wavery walked to the Abyla Swimming Club where he swam twenty lengths of the open air pool in as many minutes. The club was situated on a cliff overlooking the eastern side of the promontory, a walk of less than fifteen minutes. Afterwards he continued to the Consulate, carrying his damp towel and swimming trunks in a roll under his arm.

At the end of his first week in Abyla, Wavery was leaving the pool when he heard a familiar cry.

"Emeeeeeleeeo . . ."

He saw the fisherman's mother a long way below. She bent her knees into the waves, bunching her dress above the water. She had worn the same dress for eight days, the colour of a wine stain.

"Emeeeeeeeleeeo."

The cry seemed to wrinkle the sea. A hand of water spread ashore, darkening her dress to the waist.

A ferry trailed smoke along the horizon. Closer to the shore a small boat puttered towards the headland. A black dog sat on a coil of rope and at the tiller sat Joseph Silkleigh. His boat

106

turned in an unhurried arc, followed in the air by hundreds of seagulls as if one of his notebooks had been torn into scraps and tossed into the air.

Wavery turned into Calle Cervantes. Already he recognised people seen the day before: women at windows of snowy Chinese bed linen, men in shirtsleeves contemplating video-recorders, a blind lady selling lottery tickets. Abyla was a hand-kerchief, Asunción warned him. You could know the good, the bad and the evil of everyone.

He entered the Plaza de los Reyes. This was the smaller of Abyla's two principal squares. The Plaza de Africa at the bottom of the hill contained the Hotel Zamora and the Church of the Virgin of Africa, but most Abylans chose the Plaza de los Reyes in which to meet. Twelve palm trees provided fugitive shade for as many concrete benches. The cold benches were occupied by old men and women who sat on cardboard cushions torn from Marie Amaral's flower boxes.

In the centre of the square there was a bust of the quinologist, Leopoldo Zamora, a metal rocking horse and an empty fountain of mustard-coloured tiles. On Fridays, such as today, a man from Algeciras sat on the fountain rim eating cockles and selling reproductions of familiar and not so familiar paintings.

On this morning, propped against the fountain, Wavery saw: "two Lancaster bombers breaking from the clouds"; "the New York skyline"; "Moses Pitti's Mappa Mundi of 1681"; "a pere-grine falcon landing in the snow".

Today the man was offering a selection of the world's great masters. Christmas being only three weeks away, he was carrying on a brisk trade.

Genia Ortiz, stood on the rocking horse side of the fountain and tapped a pile of Murillo Virgins with her baton. She wore a fox-fur boa and a green tulle dress with a collar slightly too high, and, fastening the collar, a cameo portrait in red hyalite of her great-grandmother, Olga.

"My spectacles – I cannot see without my spectacles – there we are." She had decided on a painting as a Christmas present for Asunción, but which one? She couldn't make up her mind between a Murillo Virgin and a Matisse casbah gate. Stooping down, a hand on each thickly stockinged knee, she picked up first the one, then the other. Her baton descended on the Murillo, raising a tiny puff of dust. How much? Ten thousand pesetas, said the man. She picked up the Matisse. It had been painted on his visit to North Africa in 1912. A seated figure – a woman could it be? – observed those passing through the gate into the medina. At the centre of the composition was a trellis dotted with pink flowers. They reminded Genia Ortiz with pleasure of her own pelargoniums.

Her hand played with the cameo. She replaced the Matisse and picked up the Murillo. The trouble was, she always felt different about something when standing than when sitting. She closed one eye on the Virgin. It was more Christmassy. Eight thousand, she said. The man shook his head. His expression said old women like Genia Ortiz should be beaten to death with their batons. Genia Ortiz balanced the Murillo on top of the pile and drew out an identical copy from lower down. She was cleaning it with her elbow when she noticed Wavery.

"Señor Consul General, help me!"

"Señora?" said Wavery, who had not spoken to Genia Ortiz since their encounter in Don Ramon's grocery. Several times he had heard the bleep of her telephone through her balcony window. Once he had seen her watering her plants.

"Which should I give Asunción? This? Or this?"

"I'm not frightfully good at paintings," Wavery said.

"No, please."

Wavery indicated the Murillo. "This one."

Genia Ortiz sighed. "The thing is, señor, I don't think it's quite Asunción." She abandoned both paintings and put Ernesto's cane into her shopping bag. "And how is the ballroom coming along?"

"Slowly, slowly," said Wavery.

She turned her better ear to him, happy to be seen in the Plaza de los Reyes in conversation with the British Consul General. A car hooted at a pedestrian and she waved.

"How are you settling into our little *presidio?*"

"Asunción's been marvellous."

"Abyla is not Petersburg."

"Indeed."

"I used to go and look at architecture books in the library. Just to remind myself of home. I couldn't talk about it without getting emotional – which was rather embarrassing for my late husband."

"Might you go back?"

"To a place that still needs to grow up? I've done my growing up, señor. Also, coming from the family that one is from, well . . . the *resentment*. People say one is oversensitive about these things. They're all so wrong."

"I'm sure you're right."

"But be warned, señor. The Abylans too are good at envy. They even realise it themselves. It leads to all sorts of nonsense. If you're going to the Consulate I will walk with you." She needed more Vic Rub, against the dust.

Along the Calle Camoes the orange trees were veiled in cobwebs.

"What about Africa? Do you go there?" asked Wavery.

"I have lived here more than a lifetime, señor. Not *once* have I been to Africa. I'd sooner visit the cinema! But your predecessor in the war, *he* chose to live in Africa," and she recalled Señor Cazes, a funny little Gibraltarian, red-haired, with impeccable shoes, who drove in from Tetuan on Mondays to conduct his affairs from a room in the Hotel Zamora.

A car hooted and again she waved.

"We do things differently today, señora."

"And the Señora Consul General," said Genia Ortiz. "When might she have the pleasure of joining you?"

"That remains to be seen," said Wavery for no reason that was afterwards clear to him.

The British Consulate was on the second floor in a building opposite the Club de Pensiones. The entrance to Wavery's building, between a bank and a jeweller, bore an oak board, pricked by woodworm, into which his Moroccan workmen had

109

yet to screw a brass plaque designating HM Consulate's opening hours: 10.00AM - 1.00PM, 2.30PM - 6.00PM IN WINTER. 9.00AM - 2.00PM IN SUMMER.

A scooter stood in the stairwell of the gloomy hallway. The walls were skirted in green tiles. Against the right wall there was a dustbin and on the left wall four metal postboxes. Wavery unlocked one of the boxes and withdrew a white canvas bag. Then, sidestepping the scooter, he climbed the chipped marble steps.

Wavery had no idea whose was the apartment on the first floor. Once a man had run into him on the stairs and hurried into the street without a word of apology, all the while pushing his arm into the recalcitrant sleeve of a black leather coat. Asunción believed he had something to do with tourism, although there was no sign to that effect.

The Consulate had a grand entrance on the second floor. It had been the offices of an Austrian bank and consisted of two rooms, the larger of which was divided by a glass panel. There were four black vinyl chairs, a low table with information about World Service Bulletins, a guide to Abyla written by Asunción's father, a copy of *Residents Abroad*. A filing cabinet contained the immigration forms, the applications for British Council Scholarships, the COI leaflets advising people on what exactly to expect of the Consulate. "In case of a fatal accident, or death from whatever cause, get in touch with the Consulate at once."

Wavery's office was the smaller room. There was a desk, a swivel chair covered in red hessian and, beneath a window he had not yet been able to open, a bookcase. Asunción had filled part of one shelf with *In Public, In Private: Their Royal Highnesses* and an old four-volume set of the London telephone directory. The room, overlooking Calle Camoes, smelled of its new wheat-coloured carpet.

Wavery arranged his towel and swimming trunks on the radiator. Out of habit he grappled unavailingly with the window, and sat down. Before Asunción arrived he went through the mail.

Abyla was too minor a post to merit the attention of a Queen's Messenger. Correspondence was diverted instead to Gibraltar. Once a week a man from the Convent crossed the Straits and deposited a small white sack in the downstairs mailbox. He was always gone by the time Wavery arrived for work.

Wavery opened the sack.

A brown envelope from his brother-in-law enclosed Wavery's passport and a note from Hoyter regretting the "matter of the pages" – these appeared to have been ripped out. Hoyter had snipped off the top corner. "I advise you to apply for a new passport as soon as conveniently possible. You might recall the temporary one I was able to supply you with last week is valid for three months only." There was still no sign of Wavery's missing jacket, most likely to be in some hidey-hole on Middle Hill. But Wavery would be pleased to learn that Johnnie had been despatched safely.

The Governor wrote:

> Dear Thomas,
>   I am sorry I was unable to manage lunch last week. Edwina told me about your skirmish on Middle Hill. Rotten luck. Please accept my congratulations on your appointment. I know I can count on your best skills to help make the Royal Visit a success and I hope you enjoy Abyla.
>   After discussing the matter with Edwina I think in the circumstances it would be better next time you visit Gibraltar you make your own arrangements.
>   Yours ever,
>   Lawrence.

A volcanic rage rose in Wavery. He wrote at once in his own fluent hand.

> Dear Larry,
>   What a crapulous, pompous toad you are. Nothing would induce me to cross your threshold again. Please do me the same courtesy. Never come anywhere near Abyla for as long as I am here. Penny, were she with me – and wish to God she were – would, I have not an iota of doubt, support me in rejecting in these terms your rudeness, your discourtesy and your insufficient humanity.
>   Yours sincerely,
>   Thomas
>   PS Do not acknowledge.

Purged, he reverted to the diplomatic bag. Four envelopes marked OHMS. A letter from Lima: Paracas, wrote Wavery's successor, had been given to the cook, who had renamed him Laurenço. The situation remained critical. One evening in October a large bomb had exploded near the residence. HE's geese had been gone for more than a week. A letter from the Foreign Office: advising Wavery of an Inspector's visit in January. Abyla was a new post. A visit was required to ascertain the level off allowances. A letter from the Foreign Office: informing Wavery of what he already knew from OED: he should expect delivery of his luggage by Christmas. And finally, a circular, distribution all posts, reminding officers of August's circular alerting officers to the dangers posed by OED-supplied aluminium kitchen equipment. The warning not to stew fruit still applied.

"The aluminum chalice," murmured Wavery aloud.

Premature senility was not the end he had envisaged over the calvados, thirty-five years before in Piccadilly. He had sat the Foreign Office exam to win a bet with friends, to enjoy their dinner at the Ritz. He achieved the second highest marks of that year's entry.

"To Our Man in Paris," was the toast at that table. "Lucky Penny, you've married a high flyer."

At the age of twenty-three, he had been idealistic and patriotic. He believed the Service remained the Service of Harold Nicolson and Duff Cooper. Orchids embellished the pillars in the Paris Embassy and a footman stood behind every chair. Above all, he had been flattered. It had not taken long to learn the dispiriting truth that flattery, like patriotism and idealism, was all very well so long as you didn't inhale.

Wavery was naturally a loyal man. These buff envelopes revived the loyal years. The years he had spent prattling to the very people he would prefer to insult. The years spent learning the gestures and the apparatus of betrayal. The years spent working with great effect on matters of no national importance whatever; the years during which it came to him that his own Service was the enemy, that all of it was about betrayal, that no one cared a damn what the Berbers were thinking.

After a week in Abyla, he was bored. The things that came naturally to him all his diplomatic life, he couldn't do anymore. He didn't see the point. For thirty-five years he had oiled wheels, polished corners, listened to people, solved problems, made everything work. The one time he had needed something to work for him, it hadn't. Consul General to Abyla. It was like one of Silkleigh's titles, echoing nowhere. He could have been Consul here when he was thirty. A week ago he was prepared to fulfil whatever duties the Abyla post required of him. Now he thought New Zealand might have been endurable. These letters were a reminder he was no distance from home. No distance at all. And on the other side of the Straits he was faced with the nightmare of Penny's brother.

He kept until last a handwritten envelope containing the briefest of letters from Penny. Before opening it, he drafted a letter to Air Vice Marshal Sir Lawrence Tredwell, DFC, for Asunción to type:

> *Dear Larry*
>
> *Thank you for your letter. You cannot imagine how sorry I am Penny is not with me in Abyla. I know she would expect us not to allow personal difficulties to develop into professional ones. Whatever we can do to make the Royal Visit a success will be worth our every effort. I was sorry about lunch, but glad to learn that you won your golf. Edwina has much to be proud of. Please tell her that she will always be a welcome guest here, as you will be.*
>
> *Yours ever.*

Penny's letter was brief and to the point. She had instructed her father's solicitors and hoped the whole business wouldn't be as messy as everyone was telling her it would be. She'd seen a house both she and Patrick had fallen for – she more than Patrick – and they were going to put in an offer. It was outside Poole, but from the top of an oak in the garden you could see Poole harbour. She hoped Tom's residence was agreeable and he had found whatever he was looking for.

He folded the letter away, experiencing an uncomplicated

tenderness towards his wife and the gallery-owner – a widower she must have first met twenty years ago.

There was nothing from Catharine. Presumably her husband, suspicious of the desperation in Wavery's voice, had not passed on the message for her to call him.

Wavery wrote out his day's schedule:

1. Put Ebbing in touch with P's solicitors
2. New passport
3. 11.00 antimony works, Calle Real, re trade links: Lavandier
4. Arrange meeting with D. Porcil, banker i/c tunnel finance
5. Letter British Council, suggestions re writer's visit
6. Letter Midland bank
7. 6.30 drinks Senator Zamora

The one thing he could not write down was "Letter to Catharine". To whom he wanted to write letter after letter after letter.

2

It was a week after Wavery's lunch with Catharine Riding at El Salto del Fraile.

He had not spoken to her since. He was sitting in his office, writing a crisp memorandum about a consignment of veterinary equipment, when she telephoned.

"I've been in Arequipa."

"Yes. Yes, you told me."

"I've been thinking of you all week. I wanted to thank you."

"I know. It was –"

"All week I've worried I've said nothing."

"You can't. What can you say?"

"We had so much . . . We got on so *well*."

"We did."

"Did you get my present?"

"Yes." Her present stood before him on the desk, a plastic rose adorned by a pair of white-framed sunglasses.

"It made us laugh, though, didn't it? That's why it's important. I want you to laugh when you think of me."

"Of course, I'll always laugh."

"Just a minute." She called to someone. "I'm here, on the balcony. What's the matter?"

He heard the drawing of a shutter and a man's voice.

She said, "It's Helen." She was speaking to her sister.

Her hand covered the mouthpiece and there was a mumble of conversation. Through her fingers Wavery heard: "Off you go, darling. I'll see you in a minute." She spoke again. "Are you still there?"

"Yes."

"You were doing something, I can tell."

"I was scratching my nose."

"When are you going back to England?"

"In about two weeks".

"For how long?"

"Until my appointment comes through."

"Time for Christmas shopping," she said.

"I suppose so."

"It would be lovely to talk to you again."

"When do you leave?"

"Thursday."

There was a pause. In the corridor he could hear the Ambassador speaking to Queesal.

She said, "Suggest somewhere."

At seven the next morning, Penny sat under a jacaranda tree at the furthest end of a sloping lawn. She was painting the mountain behind their house. She did not look up from her easel when Wavery lowered himself into the pool and began his daily stint. The air was calm, the water reflecting faithfully the sky, the mountain, a bird flying south. He pushed out in a slow, methodical breast-stroke, obliterating the images. The water poured into his ears, muffling the scream of children from the playground beyond the hedge. On the lawn Paracas loitered over a purple leaf. Wavery swam

115

towards the mountain, organising his responses to Catharine Riding.

People do not suspect what they start with a simple gesture. When Wavery had looked into Catharine's eyes on Rita's patio and at lunch at the Friar's Leap he had focused on the possibilities of life. He had been impelled beyond the bounds of his normal existence into new latitudes. Catharine had disturbed a muscle he had put to sleep for more than thirty years.

After swimming twenty lengths, Wavery climbed from the pool. He dried himself, scrubbing a towel over his head. "Breakfast, Penny?" he called. He crossed the lawn, to the house. The children had disappeared inside their classrooms. Near the hedge, the tortoise was mounting an imitation *chimu* pot.

Should he have agreed to see her again? Or was it a selfish thing to do?

"What about tomorrow?" he had said, feeling his absence of power over himself; also a sense of his power over her and a wanting to enjoy that too.

"Where?"

He had suggested the Hotel Bolívar. One o'clock. They would have lunch in the grill room.

Wavery threw the towel onto a chair. He began to dress. It wasn't selfish, he reassured himself, unfolding a white shirt Penny had given him for Christmas. He had formed an intellectual sympathy he would like to explore.

He buttoned the shirt and was attacked by doubts. Fifty-eight was no age to form intellectual sympathies. Lunch had not been just the purest bliss. It had offered glimpses of a companionship he had not hitherto known. Drawing out Catharine Riding, sharing the have-you-ever-seens, were-you-also-ins, did-you-feel-toos, Wavery had been taken out of a place he had long ago fortified for himself.

He made his decision while knotting his tie. He would cancel lunch. When he reached the office he would write her a note. He would fold her away in a buff-coloured envelope which he would arrange for the Embassy driver to deliver, as soon as he could, but not later than twelve-thirty, to the head waiter at the Bolivár.

Penny collapsed her easel and carried in the mountain. The mountain was a massive lump of grey dust. She saw it as livid yellow, enlivened by two horns and an eye. At the edge of the exhausted landscape stood a tree. Wavery felt if he pushed it the tree would fall over, never to grow.

"Lovely, darling," he said with feeling and she smiled.

"Why are you crying?"

She said, "I'm not crying, you idiot. It's this bloody hay fever." She squinted at the tortoise. "What on earth is Paracas up to?"

"I think he wants to go back to the desert."

Wavery was late for the Tuesday prayer meeting: he had been waiting for the driver to return from the petrol station. The weekly meeting was an occasion for the Ambassador to demonstrate his seniority and for everyone else to circulate ideas which might appeal to him as useful. In his first year he introduced from his previous post the habit of settling the staff around a table and combing the newspapers for items they thought merited discussion. This ceremony had been abandoned when someone found an article revealing that the Ambassador's name had been found on a death list. His nerves had frayed a good deal since then. The only creatures he regarded with any degree of trust were his geese, of which he kept a flock in the residence compound.

Until his posting to Lima he had been regarded as a successful diplomat. "Which means," observed Penny, "he's been away at the right time and ill at crucial moments." But his Peruvian tour coincided with the counter-revolution. He had grown a frothy beard as a security measure and taken to arriving at the Embassy under a blanket.

"The Labour MPs were flying Eastern." Queesal, the First Secretary Commercial, was speaking. "The strike will mean reorganising their schedule PDQ."

The Ambassador shifted in his chair, plucking a feather from his sleeve. He suspected the MPs were interested in political developments only in so far as they affected British interests, of which in Peru there were relatively few.

"Is it a vital half day or what?" said the Ambassador. He regarded Queesal as "very dynamic". Penny, too, was fond of the Commercial Attaché: "He does a good job in a talkative way." But Wavery could never take him seriously. In George Queesal he saw his own faults writ large.

The Commercial Attaché was a great one for doing what was expected of him. A creature of tidy habits, he had a primitive attitude to inefficiency. Wavery suspected a swirl of chaos beneath his pert appearance. He had been married twice. Both wives had left him, in each case for a local man. Bernice, for a public relations executive in Panama City and Shirley, four months ago, for a young graduate at the International Potato Centre. In the office his ideas were made exclusively with the Ambassador in mind and packaged to his own preferment. Whenever he could, Wavery booted them into touch.

"They've lost all their talks," said Queesal.

"That's fine. They can spend another day at Macchu Piccu. Anything else?"

"On the drugs front, the US Attorney General is in town to see the DEA. Fourteen planes were impounded last week."

The Ambassador looked at Wavery. "Remind me to tell you what Denver told me the other night."

Wavery nodded. "Right."

"George, we might talk to the Americans after he's gone. Or I'll talk to Denver. Either way, let's talk. There should be some useful ideas there. Anything else?'

"I've had a call from Smock, our ex-Consul in Tumbes. He wants to know why he's not coming to the Queen's Birthday Party. Sounds unhappy."

"We're not here to keep the British community happy, dammit," snapped the Ambassador who had promulgated a despotic reduction in the number of invitations. "Deirdre?"

Penny described Deirdre as "one of those fragile English ladies who leave England for reasons of health only to blossom in places where conditions were ten times worse". Under Wavery, her responsibility was to oversee the Embassy's aid programme. In the Ambassador's view, the aid scene was a "bottomless pit", but in Peru, as elsewhere, aid was the means by which you bought political importance. A country was judged by the amount it donated and its ambassador was respected in proportion. According to Deirdre's computations, Britain gave a fraction more to Peru than did Gabon.

Deirdre described her arrangement for the delivery of a wheel-barrow and three shovels to a clinic damaged by flooding. She glanced over at Wavery. She would leave it to Wavery to explain the matter of the veterinary equipment in Cajamarca, which, having remained unpacked for six months, they now learned was missing crucial elements.

"Anything else?" said the Ambassador.

Deirdre doubled as the Cultural Attaché. "At least the Eastern Strike doesn't affect the British Council visit." A feminist science-fiction writer was arriving for a week.

"You've done a programme?"

"She's staying with me."

"I suppose that's a good idea? What do we want to achieve?"

"The Council rather hope you might host a small reception," Deirdre said stubbornly. "We have so much competition from the Goethe Institute and the Alliance Française.

Deirdre's remark provoked an Ambassadorial riposte. "We don't want to get into competition. We want what's most appropriate for Anglo-Peruvian relations. You know my position on that, Deirdre. Three words. English. Language. Teaching . . ." From his manner, it was unlikely he regarded the Council's science-fiction writer as fulfilling his criteria.

Wavery gazed out of the window and down into Plaza Washington as Deirdre became an excuse for the Ambassador to remind all those assembled of the banner, and the words Caring but Cautious, beneath which he expected them to march.

Wavery looked ahead to Lisbon. He promised himself he would conduct his prayer meetings differently. But he could not think clearly of Lisbon. He could think only of Catharine. He watched a police car speed through a red light. He imagined her entering the Hotel Bolivar. He followed her in quick steps into the foyer, up the stairs, into the grill room.

"Señora Riding? Please. This is for you."

". . . and in providing such teaching, let's go for doctors and scientists in preference to someone who can talk about the sororities of English literature. It's the technocratic spectrum which is directing life in our country, not raccoons from outer space. It's all about priorities. Which reminds me. Gifty? What's the programme for direct dialling?"

"October is promised," said the Ambassador's Trinidadian secretary.

The Ambassador nodded. "Good. It took me all of two hours to get through to Personnel Department yesterday."

"And you said to remind you about the saucepans."

"Ah, yes. Thank you," said the Ambassador. His face assumed an expression more ominous than normal. "Quite right. The saucepans. Where is it, Gifty?"

Gifty identified the relevant paper on his desk.

To the threat posed by Maoist guerrillas, the Foreign Office had added a sinister anxiety of their own. "I've had a message from London warning us of a link established between the metal in the saucepans issued by Overseas Estates Department, and memory loss. OED promise to disconnect the supply, but as yet no funds are available to replace all existing kitchenware. Meanwhile, we are advised not to stew fruit."

He gave a deathly little smile. He flicked the page with the back of his goose-stroker's hand. Drily he said, "I suspect this warning has come too late for many of my *chers collègues*."

He turned to his Deputy Head of Mission.

"Tom?"

At two thirty-five Wavery's secretary put through a call.

"Well? So where are you?"

"Didn't you get the message?"

"What message? I've been here two hours."

"Something cropped up –"

"What do you want to do?"

His secretary tapped on the door. Wavery waved her away. "It's all right. I'm here," he said. "Listen, I can't talk now. Catharine?" But she had gone.

He met the Ambassador in the corridor. "Tom, do you have a second?"

"Not a good moment, Ambassador," said Wavery. He knew what the Ambassador wished to discuss. Undercover agents at Denver's embassy, following a trail originating in Miami, had been led to the guardhouse at the British residence. There was evidence that two of the guards responsible for the Ambassador's security had been making long-distance telephone calls to Bolivia.

Wavery told the Ambassador he was due at a meeting with Petro-Peru's Vice President. Tenders were expected next week for a drilling project on the Huallaga. "There should be useful opportunities for UK suppliers," said Wavery. For the first time in his career he had told a direct lie.

"Then when you have a moment. By the way, I thought the artist was looking splendid at Rita's."

"I'll tell her."

"I never used to think so, Tom, but she'll make an excellent Ambassadress."

Catharine Riding sat in the lobby on a tall pink chair. There had been a press conference and the lobby milled with journalists. "They've discovered the world's longest natural bridge," she said and gathered up her coat. She had been waiting since twelve-forty-five. "I never thought of trying the restaurant. You are exasperating."

"Are you hungry?"

"No. Exasperated."

He drove out of the town centre, through Miraflores to Barranco. He parked on a cliff overlooking the sea. They left the car and she slipped her arm through his, quickening her step until they walked at the same pace.

They walked over the wooden bridge and along the Malecon

Paul Harris where security men stood on neatly tiled roofs, confessional with their handsets. The cliffs were softened by moist fog, the Lima *garua* which curled off the sea as if it were not fog at all but steam from a witchdoctor's cauldron, thinning and thickening to reveal or smother a couple in a parked car licking ice cream, two children chasing each other round the base of Admiral Grau's statue, a figure coiled in a manhole, half-asleep, a hand moving inside torn trousers, nurturing itself.

The fog covered the road, the grand houses. Through the fog came the scuttle of rats on the garbage, the bark of a dog inside a car, the distant roll of the waves.

The fog lifted, and standing on the verge ahead of them they saw a one-armed man wearing a loose coat. He unloaded a cart of burning rubbish. He applied the stub of his left arm to the handle and pushed upwards. The contents slithered over the cliff and the air became warm with ash.

They walked between the grand houses and the smoking rubbish and Wavery was gripped by the urge to jump. If they jumped now, hand in hand and one two three . . . He saw himself and Catharine rolling through the cracked shoes, the melted shampoo bottles, the intestinal spews of cassette tape caught in the cactus while above them, urged on by the one-armed man, the ice-cream lovers abandoned their car and the vagrant stood erect in his hole and the children mounted the admiral's shoulders and they peered down at two specks on the sand where the waves wrapped the shore in a tattered ribbon.

He rubbed an elbow. "It's cold."

She had the fog in her eyes. "Listen . . ." She was unable to complete the phrase.

"Yes?" The *garua* must have frightened her. That and the tension in the streets. You could never underestimate the tension. It was everywhere around them, like the fog.

"It doesn't matter."

"No, Catharine. Tell me. It's what I'm here for."

She said, and it was not what she had been going to say, "Have you ever felt you had a protective spirit?"

"Early on," said Wavery. Once he had thought himself invincible.

"Or yourself to be one?"

"Catharine," he said at last. "What's this about?"

A young girl searched his face. Then the much older woman elbowed her aside. "When we had lunch you were like a very good father. It was a luxury for me to have someone who listened and talked in that way."

"I'm still listening, Catharine."

She said, "That week – when Adam was in Ica – I began walking round myself, trying to catch myself unawares. I was looking for a means of convincing myself that I was no different from anybody else. I wanted someone to say 'No, you're normal. What happened then was of no significance. It's got to be allowed out.' I was ready to explain this to your colleague, whatever his name was, at Rita's party. But . . . but he didn't want to know."

"What didn't Queesal want to know?"

"Oh, nothing that doesn't happen to thousands of other children. Parents not getting on. Parents saying to you, 'We're only staying together for your sake, because of you,' and you saying to yourself, 'My God, if only I wasn't here.' Parents passing their guilt onto you, which isn't right because if they really couldn't stand each other then they would have left. Wouldn't they?"

"Generally," said Wavery.

"Your mother then taking you away. You saying, 'It must have been something I did.' Your perpetually unexplained guilt." She pushed the words out one after the other. "Those days when I was alone here – I saw things clearer."

When she failed to go on, Wavery took her arm. "Catharine? What did you see?"

"I saw that what then happened to me stole my freedom to choose. I saw how I was forced to imitate. I saw that all the time I was saying to myself, 'I will be like everybody else, if it's the last thing I do.'"

It was as if she was gnawing at some wrong bone. Could her

parents' separation really be what troubled her? Or was it her father's suicide?

"You'd never felt this before?"

"It was like a pool of water that came seeping under the door. Before, it always went back. But now – now I feel there's no stopping the flood."

"Why now?"

"Because in the end a point is reached when the truth *has* to be spoken."

He pointed to the smudged-out city. "Are you saying Lima caused you to see this?"

"No, Tom, not just Lima." She stepped away, facing the rubbish slopes, so he was unable to see her expression. She folded her arms and her voice was tired. "You can't tell the truth without destroying the aura of family life. I married Adam because he brought me a patch of sunlight. I don't think he could handle that – well, that's what it is – darkness."

"You think I can?" He was touched.

"Oh Tom," she spun around, and he saw confusion lapping at her eyes. "Just being able to talk. It's been such a boon, you can't imagine. I've not been able to say this before."

It was his turn to sound awkward. "It doesn't have to end here, you know."

"But I leave tomorrow."

"We can write. Why can't we write?"

"Would you write to me?" She was animated. "Oh, would you? I would write back, I promise."

"I'll give you our address in London."

They walked back to the car and she held his arm again. "I feel you're somebody I can say anything to."

As if to a child, Wavery replied, "And I would like to be somebody for the rest of your life." He knew if he was not careful he could be somebody completely different. But he was a careful man, a diplomat who had made a marriage vow. He was able to stop just there, on a clifftop in Barranco, not laying a finger on her.

Chapter Six

I

SENATOR ZAMORA HAD arrived home late from the baths. He had forgotten that Wavery was invited for drinks. When Asunción reminded him he opened his cupboard and surveyed the cardigans hanging there.

He possessed three cardigans, knitted by his late wife in three separate colours and he wore them according to his moods.

A purple cardigan, such as he had worn to Cap Spartel, indicated he was happy. Senator Zamora wore this on the days he spent at the Museo de Arqueología near the harbour where he was employed part time as a director and where he enjoyed nothing so much as to work on his thesis.

Senator Zamora's thesis was something endured by the Zamora household for as long as anyone in it could remember. The thesis was supported by a simple proposition. It argued the case for Abyla as an important Phoenician city when Athens was an unwalled settlement.

In Abyla, Senator Zamora believed, the Peoples of the Sea had perfected their alphabet. In Abyla they had recognised in an ox-head the possibility of the letter "A" thereafter giving all men access to learning – even their ox-headed Governor, Sexto Menendez.

In Abyla the Phoenicians had filled their tetremes with tortoise shell, elephant's teeth, odoriferous gum, mallow-coloured cotton, stibium to tinge the eyes and honey from the cane called sugar. And from Abyla, they tacked off into the unknown –

125

beyond the Pillars of Hercules, to Africa, India, even to South America whither Senator Zamora's great-grandfather had migrated in 1870.

Senator Zamora's thesis argued that Abyla was the Phoenician settlement of Exilissa mentioned in the *Hecatæus* of Miletus and in the works of Pliny, Strabo and Ptolemy. For the enlightened professors at the University of Oran, Senator Zamora's intepretation of Abyla's role as a Phoenician staging post had its undeniable fascination. "There is no need to worry about the state of learning in North Africa while works like this one are being produced. A work of genius, and we do not use that epithet lightly."

Its submission to Oran had followed a rejection by the University of Cadiz, which found it a work of paralysing tedium. The expression of Senator Zamora's conviction, while admired for its earnestness, had, however – and this was something regretted by his examiners across the Straits in Cadiz – not been accompanied by solid evidence.

The Phoenicans of Senator Zamora's Abyla had neglected to leave behind either literary or monumental evidence of their existence. In the absence of records, the University of Cadiz had judged that Senator Zamora's thesis, while in his words "sanctioned by every probability", would not survive searching criticism.

Lesser men might have been content with the honorary doctorate from Oran, or else consigned the thesis to Señora Criado's oven. Not Senator Zamora. The reason no particulars from that remote era had arrived at his desk was this: the events took place before the first stirring of Greek history. That the truth of his argument should be repudiated by some learned barbarians across the Straits who lacked imagination to envisage a time when every sail from Carthage to Cornwall was a Phoenician sail was not merely unreasonable. It was *incredible*. Not for nothing was Senator Zamora a correspondent member of the Spanish Royal Academy. In time, he would shake their faith.

There was one catch. Senator Zamora had reached a point where he could not read his own handwriting. He had never learned to type, not even in the period when he had been editor of *El Faro*. What did men do in these situations?

This was the question Senator Zamora had been asking when Pablo gave him the estimation made by his computer of Hercules' height.

On the other hand, a green cardigan such as the Senator had worn for the emergency debate on Tuesday, signified to his household that he would be spending the day at the Casa del Gobierno.

Green was the colour of the opposition party, Abyla Independiente, of which Senator Zamora was reluctant leader. The party was opposed to the terms of the Straits Treaty and to Governor Menendez' tunnel, both guaranteed to rob Abyla of its patrimony as Tyre was affected by the causeway Alexander had constructed from the mainland.

Senator Zamora suspected the Governor of using the tunnel to advance a political career on the mainland. Not a day passed without him coining a new epithet to describe the Governor. This week Menendez had earned himself further opprobrium for removing the black Seville hat belonging to Senator Zamora's father from the antler stand in the Club de Pensiones. Senator Zamora was not persuaded the Governor had mistaken it for his own.

After the hat-thief, Senator Zamora blamed his King. He should have stamped on the Straits Treaty from the outset as he had stamped on that Colonel who dared suggest that Abyla, the pearl of the Mediterranean, be exchanged for Gibraltar.

For five years Zamora had listened to Menendez' promises. The Treaty would transform the Mediterranean's pearl into another Hong Kong. It was desirable from every ethical and moral point of view.

In Senator Zamora's experience, only gangsters talked of ethics. Only prostitutes of morals. How, señor, do you secure our future, he would ask in the Chamber, if you hand our beloved *presidio* – Spanish for longer than America has been a nation – to the mercy of a European Parliament? If the pensinsulares in Madrid had done nothing for their sovereign territory, what chance the EC? No, gentlemen. This was a political chimera foisted on businessmen. Its objects were to make money for shareholders and to rid itself of two relatives born embarrassingly the wrong side of the bed. It was led by no popular demand – unless you counted the Moroccan King who wanted anything which might link Morocco closer to Europe.

For five years, Senator Zamora had done his duty. All work relating to the tunnel was subject to planning permission. Of the three hundred and forty-five planning applications submitted so far, only seventeen remained unaffected by Abyla Independiente's amendments.

He had wasted an awful lot of the hat-thief's time.

The third cardigan was dark grey, and a warning to stay out of his way. It was the shade of his wife's gravestone. Señora Criado would keep to the kitchen, humming inoffensively, whenever her master wore this particular cardigan. He rarely remained in the house. He would scrape the keys from a bowl in the hall, start the Seat and in an aimless but repetitive circuit drive round and round and round the rock.

This was the colour he wore to greet the British Consul General.

"It's very exciting," Asunción was saying, with more enthusiasm than she felt. "Daddy's been made president of the *corrida*." She looked over at her father, standing by the tea-tray, the thick hair gushing around his ears in ash curls.

"Congratulations," said Wavery.

Senator Zamora grunted. It was nothing. It was Menendez trying to buy him out. "How do you like your tea? Strong or weak?"

"It's an enormous honour," insisted Asunción.

"Strong," said Wavery, who would have preferred a whisky.

"Good. So do I," said Zamora, who had only served tea to make his guest feel at home. "Do you smoke?"

"No."

"I do."

Zamora lit a cigarette and tossed the match into the fire. The

128

Senator's suspicion of the English was automatic. The Phoenicians knew Señor Wavery's country as a land stocked with Belgians, of interest for its tin. As a Spaniard, Senator Zamora inherited a conviction that Wavery's countrymen had clung without justice to Gibraltar and, more damaging, they numbered Joseph Silkleigh. Clotilda should be encouraged to marry anyone, anyone at all, but, Santa Maria, please not the English diver.

After Asunción had circulated the nut bowl a third time and Zamora, kissing Pablo goodnight, had recoiled in horror from his grandson – "Pablo! You stink of smoke. Have you been smoking, child?" – and Wavery had exchanged some anodyne remarks about the attractions of Abyla (having been alerted by Asunción it was best where possible to avoid mention of the tunnel), there fell an uncomfortable silence in which the only sound to be heard was the sound of three grown-up people eating peanuts.

It had seemed such a good idea! thought Asunción. She could not have foreseen her father would choose to elect today a grey cardigan day.

Zamora had woken from his siesta downcast. After lunch he had needed a walk. Señora Criado, having basted a leg of lamb with olive oil, fresh rosemary and crushed garlic, had served up the dish with no small pride – only for Zamora to discover the meat was in fact beef. He knew he was prone to exaggeration but it was possibly the most revolting meal he had ever tasted.

As he walked by the sea he thought he heard his name called by the familiar voice of his dead wife. "Teodorooooo." He looked into the dusk and was overwhelmed by the memory of Minerva's nonchalant beauty – the same as Arletty's in *Les Perles de la Couronne* – before the throat cancer ravaged her.

"Teodoroooo . . ."

She was warning him! Teodoro, don't do it. Do not consign all the beautiful ideas in your head to the green machine. Do not abandon your own nature for children's toys. You are a man of scholarship. How can you expect to master Pablo's computer

129

if you do not understand the instruction manual? Remember the fate of Leopoldo! As he stood on the Playa Benitez, there floated into his mind the usually welcome, but on this evening disagreeable spectre of the quinologist.

His great-grandfather, the generous donor of Santa Maria's bell, a lover of cold grapes and marzipan, a pleader for stowaways, a founder member of the Club de Pensiones and Abyla's most brilliant after-dinner speaker, a man whose qualities were known wherever venereology was respected as a science and who with his *chinchona* bark had treated politicians of all parties and priests of all denominations, had sunk with the *Santarense* off the Gulf of Mexico in 1896. Lost with the marble staircase intended for the Teatro Amazonas had been Leopoldo Zamora's life work.

Senator Zamora wondered, after another day exposed to the technological elements: Was this the fate awaiting his own decades of research?

"That man," said Wavery to break the silence and also because he wanted to know. "Who is he?"

"Who?" asked Senator Zamora and Asunción together.

Wavery nodded at the soldier over the fireplace. It was the portrait he had seen hanging in the Café Ulises and on a panel composed of red ceramics outside Governor Menendez' office. The same portrait was reproduced in Senator Zamora's hallway, on the staircase and in the downstairs lavatory, where pinned to his feet a couplet celebrated "*la perla del Mediterraneo*" in faience.

> *Blanca. Celeste. Perfecta.*
> *Una ciudad luminoza. Corazon de España.*
> *Abyla.*
> > *Abyla.*
> > > *Abyla.*
> > > > *Abyla.*

Zamora examined Wavery from the embrace of his winged chair.

Sombrely and with immense pride, he answered, "That man, señor, is my father. He died to keep Abyla Spanish."

"In the African War?"

Zamora bowed his head. It was a matter too close to his heart. He did not wish to say more to satisfy diplomatic nicety, but Zamora was wrong. Wavery positively did wish to know, and the effect on his host, who judged a man by his bookshelf, was instantaneous. Wavery had studied classics? At Cambridge? Ah! Then he had read books. This placed him at an advantage to people in Abyla. He took Wavery's cup, an infusion of hot milk and water to which had been added a Stallion tea bag.

"A drink. A drink. My dear, will you ask . . ." Zamora found a forehead to clap ". . . I have known her for thirty-five years and I cannot remember her first name. We are all crazy here."

Wavery said, when Asunción had left the room, "Asunción was telling me of your work at the museum. I did not appreciate that Abyla was so old."

"Old! Old!" Zamora sank into the chair, a hand on his chest. Early Man had come from North Africa. And before him the hero of Hesiodic theogony. "Hercules," he told Wavery, and his finger pointed several times to the carpet onto which was woven a map of the promontory. "Can I allude to him?" Hercules had built Abyla with his own hands. The Garden of the Hesperides was most probably situated on Monte Hacho. In Abyla Ulysses had passed several years drinking the local waters to forget Calypso.

When Asunción returned from the kitchen her father was rowing to the peep of a Phoenician flute. And then Nebuchadnezzar's Babylonians. The Romans. This was Flavio Suintilla's capital, built on seven hills like Rome. Then, after Governor Julian had invited Tarik to avenge his Florinda's rape, there had then been an unfortunate spell in which Abyla was occupied by Arabs. But this period had ended in 1415 when the promontory was secured by Henry the Navigator – a grandson of England! In Abyla, Henry had found the maps which allowed his captains to sail beyond the edge of the world. Asunción said to Wavery, "Will you –"

But her father had found new breath. Had Señor Wavery

131

read Camoes, the author of *Los Lusiads*? He was exiled from Lisbon to Abyla – where he lost an eye in a sea fight with the Moors. He loved a lady in waiting at Court! "And Franco?" The very same. From Abyla, General Franco, head of the Tercio, had launched the Civil War.

"Abyla," Zamora concluded, at last, "is the navel of the world."

He placed his glass on the carpet. Emotionally he said, "I'm happy to give you all my knowledge, señor, but I haven't organised myself for it."

"Perhaps you could suggest some books," said Wavery.

"But of course. Here. Let me remind myself or I will forget." And down he scribbled on a white pad in capital letters, "Reading. List. For. Señor. Wavery. I will write it this evening!"

For the first time since his arrival, Wavery's spirits lifted. In Zamora's enthusiasm he saw a path ahead in which he might escape his despair. Why should he not take advantage of his time in Abyla as Scaley had in the Gabon and Dardle in Prague – as had any number of senior diplomats, now he came to think of it? He hadn't the energy to write a book, certainly, but he might be able to submerge himself in his host's reading list.

"Which is why Abyla should be independent," Zamora was saying. There was a new note in his voice. It was the note of lament which crept in whenever he considered the threat to Abyla's heritage. After twelve thousand years of history, Abyla did not deserve the fate awaiting it, to have its identity removed at one blow by this tunnel – this mousehole, this sewer, this ditch in the ground – to be forgotten as the Tangier mole, which had taken thirty years to build, had been forgotten! He rattled his ice.

"Then do you not feel Spanish?" asked Wavery.

Yes, Zamora felt Spanish, but Abyla was his first priority. Nor must he forget Melilla, Spain's other enclave on this coast. Abyla and Melilla were like two daughters of divorced parents. They had been brought up by one parent against the wish of the other.

"I'm sure my younger daughter would enjoy meeting you,"

the idea suddenly occurred to Zamora. She was out this evening, unfortunately. The second evening in succession! He was very much afraid that the driver of the white car was none other than Joseph Silkleigh, a man he wouldn't trust with his tomcat.

"You'll stay for dinner?" Asunción asked.

But Zamora had grown intimidated by the smells issuing from the kitchen. He threw an arm from the chair.

"Darling . . ."

"Actually, I can't," said Wavery. Halima was expecting him. Senator Zamora rose too. His leg had gone to sleep and he stood at the second attempt. "I will lunch you at my club," he promised. Then, once the hunting season began, Wavery must come to dinner. They would eat roast duck. And Wavery would meet Clotilda.

On the doorstep Zamora kept a long hold of Wavery's hand. He was no longer the tetchy Anglophobe. In the Englishman's reserve he saw plenty to admire. Their armigerous neighbour Genia Ortiz had a tendency to dominate the conversation without leading it anywhere. Señor Wavery was not a man who dominated in this way. He had a sensitivity about him that reminded Senator Zamora of himself, but fifteen years younger.

"I envy you, señor. What I would give to see Abyla for the first time!"

2

"Señor, señor! It's unbelievable what has happened." She directed her baton to a spot five feet away. "Yes, sit on that wall. Now listen.

Highly Esteemed Evgenia Nikolaevna!
  Our Consul in Oslo has furnished me with your address. I have no way of knowing if it is correct. Nor do I know if you are alive. I am writing in the light of recent events to declare it the unanimous pleasure of your family's village that the estate and lake of Balnasharki should be returned to the rightful owners. It is my humble hope this

letter finds you in good health and that you have been blessed with the longevity traditionally associated with the Polotsevs.

Vladimir Paskin
Mayor of Balnasharki.

The letter was written in Russian and had taken seven weeks to reach Abyla. Genia Ortiz translated it to Wavery. He had been eating breakfast in the shade of the handkerchief tree when she summoned him. Now he sat on the low wall, listening to her across the gulley. There was some stumbling because one or two words were unfamiliar, but as she read her wrinkles disappeared and her cheeks glowed.

"Well, what do you think?"

"A lot may have changed," warned Wavery.

"Oh, señor, you can't believe what a wonderful house. Wait. I must show you the photographs."

"Señora Ortiz, I'm so sorry. I have an appointment. Perhaps I could look at them another time?" said Wavery, hearing the shifting templates of his own displacement.

Wavery was thinking about Genia Ortiz and her house in the Ukraine when, on the way to the swimming pool, he bumped into Silkleigh. The diver was wearing an oilskin and over one shoulder he carried an oxygen cylinder, strapped to which were a pair of goggles and two green flippers.

"*Ambasadoro*! What goes grunt, grunt, grunt from one cocktail party to the next?" He waited for Wavery's reaction. When none came he scratched an armpit and uttered a simian whoop. "An ape with a diplomat's passport," he said. "Chap in Main Street told me. One of my diaphragms was getting a bit sucky so I thought I'd za-za over to Gib. You've got to laugh. I mean you've got to laugh."

"I suppose so," said Wavery.

Silkleigh fell in beside him. "Don't worry yourself. What does it matter anyway? All men spring from monkeys. Jesus. You're probably the one human being in the Foreign Office. I judge people by the odour they leave behind and let me tell you, *kara mia*, you leave a very good odour."

They walked up Millan Astray. "I'm not actually going this way, but never mind," said Silkleigh. "It's nice to have a chat. I feel we understand each other, *ambasadoro*. And while I'm here, is there anything you want to ask me? Are you settling in? How is your neighbour, the Russian bat-head? I mean nightmare or what. She should be in Paris or Rome or wherever it is White Russians hole up. Not in Abyla."

He licked his lips, and spoke in a falsetto voice, "'Mr Silkleigh, I know it's a terrible thing to say, but in my day they wouldn't have let you through the green baize door.' Which is beyond the pale, frankly, even if I do happen to come from Yeovil. If she was English she would probably come from Yeovil. She'd be called Mannering and insist you pronounced it Mainwaring. She also has that thing I never really admire in a woman. A slight cast in one eye. Still, she's an improvement on her husband who taught Rosita to sing those terrible songs. I *hated* the man. When he dropped dead, I thought, Good. Bloody justice. Sorry. Oh, yes, *ambasadoro*, anything you need to know about Genia and Ernesto Ortiz," and he thumped his yellow chest, "ask Comrade Silkleigh. I know it all. It's all going into that book of mine, every word."

Wavery had met Silkleighs the world over. Watching him hurt Rosita in the Café Ulises, he had thought, Yes, I know your type. Silkleigh was one of those who saved the true expression of themselves for the right time, the right person. The time had gone by and the right person had not come along and the day had arrived when in the middle of some mundane action – inserting a key in the lock, paying for a coffee – he found he had lost all awareness of his best expression. The only person left to him was himself and the only solace creativity, and that, no doubt, was why he had taken refuge in autobiography.

"It's going to contain everything I know and quite a lot I don't know."

"Tell me about Genia Ortiz then," said Wavery.

"Evgenia Nikolaevna Polotseva Ortiz," began Silkleigh.

Oxygen cylinder on shoulder, he followed her towards the

lake. He knew which tree she would pause before, what she was thinking.

Her summer memories were of this lake. It was her mother's lake and stocked with large, red mirror carp. As a wedding present the Tsar had instructed his water-bailiff to net from the lake at Gatchina fifty-eight of these fish – her parents' combined age in years. Rings on four of the carp proclaimed them to be as ancient as the walnut trees on the drive.

Every evening at six the shoal swarmed towards the sound of a cow-bell on the south-west bank. The bell was shaken by Genia's mother, ambling between the trees. She carried a basket of bread and over her shoulder, if the weather was warm, a towel the size of a sheet. At the edge of the lake she stopped. She dropped the bell in the grass and she stood a moment on the bank savouring the sight of her water, calm but about to erupt, goosepimpled by whatever moved beneath the surface. Then she peeled the cloth from the basket.

In summer Genia would find her mother floating naked among pieces of bread, feeling the carp swirling against her long legs, nibbling at her skin. Genia was too young to understand such sensations. On summer evenings she collected mushrooms in the walnut drive. It was like gathering stars, she told her father. Her winter memories were of snowfights in the dark on Christmas Day. After dinner the household would spread out along the frozen banks. They divided into groups, each holding a torch. During their last Christmas together a snowball landed against Genia's throat. The ice slipped between her shirt and coat, down against her skin, dagger cold, knifing away her breath. She fumbled with her coat, but she couldn't find the ice. It spread out into a cold patch on her heart where it had remained ever since.

The question she never stopped asking herself was, Who threw that snowball in the dark? Her mother? Her father? Or her mother's friend, Colonel Slava, whom Genia with a child's crush had always thought handsome until he ransacked Balnash-arki in the autumn of 1917.

That was her last memory of the home. She heard the Colonel's arrival from the lake as her father rowed over the water, disturbing the midges. Her father laid down an oar. They listened to the canter of hooves in the trees.

"I'll talk to him, Nikolai," said her mother. "Just get Genia away."

No lamp-light swayed on the water. On the far side the boat hit a sandbank. Her father stood unsteadily. Cursing, he tried to push them free. He thought he knew the shallows, every inch. He'd left his cigars behind. The boat didn't shift. "It's your trunk weighing us down," he whispered. He plopped off his boots and pushed the boat to the shore. There was a scuffle and the reeds parted on a nervous face. His ADC would take Genia to the dacha in Kirov.

"Goodbye, my child." He kissed the top of her clean head. "I must go back to your mother." Genia last saw her father pulling out of the reeds, rowing back to the house, ominously silent, until the darkness and the midges ate him and all she heard was the squeak of metal, a muffled clatter as an oar slipped its rowlock and the slap of his hand on his cheek.

From Kirov she journeyed north to Archangel, where she was left in the care of a pomor trader. Her father had given her a leather envelope of jewels, some Kerensky notes and a letter to this man, the uncle of a colleague in the guard. His ships carried flour and timber and rye to Norway, returning with a cargo of dried cod. In December his cargo included the twelve-year-old Evgenia Nikolaevna. She travelled in the guise of an under-maid. She was returning to the household of his daughter in Tromso. The captain explained this in a hybrid dialect of Russian and Norsk.

Deep into the second night, the Captain shook her awake. He held a bowl of buckwheat porridge. "It's all right," he said. "We've passed Posvik. We're in Norwegian water." She could tell by his face they were safe.

They dropped anchor in Tromso, the world's most northerly city. They arrived in the *Morketiden*, the Murky Time. It was midday and snow ripped from a grey sack of sky. It fell on her cheeks like pieces of wet bread. There was no sun. The sun, which had sunk into the sea beyond Bensfordtind mountain, would remain underwater until January.

Over Russia strange lights rippled the dark where the sky was clear. She thought it was gunfire, but the captain laughed. He hauled her trunk on deck. They were rowed to the quayside and a cart carried them to a house in Karlpedersengate.

Evgenia Nikolaevna paid for her passage and lodging from the envelope of jewels. She heard nothing from Balnasharki. On each trip the pomor trader produced another fragment of news, none of it concerning the situation in Kiev. Then in June he received information from his nephew in the White Guard. The regiment had scattered. Many had been executed. These included Genia's father. His body and also the body of his beautiful wife had been found deteriorating in the lake.

They were surrounded by hundreds of rotting carp.

"The fish too had been shot. Right through the gills," said Silkleigh in a shocked voice, placing a finger to his ear.

Genia would not know the details until the eve of her departure from Tromso. She spent most of the next six years in an unhealthy daze. She attended the gymnasium, she helped out in the house and she passed the evenings alone in her room, looking at the northern lights misting the night sky.

According to the trader this phenomenon was caused by thousands of swans. They had slept on the ice, their wings had frozen in the night and they were beating their way free. His daughter said it was the hair of women who had died as virgins floating on the night winds. She wished no such fate for Genia. When an orchestra from Bergen visited Tromso she gave a dinner party for its Spanish conductor. Genia was instructed to lead him home after a programme which included music from Bartók's ballet "The Wooden Prince" and Sibelius' "Valse Triste".

"Come here, Genia. You make the arrangements. He speaks only French."

She accepted the telephone.

"How will I know you?" came a young man's voice.

She thought, I don't know. She had a small nondescript face and long brown hair which everyone said was beautiful once she had brushed it a hundred times.

"Why don't you wait for me by the ticket box looking helpless?"

He said two people who have never seen each other before, but who are looking, always find each other.

She arrived late and sat at the rear of the hall until Ernesto finished conducting. Afterwards she made her way to the ticket office. Suddenly she felt a stroking movement on the back of her legs. Something hard was touching her skin, causing her to shiver. It lifted the hem of her skirt and rose ticklishly up her calf. She twirled about.

"My magic wand!" said Ernesto, spinning his baton into the air and nearly dropping it.

He shook her hands while Klebst, owner of the concert hall told him how wonderful she was, how pretty. The more Klebst told him, the harder the conductor squeezed.

Ernesto Ortiz was a tall, thick-set man, with a large chin and a perpetually moist upper lip. His darkish blond hair was unkempt and wiry, as if the strings had snapped on a thousand violins. He was twenty-five and conductor of the orchestra he had founded two years before. Nineteen twenty-four, while a remarkable year for claret, was no *annus mirabilis* in the short history of the Abyla Philharmonic. When offered the position for six months as guest conductor of a Norwegian orchestra, Ernesto had accepted, as he had profited from his term at Manaus's Teatro Amazonas. He might also meet some musicians whom he could attract to Abyla.

One of the few persons whom Ernesto would ever attract to Abyla was the seventeen-year old Evgenia Nikolaevna. Paraphrasing Goethe, he told her she was the eternal feminine who had transported him to higher spheres. She was the halfness he had always been seeking. The eagerness with which he pressed his suit melted something inside her. He was an apostle from a happier world, a world echoing to the slurred cadences of Sibelius. On the day following his proposal, after consulting with the captain's daughter who told her it was a brilliant match, Genia consented.

The couple arrived in Abyla at the end of March 1924. Genia expected to find lions and elephants with long teeth and vegetation that towed the houses back into the jungle. She did not believe Ernesto when he described his city as a donkey-grey fugue on the banks of Africa.

They stepped through the black veil of flies into a city under siege. There were no lights. The water supply had been cut off and Abdel Akbar perched on the brow of La Mujer Muerta whose slopes crumped with mortar fire.

Genia's first impression was the silver dirigible above the church from which a man with a mirror directed the mortars (including the shell which late in the war plummeted onto the bell tower of Santa Maria).

"*Qu'est ce que c'est que ça?*" she asked, opening the window onto the balcony.

"A dead cat, it looks like," said Ernesto.

"A dead cat!"

"Someone's shot it through the head."

A great hollering rose from the street below. Genia leaned over the balcony. She saw a man in a corset brandishing a sabre.

She hated Abyla from that moment, this rare and ugly orchid which sprouted on what was, without any argument at all, the wrong side of the Mediterranean. Five centuries of Europe in Africa, she would remind herself, peering down over the General's terrace and his handkerchief tree – for this!

The feeling that she was tantalised by something in which she could not participate was not exclusively an Abylan emotion, but the Straits, and the fact she could see Gibraltar across them, encouraged it. From the very first, Evgenia Nikolaevna judged a day by whether she could see Europe.

Neither was there solace to be found in the church where Padre Ruiz married them. Santa Maria de Africa had been converted into a granary. To scare the rats away, Padre Ruiz had permitted a number of the city's cats to seek refuge from the General's shotgun. His bell tolled to warn of an enemy attack as often as it tolled for prayer. Twice in her first month, Genia Ortiz solemnly made her way to the Plaza de Africa believing she had been summoned to a late Matins.

When she learned to read the newspapers, her feeling that she was trapped was confirmed. She was trapped between a Europe that no longer existed, a continent of midday darkness, and this Africa of Abdel Akbar. Beyond La Mujer Muerta they tumbled over themselves to embrace death. To what end? It was all as pointless as the heroic end of Lieutenant Zamora who died to keep Abyla Spanish.

Genia stood on Calle Camoes and watched the General lead the Lieutenant's body through the streets. He was cheered loudest by Abyla's women. Were the Moors to breech the massive ramparts of the fortress of San Felipe, a group of Abyla's richest wives had decided to flee to a cave in La Mujer Muerta where they proposed to live on the same deciduous barks as the apes.

Genia wore a Goya veil in the funeral cortege. She walked in the third row of mourners. Ernesto, leading the band, conducted at a smart pace and she had some difficulty keeping up with the shiny black coffin. She followed it into the Virgin of Africa, where after a short prayer for Lieutenant Zamora's soul, she turned to the matter of her own. Clasping her fingers, she bothered the Virgin to be a dear and keep Ernesto from touching her.

Ernesto Ortiz and Evgenia Nikolaevna Polotseva were married under the same roof six weeks later. In the evening, she floated on the bed while Ernesto undressed. Her husband sat down awkwardly beside her. She was her dead mother on the lake. "Genia," he whispered, crawling on top of her. She felt a carp swimming inside her legs and became hysterical.

Ernesto was too terrifed to ask what the matter was, but he could see she was living through a horror he didn't dare experience at second hand. The carp swam away, and in the morning when they looked at each other, each saw the stranger to whom they would be married for the rest of their lives.

Genia Ortiz remained a virgin until she was forty. She satisfied herself with thinking of the old days. The old days were always good. No other part of the world had the power to replace Balnasharki in her heart. The memories trembled through her head like feet across the slats of the old bridge. She saw the house like a slice of christening cake, the storks bouncing from the toothpick reeds, the walnut avenue with its pothole which caused her body to clench every time they drove over it, the spires of the town through the trees, her father fanning away the midges from his mournful face with the cigar he only smoked on the lake.

In Abyla such clamorous images grew and bred. She only had to pass her nose over an empty perfume bottle to be circled by moths of nostaglia. The fabric belonging to the rest of her life had been consumed by these moths until it seemed her entire existence might have been squeezed or buttoned into her first eleven years.

Just as early photographs blurred moving objects, so few other people existed for her. In the stopped clocks of her imagination she referred not to General Franco nor La Pasionara nor King Juan Carlos, but to a grandmother who had argued with Pavlova or a twelfth-century Boyar or an ancestor, an insane cossack – the nearest she ever came to a black sheep – who had fled Kiev to become a stargazer in Rudolfine Prague.

In her lonely exile, Genia Ortiz dropped names – Golitsyn, Meyershensky, Oblomov – which stayed where they fell because no one knew who on earth she was talking about.

After more than sixty years, Genia Ortiz had talked herself out of a large percentage of the *presidio*'s goodwill. She was conscious of her effect on people, and minded, regretting it in the way a smoker regrets the taste in his mouth, but she was powerless to prevent herself from advising anyone with two good ears of her father's descent from Grand Duke Polotsev, of the eighteen servants who infested the house, the paquet floor in the principal bedroom – where no less a person than X had stayed on his way back from the siege of Vienna, and the occasion, as an eight-year-old child attending the Kiev School for Young Ladies of the Nobility, when she had very nearly been bitten by one of Anna Pavlova's bulldogs.

In the early days, Ernesto told her to be quiet, Genia, for the love of God. Vexed, she looked back, her eyes locking, then unlocking, not thinking about him at all. He knew it wasn't snobbery that had given her a squint – as many suggested – but from time to time he did wonder if the non-alignment of vision that entranced him once in the foyer of an arctic concert hall had deteriorated with the century.

She would respond by saying she had been hurt, that was all, and fall into a proud self-consolatory sulk almost as irritating to Ernesto as whatever had precipitated it. Eventually he learned to say nothing.

Genia remained a virgin until the night in the twenty-third year of her marriage when Ernesto was scratched by a wounded tomcat as he left the Club de Pensiones. He had given up approaching her long ago, but as she washed away the blood, one hand remained squeezing his left ankle. Her other arm rested on his knee. Ernesto, sitting with no trousers, gently spread her fingers and laid them without a word upon the mound shifting inside his underpants.

Since his marriage to Genia that mound had shifted for many women. After all, what does a man do when his wife denies him, when instead of performing her conjugal duties she treats him to stories about the *beau monde* in pre-revolutionary Kiev, a diet far richer than the Hofbauer truffles with which Ernesto learned to commence his overtures? While he regretted Genia's obstinacy, his position as conductor and his gamey good looks guaranteed a certain success.

The idiosyncratic justice he liked to administer on the flanks of aspirant cellists was a punishment he would much rather have wrought upon his wife.

Genia Ortiz, uncovering the mound, remained ignorant of her husband's *nuits folles* and that part of his soul he allowed out to hunt. Because the same part of her own soul had not been awakened, she had not taken account his infidelities. Yes, she saw that women liked to mother him. Yes, she watched waitresses feed him pieces of almond cake she hadn't eaten. Sometimes she wondered if she should mind. But until the night he was scratched by a cat, she had not coveted an area he had surrendered to others.

On the verge of making love for the first time with his wife of twenty-three years, Ernesto felt the nerves of a small boy whose bluff has at last been called.

At first sex terrified Genia Ortiz as much as the prospect of pregnancy. Under a delusion about the motility of semen, she lay back as clenched as when the cart approached the pothole telling Ernesto in a small voice to do as he pleased.

He didn't like to do much. Jelly made her slippery and Hüter's vaginal powder which she applied in large doses, caused him grave irritations. Possibly such sexual contact as they enjoyed in their first year would have ceased altogether in the second had not Ernesto returned from a season of Mahler concerts in Prague bearing a curious contraption described by its inventor as a Venus Apparatus.

"What is it?"

Ernesto said, "Something to make us enjoy ourselves more." Determination had made him pale.

In her forty years, Genia Ortiz had never seen anything so ridiculous as the "instant orgasmic douche" of this Dr Linz. A perforated rubber ball, the size of a greengage, was connected by a thin tube to a transparent football. When squeezed, the liquid in the football released itself through the perforations in the greengage. "Undress," he whispered. She removed her clothes in a trance. The conductor stood at the basin, filling the larger balloon with vinegar, lysol and warm water. She saw the furtive caresses as he coated the long tube with vaseline.

"This goes there," he said, holding up the greengage. He kept his back to her. He unbuttoned his shirt and trousers while she inserted it.

"Ready?"

"I think so."

He turned, naked, and picked the warm balloon from the sheet beside her.

"At the moment of ejaculation," he read out, "we both squeeze."

Dr Linz's apparatus would involve the Ortizes in some improbable contortions, but nothing would match the occasion of their first experiment when after less than a minute Ernesto screamed, "Squeeze!" Tense with fright the two of them fumbled for the football which they dislodged from the pillow next to her head, dilating the sphere so frenetically that it slithered from their grasp, bouncing once, twice, three times on the floor before it was jerked back by the umbilical entrail tugging at their loins, coming to rest with an audible shudder against one of Ernesto's shoes.

Ernesto was filled with shame. Not so his wife. Rigid with panic at the outset, she found herself stimulated by the tube linking them. There was something about the preliminary preparations which also aroused her – even if Tromso's birth exactly nine months later testified to the inefficacy of the Venus Apparatus as a contraceptive device. And experiencing a sensation entirely new to her in bed, she found the operation comical.

In a way she had fallen in love, and falling in love she brought to her love-making all the fervency she might have given him in her twenties.

After experimenting for a week with the Venus Apparatus, Genia Ortiz discovered her preferred position. She sat astride Ernesto on the blue arm chair, looking into the malleable globe between them. It was a position she favoured for five years until out of the blue she received a note "on behalf of one who wants to see justice in this matter". The unsigned scribble informed her of Ernesto's ministrations to an assistant cook in the asylum on Calle Silvestre.

"From then on, it was downhill," Silkleigh told Wavery. They stood outside the Abyla Swimming Club. "But you are never innocent in how you choose to be destroyed, old soul. You should know that."

"But how do you know all that?" asked Wavery.

"If you live in a city of exile, you become *aware*. And I'm a writer, remember. I know who's telling the story and what the story is and why the story. I can sum up these people's lives in a *minuto*. Where they've got to and how, who has been felled by sloth or greed or sheer bad luck, or driven by the power of love. Oh, yes, old soul, I'm good on others. It's simply myself I can't work out."

3

In the Plaza de los Reyes a pigeon settled on a palm frond, dislodging a cough of dust. Marie Amaral observed its powdery descent. It tumbled into the waterless fountain and over the bucket she had left out overnight, filled to the brim with rock roses.

This morning when she opened her stall, the bucket was empty. It was a metal bucket with a handle that squeaked. In such a bucket Captain Panteco's grandfather, a veteran of Cuba, a minor poet, and for twenty-three years the city's night watchman, had carried the blood from the old bullring in Santos Vilela and tipped the contents into the ground at the base of the palm trees. The recipe was effective. The blood strengthened the roots and almost seventy years later the carnivorous trees spread a generous shade over the benches.

Marie Amaral loved this square. It was her luxury to sit here when the flowers did not require her. She would sit for an hour, a newspaper on her lap, now and then looking up to watch her stall. She could have her shoes cleaned or her palm read or a silhouette of her profile scissored out of card. In the bull-black shade, she sat out the heat.

In the shoe shop on the corner Marie Amaral saw her stepdaughter arranging shoes in the window. Immediately, she became cross with herself. I'm full of emptiness, she thought. I am moved to sentimentality by a pair of children's gumboots, yet I remain immobile in the real face of my stepdaughter's unhappiness.

How she wished she could have found some words to say an

hour ago. Anything. And she had been going to be a teacher! Ah, Marie Amaral, if you could know now what you knew then.

Into the stall had walked Rosita, tortoiseshell comb in her hair, red nails, rabbit-skin coat on her shoulders. But inside, dry earth.

"Is something bothering?" Marie Amaral could tell when her stepdaughter was distressed. She didn't wear make-up or wash her hair.

"Silkleigh," said Rosita. She picked up a piece of cellophane and tore at it with her teeth.

"Don't do that. It ruins the enamel."

"Mama, help me."

Rosita sought Marie Amaral's comfort as she had never sought it in the days of her marriage to the unsuitable guitarist, or afterwards when she lived with the policeman. Silkleigh was another matter.

Rosita wanted help and Marie Amaral couldn't give it. She was useless, without a tongue, emptier than the *babouche* mounds in Oran's medina. Something vital had gone. That broken mirror, its fragments, they had been reassembling ever since she had dropped the vase. Like a film in reverse. Sweeping off the floor, showing the world as it was before Abyla.

Marie Amaral retreated indoors. She needed to distract herself. She made some coffee. She wiped last week's prices, written in felt pen, from a bunch of plastic tabs. She cut open a cardboard box, one of five purchased from the Dutchman. She removed the bouvardia. "In God's earth till yesterday, señora."

The Dutchman operated out of a large lorry in the Algeciras flower market. Winter and summer he stood on the trailer dispensing fresh-cut flowers, fifty stems a box. He never failed to recognise the scents worn by his clients. "That's a new one," he would say approvingly. Marie Amaral bought most of her flowers from the Dutchman. Thirty years ago when she opened her stall, the seasons determined her stock. Now, thanks to the Dutchman, she was able to offer flowers of all seasons, most of the year round.

The stall was a glass cabin eight feet by eight. A plastic sheet covered the door in case it rained. On market days she watered and drained whatever plants she might have carried back from the Peninsula. Then she unpacked the boxes, cutting the soft stems at an angle and hammering the tougher ones on a low formica table. In summer she brought freeze bags to put in the buckets. In winter she boiled a kettle.

Marie Amaral smelled her flowers for two or three minutes after she unlocked the stall. Thereafter she became impervious to the scents. She took her vicarious pleasure in watching others. She didn't know about their hearts, but the corners of their mouths turned up.

She picked up her coffee. There was a milk skin on the surface, like the caul which had smothered her face at birth. "A sailor would give his mizzen mast for that," her father had said. She kept the scrap of dry brown skin in a matchbox. She was thinking, "I should have given it to Emilio," when there was a tap on the glass and a voice said, "What terrific bouvardia!"

It was the British Consul General.

In the early mornings she sometimes noticed him pass the door. A man's hair told her whether he should be taken seriously. She remained undecided about Señor Wavery. She had only seen him with wet hair, but his manner had a diffidence which intrigued her. And there was the sympathy she felt instinctively for another foreigner in Abyla.

"But you have everything!" said Wavery. He looked at the shelves. He had the pinkish-grey skin you only see in Englishmen.

"I'm afraid they have to fight for existence, señor."

"Do you buy them from Africa?"

"From Algeciras."

Wavery, listening to her accent, said, "You must be French?"

Marie Amaral gave a frightened laugh. "I've been here thirty years."

"But your accent."

"I was born in Algeria." She busied herself with ribbons.

He saw she wasn't about to answer and said, "What about

some mimosa?" He wanted to brighten his empty house and to chase away the plaster smells.

He waited while Marie Amaral wrapped it. He was about to leave when he noticed the begonia. "What is that?"

"The begonia?" said Marie Amaral. The horrid thing was flourishing.

"I meant the pot."

"It's just a teapot."

It was not until after Wavery had left that Marie Amaral found the courage to approach the shelf. By noticing the teapot, he had made it real. This was not just a teapot. This was the only memento she possessed of David. She held the teapot to her face as if she would see her husband there and not herself, upside down in the convex metal. She looked, and upside down behind her appeared the square, the benches and the palm trees of a hotel garden in Oran where David Utor the medical student had courted her, turning over in his hands this same object.

He had bought it from a Berber girl in the Rif. That was all he could talk about when they first met. This girl and her teapot. Think of something else, Marie Amaral told herself, not a Berber dancing girl from the Ait Haddidu. Her attention slipped to his wrist. He had no watch. What an affectation, she thought.

"She amazed me very much." One night the girl had danced around the fire. Towards the end of the dance she held the teapot to the faces of the three medical students. The flames on the distorting metal – he thought it was silver, like her bracelets – made his handsome face go on forever.

"What do you drink?" asked the girl. Her eyes mocked him. They had been emboldened with antimony and her eyebrows arched with soot. There were indigo tattoos on her chin.

"Champagne," he joked. He held up his metal mug. The girl lowered the camel-neck spout and poured.

"It wasn't a vintage, and it was warm. But it was champagne."

The student next to him, also from Oran, asked for vodka.

"And what came out? Vodka!" The action was repeated, this time with wine, after which David determined to buy the miraculous vessel. The girl refused. It was an heirloom. She stroked the lid, mocking him. It had passed into her family when her ancestors defeated King Sebastian. It had belonged to the ten-year-old Duke of Barcelos. It had been made in Cordoba under Abd-ar-Rachman III. "It is magic."

David held out his mug for more. Again she poured. She could name her price, he said. She shook her head, jingling with armillae. He mentioned a price she could name. The armillae jingled again. He raised his offer. The fire was dying when her head grew still and she parted with her magic heirloom. He took the teapot to bed. "Only the teapot, Marie."

The girl was gone when he woke, so he was unable to question her about the words engraved on its base which included the name of an industrial town in northern England.

When in 1962 she left Oran, Marie Amaral tidied the teapot away. It was all she had of her husband and it made her jealous.

Memory was a rapist too. She only had to look into her son's face to be gripped by the sight of his father and not the man she had loved. How often had two never-experienced-madness eyes escorted her back to the present dinner table and she heard herself say brightly, "Where were we?"

Periclito never asked. But now and then Rosita would say, "Mama, tell me about Daddy."

There was little to tell. She had met Rosita's father in the winter of 1959 after he had spent a year in the Rif studying plants. He was a Portuguese Jew, a doctor, a passionate believer in the healing properties of herbs, and a lover of football. He was also a widower. His young Portuguese wife had died in childbirth. Two months later he put Rosita in the care of his sister in Lisbon and departed for the mountains.

They met on his return, in the hospital in Oran. Marie had a lump on her left arm and David Amaral was the doctor. The lump was benign.

She was a nineteen-year-old *pied noir*, studying to be a teacher. At weekends she read Shakespeare and Dickens and

Evelyn Waugh. To earn her way through teacher training, she worked for a dressmaker in the Saint-Pierre district. She rarely saw her parents. Her father had a citrus farm south of the city and a temper like the *levante* which blew lemons through the windows. He would die in his bed, betrayed by his only daughter, and with bitterness in his heart when he considered the fate of Algeria.

David argued with him on the one occasion they met.

"What do you think of the situation?" demanded Marie's father. There had been an FLN attack on a neighbour's farm. A baby's slashed body had been replaced in her mother's womb and the mother's ventricles stuffed with bottles from the dressing table.

David looked awkward. In the days before the Evian agreement it was possible to be twenty-five and not interested in politics.

"I don't know, monsieur," he said.

"You don't *know*!" Marie's father stood up. He walked to where David sat and leaning over him he filled the young man's glass with vinegary red wine. David drank nervously.

"You know what the Arabs do to those who drink alcohol?" Her father's voice was cruel now. "Do you?" He bent his face until his cheeks touched David's. He placed the bottle on the table and opened his hand. Very slowly he wiped a palm over his mouth. "They cut off their lips."

"Papa!"

"Louis, I think . . ." said Marie's mother.

He straightened. "Now," he said. "I ask you again. What do you think of the situation?"

He told Marie's father he was not dedicated to the preservation of Algérie Française. He said that, for him, the problem of the white man in Algeria began with his arrival.

"I'm going to bed," said Marie's father, whose family had farmed here since 1883. Silence replaced him in the room. Marie's mother had followed in his wake, and they heard her quick steps upstairs and the father's voice bellowing "bloody Jew."

Marie stood up, but David said, "No, Marie. No. It's not our business."

She came over to where he sat and stood over him, stroking his black hair away from his eyes. "You know," she said, "I've never met a Frenchman." Oran was very much a Spanish city. The only French she knew were *pieds noirs* like herself.

"One day I'll take you to Paris," he promised.

The young couple left in the morning. They were heading for the sea, in a cart drawn by two bays, in the swaying back of which Marie remembered a carpet spread with food and drink, and, balanced on a large cream cushion so the needle would not slip, a phonograph that played "The Horn Sounds at Midnight" as David held her in his arms, promising when they were married he would lose his head between her breasts and listen to the gunfire in her heart.

Two months later he proposed in the garden of the Hotel Saint-Sulpice. There were names on the trees in Latin and French and in the branches a blackbird. Once in their conversation they heard a different bird. David turned and there behind their bench stood Hacine, a poet he had known at university. Hacine was drinking rosé from a bottle, and whistling. "I can do warblers, starlings and sparrows," and he threw back his head. The wine burst in tiny bubbles on his tongue. "And cuckoos, of course."

David proposed after a conversation about the healing qualities of herbs and the protection certain herbs were believed to offer against thunderbolts and witchcraft. "Mimosa bark for diarrhoea. Persicaria for mouth ulcers. Chicory for . . ."

Marie never learned. She could tell David was not concentrating on what he said. Their heads were so close she could smell his skin. He leaped back crying, "My God, what am I talking about?"

(Very occasionally through the Abyla dust, David's odour would cross the square to her, unaccountably erotic and smelling of chicory.)

They spent part of their honeymoon in the Aurés, part of it beside the sea. He could not yet afford Paris. That city could

152

wait. On the sea they rented a villa at Tipala, near the Roman ruins. In the afternoons they slept on a bed of blue saxifrage, his head between her breasts.

They had been married for six months when David was murdered by the OAS.

He was killed a few days after Evian. The treaty had enraged the *pieds noirs*. Attacks. Reprisals. That was Oran in the weeks of March and April. But his murder was an accident. She returned home late, about nine in the evening. She had been working in her shop, on a dress for the Mayor's sister. There were no trams. A bomb had exploded in the baths. OAS soldiers had fired on Arabs who ran into the streets in their towels. "There'll be a rat hunt tonight," warned a young man in the tram queue. She waited half an hour, then decided to walk home. The night was filled with car horns and people beating pan lids, shouting *"Al-gé-rie Française! Al-gé-rie Française!"* The *ratissage* had begun.

Their house was in Mers-El-Kebir, four blocks from the sea. She opened the gate, climbed the steps, unlocked the door and walked into the sitting room. She did not turn on the lights. The curtains were open. The city was blacked out, but there was a fire burning in the road below, beyond their little garden. The light from the flames leaped up a tree. She heard a scream from the fire in the road. The stench of smoke was horrible. A car was alight and around it dark figures were cavorting. *"Al-gé-rie Française!"* they chanted.

There was a noise behind her.

"David?" She turned. For the first time she noticed something unusual about the furniture. The room was untidy, chairs awry, books on the floor, the mirror given by her father as a wedding present at a strange angle.

"Rosita?"

And still the pan lids, the car horn, the chants in a terrifying rhythm. *"Al-gé-rie Française! Al-gé-rie Fran-çaise!"*

"I love that sound," said a voice not David's.

A shadow detached itself from the wall near the bookcase, moving across the mirror. A man stepped into the light of the

153

burning car. He looked out of the window, not looking at her.

"Who the hell are you?"

The head turned and the orange light fell onto a large chin and close-cut hair. The hair was white, as if dyed. "Madame Amaral?"

"I am, yes. But where's David? Who are you? Or are you from the hospital?"

He laughed and she could smell the *anisette* on his breath and what could have been *merguez* sausage.

"No, not from the hospital."

"Then who are you?"

"Merimée. Just call me Merimée." He spoke in mainland French, without the inflexions of Africa.

"Where's Rosita?"

He put a finger to his lips. "In bed."

"Where's David?"

"Your husband?" His voice was solicitous. He tapped the window, the light bouncing off his eyes.

He said, "But isn't that his car?"

That they had killed the wrong man, they would not know till morning. The man they wanted to kill was a Trade Union leader, Diego Amaral, who had spoken on television in favour of independence.

Merimée was in charge. He had come from Strasbourg in March. This was his first mission for the OAS. After he watched the television interview he had issued his *ponctuelle*. The name D. Amaral was written in red on a page torn from *L'Echo d'Oran* and delivered to the executioner, a maker of garage doors known as Le Cygne who looked up the name in a telephone book. There were two Amarals one with the initials A.D., the other D.P. He wrote down the address of the second, belonging to David Paco Amaral.

Returning from the hospital, David was ambushed by Le Cygne's men. They poured petrol on the roof of the car and over the bonnet, and when he tried to open the door they kicked it shut.

That night, re-enacting the scene, the man called Le Cygne said, "It was like taking a photo." He struck a match and as if to the car applied it to the paper on which had been written his victim's name. When he discovered he had killed the wrong Amaral, he had a good laugh. Sometimes mistakes were made. He would shoot the right one two days later. He would draw up on his motorbike, its number plates smeared with lipstick. "Señor Amaral," he would say, rapping the window of the official's car. "Señor Amaral," he would say again and hold up a woman's handbag. Puzzled, the other Amaral would wind down his window. Le Cygne would shoot him four times in the face before driving off.

But that was later. Tonight, on the night of the mistake, there was one dead Amaral. "He was a coco," Merimée told Marie. "A liberal. That's why we rubbed him out." Marie couldn't remember her words. She wanted to rush to the street. Merimée held her wrists. The pressure seemed to hurt him – there was something wrong with his hands. She pulled away, but she couldn't escape.

She didn't understand. She simply didn't understand. David was not interested in politics. Once he had argued with a doctor who kept the Maréchal's portrait in his surgery. And he had read without finishing it, Henri Alleg's *La Question*. That was the sum total of his political activity. She hurled the words at the man who held her arms. Merimée did not hear. A tiny grimace contorted his face.

That night was the night of her husband's death, and of her son's conception.

A thud startled her. The fisherman's dog was beating his tail against the door. His tail swept through a bucket of Stargazer lilies, spilling a lily to the ground. He spread the pads of his feet and rolled his tongue along the stem. The poor thing wants water, she thought, and she filled a bowl from the kettle. The dog drank noisily. Then, trailing his lead behind him, he trotted out into the square, reaching the mechanical rocking horse at the same moment as Senator Zamora and Pablo.

Marie Amaral watched Senator Zamora crumple onto his haunches. He was inspecting the collar. The dog lifted his nose and licked the Senator's face. "Oy!" exclaimed Zamora, crinkling his eyes. He fell backwards onto one hand, wiping his cheeks with a sleeve of his green cardigan, laughing.

Inside her flowerstall, Marie Amaral also laughed. If ever she let herself go again, it would be to a man like Senator Zamora. People are happy with those they understand. More than anyone Senator Zamora understood her. He was the only person in Abyla she had told about the French soldier called Merimée.

She had told him five years before, when Abyla was invaded by the tunnel workers.

She told him one day, out of the blue, after walking into him in the Calle Camoes. "Marie Amaral!" exclaimed Zamora, who had been playing dominoes. He stood on the steps of the Club de Pensiones and raised his hat. When he saw her face he was moved to take her arm.

"I don't want to join the *paseo*, Teodoro." She felt a stitch in her side.

"Then a walk by the sea?"

"That would be fine."

"Would you like a drink?" asked Zamora. They were passing the Café Ulises.

Marie Amaral shook her head. Silkleigh would be there.

They walked past the construction site, parallel to the shore. "Is it the tunnel?" he asked, with a shudder.

"Teodoro, can we talk?" This time it was she who held him. She led him onto the beach. "Sit on that," she said, offering Zamora a rock. She squeezed onto the rock beside him.

"Well, Marie?"

Looking straight ahead she told him of Periclito's father, the OAS officer from Strasbourg.

Zamora listened, his long legs stretched out in the sand, crossed over at the ankles, his chin on the back of his hand, his hand on the chest of his cardigan.

In a strained voice she said, "Sometimes I think does it really matter?"

"Have you told Periclito?"

"How can I? I used to see things in him I recognised in his father, but I couldn't tell him why I cried, 'Out!' And now it's too late. How can I tell him I feel as much guilt as love? That guilt is stronger."

Zamora uncrossed his legs. He picked up his father's hat from the sand and leaned forward. He held the hat between his knees, allowing his gaze to fall into its bat-coloured bowl as if he would find there, on the label reading SEVILLE – CALLE DEL GATO, 34, the words she needed him to say. He looked back at her. When he spoke his words were candle-light kind. He didn't speak of the rat-hunt, nor about betrayal, nor about what David might have thought. He talked about the Phoenicians. "People laugh. But they had many answers," he said. He asked Marie Amaral to imagine herself a woman of Byblos.

"Byblos?" said Marie Amaral, doubtfully.

He explained. Once in the course of their lives, it was incumbent on any woman born in Byblos to visit Astarte's temple and there to associate with a stranger. Only foreign pilgrims were permitted entry to the temple. When these women – "all honourable women, Marie" – had offered themselves to a pilgrim they could return home, their duty fulfilled.

"Major Merimée as a *pilgrim*?" said Marie Amaral, astonished.

"As a pilgrim," insisted Zamora who all along had suspected what everyone else in Abyla suspected.

"Look at his ears, look at his ears," Marie Amaral would say in the early days. "They're just like David's." Zamora had been glad when her appeal ceased. There was no one in Abyla who could verify whether or not the owner of the Café Ulises had David's ears. One thing was unarguable: he did not have his mother's uninheritable grace.

Marie Amaral pressed her side as if she was about to say something, but Zamora continued. It was wrong to grieve forever. Too much grief made a cobblestone of the heart.

"But when Minerva died?"

"When Minerva died, I grieved – for a while," and he thought of those soupless days, sitting on the bed with her photograph. "But old love doesn't rust."

Marie Amaral remembered the iris he bought on Minerva's birthday, every year an extra stem. "If she lives to a hundred you'll have to sell the car!"

On the rock beside her, Senator Zamora said, "And God? I don't suppose he helps?"

"No," she faltered. "What do you believe, Teodoro?"

"I believe – No. What do I believe?" Telling someone what you believed had the same effect as looking them in the eye. He sat back. An hour ago he was routing Porcil at dominoes. He sat forward, groping in the darkness of his father's hat.

"If I think of what you have seen, Marie, I have seen nothing," he said. "Yet I have lived through six revolutions. And you know what happens? After each revolution everyone becomes a hero. I was never a hero. I tried to be honest, that's all. But one thing I have learned is this: neither intelligence nor art is a weapon against the beast in the human heart. That said, I do believe all of us at some point experience what it is to be beautiful as well as to be ugly. To be strong and also to be weak. To be good and bad, funny, boring, rich, poor, a flower seller, a senator, I won't go on. We all become Hercules. We all become Menendez. One cannot avoid the fate. That is what it means to be human. The important thing is to be yourself when it happens." He looked her in the eye. "It's time to be yourself again, Marie."

What he had said impressed her more than his Phoenician anecdote. Her nose wrinkled. "Menendez?" she said.

Zamora nodded. "Even Menendez."

She began to giggle, a superb rich giggle that caused Senator Zamora to begin laughing himself and Marie Amaral to respond until she had to wipe the tears from her eyes.

The wrong man had been killed, the wrong woman raped. She knew what she had suffered was nothing, nothing, nothing compared to the experience of many others in Oran. But she knew after that night she never again wished to be in Europe.

Death came in nibbles. Stress locked her jaw. She ceased to

menstruate. It was natural for women in a state of shock to cease menstruating. When she discovered she was pregnant she cut her wrists. She nearly died, but she had no talent for death. She shaved off her beautiful hair. In the mirror she saw a face such as she would later see in the asylum in Calle Silvestre. She tapped the window, grinning. She cartwheeled about the room uttering hideous cries. She squatted in the corner, not bothering to go outside.

It was curious. By the act of pretending to be someone else, she preserved her sanity. "I survived because I played a madwoman, Teodoro."

She played a madwoman for a month. Her head began to blacken again. Her stomach grew.

In September she was stopped by two policemen in the Rue Balzac.

"Why the veil?"

Don't scream, she told herself. They can smell your fear. Look at him. What does he remind you of? She could only compare the small hard peak of his cap to a bitten fingernail.

"It's hot. It's not illegal. I was seeing a friend."

"An Arab?"

"She is, yes."

"Any Arab is a rebel."

"Let her go," said his colleague. "*Elle avait la frousse.*" He could see she was no more than what she said, the daughter of a colon. He waved her on, not bothering to flatten the hand which held the address of the woman in the next street.

Marie Amaral had read of her in the newspaper. Absolute success in discrete matters. Feminine ailments quickly and economically cured in strictest confidence. Many testimonials. It would be more expensive than she could afford. The Abortion Act meant not only the mother risked prison, the abortionist too.

"I won't ask who's given you the big stomach," said the woman, drawing her lips on a cemetery of yellow teeth. Marie Amaral lifted the gold chain over her head. "I can only pay with this," she said in a voice further away than the mountains. The woman trailed it from her fingers. She nodded.

Marie Amaral stripped. She lay on the couch, her folded shirt a cushion under her head. The woman strapped her ankles into stirrups. She prattled from the basin. She believed it soothed her clients to know exactly what she was doing. She was preparing a salve of camphor and saffron which she was now injecting through this tube, a little wider, no – a little more, that'll do, into the uterus. To poison and dislodge the foetus.

Marie Amaral's legs were drawn up in the same position as Merimée had raised them when he entered her. The syringe was old and the contents leaked through the nozzle over the abortionist's hands.

Later the tube was removed and the woman swabbed her with carbolic soap. She returned to the basin. At this age it had a heart but no face. Her interminable talk rose over the sound from the bed. The sound was not describable. Every woman had her own sound, but uttered through the same snarled-back lips. She had wanted to be a chemist, not an abortionist. She dropped the syringe into a wooden box. There shouldn't be any problems. In case there are, remember – every day the horsie!

When the abortion failed, Marie Amaral did not return to the apartment in the Rue Narbonne. She drank foul-tasting lavender tea and ate plants containing volatile oils. In October she swallowed four packets of matches, heads only, hoping the phosphorus would kill. She was sick for a week. Under its smock her stomach grew. In November she jumped from a charred branch into the garden, spraining her knee. A day before Periclito was born she made a vow. If the child lived she would hurl it into the sea – towards the country of its father.

A bark returned Marie Amaral to the square. Pablo's rocking horse had excited the fisherman's dog. Once he became accustomed to the motion, Toribio returned to Zamora's side. He slumped to the ground, watching Pablo on the horse, his tail slapping in the dust.

Zamora's grandson wanted always to know everything.

He would visit her stall when he should have been at school.

"Why doesn't Periclito look like you? Why does he have to fight bulls? Why isn't he at home ever?"

"I don't know, Pablo," she said. "Maybe he just doesn't like Abyla." But it was a lie. The truth had a different smell. The truth had its own smell, but how could she convey it to an eight-year-old boy, still less to her son or her stepdaughter.

Periclito had looked and behaved much as Pablo had behaved at the same age. Marie Amaral, watching Pablo on his horse, realised she had done nothing about the red bouvardia stems. Every bucket in the stall was full. The only spare bucket was that by the fountain which she had left last night filled with rock roses. She walked outside, into the square.

"I'm a picador!" Pablo's arm was a lance, the dog at his feet a bull. *"Olé!"*

She thought of Periclito. She had failed her son, as an hour ago she had failed Rosita.

"Olé!"

She thought of Periclito at Pablo's age, more than twenty years before.

"Maman, did you get my bull?" He was running through the marigold field on the other side of La Mujer Muerta. She had taken a house for the summer, where Teodoro Zamora shot his duck and wild pig. A flock of doves flew low over the marigold field, catching the sun on their wings, fading, catching the sun again, settling, rising as he panted towards her.

His voice piped over the field. "Did you get it, Maman?"

Before they had left Abyla, her son had seen for sale in the Plaza de los Reyes a daguerreotype of a bullfight. He had entrusted her his savings to buy it. But the man wasn't there. There was no one in the square. Marie forgot her own business and spent the afternoon passing from shop to shop, desperate for a hat, a cape, the plastic model of a bull, anything to do with the *corrida*. But there was nothing.

Determined not to return empty-handed, she bought him a straw sombrero outside the Hotel Zamora.

At thirty, Periclito's head had grown too large for the

161

sombrero, but in his own eyes he remained the figure in the daguerreotype, his throat outstretched to the crowd as if he was a goat nibbling at an argan tree.

"Oh, Periclito," she said aloud while concentrating in an abstract way on the Senator and his grandson. She had last seen her son three years ago.

"*Olé!*"

She saw him circled by oxcarts, lunging at something or other somewhere in Venzuela, not yet a matador. When would she see him again? Perhaps he would come for the celebrations next August. Perhaps – how could she not have thought of it! *The feria de toros!* The bullfight for which her instructive and lovable Senator Zamora had been appointed President.

At the fountain Marie Amaral stooped to pick up her bucket, and an idea thrilled her.

4

Rosita saw her stepmother through the window. As soon as Marie Amaral was back inside her stall, Rosita slipped the rabbit-skin coat from its hanger, tucked the collar against her ears and said to her assistant, "I'll be back at two."

All morning she had been modelling shoes and clothes for Portuguese tourists. All morning they had wanted to see if this boot or that leather coat or that gum-pink slipper would suit their wife, their girlfriend, their mistress. All morning they had gazed at Rosita unseeing. They saw her taller, thinner, fatter, prettier. For one hour she would be her unhappy self.

She circled the empty fountain to the bench where she usually sat.

"Now that's what I mean by not using your intelligence," Teodoro Zamora was lecturing his grandson. Pablo was crying. He had offered the dog a lick and the dog had eaten his whole ice cream.

"Naughty Toribio," Zamora. The dog licked his fingers. "See those feet, Pablo, webbed like a duck's? They help him to swim.

He swims like this, rope in mouth, to the shore. In times of war he used to carry messages across the Tagus. Didn't you?" But Toribio the Portuguese waterdog must have had water in his ear. He licked the last flecks of ice cream from his mouth, yawned, and trotted down the hill.

Zamora stood up. "I'll buy you another ice cream." He set about cleaning Pablo's sticky cheeks with a sleeve of his cardigan.

"Hello, Pablo," said Rosita.

"Speak, child! You'll never get lost with a tongue in your head."

"Hello, Señorita Rosita." But his face was a playground robbed of its swings.

She moved on. Old men and fatherless children. That was Abyla. And a few hairy-arsed soldiers. As soon as they could walk up the gangplank, the young crossed to Algeciras.

Rosita hadn't followed them. Like her stepmother and Senator Zamora, she disliked the Peninsula. Her husband had been a *peninsulare*. He had walked off the ferry with his guitar. He had wooed her on the Playa Benitez under the stony gaze of La Mujer Muerta and with the hard tips of his fingers. In Abyla a lot of love began on the Playa Benitez. In Rosita's experience a Playa Benitez love lasted two weeks.

Old Lady Fortnight, she described it to her friend Dolores.

Rosita had hoped Norberto would teach her the secret of song. He had been so nice. He wrote her poems. He promised to give up drugs. He would find work. On their wedding day he bought her paella and Black Forest gateau. Then one evening he had ridden up on a duty-free motorbike and shouted "Whore!" He tried to stub out a cigarette on her face. He ripped the first and last pages from her favourite books and wrote "adulteress!" in lipstick on their wall.

He'd heard from someone who'd heard from someone else that she was having an affair with Señor Ortiz. But she wasn't. The conductor had promised to give her singing lessons. That was the limit of his attentions. It was Norberto who had been unfaithful – although not until he'd accelerated his bike onto the ferry to Algeciras for the last time did Dolores tell Rosita.

There was no one else until Panteco. She went with the impatient policeman because it was better to be wanted than not wanted, but she hadn't wanted his child. That was the reason she left him.

"Why, Rosita? Why?" he would demand, barging into her shop and then marching off in the middle of her attempt to explain, only to come pounding on her door in the evening. "Why?" She dreaded the sound of his steps on the stair, his booming voice. It upset her, the childish speed with which he raced through life, spilling everything to the ground when there was no need to hurry like that. And he would have spilled her. For months after the miscarriage she couldn't bear the sight of him, as if she'd eaten something that would forever after make her sick. She could not bear the touch of any man until one night as she sang *fado* in her brother's café, she looked down through the peacock lights and there, sitting at the bar, looking slightly lost, was the Englishman.

The love Rosita would grow to feel for Silkleigh was out of her realm, but there was no one in Abyla with whom Rosita could discuss him. She could not confide in her stepmother. "Don't glamourise him," Marie Amaral said this morning, embarrassed to talk of emotion. Then, as if it was the wisest thing in the world, she had said stiffly, "The horse one can't have is still a horse."

"I'm not going to glamourise him. He'll have to walk on his knees up the Calle Camoes before I speak to him again."

Or ring, thought Marie Amaral, seeing her stepdaughter's peach-soft resolve to hate the man.

Rosita could not talk to Dolores, who only wanted to talk of herself and Ernesto. She could not talk to her brother. Periclito was in Caracas. Only Clotilda could have helped her to explain the phenomenon of her attraction to Silkleigh. But Clotilda Zamora was not speaking to anyone.

"Is that taken?" A man, an Englishman, was asking her something. She could tell he was an Englishman by the V-neck, the

164

tweed jacket, the hair falling over one eye. This one was clutching an armful of mimosa.

Rosita moved along the bench, creating space for him. She knew the amount of space an Englishman needed.

"I was looking at the children," she said.

Wavery said, "Is that Pablo?"

"God loves men who love their children," remembered Rosita from somewhere. "Do you have children, señor?"

"No." Wavery recognised Zamora who cupped his mouth and called, "Did Asunción give you the list?"

From his pocket Wavery produced the computer print out. He brandished it.

"Thank you," Wavery called back. "I'm going to the library now."

Zamora looked about for Pablo. "Come on, Pablo," he said. In an attitude of grandfatherly despair, he propelled his grandson across the square towards the ice-cream kiosk. Wavery watched the motionless rocking horse, the man from Algeciras by the fountain, the eyebrows of shade made by the palm leaves in the dust.

Next to him Rosita placed a tortoiseshell comb in her mouth and flipped her hair forward, over her face. With the comb she fastened her hair into a loose chignon, tucking it up from the furrow of her neck where the fine black hair grew silver. She gave several shakes to make sure it was secure and sat back.

She said, "Señor Consul General, how does one sleep with an Englishman?"

"Silkleigh?"

Her face sank deeper into her collar. In the white fur she nodded.

"Are you positive you want to?"

They both laughed, Rosita's laugh lost in her coat. She said, "I know everyone is suspicious of him. Silkleigh is dangerous, they say, but I don't feel that. With me he's just rude. 'Rosita, you're the only person I have to hurt.' As if it's a compliment."

"He does rather pretend to know about everyone."

"Psssh. It's all in his mind, in his English imagination. You know what I think about Silkleigh, señor? I think he's a mytho-maniac. How can he know *anything* of other people when he is such a hopeless judge of his own character?"

"Do you know what he thinks of you?"

She stretched out a finger and pressed it against her long nose. "He thinks I'm cheap." She said the word as if she were saying "cheese" to one of the street photographers in Calle Real. "If men think you're cheap, they tend to think twice before signing up."

"Why does he think that?"

"Panteco," she said simply.

"And what happened with Panteco?"

"The usual. At the beginning I exaggerated his good bits. At the end his bad bits. He's not so bad, but he wasn't for me." She tidied away her smile. She inspected her red nails. "All my life I've been attractive to bastards. A man gives you the come on, you come on and then he goes. Men want to possess you in order to kill you. They see something lively and they want it, and when they've got it, they can't bear it being lively. But because I'm *loca completamente* I think Silkleigh is not like that."

"Really?"

Oh, he wanted to be. Silkleigh wanted to be like her brother, Periclito. He wanted every women he saw. Not that they were at all discouraged by his intolerable banter. What discouraged them, what sent them scattering likes ewes from a jackal, was the overwhelming dimension of his self-delusion.

"You mean his books?"

Rosita made a sound, somewhere between a snort and a wail. "He wants to be a writer. He couldn't write 'Shit' in the dirt on the side of his boat. It's his crazy refuge! He has no interest in human nature. He never has been in love. So how can he feel a love story, which is what novels are about?"

"I thought he was writing an autobiography," said Wavery, "with special emphasis on what we're doing to the sea."

"That's what *he* says! And last week on the ferry he tells me he has a great title, *Sunglasses on a Rainy Day*. But it would have to be a detective story. I said, 'Silkleigh, you're writing your life story. What is it with this detective crap?' And he says, 'Well, if the title is right, perhaps I'll write fiction.' You see! You can't trust him. He changes with the current, with every wind. He doesn't understand real people can't be actors. But most of all, señor, he doesn't understand it's not enough to live to write the story of your life. This talk, talk, talk about titles. It's all an excuse. *Letters to My Ego*. That's the book he should write. Oh, I don't want to think about him. He's so obnoxious."

"There's no one else?" Wavery asked.

"No. They never look back. Ever. Who, I ask you, is the one idiotic person who has looked back?" Her thumb jerked towards her own chest. "I'm sorry, señor. But if I have something in my heart, I tell it. There's no difference between my mouth and here. The English make everything a great secret. When they talk they are all lying. I suppose it's the same if they speak to each other."

"Yes," said Wavery. "I dare say you're probably right."

"Some days I think Silkleigh is no different from a matador. Each new girl is a mirror to fiddle with, until she reflects his face. Then he throws her away like tissue. He looks for another shiny pair of eyes."

"Silkleigh has a lot of days like that?"

"Only when he is drunk. And then he becomes the man you saw."

"And other times?"

"On other days he is the calmest of men. He talks about the sea, about the songs he hears underwater, about the turtles he makes shine with his fingers. On these days he becomes like his hands."

"His hands?"

"He has beautiful hands. Women look at the hands of men they wish to touch them, señor. I want him to make me shine in the night. Like his turtle."

A bell struck eight. Wavery looked involuntarily at his watch, his hand. It was two-fifteen.

"I have to go to the library," he said.

167

Chapter Seven

I

AT WHAT POINT had Wavery understood the force which bound him to Catharine? Not in the two months of their correspondence. She was a pebble in his shoe, no more. So he told himself.

He wrote every week. On paper he discovered things to say that he had never said to Penny. These things he hoarded for Catharine. He described his last days in Lima, his surprised regret over leaving Peru, his first homecoming in four years. He took pleasure in the most ordinary details. The Dutch lodgers had left their flat in an appalling state, "but I can turn on the tap without worms tumbling out." There was still no confirmation of his last posting, and this was annoying his wife. He had two months leave owing. He was in no hurry to begin work.

Catharine's letters were confessional. In one of them she talked of her mother. "What was the first thing I did when she died? I watered the plants. I felt alive and intense and when Adam returned he said 'What's happened? I've never seen you looking so beautiful.' Isn't that terrible?"

Then early in September Wavery wrote to tell her of an extraordinary piece of luck. Did she remember his hankering to retire to Sintra, outside Lisbon? He'd had a letter from a friend of more than thirty years ago. This man's elder sister had died and he was looking to sell her estate below Pena Palace. From his description of the house there was a sporting chance it might fit Wavery's requirement exactly. Penny, unfortunately was busy preparing for an exhibition in the west country. "I've decided to have a look anyway," wrote Wavery.

In her next letter Catharine wrote, "You know what I'd like more than anything? To come with you."

They came as a brother and sister might, in the middle of October. Wavery booked rooms at a hotel in the Bairo Alto. He would fly out a day earlier to make arrangements. They would meet on Friday at a café near the Moorish castle. In his last communication to her was simply, "Café Queluz, Praça dos Pássaros, three o'clock."

His conscience was clear. They were spending a weekend together because they needed each other. He was going to be very good for Catharine in some way, and she for him. Their trip was innocent, just as his feeling for her was innocent. He was sure of that. At the Lisbon Embassy he was about to come into his own. But before coming into his own he wanted to be, by God, in a simple way a little bit happy. For thirty-five years he had been married to a woman whose behaviour suggested it had been a waste of everybody's time. If only for a weekend, he saw redemption staring him in the face.

"Does your name start with a W?" A gypsy stood by his table in the Praça dos Pássaros. Pigeons clattered through the golden leaves, chesting the cold, briny air like ladies settling down to bridge. From the little square, full of blue-tiled houses and drying sheets, his eye followed two streets down to the Tagus.

The old woman crossed his hand with a sprig of rosemary.

"Yes."

"Lots of changes."

He accepted the rosemary. "Thank you."

"Five hundred escudos."

He paid. He ordered another coffee. He was cold. She was seventy-nine minutes late.

Black hair, white face, lilac dress. "Remember me?"

Wavery leaped to his feet, spilling coffee. They bumped noses. He said, "You're here, you're here. I don't believe it." His heart slammed against his chest.

She said, "Time has got to stand still now, hasn't it?"

He took her suitcase and they walked through the streets. She breathed in the bracing air. "I knew I was going to have a marvellous time, as soon as I stepped out of the taxi. If you didn't turn up I was determined to enjoy myself."

"You thought I might not turn up?"

She said happily, "The hotel in Lima! Or had you forgotten?"

Her room was identical to his: small, with green handpainted furniture and a view onto a church roof. Above the pediment an angel blew a chipped trumpet.

"I'll leave you to unpack," he said. "I'm in 402. End of the corridor, turn right."

Moments later there was a knock. Her telephone was not working. A man had come and fiddled. He could not fix the fault until Monday.

"I have to ring home."

"Use mine," said Wavery.

He put on his coat and went out into the square. He explored the damp-smelling church. He kicked a ball back to a small boy. He looked in the window of an antique shop. There were bits and pieces of a glass chandelier, a leather holder for playing-cards, a tin slipper ashtray and a row of black and white carnival masks with beaks for noses.

He glanced up at his hotel window. She must have finished speaking because she was standing there, looking at him. She opened the window and waved, and thereafter an open window became a sign that one or other had finished on the telephone.

He came back into the room. He tried to smile. "All well?"

"Oh, yes. Bowling along." She stood up to leave. By the door she touched his shoulder. "What is it, Thomas ?"

"Who does –?" He could not bring himself to say her husband's name.

"I'm with my sister. And you? What does Penny think?"

"I'm here to see the house in Sintra."

"Alone?"

*　　*　　*

170

They dined in the back room of a fish restaurant behind the castle. Later, if he thought hard, he would be able to bring back to mind the wooden tables, the metal coatstand, the large man in a red shirt who served them fresh clams and a chilled Casal Garcia.

She said, "Thank you for letting me be here."

"Don't be silly."

"You can't know the effect you had just putting 'Café Queluz, Praça dos Pássaros, three o'clock.' Ever since I was a girl . . ." But she stopped.

"Tell me," said Wavery.

"There's something I've always hoped, all my life," she said. "It sounds mad, like a faith. But I've always hoped to meet someone who was so close in spirit that separation for all its pain did not count. Someone to whom I could say, 'I'll see you there – some far-flung place – at such and such a time, in a week, a month, a year.' And know that meeting would happen, would come to pass." She went on, " What I suppose I'm saying is that I've always wanted a relationship where I can say, 'Café Queluz, Praça dos Pássaros, three o'clock.'"

"Here we are then," said Wavery gladly. He refilled her glass with the tart white wine. He looked up and she was staring at him.

"Well, what are you searching for? You're only going to see a short-sighted, middle-aged diplomat."

She accepted the wine. "Funny, I have a different image of you."

"Really?"

"It's the little things you remember, not the obvious ones. Your pigeon toe. Did you know your toe had a pigeon?"

Next morning they travelled by taxi to Sintra. Sciatica prevented Wavery's friend, a former head of the British Council, from personally showing them the estate. His lawyer would meet them at eleven outside the main gate.

The house lay behind a crumbling chest-high wall beyond the hotel of Seteais, at the end of a drive which had once been tarmaced. It was painted white, with broad bands of blue along the edge of the walls and about the windows. The building was single-storeyed and arranged around an open courtyard. Oak trees brushed the roof and through the oaks they could see a small chapel.

In the courtyard there was an inquisitive cat, a chicken in a cage and a girl wearing a grey school skirt. There was a smudge mark on the girl's shirt from where she had leaned against the wall, watching them walk up the drive. "The cook's daughter," murmured the lawyer. He stood aside for Wavery and Catharine to enter. Above the door into the hall there was a cactus cross. In the hallway was a huge Kelvinator fridge, its plug removed. On the walls were pale rectangles where paintings had hung.

Catharine opened a cupboard. There was an old radio on the shelf and an almost empty bottle of island malt.

"Was she married?" Wavery asked the lawyer.

Twice, the man thought, although she had been alone by the time she died.

They walked into an anteroom. The architraves were decorated with dusty putti.

"This is where she came to get away from her husband," said Catharine. There was thick dust everywhere. "Or where he came to drink whisky when she was in church," said Wavery.

"Oh, I don't think she was very religious," said Catharine. Idly, she drew something with her finger in the dust

"She kept an antique pistol in her desk," said the lawyer.

"To shoot lovers when she'd finished with them," said Catharine. She brushed away her telephone number and stood up.

She opened more doors. "Look!" she said, passing into what had been a bedroom. "The sea." Excited, she seized Wavery's hand. "Oh, Thomas, you could have your bed there. But you'd want the walls a different colour."

"Light blue?"

"Yes," she nodded. She was approving. "Light blue would be fine."

There were three bedrooms, each with views to Colares, and

172

a large drawing room which led down four steps into a huge garden. The air was humid and chilly. On a hill to the right was the red roof of another house and through the olives they could see the sea.

"You'd think you were in the tropics," said Wavery. "Look at those palms. They are rather terrific." He stepped outside. No one had tended the garden. The grass was long and blunted with leaves. Here and there in the undergrowth peeped large blue and white flowers.

"Verbena, nicotiana, camellia, camellia, camellia," said Catharine behind him.

"I'd plant more olives. One or two, over there."

"They take too long. You want something quicker. Robinia's quite fast."

"I don't think I like robinia. I want olives."

"You could talk yourself into liking it."

He sat on what had been a retaining wall. After so many years, the landscape was coming back to him. Yes, he could imagine planting himself here. He said, "I always longed for a settled place where I could watch the seasons." He wanted a garden with all sorts of secret corners, nooks where he might get right away. He conjured to Catharine a grass path through the foliage. It led to high hornbeam hedges and arches passing into separate gardens, each like a room. This was his fantasy: to arrange the smaller gardens with plants from the countries he had lived in. Sintra's climate made it possible. Everything grew miraculously.

"While Penny is painting, I can wander around smelling Argentina, Jordan, Hungary, Peru."

As they walked through the empty rooms, exchanging fantasies, Wavery felt he was coming out of the dormant season. Secretly, he was saying to himself, Oh, Oh, Oh, if we allowed ourselves to live . . .

"This is charming, Thomas," Catharine was saying. "Lovely, in fact."

"So I should put in an offer?"

"Definitely."

173

They had lunch at Seteais and late in the afternoon returned to Lisbon.

Before dinner Wavery telephoned Penny. He wanted to discuss with her the house and the price, but there was no answer. She had gone to Poole for the day, to plan the exhibition. She must still be in Dorset. He opened the window. In a while Catharine knocked.

He said, "I called my other reality and she's not there. There's only this."

"Shall I now, then?"

But neither did Adam nor the girls answer. "Can I try again after dinner?"

Half an hour later Wavery collected Catharine from her room. She wore a cinnamon scarf, and the rust-red jacket she had been wearing on the night they met. "I haven't had it cleaned since," she joked.

They dined in the Alfama, in a restaurant they had seen from the outside and liked. A *fado* was playing through a loudspeaker. *"E quem me dera, ter outra vinte anos,"* sang the waitress, joining in.

Wavery ordered champagne. They touched glasses too soon and their champagne overflowed into a bowl of salt which turned blue. They ate vegetable soup and grilled fish and didn't finish their wine. "You're not drinking," he said. But she was untying her scarf. She was reaching over the table and in a voice so soft he could have wrapped it also round his neck she was saying, "A present."

His hands moved over the table. They held her face. When he had begun the gesture he wanted only to thank her. Calmly, without excitement, he drew Catharine to him and kissed her. She did not respond immediately, but she allowed her head to stay against him, very still, to let him know he had not done anything wrong.

In the square outside their hotel, she said, "Tom, I do have to make that call." He gave her his room key.

"I'll wait here."

She kissed him quickly and passionately and went indoors. He waited half an hour in the square. It was cold and there was a winter mist and in the mist he heard the sound of cats howling. In another month he expected to be living here, in the large residence in Lapa. He would know on Tuesday.

He looked at his watch. It had been more than an hour. There was no sign of movement in the room. No shadows on the ceiling. No window opened. At last he went up.

She was sitting on the bed, receiver in hand, staring at the floor.

"Catharine?"

Her voice was faint. "He said, 'Are you tired of me?'"

Wavery closed the door.

"He said, 'You won't ever leave me? Promise you won't leave me.'" She wrenched her eyes to Wavery. "Tom, I promised."

He took the receiver from her hand, replacing it.

"I don't feel guilty. Not about that." Violently, she shook her head. "What I've given to you is something nobody else wants."

"Catharine, what do you –"

"That's not the only reason for ringing home." She opened her arms to take in the room. "Can't you see?" She wasn't merely discharging a duty. She wasn't just putting her maternal conscience at rest and patting the rest of her world on its head. "I'm confirming all this. I'm making our happiness more real. If I were to say, the world doesn't exist, and draw down the blind, then I'm saying this is a dream. But it's not a dream." She shook her head. "It's not a dream, Tom. But the only way I can help myself is not to take any step towards it."

Wavery sat down beside her on the bed. He tried to hug away her pain and for a moment she allowed herself to be held like this. Then she snatched herself away. When she leaned back, he could see that she had tears in her eyes.

"I want you to know something, Tom. After this weekend, I'll never ring you."

"Never?"

"Promise."

"Why ever not?"

175

"You can talk a friendship away on the telephone. You know how writers say you can talk away a book? Well, you can do the same with a friendship. If we talk on the telephone, the chances are we'll misunderstand each other."

"It's all right. I hate the telephone too."

"Oh, Tom, you are wonderful," and she laughed through her tears. "One day you'll appreciate the gift I've given when I say I'll never ring. It's like the gift you gave to me when I told you I hadn't said as much as you and you said, 'You can't.'"

He pressed his lips to her eyes, closing them. "What do you want to do?"

"No, Tom. What are *you* thinking?"

His throat was dry. He thought, People do this every day. "I don't know the rules," he said softly.

She placed her room key down on the table by the bed. "And you think I do?"

She stood up and disappeared into the bathroom. The cistern flushed. She came out of the bathroom. He took off his jacket and walked to where she was standing. He touched her face, then her hair, watching all the time, fearful of disturbing her. Sex was a hideous solemnity. Nothing had prepared him for the emotions he felt. There was no experience he could use to ride them. "You're so beautiful," he said, caressing her.

"Shh," she said and touched his face. In the touch he could feel her concern for him. She unfastened the buttons on his cuffs, his belt. "It's going to be all right." It was to reassure herself as well.

He woke early, waking her with a kiss. She turned into him, removing a hair from her mouth. She traced the contours of his cheek.

"Oh darling, it's your face. It's your face after all."

He said, "I'm happy." His love was innocent and permanent, a heart carved into a school desk. He had fallen asleep in her arms, her taste on his tongue, her cry in his ears, her fulfilled face against his, not realising until then how much love he had to give, as if the earth had welled up through him.

He said, "What would have happened if I hadn't kissed you."

She stretched out a leg and rolled onto him, her hair falling into his face. She said in his ear, "We'd still be having dinner." His fingers moved down her back, over the peach hair in the hollow of her back, between her buttocks, into her darkest hair.

Lying beside her, he saw where their hair meshed grey and black. She whispered, "What is it, Tom? "

"I'm seeing where we join." He rang with a clear sound. "The indians exterminated by the Argentines had eight different ways of saying 'I love you'."

She ran her hand back and forth over his stomach. "It never occurred to me. Not this."

"What didn't?"

"That you'd find me attractive."

He waved at the brown blanket, the sheet.

She rescued him. "Have I done this before?"

"I suppose so, yes."

"No, Tom."

"Then why with me?" She was young enough to be his daughter.

"It was unthinkable before."

He stroked the back of her hands, her arms. When he touched her shoulder, she flinched. She tried to sit up, but his body hemmed her in. She threw herself back against the bed-head, her face turning from side to side. "Wait," she said. "Listen. Listen –" Pain clawed at her face. He gripped her hand, to give her his protection. He listened to what she was saying, but realised she was trying to protect him.

"Don't, don't, don't," she moaned. "I'm not safe for you."

"Oh yes, you are," he managed through kisses.

"I'm not safe, Tom," she warned him.

"Yes, yes, yes, yes."

She pushed at him, but he held her. "Catharine, what's wrong?" Don't worry, he was saying. He understood her panic. She had not been unfaithful before. He might be expecting too much. Her innocence matched his own.

"I'm not reliable," she said, willing herself to be understood like this. "But I don't mean that. I don't mean that." She reached for him in the half-light, squeezing his arm, but what she thought was his arm was an empty fold of the blanket. "Oh, God, I don't know what I mean."

It was their last day and she tried to be happy, but her mood infected the day. In the morning they visited the Gulbenkian Collection. After lunch they saw the Moorish castle, and then returned to the hotel.

"Look!" said Catharine as they came into their square. She had seen the lopsided, ill-lit window and the row of masks.

There were more masks inside, but new ones. A man was painting them from a pile on the counter. He was listening to a football match on the radio. Behind the counter he nodded support for one of the teams, dipping his brush into a bowl. The room smelled of glue and turpentine.

Catharine looked at the eyeless carnival faces: black and white, silver and gold, mauve and vermilion.

"You should buy one for your husband," said Wavery. He deluded himself he meant it kindly, but he was giving in to anguish. He was proving his dominion and striking back at pain.

"I don't think so, Tom."

"Then one for you," said Wavery. "What about an unpainted one?"

"That one," she said.

"This is a present from me," he said. He took the face from the bottom of the pile.

The man watched them. His narrow eyes minnowed from one to the other. He wiped his hands on his apron and wrapped the mask in crinkled brown paper, biting the corner of his mouth and taking forever.

They ate dinner near the hotel. Afterwards they walked back through the empty streets. Their steps echoed against the church and a cat's howl ricochetted up into the night.

He followed Catharine into her room. "So after this we mustn't see each other?"

"Do you want to talk about it?"

"No," he said, and then, "All right, you talk." He sat on the mini-bar, picking up the mask which rested there, wrapped in its stiff brown paper. She lay down on the right side of the bed. She spoke as if she had learned what she was saying by rote. "It will be much easier if we say, 'This is it'."

Unthinkingly, he began to untie the string on the parcel.

She said, "I will never be able to say to you, 'Stay for Christmas', or 'Let's have friends to dinner', or 'Let's go to Venice'. Think of all the things I cannot say to you."

He pulled away the string.

She said, "I have tried to give you everything in these days. Have I failed you in anything? But it's better this way. You to your wife, me to my family."

He removed the paper wrapping.

The mask lay in its untidy brown petal of paper. He took out the unpainted face and placed its rough surface to his own.

"*E quem me dera, ter outra vez vinte anos,*" he chanted throught the puffed plaster lips.

"What's it mean?"

He translated. "'I wish I were twenty years younger'."

"Here." She stretched out a hand. "Let me try."

He went over to the bed, where she pulled it off him. He raised her head from the pillow and knotted the two black ribbons behind her ears.

"How does it look?"

His tongue sought hers through the rough, expressionless hole.

Then something terrible happened. He was kneeling above Catharine, undressing her, and she was unbuttoning his shirt when suddenly her body tensed and what had been a caress became a struggle.

"No." Her hands were trying to scratch him and he was frightened to let go. He realised she was saying something, but what she was saying was at odds with the violence in her body. She was beating his chest and his face, imploring, begging, "Please, keep away. Please. Please."

179

He threw off the mask, pulling the ribbons through her hair. He held her face. "It's me, Catharine," he said. "It's not anyone else."

But she was slithering down some perilous slope of her own. She whispered, sobbing, catching her breath, "Yes, but who are you?"

Her head was pressed against him, a dead weight moving with the coughing tears.

"Don't hate me," he said. "Say something."

She spoke into his chest. She lifted up her reddened eyes. Her mascara had left two smudges on his shirt. "It's horrible here."

"You don't like your room? Lisbon?"

"The place where I am."

A third reality, separate from the other two, was creeping up on them. She sat up and shivered. "There, then. That's the sign. We've come to it. I knew it would come and I wish it hadn't come so soon. That's STOP, isn't it?"

People only ask about what they can handle. Wavery did not ask about the sign. He did not ask again what was wrong. He had not insisted this morning and he did not do so now. Instead he talked and as he spoke, she stole back to him. He talked about whatever came into his head, about his childhood in Mathon, the view over the Beacon one way and Hay Bluff the other, his schooldays in Oxford, the Sundays on which he had waited for his parents to take him out, sitting, dangling legs on a pillar box in the Bardwell Road, knowing they would arrive late and leave early.

"I love you," she said.

He went on talking.

"Did you hear that, Thomas? I love you."

"You don't have to say it."

"I love the way you say my name. I love your hot head, your lovely face, your laugh. I love your pigeon's toe. I love you for having shared with me your garden." She rolled on her back. She waved her arms. She was holding back more tears. "I'll see you at a party one day talking to someone, your arms waving,

180

and I'll come up behind you and say 'Bob Hope' and you'll turn and hug me and no one will know why." She turned towards him. "I love the way your body moves around me at night, that whenever I move you adjust yourself and bring me back." She said, "I don't want to betray your fantasies of me."

Her face was wet. He licked the tears, not speaking. They slept.

He woke, feeling her warm skin. Was he never to feel it again? "Catharine?" Outside it was still dark. "Six-thirty. We ought to be getting up." She said nothing. "Are you there?"

She said, "I love you, Tom. I love you, I love you, I love you."

They landed a few minutes before noon. They queued to present their passports. The man, noting Wavery's profession, inspected with curiosity the scarf around his neck. He had smelled it four passports away.

"Will you spray it?"

She sat on the bed and applied her scent. "All the girls will come running," she had said.

They walked to the baggage reclaim. He lifted her suitcase from the conveyor belt. His eyes remained on the trolley. She opened her arms and held him. "This is just horrid . . . Thank you for everything . . . every single moment."

"Goodbye then."

"I'm going, Tom. I won't ever look back."

"Yes, yes, of course you must," and he held her hands incredibly tight to his face.

He kissed the top of them. He put the knuckles into his eyes to stop the tears. She pulled away and he opened his eyes. There was someone over her shoulder, a man he knew from somewhere, watching him.

Chapter Eight

I

ON SATURDAY MORNING, Genia Ortiz closed the door and kneeled on a cushion beside her bed. She pulled the trunk towards her. It was made from hardwood and covered in green canvas, studded with brass buttons at the corners and hooped in steamed ribs of cedar. She wiped the dust from the top. She opened the lid wide enough to be able to slip a hand inside. Steeled by two glasses of vodka, she delved for the photographs of Balnasharki.

The first object her fingers encountered was Dr Linz's Venus Apparatus. The rubber perished at her touch. Her hand closed next on a sheaf of paper. Sheet music for "On the Promontory"! She threw back the score.

Two hours later, at twelve-thirty, she tottered onto her balcony. "Señor Consul General! Look!"

She beckoned Wavery from the chair where he had been reading, to the wall. "Forgive me, I didn't wish to disturb your reading. I can see it must be very important, but I had to show you these."

"By all means, señora."

"If you will join me, we can look at them together over a drink. I can explain them to you. Do you like vodka?"

"That's kind of you, señora. I would like so much to say yes. But I do need to go out."

Genia Ortiz looked at Wavery. He was so polite, so considerate, so unlike Tromso. She was reluctant to let him go. A brilliant idea inspired her. "Then why don't I show them to you now? Can you see?" Five feet away she held up a blurred rectangle.

"Wait, I'll get my other glasses," and Wavery went indoors, hoping by some miracle that she would have disappeared by the time he returned to the terrace.

"A portrait of myself at thirteen." She stretched a hand towards him over the gulley. Wavery looked down at the dustbins thirty feet below. He accepted the ancient black and white photograph.

"How very pretty," said Wavery. He turned it over. The photographer's name was stamped in violet on the back. *A. Vyotsky photographe de la cour de S.A. Imperiale Alexandra S.*

"My mother insisted on the retouched pupils.

"Myself, a year later." Sharing a joke with Prince Orlov, who always carried a thousand roubles in his pocket and considered it bourgeois not to decant vodka.

"The prince with his morganatic wife." A founder member of the Kiev Temperance Society.

"My mother." Ravishing, at the ball of the coloured wigs given by Stolypin's niece, a collector of menus. If only Stolypin had lived!

"My father." The cavalry officer, a melancholy study in damp elkskin breeches, already suspecting their age was under the gavel.

Wavery returned the photographs one by one. Like Penny, Genia Ortiz seemed to require of him a response he was unable to give. "Marvellous," he said, but her images had unleashed in him an awful romantic despair.

She continued dealing. The photographs of Balnasharki lay at the bottom of the stack. They had been taken by Vyotsky's rachitic assistant on a cold afternoon before Christmas. He had trimmed the edges with pinking scissors and written at the foot of each *Balnasharki, January 1917*, the date they were developed. He smelled of carbolic soap and his camera lens was scratched. Each print was marked in the bottom left-hand corner by two long white lines, one above the other like the wires of a fence.

Her father had objected to this recurrent imperfection. Peevish, raising his voice, as straight as the cleft in his chin, he succeeded in reducing Mr Vyotsky's bill.

She held another rectangle of stiff card to her nose. She moved her head, passing one eye and then the other over the surface before allowing it across the gap. Reverently she offered it to Wavery. It was the photograph of a house at the end of a tree-lined avenue.

"Balnasharki," she said.

Those walnut trees had been heeled into the earth by her grandfather, a pacifist, on the morning he joined his regiment in Kiev. One tree grew this way, one that, repeating his turmoil in an avenue of conflicting trunks, this tree bowing towards the house he loved, the next away, towards the battlefield where a July evening would find him basted in mud, his guts spilling from a neatly buttoned tunic.

She retrieved the photograph. She savoured it again. Balnasharki, she was thinking. The Motherland had called her!

Tentatively, she was unleashing her childhood demesne. She could see the fir-cone dome through the trees, the farm buildings beyond and the pothole in the drive and her father saying to her mother, "Really, Alexandra Andreevna, we must fill that hole in." But they never did.

The drive continued, past the lawns where they had had snowball fights in the dark, to her mother's lake of carp. There was vodka on her lips, but Genia Ortiz could taste that lake as she had tasted it from a carnival mask on her last summer, scooping into her mouth the tannic brown water before returning to the dance. Her parents had been married thirty years. Her father watched his wife dancing with Colonel Slava. She leaned close, laughing. "Let me show you the lake."

"Evgenia Nikolaevna, will you dance with an old man?" They danced and a breeze carried champagne bubbles of air into her mask. She sneezed and her father said, "If only we could blow our noses to clear our minds." Less than a year later Colonel Slava's men were prising up the parquet floor for firewood.

Reluctantly, Genia Ortiz put down the photograph. She lifted a hand to her white hair, and thought of Balnasharki in the days after the Duma. A war orphan's home, then an agricultural cooperative, today deserted. The wind cutting itself on the broken glass, slime on the lake, the walnut trees neglected in the avenue, only the argument of leaves the same. She dared to entertain these images because of the letter she carried folded in her sleeve.

"I have made a decision, Señor Consul General. I am going back."

"I'm glad," said Wavery. "I hope you won't regret it." But he was not thinking of Balnasharki. He was thinking of a house in Sintra he would never see again.

His expedition to Sintra with Catharine was the end. This he now saw. At the time neither of them had been aware of it. For one morning in an empty house, Catharine had realised his fantasy. In so doing she had blighted his favourite place. He could never go back there because it would always reek of her. There was another, plainer reason. The idea of Sintra, in so far as he had taken time out to think beyond the garden, had depended on his retiring from the Lisbon Embassy. He had seen himself enjoying non-executive directorships and other respectable sinecures that might come the way of a retired ambassador, while gazing at the miraculous stages of growth of his every plant. But Thomas Wavery, retired early, last post Abyla, was not the same thing as Thomas Wavery, retired Lisbon.

"I'm sorry, Michael. I'll have to say no."

"It's not overpriced."

"It's not that."

"What then? Did you not like the house? I can't believe that. Isn't it just up your street?"

"We felt it wasn't quite right for us."

"Well, if it's not right, it's not right."

"You'll have no trouble selling."

"None at all. There's no problem about offers. I just wanted to help two old friends. Now when are you and Penny –"

There was the chastening sound of a baton tapping on wrought iron. "But here am I, talking all about myself! What

185

about you, señor? How is the house? The drains – have they been naughty with you?"

"Not yet."

"I see scaffolding everywhere, *mais où en est le travail?*"

Wavery explained that his foreman was still in Morocco.

"And your luggage – has it arrived?"

"Tomorrow, I'm hoping."

"What a relief that will be." Through the French windows she could see the corner of a bed and draped over a chair what might have been a woman's scarf. "I too can remember what it is to live out of a suitcase! And will Señora Wavery be here for Christmas?"

"There's no longer any Señora Wavery," said Wavery.

"Oh," said Genia Ortiz. But she was in no frame of mind to be glum on his behalf. She gathered up her photographs. She was going back and she wanted to celebrate. She had settled too long on this sliver of rock. People who settled this long generally died of Rock Fever. "Consul General, you won't change your mind about a vodka?"

"Again, it's extremely kind of you, Señora Ortiz, but the library closes in half an hour."

From inside her apartment came a bleeping.

"My telephone!"

2

As on most Saturday mornings, the library in Calle Real was empty. The one sound was the buzzing of a defective light bulb.

Dolores sat at a large table near the stacks devoted loosely to Local History. (The tolerance of Franco's authorities towards certain authors not judged to be dangerous explained the continued presence on this shelf of Teodoro Zamora's *History of Abyla*, Strabo's *Geography*, in the 1458 translation by Guarino of Verona, the works of Diodorus Siculus, two copies of the first volume of *Discours sur l'Histoire Universelle* and several bound copies in blue leather of the *Illustrated London News* for

186

the years 1897–1914, a gift of British Consul Cazes.) Dolores inspected her face in the blade of a paperknife. She was concerned she might have caught a spot off Captain Panteco with whom she had slept the night.

The telephone shrilled. "Abyla Public Library."

"It's Lustrino."

"I was thinking of you," she said truthfully. Her windmill earrings were too large to wear when speaking into the telephone. She picked them off and played with them on the table.

"Mohamed give you a good breakfast?" This morning Panteco had dropped her off at the Café Ulises. He demanded a farewell kiss, during which Toribio had taken the opportunity to leap from behind.

Dolores considered. "Bran flakes, orange juice, tea, toast, butter, jam, a boiled egg."

"Milk?"

"Milk –" She couldn't remember.

He wanted to see her tonight, he blurted.

"Yes?" She laughed, then realised what was being said. "No."

Panteco. What did she care for Panteco? He was no oil painting – unless one thought of that Flemish painter Ernesto had liked. He had bad skin and never listened and his kisses were more slobbery than Toribio's. Dolores thought she preferred the dog's kisses. Last night, Panteco had insisted on taking the animal back to the rooms he rented in Alfau. Emilio's mother was so godamn crazy she hadn't fed him for a week. Panteco had all sorts of plans to train him as a drug-dog. If he didn't take care of Toribio, there were plenty of El Callado's men who would. The hash-heads would cut off his ears and tail so he wouldn't make a sound when he came out of the water.

"Oh, no, you can't let that happen to Toribio," said Dolores, sitting on Panteco's floor, stroking his ears, knowing Panteco was not thinking about Toribio, but how to make Dolores move from where she sat, useless for his purpose, and onto that mattress where he might place his hand on her knee, all the while talking of Toribio but looking for a sign that might give him the courage to say in his loud voice, without her laughing at him,

Dolores, shall we go to bed? So to spare Panteco the trouble, and not wishing to hear his booming sales pitch, Dolores stood up, walked over to the mattress, sat down, moved the instep of her ankle into vision and said: "Oh shit, my tights have laddered."

Panteco advanced to touch the spot where the tragic laddering had taken place, scattering a pile of magazines, knocking over a fishing-rod and dashing his head against the overhead light shade.

"What does it matter anyway?" she said, as the shadows rocked still on the wall. She looked at him with the round eyes of a turkey-cock. She felt nothing for Panteco, but she didn't want to hurt him. It was nice to be liked. She had few more expectations than to capture the hearts of men who loved stereotypes. She was a passive girl. Men invariably made the initial move and with few exceptions – Mohamed, Ghanem the Mute, Gallo, the bellboy – she didn't resist. She never mistook their attentions for affection, yet that is what she sought. The saddest moment in each relationship was the moment when she understood she fitted into a pattern. Gradually she had renounced all claim to the love which appeared in those romances she was always having to find for that inflamed jellyfish Señora Menendez. Dolores had been too free with her body for that kind of love. She was a car who had spent her time off the road, parked on the cliff by La Mujer Muerta where the tarmac ended, exposed to the sand and the spray. She never counted the men she had known in the back – out of superstition, she supposed. Ernesto, of course. Periclito, caterpillar-fat, making her laugh, hardly able to squeeze over the seat. Emilio, the fisherman, who hadn't been particularly keen on The Act. Rosita's husband, tenderer with his guitar, left carefully on the front seat, than with Dolores. And one night in a strange language she didn't understand, Joseph Silkleigh – although this she had never told Rosita.

"Do you like it – the flat?" These had been the only words of Silkleigh she had understood. She inspected the two rooms in Millan Astray. When she saw the unwashed plates in the kitchen and the bath still full of water and the goggle-heaps, but above all the hurriedly kicked notebooks beneath the sofa, she decided after all not to let her heart flare for him. She worked in a library, but if Ernesto had taught her a thing, it was never to live beyond her mental means.

If she told the truth, sex bored her. She agreed with Ernesto: "The great pleasure comes if you do nothing! Sex is about restraint." But how did you tell that to Panteco? As she coaxed an erection from Panteco, she felt she was handing a loaded revolver to a man who couldn't shoot. Dolores closed her eyes as he kissed her brow. She didn't want to see his face. With Panteco, she swiftly discovered, it was but a matter of time before she could open her eyes.

"Do you think there's sex in heaven?" she asked. She kneeled on all fours, watching her favourite soap opera while at the same time luxuriously arching her instep against Toribio's tongue at the edge of the mattress. She was confident the man behind her was thinking of another person, and that when he released the words, "Precious, my precious," it was not Dolores he addressed (nor Toribio, who lifted his head and slapped his tail against the cupboard door), but her friend the *fadista*. The knowledge didn't make Dolores jealous. Rosita was her ally. With Rosita she could talk about men, men like Lieutenant Casares, in Abyla to complete his military service. Unfortunately, Casares had caught the eye of Señora Menendez. With Rosita she could talk also about Panteco.

It was not like sex with Ernesto. The conductor, had excited her. Would she ever feel something of the same for Panteco, this loud, tall, stubborn, gauche, proud policeman who treated her so off-handedly, although she could see he didn't mean to, who now plunged his face into the pillow, away from her, panting like a tunny fish. "Dolores, why do you have to ask such stupid, stupid questions?"

Probably not, she decided.

"Dolores, will you listen to me." Over the telephone Panteco listed several reasons why she must change her mind about tonight.

Dolores picked up the paperknife. She inspected her face again. "Lustrino, I'm listening." She had the night before on her face. Her body was telling her she wasn't beautiful. The coffee in Panteco's flat had made her skin dry and ruddy. When she made love regularly she felt good. If she didn't make love regularly, her body grew stale, she became neurotic and aware of a tremendous physical unhappiness. It was no good Panteco telling her she was beautiful.

Dolores tilted the blade from one eye to the other, to her nose, to the definite spot on her chin, to the unending stacks behind her, unread and smelling of mildew. The insecurity of a beautiful woman wasn't something a man like Panteco could appreciate. It was something a lot of women couldn't understand, but Ernesto had understood it.

Not a day passed without Dolores thinking about Ernesto, the conductor whom she had met on the Algeciras ferry in his sixty-eighth year.

"I'm in love, Rosita."

"The big L?"

"No, the little o," she laughed. She was young then, about seventeen and thin as a fish-hook. It was her first job. Ding dong, the restaurant on B deck is now open, that was her. It didn't amount to much, but it left her free to talk to the man who appeared in the cabin on the pretext of looking for an aspirin. She was too young to know her part in the pattern. The conductor gave her a box of chocolates and promised to teach her the triangle.

"He told me I am the eternal feminine and I transported him to higher spheres." But Dolores it was who transported Ernesto thither, and fifteen years after his death she continued to experience nightmares of their final afternoon in the Hotel Zamora: of his sea-gull cry which she mistook for triumph – something that happened less and less often – but was Ernesto's imitation of the bird crying out at the end of "Grosse Appell"; of his eyes resolutely closing, his arms tensing about her, his body folding as if taking a bow, humbled by the surge of applause. It was twenty minutes before she could extract herself from his embrace.

"Never come back," said the manager, who spirited Dolores, wrapped in Ernesto's brown coat, through the laundry-room and out into the street. The Hotel Zamora had been a mute witness to many events, but not to the "Grosse Appell". Traditionally it was a song reserved for Bishops and for Portuguese politicians. It was sung only on the Peninsula.

"I've left my keys." The manager stood over her while she fetched them. Ernesto's lips were bluer than the ceiling.

"Ever again."

In that room where Ernesto had furled his wings, beside two complimentary mints, Dolores had left behind an important part of herself.

The librarian was looking at her eyes, when she caught a movement in the blade. She tilted the paperknife. Señor Wavery was standing in the doorway.

"Lustrino, I've got to go." A hand loosened on her tress and slowly she pulled her fingers through her black, black hair. "I mean really go."

3

"I see you've been sniffing at the library, old soul," said Silkleigh. He hailed Wavery from below the Marina Española. He had been tethering his boat to a bollard on the quay.

"I have a reading list from Senator Zamora," said Wavery defensively.

"Yes, yes, yes, they all finish up at the library sooner or later."

"Come on, Silkleigh," said Wavery. "You see the worst in everyone."

"Oh, no. I know all about Dolores. Dangerous murderess, old soul. Ask your friend and neighbour the widow Ortiz. Wave your library books under her nose, ho, ho, ho. If Ernesto hadn't toed up in the Hotel Zamora, nobody would have known a thing.

Instead, the world was suddenly saying to his wife, 'Any library books to go back, sweetie?'"

He twisted his head. "So what have you got there? Ideas for me? I say," said Silkleigh, reading the titles. "Doing your homework, aren't you?"

The man was a kind of purgatory. "How is your writing?" said Wavery, wishing he was simply elsewhere.

"I'm too busy diving for Emilio to write a single lucid word, old soul."

"How's the search going?"

"Absolutely hopeless, *ambasadoro*. But they have found his ring."

4

Genia Ortiz, hurrying inside to answer the telephone and hoping it might be Tromso, found Pablo sitting on the window cushion, his feet stretched out, wearing his BIG CHIEF T-shirt.

"Get your feet off that cushion!"

Pablo remained where he lay.

"Age, Grandpa's inviting you to Christmas lunch,"

"That's nice of Grandpa." She placed the photographs on the desk, next to the painting of the Virgin. "Who was that, Pablo? Did you find out?"

"It was no one."

"I was hoping it might be your father."

"Is Daddy coming for Christmas?"

"I don't know, dear."

"Is that the famous letter from the Soviet Union?" Pablo laid particular emphasis on the last two words.

"The Ukraine, Pablo. The Ukraine."

"Can I –"

The telephone rang again. "Hello, the residence of Señora Ortiz." He listened, puzzled. "Nothing," he told his grandmother. He returned it to his ear. "Sounds like someone breathing."

"Give it here, dear. Hello? Hello? Hello?" But all she heard was the dialling tone. "Probably one of Periclito's women." Marie Amaral's son was always meeting women on a bench at the end of the world, then leaving them an Abyla telephone number. There had been a tiresome period five years ago when the number he supplied was her own. Now he gave the number of the kiosk outside the Café Ulises.

"Tell your grandfather I'd very much like to come for Christmas lunch."

"Goodbye, Age. Take risks."

Genia Ortiz loved her grandson and she spoiled him. Since he was a baby she had seen in Pablo the finer characteristics of her own family. He possessed her mother's long lashes and the intelligent forehead of Constantin, the most remarkable of the Polotsevs. To Asunción, Pablo looked identical to portraits of her father at the same age. As the boy grew more unruly each side of the family had chosen to see the other's side predominate.

Genia Ortiz had embraced Asunción in a terrific rush at the time of her marriage to Tromso and then had retreated. After several years of thinking her too good to be true, she had ended up quite fond of the woman. Since Asunción's separation, four years ago, the two of them had grown to confide in each other.

She would recall for her daughter-in-law Ernesto's jodhpur boots, the yellow socks, the one smart suit which he always took care to fold away when he came home. "He depended on me, Asunción. I knew he would never leave. That would have been too easy." When it came to hindsight Genia Ortiz had very sharp vision.

"Your husband was a passionate man," Asunción said once, with a trace of envy.

Genia Ortiz responded, "Ernesto was more a man of passion than of love. He was for mixing the two. I never did, you know. Love can be repeated, he used to say. But it can't. Isn't it so, Asunción? Isn't that the truth? I would always know when Ernesto had been unfaithful. Because he'd be so extremely nice – and then tell me utterly unnecessary details about what he'd

193

been doing. What did I care if for lunch he'd eaten a cassoulet with delicious cheese sauce at Periclito's café?"

Asunción agreed. While their two experiences were not entirely similar, at least not so similar as Genia Ortiz, in her pressing need for an ally, would have liked to think, infidelity *was* infidelity. It was the same, whether you ran off with another woman or your clipboard.

Alone again in her room, Genia Ortiz retrieved the Ukrainian letter from her sleeve, poured herself another measure of vodka, took a sip, reread the letter, looked at the Virgin, took another sip, reread the letter again and sat down. She lifted the telephone and dialled a number. She waited, her gaze passing from the Virgin to the photographs on the desk and back to the letter.

"Tromso?" she said, hearing a voice. "Tromso, it's your mother."

Genia Ortiz's relationship with the son of her middle age had never been easy. He was a workaholic who had married late in life, like the General. He separated from Asunción three years later. He had not lived with anyone before, so when he put down his glass and she moved it, he could not cope. He had advanced to the age of forty-eight having learned to play one or two simple theme tunes on the keyboard of a relationship, but little more. So far as Genia Ortiz knew, there was no other woman in his life. He was wedded, more successfully than ever he had been to Asunción, to his work. While wealth and prosperity had followed the success of *The Strong Tend to Leave*, Genia Ortiz noted in their recent conversations a grub of dissatisfaction. The industry did not regard him seriously enough. He wished to find a project which would attract recognition too. "Something of quality, mother. Like a documentary."

"You could make a documentary about Abyla, Tromso."

"Mother, *there's nothing in Abyla*."

"I'm sure Senator Zamora would talk to you about the Phoenicians."

If television was Tromso's mistress, he would never want for female attention. He was good looking in a supine sort of way – the way that is one step beyond handsome – causing old women to think him charming and men to dislike him.

Tromso's charm had no effect on his mother, who had become jealous of him in the way that parents do who make sacrifices for their children in order to give them every opportunity. Once Tromso had seized his opportunity a bitterness crept into the relationship. Ernesto had been more in awe of his son than bitter. It fell to Tromso's mother to experience the more elementary feeling.

She pressed the telephone to her ear. "Tromso, are you coming for Christmas?" If he said yes, she would tell him about Balnasharki.

"I'll try, Mother. I really will. What worries me slightly are the dates."

"It's always the same date, Tromso."

"Dates for the video-edit, Mother. And the dub. You know how things are. They are *crazy* at the moment."

"You should come, Tromso. It's important for Pablo. It's important for Asunción too. It's important for me."

"Mother, I'm going to try."

"What do you think your father would have said?" A futile appeal. Genia Ortiz could not care less what Ernesto would have said.

"Mother . . ."

She heard him soften his voice, tell her about the present he had seen, that he was going to buy her for Christmas. He infuriated most when trying to mollify.

"But I have a desk," she said. "I have a huge desk."

"That's too bad, mother. You were always complaining how –"

"Can I just say something? When you're in this mood, I find it hard to feel anything for you."

"But, Mother –"

"Tromso, is there anybody else?"

"Mother, there's no one else."

"Tromso?" He was forty-eight, but Genia Ortiz found it impossible to keep from her voice the tone in which she had addressed him as a teenager. She hoped there wasn't anyone else, for Asunción's sake and for Pablo's. A man's second family could mean much more to him. He gave them all the gentlenesses he'd picked up on the way.

"You remember Tania?"

"The one who became a nun?"

"That was her sister, Teresa."

"I do not remember Tania, Tromso."

"I might – I say might – have Christmas lunch with Tania. If the dates for the video-edit are what I think they are."

Genia Ortiz was silent.

"Mother ... I don't suppose you saw last night's programme?"

"No, Tromso. I did not."

"She's a very good actress."

Genia Ortiz could no longer contain herself. "You told me she never had speaking parts."

She slapped down the telephone. Just when she wanted to celebrate, to tell him about Balnasharki. His selfishness was *fantastic*. He was always, always talking about himself. Where his sense of filial duty should have been, there was one big, black, screen-sized hole. He deserved to be lonely. Why on earth had she wanted him to come for Christmas ...

And he would buy her off with a desk! Her eyes met the eyes of the Virgin. She decided she disliked the engraving intensely. All along she had preferred the Matisse of the casbah gate. Asunción deserved the best. She poured herself another measure of vodka. She unhooked her shopping bag and slipped the painting inside. She would exchange it now, before the man returned to Algeciras. She would refuse to allow Tromso to put her in a mood. On this day of all days.

196

Senator Zamora had arrived late at the Tercio Museum.

"Pablo, I'm sorry," he said, excited. He had been walking on Playa Benitez.

"Did you find the conger eel?" asked Pablo, sitting above him on the wall.

"I did not," said Senator Zamora. He had been monitoring the shoreline for oil. "But I did find – this!" Triumphantly, he held up a small and spiky object coated in tar.

"What is it?"

"A *murex brandaris*!" From such a shell the Phoenicians had extracted their dye, the exact shade of his purple cardigan. He raised his fist to Cadiz. The evidence, if not yet irrefutable, was mounting.

Pablo, unimpressed, jumped off the wall. He wanted to hear about his great-grandfather's death.

Senator Zamora replaced the shell in his pocket. He waited for his grandson to pick himself up. Over Pablo's head he caught sight of Wavery and Silkleigh. The two men were walking up Paseo Colon.

"Señor Wavery!" said Senator Zamora, thinking if he had been the Consul General he would have been only too delighted for an excuse to extricate himself from his frightful compatriot. He grasped Wavery's arm. "I am taking the boy to see my father's relics. If you have a moment . . ."

"Chance of a lifetime, old soul," said Silkleigh, cheerfully.

Wavery gratefully allowed Zamora to escort him into the museum.

They stood in an empty room, before a flat glass cabinet. Mindful of the sign SILENCIO, Zamora bent over the glass and in a low voice told his small audience about the man who had worn the uniform displayed there.

Now he was here, Wavery was curious about the man whose portrait, without his later double chin, bloomed everywhere in the city. Pablo less so. There had been no competition for Hercules as subject for one of his two holiday tasks. But the choice of the Tercio's history in Abyla had been emphatically his grand-father's. Zamora had lured him to the Tercio Museum with the promise of several ice creams afterwards. "And four rides on the rocking horse," said Pablo, whose preferred vision of the Tercio was the rout caused every week by the bread delivery. "Yes, yes, child. That too."

Zamora described his father's end, asphyxiated by dust in a valley behind Abyla, in a garrison besieged by Abdel Akbar. "His battle cry was *viva la muerte!* He was one of the Death-Betrothed. He made war against the shadows. He was a hero, child."

Lieutenant Zamora had been the garrison commander. He respected his enemy. The Moors were not women with beards. Soon Abdel Akbar's army would descend on Abyla. The garrison was all that stood between them.

Abdel Akbar, the dropsical gallows bird from the mountains beyond, had smelled the weakness of the men who defended Abyla. Among Lieutenant Zamora's garrison he had smelled it in the Colour Sergeant who had done everything in his power to avoid another tour of duty. One night Abdel Akbar's men squirmed over the blockhouse wall and carried him away.

Sun found the Sergeant's body by the gate, his empty stomach filled with straw and amethyst. As he decomposed, the coin marks disappeared from his legs. Sergeant Pisac had hoped to pass them off as ulcers until the Tercio doctor, puzzled by this strange chain of sores, suddenly discerned the contours of a familiar face and, scorched into the Sergeant's flesh, the head of their long-nosed monarch.

In the night the Moors burnt the body and the fumes drifted through the camp. The Lieutenant's men had no food. Water was low. They remembered the question asked of the General in Chauen, "Do you have meat?" They remembered his reply, after sticking a hand under his arm and producing three lice. "These are the only cattle here." Lieutenant Zamora's men ate their lice. They drank vinegar, cologne and ink, and urine stirred with sugar. And so they waited for their betrothed.

One morning they saw in the sky the swollen shape of a

dirigible. They flashed a mirrored message at the silver balloon. Later a plane chirred over the mountain. The Moors opened fire. The plane tilted in a circle over the garrison, dropping two objects from its belly. One, a sack, fell onto the garrison's corrugated roof. The other was a huge white bar of ice, the size of a bath. The ice landed twenty yards outside the wall. They watched its whiteness darken the sand. They rushed onto the roof. They tore open the sack. Medals clattered over the hot tin. Engraved on the medals they saw the same disagreeable profile that had decorated the Colour Sergeant's leg.

The General's relief came three days later. The General found Lieutenant Zamora's body in the dust, a goat chewing on his still-growing beard and onions in his eyes. His legs had been soused with kerosene and burnt, his tunic was growing into his skin and his hands had been tied with his bowels. One hand closed over the medal now in the glass cabinet. He smelled of cologne.

Lieutenant Zamora had been awarded the *Medalla de Africa*. *Palajox laudenus viros gloriosos*.

The medal, the uniform and a cuirass were the museum's only relics. Otherwise the Zamora Room contained nothing but newspaper reports and photographs of items on permanent loan to the Museo Militar in Cadiz – a further source of Senator Zamora's gripe.

Longingly he lingered over the black and white reproductions of his father's straw slippers, of his binoculars, of an unused match erect beneath a glass dome, of his watch captured at four minutes past twelve, and of the full-length portrait, also in Cadiz, of the Lieutenant leaning on his sword, one hand inside his tunic.

The most substantial exhibit hung on the wall, beneath the sign for silence. In a florid ode composed by Captain Panteco's grandfather was celebrated the world's cruel ignorance of Lieutenant Zamora's glory.

"*O Zamora! Tu solamente Zamora! La sangre que corre por defender a la patria/ no corre inutilmente*," it began. In a concluding image, the sky over Abyla reddened with the Lieutenant's blood and the sea grew green with his laurels.

"He died to keep Abyla Spanish," whispered Zamora, standing with bowed head before the cabinet.

"Can we go now to Plaza de los Reyes?" said Pablo whose concentration had strayed to a corset on the wall in the next room and a cabinet containing the pickled left eyeball of Abdel Akbar. But Zamora had not finished. He was caressing the glass, tracing the contours of a badge, a globe ridden on eagle's wings. "Our family motto," he said. "You know what it means?"

Wavery read the words *Plus Ultra*.

"There is more beyond," he told the old man.

6

Genia Ortiz, tame carp of Balnasharki, gaze full of Polish vodka, her bag bulging with a plastic-framed Murillo Virgin, walked left into Calle Zamora and left again up La Legion, rising fairly steadily towards the Plaza de los Reyes. At the corner of Fernandez Solis she searched in her bag to make certain it contained the keys to her apartment, crossed the road, stepped onto the pavement and – there! – caricoling up the street two yards ahead was that lynx, Dolores. Dressed in yapping colours, in a skirt too small for her, in Ernesto's coat!

Her lower lip trembled. Her fingers tightened about the gold-topped baton as all at once the afternoon rushed back to her, that devastating afternoon when she had opened the library door and seen on the front desk the book reserved for her husband, his name on a tongue of red paper, and crossed the floor to collect it and heard the telephone ringing in the empty room and called out anxiously, "Dolores! Dolores!" and listened to the noise – ring! ring! ring! – until at last she picked up the receiver only to recognise at the other end in a voice she had never heard him use and before she could so much as say "Hello?", Ernesto, her spouse of fifty-four years, undertaking to butter her little buns.

It was inevitable. Now she had broached the trunk beneath her bed, Genia Ortiz had rolled away the stone behind which she had successfully concealed the conductor. Deliberately she had left the photographs of him inside the trunk, but he had climbed out anyway. She felt his tap on her leg and she kicked out. For fifteen years he had been locked up with the hosts and hostesses of pre-revolutionary Kiev. Now he was avenging himself. Someone whistled in the street behind. Genia Ortiz revolved. The whistler dashed into a Fiat salesroom.

Dolores, without turning, trailed a hand down her long dark tresses. Perceptibly the librarian accentuated the motion of her walk.

"That itchy bitch would give herself to a tree," thought Genia Ortiz. If she was fifty years younger she would have torn Ernesto's coat from the hussy's back.

Mercifully, at the top of the street Dolores took her tresses left, in the direction of her apartment in Calle Real. Puffing, Genia Ortiz turned right into the Plaza de los Reyes. Over the rooftops and between the houses she saw the mountains behind Abyla. Nothing could be more intimidating to her than those mountains, where Senator Zamora shot his pig and where Lieutenant Zamora had been found with onions in his eyesockets.

But if the letter in her sleeve spoke the truth, if Balnasharki had indeed been returned to her . . . The knowledge returned as powerfully as the sight of Santa Maria de Africa in floodlight: she could leave Abyla!

In that moment Genia Ortiz saw the Straits Tunnel as an unequivocal and glorious symbol. It was a link connecting her again to the Europe that had prospered for the first eleven years of her life. As soon as the tunnel was open, as soon as the Royal Visit was over, she would leave this roofless cell. Never again would she have to set eyes on the mountains of Africa. Never again would she have to see the dead woman's face. Never again would she have to worry about what might be fomenting on the other side of the mountains, where duck-sized bats thrashed the darkness.

Genia Ortiz regained her breath. She was preparing to cross

the square, to do battle with the man from Algeciras when her attention was drawn to Senator Zamora and Pablo. They were taking their leave of her neighbour, Señor Wavery. There was no way of avoiding the three of them if she wished to exchange the picture in her bag. If she continued towards the fountain, it would be bound to come out that Tromso was not going to be in Abyla for Christmas.

Genia Ortiz ducked instead into Marie Amaral's flowerstall. She drank the air. "What lovely smells!"

"Can you be helped, Señora Ortiz?"

Marie Amaral emerged, smiling, from behind her bucket of bouvardia. "Or are you trying to avoid your neighbour?"

"My neighbour?" Genia Ortiz bent forward, to see if she could see him outside. "No, it's not that. I didn't want to . . ."

"I like him, I must say. Don't you like him?"

Genia Ortiz tracked Wavery to the fountain. He was thanking Zamora for something and patting Pablo's head.

"Madame Amaral, I have never found in myself an affinity for single men."

Now when she thought of the British Consul General, Genia Ortiz realised for the first time how disappointed she had become in her neighbour. When he first arrived, she had been willing to treat him as her ideal son, which was why this morning she had privileged him with the most intimate and precious parts of her life. She had selected him fom the whole of Abyla to share Balnasharki – and afterwards, what had been his immediate reaction? To make a beeline for that hussy's library!

"You know what they say, madame. A bachelor is a dangerous man."

"But he's not single, is he?"

"Even so. Perhaps he's like the General, not entirely committed to women."

"Perhaps he is not well?" said Marie Amaral, who didn't believe he was another gay Englishman. She had become fascinated by Wavery. She could see his lightest veins were drying up. He was scarred by loneliness.

"That could be it, I suppose." Genia Ortiz attempted a wise

cluck. "But then to be ill today. You look at someone who's ill today and you feel awfully suspicious."

"Some flowers, then?" suggested Marie Amaral.

Genia Ortiz rested her bag on the counter. "Well, I'll tell you," she confided. "I didn't want to have to share my sad news with the Senator."

"Oh, forgive me, señora. What is your sad news?"

Genia Ortiz told her about Tromso. "But I have some good news too! I haven't told anyone else."

"That's wonderful," said Marie Amaral, responding to the contents of Genia Ortiz' letter from the Ukraine.

"Yes, Marie Amaral. I was wondering . . ." Through the open door, she could see Pablo riding the horse. "I thought I would celebrate with a new dress."

Carefully, Marie Amaral wiped her florist's scissors. The blades could cut through bone. "You would like me to make you a dress?" she said.

"I would, madame, if that were possible."

"Of course, I will make you a dress."

"Then I must have some flowers. Those. What about those?" She waved at the same bucket of Stargazer lilies through which the fisherman's dog had wagged his tail. Marie Amaral lifted the bucket onto the table. She cut a strip of paper and a length of ribbon. "You've heard about Emilio's ring?" It had been found by Berahu the dustman, inside a conger eel.

"Poor man," said Genia Ortiz lifelessly. She scanned the square.

Marie Amaral scraped her closed scissors along the ribbon, watching it curl into a multitude of tiny bows. Sandra the Rapist was loose again. People were talking about a funny little episode during last night's soap which involved an antiquated contraceptive device. Apparently –

Genia Ortiz turned, the coast was clear! "Madame, if I could collect these in a few minutes," and she seized her bag and tacked across the square towards the man from Algeciras.

Normally when he walked home to lunch, Wavery approached the inviolable territory of his residence along the Marina Española. On this Saturday lunchtime he approached from the west.

As he walked along Calle Silvestre, he thought of Zamora in the museum. His guide was consumed by certain obsessions, yet he impressed Wavery as a considerable civic figure. Unlike the man Wavery could see standing on the residence balcony.

Plaisir des Yeux had not seen Wavery. Every so often he rotated his head in the opposite direction, after which his eyes reverted to the tunnel. Wavery knew this expression. Those on the esplanade below looked at the tunnel with mulish curiosity: members of the Club Nautico would skim in blue kayaks to the edge of the concrete barrier; fathers strolling with their families in the early afternoon would point and then boast inaccurately of how far the shaft went down into the sea; the snub-nosed Land-Rovers would slow down, windows lowered, before accelerating towards Monte Hacho. Plaisir des Yeux, the simple tiler, did not look with mere curiosity. He gazed with longing.

There was something dangerously distracted about Plaisir des Yeux. On his neck he had a scar where a tube had been inserted after a fall from the minaret he was tiling in El Hadu. In the fortnight since Wavery's arrival in Abyla, Plaisir des Yeux had done little save screw a new lock into the front door with the keyhole upside down and chisel a phallus on the wall with the goalpost. "Against the evil eye, señor," a statement accompanied by a gesture of his index finger.

Twice Wavery had come across him watching a fly flying figures of eight in the room he was supposed to be tiling. Wavery rarely heard him utter a word. The way in which he held himself suggested Plasir des Yeux had taken to heart the saw about a bowed head not being cut off. Halima had no illusions. "He doesn't do anything," she complained. "He smokes. He eats bacon. He wears his mother's beads under his shirt –"

"Then why do we employ him?" said Wavery.

"Ask Pas de Problème." But this Wavery was unable to do. According to Plaisir des Yeux, he was still in Morocco collecting building materials.

"Morocco!" tutted Halima. Most likely he was dragging some poor girl into a field on La Mujer Muerta, or weaving with the whores of Bni Tidir.

Wavery inserted his key upside down in the lock. He left the books in a pile on the table in the hallway. There were voices in the kitchen. The door was open and through it, sideways on, he saw a man sitting on the table. One of his cheeks was patched with a large strip of plaster and he was shouting at Halima in Arabic.

When he saw Wavery he slunk to his feet, his face transforming itself into a grin.

"Pas de Problème," Halima said, introducing Wavery to his foreman.

Pas de Problème, who was called but never answered to the name of Abdul Hadi, was a compact Berber with high cheekbones. He had prominent velvety eyes and the thin moustache of someone who paid too much attention to himself. This possibly explained why the plaster, bulging on either side with cotton wool fluffs, exerted such a grotesque effect.

Wavery took Pas de Problème out of Halima's hearing, to give him his dressing-down. "I am extremely upset by what I have found here," he began. An Inspector from London was expected in the New Year, less than a month away, yet the only finished room in the house remained his bedroom, the telephone wires continued to dangle against an unpainted wall, the window in the consulate still refused to open and the grey plaque in Calle Camoes remained punctured with woodworm. Pas de Problème held up both hands. "Everything is OK, monsieur," and he beamed the wonderful news of how he had managed to make a very good reduction through a very good friend on a consignment of drainpipes and sprinkler valves. Wavery was unable to muster the anger he knew he ought to feel. He hadn't sounded angry, only pompous. "I'll also need you tomorrow," he said severely. "To unpack the luggage."

His foreman's expression was beatific. "*Pas de problème, monsieur.*"

8

On Saturday Pas de Problème arrived early and made a lot of noise so Wavery would know. The thirty plywood cases had been cleared by Captain Panteco's men and were now stationed in the hall. Pas de Problème yanked at a nail with his crowbar. He was demonstrating to Wavery that when Wavery wasn't here, this was how he worked. He lifted the top from a box of books, ripping the silver sheet underneath. He carried the volumes upstairs on his shoulder. As he passed the kitchen he whistled.

The cases blocked the window on the Marina Española. Cases of wine Wavery had been compelled to buy sight unseen and exorbitantly priced from his predecessor in Lima; of Cambodian buddha heads and onyx grapes and framed certificates of the freedom of various obscure villages in the Altiplano; boxes of cornflake packets turned to dust and half-empty bottles of Worcester sauce and concertina folders containing recipes copied from flattered hostesses, but never used.

The same cases had accompanied him to Lima, to Amman, to Phnom Penh and they would have accompanied him again to Lisbon. They contained the life of a man who had lived the world over; also Martial's truth that he who lived the world over lived nowhere.

One case was packed with seven of Penny's canvases, painted in Peru. They showed the influence of the Cuzceño school. Beasts with peculiar noses. Christs with women's thighs. A pair of pliers floating beside a severed hand.

Wavery drew out the largest canvas. The figure of a man lay suspended horizontally across the summit of a mountain. His arms were crossed and he lay calmly, without a head, the severed neck-bone like an eye, while a squadron of low-flying angels lifted him heavenwards in a shroud of grey and pink feathers. One angel carried his head separately by the hair.

"Lovely, darling, but what is it called?"

"'Sisyphus Happy or The Diplomat'."

Penny, dipping her brush into the core of her misery, had found it to be the colour of Wavery's face.

Pas de Problème came into the room. From a crate he picked out a tennis racket and some bald yellow balls. "In Morocco very popular is the golf sport," he said. He looked at the canvas against the wall, then at Wavery.

"*Mais c'est vous, monsieur!*"

Wavery tore open another lid, slitting the foil, releasing a zodiac of houses, cities, countries where he had shed bits and pieces of himself until what remained was a man standing in a bare unpainted room holding a grotesque rose which twitched if you so much as whispered to it.

The thought of Catharine darkened his darkness. He had nothing with which to build a fire against the darkness except this plastic flower and the promise which fluttered over its white-rimmed spectacles. He carried the pot to his bedroom. He planted it on his bedside table and pressed the red button. "Boo!" he said. There was no response. He licked his lips. He hovered over the petals. "*E quem me dera, ter outra vez vinte anos,*" he chanted. The sunglasses dipped in a desultory shiver. The battery must be flat, or else the mechanism did not respond to Portuguese. "Pack up all my cares and woe," he began furtively and he felt the private embarrassment of a man alone in a room who is trying to make a plastic rose dance. "There I go, singing hello . . ."

The plant lurched.

Halima's voice at the door: "Is anything wrong, señor?"

9

Penny said, "So you did like the house?"

It was the second time she had asked. He had described his visit to Sintra, but there was a hole and she saw it.

"And Michael – did you see him?" she asked.

"No. He was ill."

"Everyone seems to be ill at the moment."

They were having dinner in a Portuguese restaurant three streets from their Fulham flat. She wore her favourite earrings.

"What time are you seeing Cullis tomorrow?"

"Ten o'clock."

"I suppose I'd better go and choose some wallpaper." On their first posting to Lisbon they had been allowed white only. As Wavery rose up the ladder so he graduated to white broken with the colour of his choice. As an ambassador he would be permitted wallpaper.

She told him about her weekend, visiting the gallery-owner near Poole. Wavery had forgotten his name. A neighbour's roof had blown off in the gale.

"There was this sweet painter staying, called Sally something. She reminded me of Edwina. She said he liked my paintings, especially the Cuzco ones." She finished her glass. "And no, I didn't."

"Didn't what?" asked Wavery, puzzled.

"Didn't sleep with him."

"Penny –"

She ordered more wine. There were tears in her eyes.

"I wonder what the cook's done with Paracas," he said. Penny had left Jésus instructions to feed the tortoise on grated carrot.

She shuddered, goosepimpling. He stroked her and she pulled away.

He returned to the menu. "What was that dish I always liked, with clams?"

"I don't know."

His eyes stayed on the menu.

"We don't know each other better, Tom, after thirty-five years. If anything we don't know each other at all."

"Oh, I think I know you," he said.

"No, you don't. I'm twenty different people. You haven't bothered to get to know one of them."

He spread a cheese paste on a piece of bread. Each time she behaved like this, she lowered a bucket into his heart, emptying

208

it of something precious. For years he had waited patiently for some internal substance to revive.

"We love each other," he said.

"Scripts are expensive, Tom, but don't – and God, you look awful when you smile like that."

He folded his glasses and tucked them in the pocket of his shirt. He continued, the clockwork in his voice running down. "It's just that, unlike you, I don't feel the need to do an inventory of our relationship every second."

Of course, there would be times when the heart didn't beat as hard, when comparisons would make the present seem less appetising than the past. "But that's because we have a history."

She played with a small pack of butter, squashing the frozen contents this way and that. She had heard it before, the useless grinding, the clang of the empty bucket against the well.

"Why don't you speak to me? You know my frailty. Don't tell me it's your work."

"I missed you."

"I wish you wouldn't answer so glibly. When you answer like that I feel this fragile paper boat I've sent out has been blown over."

"I missed you."

"You didn't miss me in Lisbon."

"I did." His voice was bloodstained.

"Oh, Tom, what are you talking about? You're still on planet Wavery. I sit here listening to you thinking, should I tell him he's a prick? No, because I'm not into mothering him. It isn't how it used to be. That's what makes me bitter. Last night, you just turned out the light. You didn't want to see my face. You just fucked me."

A head turned at the next table.

"Penny –"

"That wasn't making love. That was fucking. This wine is awful."

"Oh, Penny."

"I'm going to complain."

"Penny, no."

"I need a man," she said dismally. A muscle flickered at the corner of her right eye. "Someone who will put his arms around me. Someone who will talk to me. Someone who won't subtly shrug off the blame for things until it's the other person's fault. And I'm going to find him. I don't care how low I have to sink. I'm fucking well going to find him. And don't you dare laugh this off. Don't you dare not take any blame."

He called for the bill. When it arrived he said, "You know, we couldn't afford to live in London." He signed the credit card chit. "I need to go the loo."

When he returned Penny was kissing the waiter. She had discovered he came from Colares, not far from Sintra. He was telling her Colares boasted the only pre-phylloxeric vineyards in Europe. She had invited him to the residence. "But after Christmas," she said. "We won't be there till after Christmas."

It was a ten-minute walk to their flat. Penny had been upset by the state of the kitchen. Wavery locked the door and joined his wife in the bedroom. She was removing her face cream.

"That's why I look so young. This gunge," she said tipsily. "Do I have anything on my face?"

"No," said Wavery. He lay in bed. He was in Suffolk, listening to her father's voice through the study window. Her father was discussing Wavery with Penny's mother. "He won't let her down. As a matter of duty, not affection."

"Why don't you wash?" she said. A hanger grated in the cupboard. "Why don't you ever wash? Women wash. I wash every night. Yet when do you wash before you go to bed? Think what it's like for us? Where have your hands been?"

"All right," said Wavery, getting out of bed and padding into the bathroom. "I'll wash."

He turned a tap. She was saying something. He continued washing. When you've been with someone so long, you stop hearing them. He returned to the bedroom. He switched off the main light, leaving on the lamp by the bed. She had stopped talking. He looked up, to see what she was doing. He saw her cradling in her arms the shirt she had given him last Christmas. She was studying the contours of two black shadows.

210

PART THREE

Chapter Nine

I

SILKLEIGH FOUND THE fisherman. It was three weeks after the *Admiral Grau* slammed into Emilio's new boat.

He had been diving in the shallows between La Mujer Muerta and Punta Benzú when he saw something caught in the springs of a car seat.

Emilio's body floated upright. He was bone from the belt up. His right hand was missing, spun off by the conger eel, but the spine was intact. The bones were black-brown with oil and his skull was wigged with seaweed.

Flesh protruded below a faded pair of denim shorts. Seaweed spores had stuck to the thigh and there was red algae along the calf. "*Asparagopsis armata,*" Silkleigh told Panteco.

"What about his boat, Silkleigh? That's what I'm interested in."

Emilio's mother waited on the quayside. Her cheeks, warmed by fresh rouge, shuddered as she approached. Silkleigh helped her into the stern. He lifted the tarpaulin and she kneeled. One by one, she stroked the leather belt hooping the rib cage, the silver chain knotted around the vertebrae, the cracked tooth where his father, a maker of prosthetic boots, had struck him when Emilio refused to enter the family business.

She looked up at Silkleigh. "Where have you put his freckles?"

Next morning the drilling stopped. For two hours no one thought to wonder why. They enjoyed the silence. It was the first time in five years Abylans had experienced this silence. It had to do with Emilio, they thought. Or Christmas. Today was Christmas Eve.

By midday the city smelled of orange trees, a medicinal smell as if invisible hands were at work scrubbing the city's hair. The clouds moving over Santa Maria were real clouds and the wind blew with the warm breath of a god, bearing to those who had forgotten them the dislocated notes of ordinary life: the gossipy tills in the Calle Camoes, the crack of Halima's duster, the band playing in the Plaza de los Reyes and the fresh shouts of children marching round and round the alarmed bust of Leopoldo Zamora.

By the time five strange birds flew into Abyla, shortly after six o'clock, the fisherman had been forgotten. Instead it was the birds that commanded the city's attention.

At six-fifteen Genia Ortiz entered Calle Zamora supporting under one arm a painting of the Virgin and under the other Matisse's casbah gate. Happy hour, said the man from Algeciras, who had to catch the last ferry at seven. Two for the price of one!

I might be as old as a bush, she thought, but I feel younger than Pablo. Her heart sounded forcibly, like a wing beat. In this silence, she could hear everything! But it wasn't her heart. The decisive wing beat came from the sky. She looked up and five extraordinary birds passed over the rooftops. They were large and black and untidy. They had bald red heads and long curved bills, and they flew with their ruffed necks outstretched, *kay-kaying* in fright.

What ugly creatures! Genia Ortiz stood outside her building and watched them. They were the size of swans. They must be tarred and feathered swans, she decided. Swans which had freed themselves from the ice! she thought, remembering the winters in Norway, the town after which she had named her son, and Ernesto as she had first seen him, conducting the "Valse Triste", stretching out his arms, his neck elongated, his dark blond curls bouncing off his shoulders, his shoulders rising above his head, filled to the scalp with immoral charm. Ernesto! She clapped her hand to her mouth. He flew out of the sunset and she saw the light beat up on his throat from the orchestra pit. But she had locked him up! This was the very last thing she desired, to summon the beaming ghost of her husband who would rather conduct Sibelius than eat. But it was no good, he had escaped the trunk beneath her bed. There he was, taking her elbow up the steps, humming "*oof, les petits pois*" into her good ear.

She reached her landing and propped the paintings against the doorframe. She found the key. She was damned if she was going to let him in. That's right, she thought, feeling his invisible arabesques. Fold away your arms. The arms that lifted into wings when he conducted, undulating up and down. Preparing the way for some intense cantabile, urging those below to flight. Under those arms, for five whole years, Genia Ortiz had become Bizet's Carmen, Puccini's butterfly.

"I thought I'd scared you off."

Genia Ortiz did not throw herself onto Ernesto's pyre, but she burnt all but one of his batons, to the same flames consigning a mountain of sheet music. The scores reminded her too much of their bedroom, which may not have been the room in which he died, but was the room in which he practised. On the nights before he conducted, it smelled like a badger's set.

Frequently he spoke of the day when he would lay down his baton and compose, an ambition which surprised his wife since so far as she knew he could only manage Erik Satie's "Gymno-pédies" on the piano. His own music, he announced, would express happiness without sounding ridiculous.

He had indeed written one popular melody, "On the Promon-tory", which everyone commended as prettily crafted.

Meanwhile he conducted from his stomach, restrained in a

tight abdominal belt to assist him in the art of correct breathing. He tapped his naked belly in the wardrobe mirror. Everything was controlled by the stomach! Oboe players had thin chests. Bassoon players looked like their bassoons. While horns – and his baton described in the air what Genia Ortiz would at a future date recognise as the breasts of his cor anglais.

In the early years, Genia Ortiz accompanied him to seasons in Spain, Portugal, even to the Residenz Theater in Munich. Her preferred seat was in the third row of the left aisle. She saw how he loved to dress up, how he loved the rigmarole of clapping, walking back, waving his hand at the orchestra, registering surprise when a small girl gave him flowers, and delight when the same girl presented another bunch to the visiting contralto – invariably selected for her looks as for the spontaneity of her amphibrachs, which would explain why the Abyla Philharmonic remained an ever larger part of the year at home.

Genia Ortiz was forty-five, in the twenty-eighth year of her marriage, when she received the anonymous note informing her of Ernesto's attentions to Sybella, a temporary cook at the asylum in Calle Silvestre. Nothing worse had ever happened to her. That day the sun set on her love and made revolting the appetite which after a fast of twenty-three years had come only with the eating. She lay on her bed, flat on her stomach as if she had swallowed a crocodile. That night when he came home she said, "I can't work out if you're a great man or a fool."

Surprised by his wife's excursion into analysis, Ernesto said happily, "I await your answer, my halfness."

Her answer arrived at dinner one week later. Ernesto, pretending to go duck shooting with Teodoro Zamora, had come home with a brace of mallard from Don Ramon's grocery. In the afternoon, when he should have been in Africa, Genia Ortiz had followed him to the asylum. "I think you're a great fool," she said.

Ernesto opened his mouth and closed it.

"Can I ask you something?" she said.

"You can ask me anything," he said, his smile made all the

more piquant by his slight buck teeth. "Anything!" When he felt seriously cornered he imitated her.

"Have you ever been unfaithful to me?"

She asked her question as he put a fork into his mouth. She had to wait for him to chew and swallow before hearing his answer.

"Never," said Ernesto growing red and looking round. She passed him the note. "On behalf of one who seeks some justice in this matter," he whinnied. He placed the piece of paper under his teacup. "Malicious, wouldn't you say? Malicious!"

"A cook," said Genia Ortiz. An irritating blond woman with dimpled legs. He had seen what a great thing a lovely figure was. She could almost bring herself to acknowledge he might wish to go off with someone more beautiful. But some bit of tat with dimpled legs! It was an insult too profound.

"Genia, you can't –" The author of this note was a sybil of misinformation. The girl was an aspirant violin player. She meant nothing to him. Nothing! Once, yes, once, now he came to think of it, he had been pounced upon by a nymphomaniac in a hotel in Avignon. But what pride Genia would have taken in his resistance. "Oh, you're so silly," he said. "But that's why I love you. Because of your silliness."

At the other end of the table, the colour had departed his wife's face. She saw the last two decades unravel. She felt very dull. Was that the fate that stretched before her, endlessly to catch him out? She looked at the man she had met in Norway's Murky Time. After a long absence a cold light had returned to the landscape. It illuminated her husband for what he really was. He was a man who avoided the truth as he avoided the sun: his constitution was too delicate for it. He preferred the shadows, the inconsequences of Café Ulises.

She said, "What do we do?"

He rose, advanced to her chair and seized both her hands. He kissed the mole on her neck and pulled his wife to her feet. "Come on, darling," Ernesto whispered, leading her to their bedroom.

For a month she ignored the note. She chose to believe

217

Ernesto. At this point her relationship mattered more than the truth. She did not want to believe she had exchanged her dreams and ideals for an everyday situation. Then one afternoon Genia Ortiz understood why it was that on certain days – invariably those days she worked at *El Faro* – she found their wedding photograph folded away in the bedroom. She returned home early to find another in its place, and Ernesto's face at the door crumpled by an expression of terror.

"Oh, my halfness, it's you."

In the photograph she recognised the sylvan features of the music prompter.

"I can explain – "

"And these?" said Genia Ortiz, who, when tossing the pot-pourri by their bed, had winnowed from the bowl three pairs of earrings, not one of them her own.

"These?" Her face was a loose web of lines in which her eyes were buzzing wasps. Ernesto confessed. She listened: lie upon lie upon lie upon lie, as if each lie he told was of no more import to him than a cup of tea when to her it was the utmost poison.

From this time on she slept in Tromso's room. Ernesto was too shy to approach her further. He left his door ajar at night. He listened to her move about the bathroom, yearning for a hinge-squeak, for her voice to say, "Ernesto?" And his answer, "Yes." "Where are you?" "Here, my halfness. Here." "This is so stupid. Can I . . . ?"

Across the corridor, she lay in bed with her four-year-old son. She noticed her husband's open door and only when she heard him close it in the middle of the night and begin snoring like a tractor did she turn. Sometimes in her most aspiriny depths, she regretted the passing of her pious but splendid copulations. For the most part she held to the belief her husband, the conductor, was a heartless, wicked, soulless skunk.

Genia Ortiz turned the lock and made a dash, but Ernesto's ghost was licking the mole on her neck, running his tongue back and forth over the hard button of flesh, smoothing out the strand of stiff hair.

218

"Ernesto, no!"

Why had she stayed with him for so many years afterwards? Was it inertia? Was it because he shored up her illusions about herself? Or was it because no one else had come along? Unlike him, she had not gone looking. She refused to expose herself to pointed fingers. And now she had padlocked a ruined place.

She squirmed away from him. But he had touched her and she was communing to herself in a whisper. She was thinking of the days when she was mad for him. Why had she cared for him so much? Hadn't he known the truth? That in all those nights she resolutely slept away from him she had nevertheless been desolate for his caresses.

She contorted her head. "Ernesto, no. I really mean *no*." She slammed the door.

She had never felt so out of breath, not even when Anna Pavlova's bulldogs had chased her in Petersburg. She stumbled into the front room where she balanced the Virgin and the Matisse on the window cushion. Very delicately, so no one would hear, she opened the windows. The evening remained silent. In the clear sky above she heard the wing beat of the strange black birds. She watched her swans conduct Sibelius with the wings they had plucked from the ice. They passed overhead, circling the bay, gliding over gardens grey with dust, the stampede of houses along El Hadu, the uplifted nose of the fisherman's dog who had found no grave to starve on.

Nothing must prevent her own flight from Abyla.

3

In the jungle-humid silence, it struck a muffled two.

Teodoro Zamora, punctilious historiofabulist and author of an article in that morning's *El Faro* entitled "The Nail in the Abyla Coffin", heard the noise of wings as he read a novel in the thermal baths of the Club de Pensiones. He arched his neck. Upside down through the overhead pane flashed five shadows. Geese migrating, he reckoned. Or wonderfully plump duck.

Like the brace in his freezer he wished they were eating tomorrow. But Señora Criado had promised to surprise them all. Something involving pork and clams which she glorified as the noon dish of Portuguese peasants. Why this was considered apposite for the Zamoras' Christmas meal, he was uncertain. Asunción had whispered in English behind her back, "This is going to be a cockup."

A drip of water from the ceiling landed on his book. The baths were silent, dimly lit and steamy. Like hell at seven o'clock, he thought. On any other day, the water would be verdigrised with tunnel dust and splashed by elderly men on their backs. Tonight, Zamora had the warm water to himself.

He sat on the submerged steps, one hand gripping a bannister. The brass bannisters on either side of the steps gave him the impression of a grand staircase leading into the water, as if a drawing room had been filled to waist-level. The water poured from the mouths of tritons chained to a wall of dark green tiles. Zamora liked to stand against their fin moustaches, the hot water coughing onto his neck and over his stomach where the flesh fell away in knobbly folds like candle wax.

But this evening he was too exhausted to stand. He needed to sit on the steps and read a book.

All afternoon, as on every Christmas Eve, Senator Zamora had locked himself in his study and stuffed presents into woollen socks. Later, as the house slept in various stages of anticipation, he would paste a white beard to his chin, dip his head into a conical red cap and stump through the corridors.

This, too, was a tradition. He had no notion he was making such a noise. Those lying in bed – if they remained awake – had learned to ignore the scrape as his left hand dislodged a picture; the ouch! as Zamora jarred his toe against the washstand outside Clotilda's room; the slow squeal of the doorhinge; the shuffle to the end of the bed; the at-long-last positioning in the crease between mattress and footboard of the stocking knitted by Minerva and bulging with this year's surprises wrapped in last year's paper. Everyone had to conspire in the reality of

Senator Zamora's Papa Noël, whether you were an eight-year-old grandson with Christmas-tree lights behind his eyes as he considered last year's computer, sent mail order in lieu of his father (Tromso busy editing an omnibus edition of *The Strong Tend to Leave*), or an adult like his wife, her eyes screwed up so tightly he never knew, not even at the moment of her death, whether she did ever sleep during their Christmas Eves together.

Which was why last year when Father Christmas crept into Pablo's room having checked the label tied to the sock with a ribbon and fumbled his way over car tracks to the bed, he was made to leap out of his skin by a strong beam shining directly at his face.

"Is that really your beard?"

"Go to sleep, Pablo."

"How do you know my name?"

"We know everything in Lapland."

"You don't come from Lapland. You come from Tromso. My father comes from there too."

"Well, this Papa Noël comes from Lapland."

"You smell like Grandpa."

"For God's sake go to sleep, you little devil."

"Daddy says Grandpa is stupid."

"He's wrong."

"I've left you a note." A request for a leather bomber jacket.

"You get what the reindeer chooses." And switching off his torch he had tucked the little devil up and out of habit rather than affection kissed him twice, leaving a smear of bread paste on his cheeks and a sock at the end of the bed with the reindeer's choice of Swiss glycerine soap, a pocket diary, a little antique book (second edition) about the Labours of Hercules, an orange from one of the trees in Calle Camoes, and a lollipop.

On his submerged staircase, Zamora forgot the strange birds. He raised a buttock. The soft wail of his flatulence was muted by the water. He returned to his book. The words drifted in the steam. He listened to the silence. It should have invigorated him, but it didn't. The silence disturbed him.

All day he had felt dizzied by it and by the newly heard sounds of the city, for so long hidden in the sediment of noise and the dirt.

There was a precarious quality to this silence. Something not quite right. He could not believe it had anything to do with the discovery of Emilio's body. In the water, Zamora felt the same presentiment he had felt when visiting the Casa del Gobierno earlier in the day. He had made an appointment with the Govenor. To tell him, formally: If Abyla had to celebrate the tunnel with a bullfight, she would do so with the contribution of her own matador. Troyano, the Cadiz matador, had agreed to sponsor Periclito in the August *feria* (an agreement costing Senator Zamora a life assurance policy in bribes since Troyano had not at this moment heard of Periclito, the Earthquake).

It was a rare appointment for the Senator to make. He and Menendez had nothing in common, but Zamora had arranged their meeting for Marie Amaral's sake. He had arranged it two days before – that is, two days before the machines stopped digging – but now he wished to hear from Menendez himself the reason for the silence.

Senator Zamora might be a thousand times glad of it, but he was suspicious of what it carried in its wake. Why had the machines stopped? Menendez boasted they could pass through rock like fingernails through soap. Senator Zamora did not believe the *ratas* had been given a holiday, as rumoured by his political colleagues. This was not money the consortium could afford. The loan had been rescheduled twice. Was the tunnel so far advanced everyone could take a holiday? He couldn't ask the workmen. Their mouths were sealed. Any *rata* found talking to an Abylan was escorted to his room and given three minutes to pack. Nor could Zamora get into the site and find out for himself. The new safety bill he had championed forbade access to the tunnel by non-technical staff.

The machines could have stopped digging for two reasons. Either they had not managed to replace the equipment lost on the *Admiral Grau*. Or the rumours were true at last. They had run out of money.

Zamora went into the Governor's office without knocking. He saw the empty coat stand, where once his father's hat had hung. He saw the empty desk. He saw the empty chair.

"Where is he, Angelita? Where's the bloated dwarf?"

"Señor Zamora, he had to go somewhere. Urgently."

"Where has he gone?"

"Africa," she said wanly.

Africa? On Christmas Eve?

Like Genia Ortiz, Zamora believed nothing good came out of those mountains, but wild pig and low-flying duck. What new baboonery could Menendez be hatching?

Another drop of water landed on his head.

Whatever Menendez was up to, Zamora would not find out until after Christmas.

For the first six years of Teodoro's life, the Zamoras spent Christmas at an uncle's ore mine in the Rif. An oak table was lowered underground and the family assembled by the light of candles to eat a feast that ran on until teatime. Since Abdel Akbar made it impossible, every Christmas had been celebrated in the red house on Calle Zamora.

This year, as for the past two years, it seemed Tromso wasn't coming.

"Has he had second thoughts?" Zamora had asked Asunción.

"I doubt if he's had first ones," she said. The news had disappointed Asunción, but he could not deny that it was a relief to him. Zamora had never taken to Tromso, nor indeed to his famous television programme, but he had done his best for Asunción's sake.

"Tromso and I are splitting up," she had told him at last.

"Oh," said Senator Zamora. "Oh, my dear," and he hugged his daughter to his lambswool chest, as if to wipe away her unhappiness. But to christen a child Tromso was to saddle him with responsibilities he would never be able to discharge. His bogus bohemianism was extraordinary. And now he wanted to be taken seriously. How could one take seriously a man whose ambition for many years was to direct a remake of *Les Enfants*

223

du Paradis? He stank of artifice and fakery, the same trait exactly which had disfigured the music of his father.

It was odd. Zamora had forgotten Ernesto's face as one forgot a joke. Everything else he remembered: his licentiousness, his attachment to music, his shallow good nature. Ernesto's heart had been relatively cold. He had not been a sentimental man. He had simply been infantile: an amiable conductor who liked spanking women.

His music was another matter. In Zamora's ears, Ernesto had been spoiled by his desire to be a composer. Music conducted by Ernesto was music that became elaborated by the conductor's truculent vision of himself as Bartók or Sibelius or Janáček. His impact on Abyla's musical history might have been less regrettable had his interpretations not been so scandalously unoriginal, without an ant's breath of life, failing wherever it lay in the man's power to avoid bathos.

While Ernesto's employment policy frequently led to chromatic uproar, his habit when in doubt of playing *presto con spirito* did not lend itself to every composition. Even in death, Zamora would not bring himself to forgive the conductor for his performance at Lieutenant Zamora's funeral service.

It was among Zamora's earliest and saddest memories. His mother had selected the music, the extra slow movement of Haydn's B flat opus 74, No. 4. From the start, the young Teodoro Zamora had disapproved of Ortiz' conducting. His Haydn – accelerated to his favoured tempo – would never be Teodoro's and indisputably it had not been his mother's Haydn. It was a wonder the funeral party had not dropped the coffin.

Over the years, Zamora was to hear each of his favourite pieces gilded by Ernesto. And if they did survive his embellishments they had then to evade the booby traps laid by his female virtuosi. The more adulterous Ernesto became the less he required of a musician providing she could press the lift button to the first floor of the Hotel Zamora.

"How's Genia?" Zamora enquired of Asunción, to change the subject after his daughter confirmed to him that Tromso was not coming for Christmas lunch after all. "Well?"

"Rather too well," said Asunción.

"Oh dear."

Since his daughter's marriage to Ortiz' son, the conductor's widow had grown to be part of the furniture of Zamora's life. He was fond of her, but she possessed no gift for intimacy. And yet there had been a time, not so long ago, when she had hinted that it might make sense if they were to . . . He had drawn a tender veil over the incident. She was many years older than he. He could not think of marrying again. Besides he was wedded to the city.

She had worked as his personal assistant on *El Faro*. It was an appointment he almost immediately wished he had not made, but to everyone's surprise it had worked out well. They made a good team, made even closer by Asunción's marriage to Tromso. It was only when she started dropping the names of the Kiev aristocracy that he reached for his smelling salts.

Equally insufferable, was the lineage she claimed for her husband. "I tell Pablo he's descended from the two oldest families in Abyla." Zamora was too polite to contradict her. Though his eyes might insist: I, Dr Teodoro Zamora, Correspondent Member of the Spanish Academy and Doctor of Letters from the University of Oran, am descended on my mother's side from the physician who cured Sancho the Fat of his obesity and on my father's side from Prince Henry's most cherished knight, and when your husband's family arrived, most probably in chains, we helped them unpack!, his lips murmured, "You are right, Genia."

Tomorrow, she would arrive in her finery. She would tap the fireguard with her baton, setting the tempo for an artificially joyful occasion. He would open the champagne. They would toast Minerva. "Minerva."

"And Ernesto." "And Ernesto."

"And Tromso." "And Tromso."

After three glasses she would lapse into Russian. After four into an overbearing recollection of someone who might have had something to do with the Duke of Albuquerque before he married. At this point Zamora would organise a competition for

225

the year's ugliest Christmas card. Then lunch, during which she would remind everyone of the occasion she had eaten a Christmas cake stirred by Peter the Great. And afterwards they would open their presents.

Senator Zamora, who had bought Señora Criado a cookbook, took up the novel he had been reading when he heard the sound of wings. He held it to the steamy light. He turned a damp page and the corner came away in his fingers. The novel had not been noticed by *El Faro*'s critic, but he was enjoying its description of the rainforests which had attracted his great-grandfather, Leopoldo, the man who had written on matters quinological but who had vanished into the sea with his life's work.

4

A car circled the empty square, mimicking the passage of the birds overhead. The birds flew over the palm trees in the Plaza de los Reyes, flying with hunched backs and shallow wing beats. Marie Amaral stared after them. She had been cherishing the *poniente* on her cheeks, gathering her energies for the evening ahead. Rosita was coming to dinner.

The birds resisted her scrutiny. They were strange and unexpected and she had not seen anything like them. They were the size of the lame stork on Santa Maria de Africa, except they were black. Black storks?

"*Kay, kay, kay.*" The call was harsh. It was the caw of something she had suppressed inside her. Had black storks brought her her son?

Silence had attended Periclito's birth.

He was born on 17 February, on the floor of Marie Amaral's drawing room in the Rue Balzac.

She chewed her sleeve, shredding it, but she did not cry out. In her silence, stretched on the floor so no one would see, grasping the legs of her bed as Periclito slithered into life, she heard everything. The sounds echoed from the world upside down in the mirror: the yap of the newspaper boy, the girls returning from the toy factory in the Rue Troyas, the foghorn of a boat loaded with families for France.

Unseeing, she reached for the infant between her legs. "I have nothing to tell my child." That was her first thought, not knowing whether to hug or to repel him, hugging him, wiping from his face the yellow creamy substance, offering him a button to suck.

She attempted to stand. The blood had dried and her legs were part of the floor. She was looking for somewhere to put the shiny blue eel of cord when Dr Blechin arrived. The hospital had sent him and he gave her morphine.

Then one day in March, a knock.

She sits on the sofa, cutting cloth for a dress. It takes a while to reach the door. By the time she opens it, the caller is walking away. He is small, with black curly hair and under his open blue shirt he wears a vest. He hears the sound of the door opening and stops in his tracks beside the gate. He returns up the path. He is European, but she cannot tell from where. He speaks in bad French, confident of his accent, nervous a little. Although he is nervous, he smiles. He explains to Marie Amaral how he was a good friend of David.

"David?"

Numbed, she lets him in. She offers him a chair, but he would prefer to stand. He casts an approving eye over the bookcase. He takes down and opens Camus' *Noces*.

"How did you know David?" she asks. He has not told her his name. But to talk with someone who has known David . . . For a second it might bring him back. He replaces the book. He takes in the room, the unfinished bodice on the sofa, the tissue patterns from which she was cutting her fabric, a play open on the floor. That's all she reads, plays. "We were at medical school together."

"Then you knew him in Algiers?"

"That's right."

227

Her head dizzies with things she wishes to ask. She wants to ask how David dressed in those days, how he looked, whether he was always so shy. But he does not want to talk about David. He produces from inside his vest a brown envelope. He talks about other friends of his, but she doesn't care to hear of anyone else. She wants to find out about David. Did his skin always smell of chicory? They admit they made a mistake, he is saying. He opens his envelope. He takes out the notes. He fans them out, rubbing them into a circle, until there are hundreds of Frenchmen's eyes, all looking at her.

"They want to give this to you," he says. "Fifty thousand francs." For the first time he meets her gaze. All around there are screams, but he does not seem to hear. "They say they're sorry." Later the screams will converge on her lips and chase him from the house. But now they scream only inside her. Looking back through them she feels something beyond expression. Staring at him, to turn them both into something else, anything else, she turns him for a moment into David.

For a while, whenever she saw groups of men in the Plaza de los Reyes, Marie Amaral imagined she saw David among them. He had survived. He could cure anything. "I used to think those sort of people survive who can mend anything, Teodoro."

But a day arrived when she became terrified of what David would say if he ever suddenly appeared in the square. What would *she* say? Would they even recognise each other?

"You look different."

"I had Periclito, you see. The boy."

He might ask something banal, such as, "Isn't it time he had new shoes?" There would be a distance, like the distance that existed between her and her son.

On the subject of what had happened in Oran, Marie Amaral was more silent than Ghanem the Mute. Once she was safely arrived in Abyla, she sewed away certain feelings. She had resolved to tell Periclito if he ever asked. "I won't lie to him. If you lie, you waste time." But he never asked.

228

He grew up to suspect David might not be his father and that if there was a secret it lay concealed in his middle name. But he had learned his silence from his mother. He never asked: Who was the Merimée in his name. He never asked: Why am I not circumcised, thin, dark-eyed? Instead of seeking out the truth, he insisted on her approval.

This was her son's need and it appalled her. All he ever wanted was his mother's pat on the back and she couldn't give it. Marie Amaral could assure him, "I'm always here for you, Periclito," but her approval was something she had sewn away also.

Only on one occasion did she talk to him about Oran. He was twenty-eight. It was December. She asked what he wanted for Christmas. Those were the days when he spent Christmas at home.

"A jersey?"

"No, Maman." He lifted up his hair. He pointed to the small scar on the left of his forehead. He said: "I want to know how I got this."

Her son had asked, so Marie Amaral told him. She told him about the Arab who had murdered his reflection and searched for it in the shattered glass. She had thrown hundreds of notes from a brown envelope to force him to leave. After he had blundered through the door and into the ranks of screaming women, their ululations louder all the time, she heard her son screaming on the mattress. His face was covered in mirror splinters and the largest splinter gouged his forehead.

A week after she told Periclito this, she learned from Señora Criado he had redecorated the Café Ulises.

"You have to see it to believe it, señora. From floor to pillar to ceiling!"

Periclito was hanging the portrait of Lieutenant Zamora when he heard his mother's gasp. To each of her thousand selves, his eyes said: You see why I had to do this, Maman. Don't you, Maman?

From then on he set out in search of the love she had denied him.

*   *   *

229

"Kay, kay, kay."

The call was fainter. Marie Amaral watched the birds, dwindling in the sky until they were no bigger than the empty cockle-shells, scattered around the fountain by the man from Algeciras.

"Señora!"

She looked down. The car which had been circling the square was parked, engine running, six feet away. A smart German car with tinted windows, such as Tromso Ortiz had driven on his last visit. The driver had an Arab face and wore a chauffeur's uniform. The uniform made Marie Amaral nervous. All uniforms unnerved her, whether they belonged to Panteco or to Gallo, the bellboy. A tourist who's missed the ferry, she thought.

He beckoned. "Señora!"

She crossed the road in small steps, wrapping the shawl around her shoulders.

The man grinned, showing irregular teeth. "The Hotel Zamora?"

She pointed behind him, down Calle Camoes. "But it's one way. Go left there, then left again at the bottom into Plaza de Africa."

He touched the brim of his cap. In the back she made out the shape of a young woman. Marie Amaral could not properly see her face, but she saw enough – long legs, gondola-black hair, nipples pressing like a cat's nose against a white T-shirt – to know she was a woman who would have appealed to her son.

The car slid away. The number plate was Moroccan. It had come down from the mountains, just as she had come all those years ago, driven in a car without lights over La Mujer Muerta and from there onto the Playa Benitez, on a mule carrying seaweed. She carried Periclito in a sack on her back and supported Rosita by the waist.

"Keep close to the fort," she was warned by the Arab who had led her through the wire. This was how she came to Abyla. No money. No doctor's pension. No documents. On a mule smelling strongly of seaweed.

We may not like them, she thought, straightening. Perhaps

230

we hate them. But at least we are no longer at war with them.

She walked back into her glass cabin. Who could be spending Christmas in Abyla? she wondered. Unless, of course, they happened to be something to do with the tunnel. No one came to Abyla for Christmas. Tromso hadn't been for three years, Periclito for four.

She folded her formica table and stacked the empty boxes. Since the shop would be closed for two days she decided on one final spray. She shook the pump gun, inhaled and began spraying a mixture of washing-up liquid, fizzy mineral water and colloidal copper dust.

She gathered up the plants which would not survive the holiday. The chrysanthemums she would donate to the square. The almost fresh carnations to Señora Criado. And the begonia in the teapot? If he had been in Abyla, she would have given it to Periclito. But he was abroad and perhaps it was as well. He would have knocked over the plant as he perfected his *mariposa*, or overwatered it.

Thanks to Teodoro, she had a wonderful present for her son. But she had nothing for Rosita.

Go on, give it to her. David wouldn't mind. Rosita might discover it to be magic after all, despite the English words on the base. Marie Amaral's lungs were hurting so much she seized the teapot. Once outside she took several breaths. Yes, she would give it to Rosita, and at the same time she would talk to her about Silkleigh. Marie Amaral would forget all she ever knew of the man. She would look upon him as someone loved by her stepdaughter.

She locked the door, peering into the cabin to see that nothing had been left undone. She gathered up the flowerpots and faced the empty square. She was not used to the quiet of the city. She addressed the benches, the waterless fountain, the carnivorous trees: Does it matter? In the course of things, does it matter what Major Merimée did to me? David, it was like . . . nothing.

The *poniente* scraped a cardboard seat through the cockleshells. From the Calle Camoes came the hornet buzz of a motorbike. In the breeze Marie Amaral thought she smelt chicory.

Wavery was reading on the terrace.

"Kay, kay, kay."

He heard their harsh unanswered sob and then the wing swish. They flew above him in an unsteady V, as if they had nowhere to go, passing so near he was able to make out five bare heads, red as brick dust, the scruffy ruff of pointed feathers, the black-green wings as wide as men.

"Kay, kay, kay."

He leaped up. He had never seen such birds. Nor had he heard such a cry. What could they be? The storks from Santa Maria's bell tower? The cattle birds of Yeats' poem? The Ambassador's geese? He looked to see if the birds had girls' necks, but the tree hid them and they flew on, over his bedroom roof, towards the withered headland of Monte Hacho.

He sat down. He remembered the origin of the image of girls' necks. It was how Penny had once described the Ambassador's birds. Wavery had begun in the past few days to appropriate many of her habits. He would catch himself wearing a particular expression, or speak with an intonation he realised afterwards was hers, or squeeze a hand between his crossed legs, as she did. This evening he had eaten one of Penny's meals. Halima had prepared it from a recipe in the concertina folder inspired by a Beef Wellington, served in Amman by the Soviets in 1969. Tonight's meal had been edible, but Wavery wondered if it might have lacked some elementary ingredient.

"Next on the World Service, a bulletin of world news . . ." Wavery turned up the volume. He was not inured to the afternoon's silence. There was news about Bosnia, South Africa, China, but over the announcer's voice he listened for the birds, their cry vibrating together with another sound.

The sound of his wife in their London flat when she found his shirt stained with mascara.

Catharine's louder cry in Lisbon.

Since arriving in Abyla, Wavery had done all in his power to stifle these cries. He reverted to a trusted habit, the trait Penny had least admired in her husband. Once she told him if ever he appeared to be flying on a magic carpet, it was only because he had swept so much under it. In the office he was better able to suppress the things that might upset him. There he was assisted by the *modus operandi* of a working consulate. He could smother himself in progress reports of one sort of another. At work he saw it his duty to encourage trade between Britain and Abyla. The prospects of commercial links, while not obvious, did exist for investors with foresight and initiative. To the DTI he wrote explaining that the antimony works were looking for a British partner. Also there might be tenders for a new hypermarket. He wrote to a merchant banker he had known at Cambridge. Might he consider taking a stake in Abyla's one and only clearing bank? He wrote to the British Council. Could Abyla be included in the British Council's "Meet the Author" programme? More humdrum was the routine demanded of him by the Foreign Office. He wrote a considered report for Pulleyblank, his Head of Department, "Abyla and the Straits Tunnel: first impressions". There had been letters to the Foreign Office Inspectorate about an Inspector's forthcoming visit in January; letters to the Overseas Estates Department on the subject of a Daimler to be relinquished after the Royal Visit; while to the Governor's office in Gibraltar he had sent a copy of the Foreign Office circular about saucepans, marked for his sister-in-law's attention. "In case Hoyter failed to warn Lawrence," he had scribbled at the bottom.

Wavery attempted to be again the career diplomat of a year ago, the man in whom the strongest passion had been habit. It was at night, when he came home to his residence, that he felt the commotion of different passions. The truth was, Wavery couldn't persuade himself he had sacrificed everything for Catharine. Just as he preferred not to dwell on his appointment, so did he not wish to bring her within the cast of his thoughts. Not to think of Catharine, he tended his heart like a bonsai tree, pruning it into a stunted shape of his own making. In the Lisbon hotel he had made a conscious decision. There had been nothing altruistic about this decision and the result was not a colossal wound. He was wounded in the way an ordinary man is wounded. For three weeks, he had listened to the diplomat in him. Don't think of her, this person said. You mustn't think of her. Not if you want to get up in the morning and go to bed at night. And soon, if you don't think of her, you will forget her.

For three weeks he had looked to be left alone, and now loneliness had installed itself. He had reached the point when he couldn't face staying at home. He found all he ever wanted to do in the residence was to sit down, spread out a sheet of paper and write the words "Dear Catharine". The longer he spent in the house the stronger became the impulse.

". . . to end the news, the main points again." The summary spoke of war and famine and political stalemate. From the table Wavery picked up Zamora's abridged history of the enclave. He found his place and prepared to submerge himself in Abyla's past. But he was distracted by the silence. He heard every noise. A scuffling in the handkerchief tree. The quarter-hour bell of Santa Maria. Don Ramon shouting to his wife not to close the shutters because they needed more potatoes.

"Christmas is an exciting time on the World Service . . ."

Wavery misread a sentence. It proved more interesting than what he then reread. He turned the page, but his mind was impossibly elsewhere. Because, Don Ramon was saying, his voice uniting with the bell and a noise from the leaves, what goes on between a man and a woman is more interesting than any book. It is more interesting than the world. You can't cry for the whole world.

For Christ's sake, Wavery, replied the diplomat in him. Concentrate. It's only Ham chasing grasshoppers in the tree. He read another paragraph, blotting out the sounds with an appraisal of Prince Henry's legacy. This time a number of black specks moved over the print. The specks were the birds he had seen in the sky. They were the marks on a trouser leg. They were smudges on a shirt.

"Tomorrow, the Queen's speech . . ."

In eight months' time, remembered Wavery, she would be spending the night in this very house. He switched off the radio.

Mohamed, pacing by the window, hands behind back, looked out between the Access, Credibank and Mastercard stickers and saw a face staring in from the night. Were those the Eyes? But it was Señor Wavery. He explained that the kitchen was closed, tonight was Christmas Eve and if he wanted a meal –

"I've eaten."

Mohamed bowed.

There were two other people in the café. Ghanem the Mute watched television and in the red and blue light of the bar sat Joseph Silkleigh. His longish, thinning hair was combed wet over his scalp. He was peeling a hard-boiled egg. When he saw Wavery he put down the egg.

"Ambasadoro!"

Wavery waited for Mohamed to take up his position behind the bar. A miniature fir tree decorated the counter, untidily draped in twinkling lights.

"So how is it among the apes this night?"

"Look," flashed Wavery, "if by chance you've got something to do elsewhere . . ."

"Kara mia, steady on," said Silkleigh. "We can't fall out. You may wish you were in Tangier, but we're the only people we can talk to. Besides, it's Christmas."

"A beer, please, Mohamed," said Wavery. He examined the grain in the counter's parquet surface, like slivers of worn fur.

Silkleigh said, "You know they came originally from Abyla?"

"What did?"

He clicked his fingers. "The apes, old soul. You see them still on La Mujer Muerta. I met a man once whose brother had been throttled by three of them. Your very good health."

Mohamed put a beer in reach and Wavery paid for it.

Silkleigh said, "When the barbary macaque is on heat she copulates once every seventeen minutes, even with her children.

She sorts out the sperm later. I believe the term is sperm competition."

Wavery sipped his drink.

"Can you believe it! I suppose there are women like that. They haven't come my way. I've been sexually inactive all year."

Wavery counted the eggs on the metal stand.

Silkleigh said, "Women are very definitely the tripwire as far as I'm concerned. When things get really bad, I go up to the hermitage on Monte Hacho. I look down at the city and I imagine all the couples making love." He rattled with his peculiar laugh. "They're probably all watching television."

"How's the book?" asked Wavery. This man was the bitter end, a ghastly albatross. But Silkleigh was nodding at Ghanem. "Now what would *he* do if there wasn't a box in the corner with two knobs on? He'd be lost. He's only as far into the twentieth century as *The Strong Tend to Leave*."

"Have you thought of a title yet?"

Silkleigh unwound the cellophane from a fresh packet of cigarettes. "*Everything I Got*," he said.

"I beg your pardon."

"As in 'I deserved everything I got'," said Silkleigh. He lighted a cigarette.

"I don't think people will necessarily understand that," said Wavery. "At least, not immediately."

"No. You're probably right."

They sat in silence for a while, Silkleigh smoking with his right hand while with his left he dipped the egg into a mound of salt. Wavery drank his beer. He was about to ask Silkleigh about his diving when Silkleigh said, "How was the Zamora family tour?"

"Very interesting."

"He's not a buffoon, by any means. In fact, he's pretty single-minded. For all that he can't sack his cook."

"He's been very kind to me."

Silkleigh wrinkled his nose. He put down his egg. "Something's burning," he said, looking down. "Maybe it's my heart." But it was ash he had dropped on his T-shirt. He flapped it off and resumed his seat. "It *could* have been my heart," he said. Only this evening he'd seen a sight which had warmed the few remaining cockles.

A large Mercedes had stopped him on the Marina Española as he walked from the quay. The windows were tinted. He couldn't see inside properly, but there was a woman sitting in the back. The sight of her wrist against the rear window had assassinated him.

"Her wrist?" said Wavery.

"Ah, but what a wrist! What a wrist!" said Silkleigh. He could tell it belonged to somebody exquisite. Somebody hopelessly exquisite. "It's weird. I felt like . . . like . . . like . . . I just hope she discovers her genius for seeking out small ugly men, that's all."

The wrist was staying at the Hotel Zamora. That's what her driver had asked for. Silkleigh would get her name from the bellboy. He would take her to the Multicine Cervantes. He would fill her with such an insane desire for him she would assuredly clamber to her hands and knees, right there in the front row, bury her head in his lap and by her moist manipulations bring him to pummel the arms of his chair and scream, "This is cinema!"

The screen went blank and he saw Wavery.

"Women not your thing, old soul?"

"I wouldn't say that," said Wavery.

"Any nippers? Where's Mrs Wavery then?"

Wavery explained he was in the process of divorcing Mrs Wavery. Silkleigh nodded several times in quick succession as if he'd seen a magpie. His face became heavy again. "Bloody time. Goes so quick," he said. "Thirty-five years. Christ, I sympathise, Mr Wavery. *Eine kleine* of the same, Mohamed. One for you, Excellency?"

Wavery shook his head.

"But objectively, because people are so loathsome, the business of splitting up should be easy. Getting together is the highwire act."

Wavery looked around for a table, but Silkleigh held his arm.

In a desolate voice he said, "Speak to me, Mr Wavery. I need a kindred spirit. Someone who understands what I feel."

"What *do* you feel?"

"A little off colour, to tell you the truth," said Silkleigh, his braggadocio waning. He pulled up his chair. "I'll be serious, promise. Promise, promise." He lit a fresh cigarette from the stub of the old. "Tell me honestly, do you ever mind you're not all the people you couldn't bear to be?"

Wavery was rendered helpless by the appeal. He had come here to escape his own mawkishness, not to share it with an Esperantist barfly up to his oarlocks in brandy-based cocktails. Silkleigh's eyes implored.

"I suppose so," said Wavery. "I suspect there are times too when all of us no longer want to be the people we have been."

"Do you think so? Well, this is a relief. You see, I don't have any of the shit you have floating after my name. Being an orphan, I was brought up by Jesuits. Twelve years with them, and I tell you, we had none of your advantageous public school muck in Father Michael's little establishment, oh no. Not in Yeovil. No friends either. Not one."

"I'm sorry to hear that, Silkleigh."

"I get terribly lonely, old soul. Except when I'm underwater."

It had not been enough for him to find Emilio's body. Silkleigh would not rest until he had found the boat. All afternoon he had been underwater. He stared over the brim of his glass. The oil had sufficiently dispersed. He lowered himself into his Satan's Whiskers, two aluminium cylinders on his back, three thousand pounds to the square inch, revolving in his neoprene suit, flippering through the luminescent sea, saying to himself: Silkleigh, remember when you're in the water you only have to think it and you see it, how if you think rainbow wrasse you see a rainbow wrasse, how if you want to see a dolphin you see a dolphin, so don't for the love of that woman in the tinted car, let's think of puffer fish or sharks or Portuguese men-of-war, let's sink ever so gently sandwards, towards blinny that kiss your ears in tiny nibbles and octopus that break when worried into the lovely opaque whiteness of their fetish, you didn't know they had a fetish for white, did you, and sea perch and crown-of-thorns starfish and triton conches, and let's think of Emilio who didn't suffer because to drown is really to fall asleep on a couch, whose boat I cannot find but which must be here somewhere.

Silkleigh hadn't found the boat, but near the surface he'd again met his turtle. It was the same loggerhead, with a bite out of her shell. She swam slowly past him, a permanent tear stain below her eyes, like a wall where the paint has run. She swam as you fly in dreams, sometimes barely touching the ground, sometimes soaring, her eyes gazing down on the world, the sun on her tiny gold flippers. She looked like an angel. An old angel with a mossy shield on her back, propelled by sparrow's wings.

"She looked like Genia Ortiz," said Silkleigh, coming up for air.

Once out of the sea, he became the T-shirted voluptuary again, ravished by a wrist. "Yes, let's have another." But it was not Mohamed, it was Ghanem the Mute who stood beside them, his eyes yearningly on Silkleigh's plate. "Hello, old thing. Has the television blown up?"

"I think he wants your egg," said Wavery.

Silkleigh took the peeled egg from his plate. He dipped its shiny end a final time in the salt and offered it to Ghanem. "Happy Christmas." Silkleigh watched him leave the café, the egg trophied above his head. "Silly fish. Where does he think he's going?"

But it was time for them to follow. Mohamed was noisily locking the till. A single chime came through the doors. Silkleigh inspected a digital watch. "Midnight," he said. "I suppose I'd better go and pull a cracker with myself."

There was a strong breeze blowing from the sea, carrying the traffic roar of the waves on Playa Benitez. The breeze scuttled an empty Coca-Cola can along the pavement. Silkleigh kicked the can at the night, inland towards Africa. He stood, listening to its clatter. As if he only now remembered, he said: "You know, there are tribes in those mountains who worship the wind as the origin of all things."

"I didn't know that," said Wavery. He buttoned his jacket.

"Oh, no, it won't be in any of your books. And there's something else extraordinary. They tell lies about liars to summon the wind. They say a liar's talk is only wind. Can you believe it!"

He thrust his hands into his pockets. "On that note, I wish you *felican Kristnaskon*," and he sidled after the can. There was another clatter and another fainter clatter, then nothing more.

Abyla lay wrapped in Senator Zamora's darkest cardigan. There were no lights shining at the tunnel worksite. When Mohamed switched off the bar lights, the only light on the esplanade shone from the telephone kiosk opposite.

Wavery breathed in the wet-wool scent of the sea. He looked across the Straits, to see if he could see the lights of Europe, where Penny was, and Catharine. But there must have been a mist. He saw nothing save the silvery froth of the waves and the faint bobbing lamp of a solitary boat, fishing by night. On such a night as this the Moors had crossed to Spain.

In the dark Wavery heard a cry. The cry came from the direction of Monte Hacho, harsh and raw nerved. He had heard the same cry above his terrace.

"Kay, kay kay."

In the kiosk the telephone began ringing. There was no one to answer it but him. Wavery ignored its appeal. He walked home. He could still hear the telephone's bleat as he entered his upturned key in the lock and opened the paint-sticky door and pressed a black finger on the switch in the hall and furiously cursed whichever of his workmen had removed the overhead bulb so that he had to shuffle in half-inches through the sharp-cornered packing cases, the signed photographs, the canvases against the wall on which his wife had brushed her white-dotted haloes, her mongoloid Christs and the levitations of her headless husbands.

Penny had left in the early hours, taking from their Fulham flat her small overnight bag and his white shirt.

Wavery felt his wife get out of bed. He felt a pause in the air above him. He opened his eyes. She reached down a hand and touched his arm. He closed his eyes and heard the hurried steps down the stairs and a door slam into the street and the car start. He went downstairs and locked the front door. He walked back to bed, looking into the sitting room and his study.

One of her sayings had been, "When you leave, it's because you've already left."

At ten Wavery was received by Cullis and half an hour later he left the Ambassadors' Entrance. In less than twenty-four hours his meticulous world had been turned on its head. He considered resigning but had the sense to understand he was in no frame of mind to make such a decision. He had been caught with every pair of trousers down. This is what his interview with Cullis had revealed. Also something else. Absolutely unforeseen, he had fallen in love.

He spent two nights in the empty flat, and then on Thursday he did what he had promised earlier in the week he would never do. He telephoned Catharine.

A girl answered.

"Is Catharine there?"

"Who is it?"

In the background Brahms was playing.

"Daddy, it's Bob Hope," cried the child.

A man's voice, concerned, said, "Hello, can I help?"

Wavery gave his name.

"Why did you say Bob Hope?"

"A joke," said Wavery.

"Thomas Wavery. That rings a bell."

"We met in Lima."

"Lima?"

"At the Tennysons. Denver and Rita Tennyson."

"I remember."

"We didn't get a chance much to talk."

"He was King Kong. Who were you?"

"Is Catharine there?"

"No. She's not here. Samantha, turn that down – hello? She's gone off somewhere. One of her girlfriends. She's not expected back till Saturday."

On the line there was static and in the distance a voice spoke in a foreign language.

"Hello? Hello?"

Wavery said, "I'm still here."

"Well, anyway. I'll tell her you rang. Any message was there?"

Wavery said, "Only that I rang."

"How's Peru? Pretty rough from what I read at the moment."

"Yes," said Wavery. "It is pretty rough."

On Saturday he drove to Suffolk. Penny was staying with her parents. He wanted to be the one who broke the news about Lisbon, to tell her the great flummery of the flag on the car, the name at the foot of the telegram, the fowl-feather hat were not for him, but her father, an avid reader of the appointments' column, had already shown her the announcement in *The Times*.

He was not at home when Wavery arrived. He had driven Penny's mother to Aldeburgh. They were both crossing fingers for lobster.

"You know how it is," Wavery told Penny. "Anything you put down, one, two, three, you don't get."

"It's only Nescafé. Do you mind?"

"Your hay fever's bad," said Wavery, but she was crying. "What's wrong?" He felt the detachment in his face, a mixture of tolerance, embarrassment, guilt.

"I want it to end." There was determination in her words, a hardness he had not known before.

"Why?"

She went into the next room and sat in a chair, blowing her nose. He followed, placing a log on the fire.

"I'm seeing someone else," she said.

"I thought you must be," he said as a reflex, not thinking she must be at all, but knowing in five minutes' time he wouldn't be able to look at her, so now deliberately looking at her, trying not to show his hurt, keeping his voice calm, as if he were saying he would like coffee. He placed another log on the fire.

"Are you in love?"

She shook her head. She would spare him that as she had spared him the question, "Who is she?"

She said, "I was closer to you than to anyone I could have ever met."

She pulled her ankles into her side while Wavery held back the tears, afraid that any word would uncover his pain.

"Come on, Thomas. Don't tell me this comes as a surprise. If you're suprised by this, it can only be because you've been so distracted."

On the table next to the basket there was a portrait of Lawrence in governor's uniform, fixed in his undoubt.

She went on, "I feel awful saying this . . ." She could probably have stomached his infidelity. But his appointment to Abyla was the last straw. She had reached a point where the prospect of packing and unpacking again was unendurable. She had wasted too much of her life running hotels for freeloaders, undoing the work of her predecessor with work her successor would in turn undo. The one thing she wanted to do was to paint. Not enough life left for anything else.

In spite of what the office said about jobs for spouses she knew they much preferred Penny to perform her Mother Teresa bit and to play bridge, which yes, might have been bearable in Lisbon, despite everything, but not in a two-horse town in Africa.

"Poor Tom. At least you won't be corrupted by power. And there's Lawrence within easy reach."

When he looked up she was sleeping. He went to the other room. He heaved with tears he didn't want to shed. He gripped the window sill and looked at where the Suffolk sky was as grey as his hair, expecting to see an old Volkswagen in the drive and Penny's father signalling, Yes – they had lobster!

He looked down. Three ladybirds moved on the lintel, creeping one after the other in a line over the white gloss. Her diary lay between his hands. He saw the back of a photograph between the pages. It would be a painting. On completing a work she always photographed it. Don't take it out, he warned himself, but he took it out, the photograph of a man in his mid-fifties, short black hair, blue eyes, open-faced. He sat at the end of a boat on a lake, a river, an estuary. He turned, smiling at the person who held the camera.

"I'm leaving."

She stood in the doorway. There was a suitcase against her knees. He could think of nothing to say. He handed her back the diary.

"How will you . . . ?"

"I'll take Mummy's car," she said.

He carried her suitcase. She must have had it packed in advance. Protectively he thought, she doesn't have the dagger of beauty to defend herself against men. "You look awful," he said, not meaning to say it in such a way, but seeing the effect of his words, appalling and indelible, like the wrong paint on a watercolour. She sat in the driver's seat. She stared at her lap, not looking at him. She smiled unnaturally. "You certainly know how to bolster egos," she said. He kneeled beside her. He opened the car door wider. He tried to kiss her. She offered her cheek, her forehead. When he searched for her lips she turned away.

He was in the house when her parents returned.

"No luck with the lobster," her father called from the next room.

"You can leave this, Tom," said Penny's mother when he went to wash up the cups.

Chapter Ten

I

THE NEW YEAR came and still the drills were silent. The days were agitated by fierce shafts of sound from the muezzin and the tapping of Emilio's mother on the asylum windows and the *kay, kay, kay* of five strange birds from their cliff-top incunable.

The birds had settled in a tumble of bronze-green fathers on a military slope the other side of Monte Hacho. They had flown from Punta Leone, smoked out of their nests by the *Admiral Grau*. They had settled in silence, because of the silence, and when in the first week of January the machines restarted it was too late: their nests were built anyway.

"They're not ordinary ibis," Zamora explained to Wavery in the Club de Pensiones. They sat beneath his father's portrait in a long wood-panelled room. At the far end there was an open hearth where four old men were playing dominoes.

"They're baldheaded ibis!"

The two had met earlier in the bank. Noting his own volume under the Consul General's arm, Zamora made the decision then and there to lunch him thoroughly. He blocked his ears to Wavery's protest that he was expecting an important visitor from London.

"The most dangerous alibi is the respectable one," he said, exhilarated at the prospect of a good meal. Last night he had typed into Pablo's computer a legend preserved by Eudoxos of Knidos concerning the revival of Hercules. Slain by Typhon in Libya, Hercules had been restored to life by smelling a quail.

Zamora looked at Wavery over the rim of his menu and ran his tongue along the skirts of his moustache. He had suffered a good deal from irregularity since Christmas. While he thought he might have found a solution in linseed oil and tarragon he was undeniably hungry.

The club had been founded by Zamora's great-grandfather, whose portrait hung above the fireplace dressed in a red poncho, white stetson and hidalgo sword and with the words *"Ecce fundator"* issuing from his mouth on a pale ribbon.

Zamora said, "The Swiss used to eat them." He had been researching their history at the library. Only two hundred and fifty pairs of baldheaded ibis remained in the world. They bred south of Agadir and in a small town in Turkey where it was considered the spirits lodged in their crop. They led pilgrims to Mecca and represented excellence, glory and virtue to the Egyptians, who mummified them. Noah's messenger had been an ibis and the moon god Thoth, the inventor of hieroglyphic writing. This might explain their presence as scribes at the judgment of the dead. The birds also acted as mediators between men and beasts. All in all, Zamora couldn't deny they were creatures of ill omen. "And they're tremendously ugly." He looked behind Wavery for a waiter.

Despite the auguries, Senator Zamora ate with relish. "Isn't this delicious?" he said as he devoured his beef.

A hand squeezed his shoulder and he smelled cigar smoke.

"Consul General. Senator Zamora." It was Sexto Menendez. Both men stood up. They shook the Governor's hand.

"Don't get up," said Menendez. He attempted to clap both men on the back, saying how much he liked them, what good *muchachos* they were and how he hoped the Doctor had now forgiven him for that episode with the hat.

Zamora looked down at him icily. Menendez passed his smile to Wavery and winked. "He wants a holy man for a governor," he said in English.

All this time Menendez was trying to gain purchase on their

two shoulders. But the men were too tall, Menendez' arms too small. "Ring me and we'll have lunch," he said finally. He grasped Wavery's hand and clapped him on the arm.

"Oh, Zamora." The Governor turned, remembering something. "I need to speak to you about Santa Maria's clock. We're going to have to install a new system." He looked to Wavery for support. After all, it was his Queen also who was coming. "We must impress Her Majesty with our *hora inglesa!*"

"You have met the Governor before?" Zamora asked Wavery, when they resumed their places.

"Once," said Wavery.

"And you took a bath after?"

Wavery maintained a diplomatic silence.

"I do not belong to his admirers," said Zamora. "He is a thief and a monkey."

"He seems in a good mood."

"The Moroccan deal!" Senator Zamora said. "I tell you, Señor Wavery, it's the thin end of the wedge."

Senator Zamora had learned of what had become known as "the Moroccan deal" one week before. He had learned of it from Dionisio Porcil, the banker now joining the Governor by the open window at the table where Menendez habitually sat, enraptured by the sound of drilling. Zamora hated men who had favourite tables! How apt that Menendez and Porcil should have gained first and second places respectively in the Zamora Christmas card competition.

Wavery had several times been to call on Porcil. As Chairman of the Bank of Abyla, one of two hundred banks to have signed a credit agreement for the tunnel consortium, Porcil had been enthusiastic to learn of Wavery's contacts in the City. Last week he had invited Senator Zamora to the domino table. As they played beside the fire, Zamora reflected that Porcil deserved to have been glummer than he appeared. He was losing the game. The tunnel had been inoperative for seven days. The latest share issue had not been a success. According to a report in *El Faro* translated from the *Gibraltar Chronicle* the Abyla Tunnel consortium was engaged in a bitter dispute over funds with the

247

Straits Tunnel Company. And there was no more money to pay the workforce.

But Porcil, extraordinarily, was happy.

"Teodoro, do you have any inkling why our beloved Governor has not been seen in Abyla since Christmas?"

Zamora did not. He played a double four.

"He was in Morocco."

"Really? How do you know?"

"I myself accompanied him to Rabat."

So? Rabat was an exceedingly dull place. Duller than Cadiz if that were possible. What had they found to do there? Paint casbahs?

Porcil ignored him. In Rabat, he went on, Menendez had used the auspices of La Société Nationale des Études du Détroit to negotiate a further loan with the President of the Greater Moroccan Company for Development and Investment. As a result, the tunnel was almost certainly saved.

For the first time in seventeen years Zamora lost to Porcil at dominoes.

Under the terms of the deal, twenty per cent of the tunnel workers would be recruited from Moroccan nationals in El Hadu. It was what Zamora had always feared and suspected: the tunnel had become the unspoken revenge of the Arabs. In allowing them to invade Abyla like this, Governor Menendez was another Count Julian!

"We consider the Governor has abandoned us to our expansionist neighbour," Zamora told Wavery, the excellence of the *bife Zamora* having failed to remove the taste which had settled in his mouth at the appearance of Menendez. "He acts as if the tunnel is an eager aspiration of everyone in Abyla. It is not. It's a crime against our country.

"They say he is a successful politician," said Wavery warily.

"He's a better politician than human being. Everyone knows politicians are not real people. You don't give them a minute if you can help it, or they'll contaminate you. You don't believe me? When Menendez took power here he said something that puzzled me. He said corruption came all the way to his front door. When a man says corruption goes as far as that, to me it indicates he has no sense of smell. Or he doesn't use that door."

"Is he so untrustworthy?"

"You can't improve on one hundred per cent. He would change the face of the moon if he could take a cut. He also steals hats."

Zamora knew how petulant he sounded. The petulance was a mask to hide his emotions. But it made him ridiculous. Sitting opposite this taciturn, courteous Englishman he felt the same embarrassment for himself as late in the Caudillo's life he had felt for Franco. There had been a time when Zamora listened to recordings of that high-pitched voice with pleasure. But the day came when he burned them all. As he watched the black discs cavort and buckle in the flames, he thought: few of us look into ourselves and discover things we like.

"Aren't you rather cold here. Let's go by the fire."

He coupled two cups and saucers from a stack on the table. "You don't play dominoes?"

"Sadly not," said Wavery, who would have shortly to leave.

"And how are you enjoying our city, señor?"

Wavery refused sugar. "So far – mainly by reading about it."

"Ah, yes," said Zamora. His eyes took on the smoky hue of his coffee. "You and I, we're in a class above," he told Wavery, indicating two green leather chairs. "We're intellectuals with a common purpose. Nevertheless," and he lifted a bushy grey eyebrow, "there can't be much for a diplomat to do."

"Oh, it's quite interesting really," said Wavery deciding he would after all take sugar. "And I dare say things will liven up."

Absent-mindedly Zamora stirred his cup, lingering over a brew that managed not to taste of burned egg. He said, "One of my uncles was a diplomat." As children Senator Zamora and his two cousins used to play charades in Uncle Eduardo's garden. When it came to acting out the identity of the Ambassador, they dealt playing cards. "That was all my uncle did. Play cards. But I'm sure things have changed."

"Asunción can tell you better than I."

"And Asunción?" said Zamora, embarrassed again. His daughter was causing no trouble he hoped. She much enjoyed working at the Consulate.

In the British Consulate Asunción could forget her poor father's obsessions.

She could forget about her husband the film-maker who had the fantastic arrogance to assume that television was in some way important, much more so than their marriage, and who was forever saying without meaning it, "That would make a *great* film, Teodoro."

And she could forget about Pablo, who had Minerva's eyes but not alas! her manners. Zamora, stirring his coffee, saw the boy with gravy on his face at Christmas lunch. He had coloured his hair with one of Tromso's presents, a sediment called Green Goo. He was refusing to eat the pork and clams.

"Come on, Pablo, one for Tromso."

"What was that?" asked Asunción.

Zamora searched for a napkin. "A regurgitated Tromso," he observed, and to Pablo: "You'll find you'll have to behave quite differently when you're older."

"When I grow up," Pablo announced brightly, "I want to be a hairdresser." So far Zamora had denied him the pleasure of a reaction.

"And do you know Clotilda?" he asked Wavery, affection returning in a rush to his voice. Clotilda whose sighs should be bottled, who would not make old bones unless she soon found a husband. But what was he to do? When your daughter is grown up, you should treat her as your sister. He couldn't tell Clotilda that Tromso's Christmas present – a box of make-up from Dior's theatrical line – was not a success. He couldn't tell her she had used the same shade of red on her lips as he suspected Tromso's actors of using to simulate bruises.

"I forget you haven't met her. You'll like her a lot. And she would enjoy meeting you." But as always when he imagined Clotilda, her image came crowded with less happy thoughts. Such as the thought of Joseph Silkleigh.

Zamora had no evidence at all to suggest that Silkleigh was

the new mystery figure in his daughter's life, but she *would* fall for a man like that. She was an absolute prey to con men.

Zamora collected the metal jug from the hotplate.

"I must tell you about your English friend," he said gravely.

But Wavery had to go. It was two-thirty already. He was expecting the Foreign Office Inspector.

2

One hour later the Consulate door was pushed open by a rubbed suitcase, made from imitation snakeskin. It was followed by a man of average height, wearing a brown suit. A tongue of white handkerchief with the initials G.Q. poked from his pocket. He had a pink face and thinning sandy hair which sweat had matted across his forehead in untidy strands. He inspected Asunción through a pair of thick glasses rimmed with wire.

"I'm looking for the Consul General," he said and he gave her his card.

For a moment Wavery did not recognise him

"Surprise, surprise," said Queesal, extending a hand.

Wavery apologised. "It's the glasses."

"The glasses?" said Queesal. "Weren't you –" But Wavery had departed Peru by the time of Queesal's ill-fated visit to Chimbote, the fishing town north of Lima where he first contracted the syndrome which encouraged his immunity system to attack tear ducts and saliva glands, mistaking them for viruses. "It's similar to leprosy. I cannot cry. Not only can I not cry, I cannot wear contact lenses."

The Foreign Office doctor had prescribed a course of royal jelly and oil of evening primrose and advised Queesal to eat a melon every day, and some onions and parsnips – but not vinegar or salt. "Because it attacks the saliva glands," Queesal disclosed, "I also have bad breath."

Professionally he was flourishing. He stretched out his cuffs. "Someone in Personnel Department must be smiling on me." Once you had served as Inspector, an unpopular

251

post, a good post would reward you as day followed night. Off the record, Queesal had his eye on Head of Department. Failing that, a minor post abroad. "You heard Wilbow's lost his memory?"

"Terrible," agreed Wavery.

"I tell you, it's an epidemic. And it's not just me who thinks so. I was talking to your brother-in-law about it."

"How is Lawrence?"

"Most impressive, I thought. Lady Tredwell sends her regards, by the way. I've been staying with them in Gibraltar."

"Let me take that." Wavery carried Queesal's suitcase into his office and placed it under the window beside the radiator.

"Sorry I'm late," Queesal's voice came to him. "But there was nothing to tell one that this was the Consulate."

"There'll be a plaque shortly."

Queesal nodded. His face had assumed the stern expression of a ticket-collector. Normally he would have been accompanied in his task by a secretary and a grade-six officer. These had remained behind in Gibraltar. When it came to inspecting the new mission at Abyla the Inspectorate's advice to Queesal was that he could manage on his own. From Calle Camoes came the sound of a bell striking.

Queesal looked at the watch chained to his waistcoat. As the chimes continued, his eyes bulged.

"Good heavens, is that the time?"

"Oh, you can ignore that," said Wavery.

"What do you mean, ignore it? It's nine o'clock."

Wavery explained about the bell tower. Queesal said, "Then why don't they do something about it?"

"I think they plan to."

"Well, you know how things are," said Queesal, unimpressed. "I'd better get on with this PDQ. Is your secretary ready for me?"

Wavery opened the door for him. Queesal made a gesture of putting his hand to his stomach and then with a little bow of the head he passed into the front room where he stood with his back to Wavery. Behind the desk Asunción waited to show the Foreign Office Inspector the local budget account.

Wavery closed his door. He sat down and removed a bundle of papers from his in-tray. From his friend in the City: apologies for replying so late and sorry not to be in a position to advise Abyla's bankers. Outside his area of expertise. Nor did he have any useful contacts in the antimony world. But it was good to hear Thomas was alive and flying high in Africa. From an anti-blood sports group in Basingstoke: protest about the bullfight in August. Copy of a letter to Prince Philip from the Chairman of the World Working Group on Storks, Ibis and Spoonbills: as His Royal Highness was aware, few avian species faced so uncertain a future as the baldheaded or crested ibis whose numbers were now perilously low. The discovery of six *waldrapp linnaeus* on the Monte Hacho headland was a just cause of excitement. But he warned it took the smallest interference to result in the desertion of a colony. Letter from the Palace explaining the interest Prince Philip had taken in these ibis. Prince Philip insisting that a tour of their nests be included in any programme the Consul General proposed for the forthcoming visit. Letter from a firm of solicitors in Aldeburgh with Penny's suit for divorce. It was not until his eyes settled on the legal syntax that Wavery registered, to the full, that his marriage was dead. He read the petition, and instantly he was sitting with Penny in a French restaurant off Kensington High Street the day before he flew to Gibraltar.

When they sat down he was reminded immediately of the reason he had married her. By the end of the meal, he knew why the marriage had not worked. Something else annoyed him. He disliked the fact that she didn't tell him to stop scratching his nose, that her eyes skidded to the people at the next table, that already she had forgotten he didn't like white wine. Her brittle superlatives had disappeared with her contentment and the image of her contentment, instead of relieving Wavery, had upset him. He made a joke about her tortoise, but she didn't bother to smile. He made a conscious effort to engage her. "Like that story . . ." he said.

"What?"

"I thought I told you." But it was Catharine he had told.

"No," she said. "It was probably her you told."

"It was you," he lied, in that instant snapping an invisible string that during thirty-five years had bound them together. He heard the sound of precious stones scattering about them.

"No, Tom." She was firm. "You didn't. Ever."

They stood up from the table together and she touched his shoulder to support herself. There was no blood in her touch. He squeezed her arm, as if he would feel there the person he had known on a summer's day at a picnic in Hyde Park. Foolishly, he tried to kiss her goodbye. He tasted the horrible sensation of her reluctance. Her hand withdrew and she said, "I don't think that's a good idea."

The letter from Penny's lawyers jabbed him into thinking of the person he was desperate to forget. Why had he made with Catharine such a ridiculous pact never to telephone, never to write? It had been her idea, and for her sake he had given way to it. Catharine had presumably not heard about his appointment to Abyla. Or else she had been trying to contact him ever since at the Lisbon embassy. Perhaps somewhere in the Foreign Office there were eighteen letters addressed to him. All of them opened by Queesal.

He took out the letter from the envelope in his hand, unfolding it. Even before he read the sentence, he recognised the hand on the page.

"Hotel Zamora, four o'clock, 3–6 July," he read.

At six-fifteen Queesal opened the door. He stood before Wavery's desk, tightening his tie and brushing imaginary crumbs from his trousers.

"There are one or two economies to suggest."

"Such as?"

"Such as the budget for servant's shoes," said Queesal. But

overall he approved of the imaginative way in which Asunción had managed her sub-heads.

Wavery reached for a paper clip and sat back, smiling. "Of course, George, things are a bit artificial at the moment. We've had no expenses – apart from the residence."

Queesal's jaw set in a mould of studied uninterest. His eyes, penetrating the glass lenses, fixed on Wavery's official diary, open on the desk at the first week in July. He twisted it to face him. He turned back the empty pages as if it were a ledger.

"How's the social life?" he said.

"We are not overburdened with society."

"Much entertaining?"

"Not yet," said Wavery, recalling Queesal's preference for buffets over cocktails. He unbent the paper clip. He explained there was no point in having people not as at ease with each other as they would be when the residence was complete. But this hadn't caused a political problem. Not yet, anyway.

"What problems are there?"

"Tourists with maps that don't show that Morocco owns the Western Sahara. The odd Gibraltarian who's forgotten he put a video under his back seat. Nothing exciting. There's tremendous goodwill here for the British, George."

"Anyone in prison?"

"No," said Wavery, wondering if this was any of Queesal's business. He excavated a rim of dirt behind a fingernail. "It's not the sort of place where Brits stay on. You eat, you drink, you sleep and that's it. People come here from Tangier to buy quails' eggs and lavatory seats."

Queesal returned the almost blank diary to its original position. His eyes were unemotional. "What do you do all day?"

"I swim," said Wavery defiantly.

"You swim!"

"You meet people at the pool. It's good PR."

Queesal's eyes lighted upon the towel drying on the radiator. "PR is no substitute for policy," he advised Wavery with the air of a man who decided then and there he had flown to a higher peak.

"No," said Wavery. "No, I don't suppose it is." He threw away his straightened paper clip and stood up. So she was coming! Catharine was coming here, to Abyla!

"I heard about Johnnie," said Queesal mercilessly.

"Johnnie?" Near to, Wavery became aware of Queesal's breath.

"The ape who stole your passport."

"Yes, wasn't that ridiculous," said Wavery agreeably, walking to the window. He put up both arms to open it and changed his mind.

"You must have been so – so *embarrassed*."

"That was our job here during the war." Wavery looked across the Calle Camoes into the room where he had eaten lunch. "Churchill's orders."

"What was?"

"To get apes for Gibraltar. They were dying out. You know the story – when the apes leave Gibraltar, so do we."

According to Asunción, who had heard it from her father, Wavery's predecessor had offered a crate of Laphroig for each new ape. His offer had been ardently taken up by the legionaries of the Tercio, Senator Zamora's eldest brother employing a tunny net on La Mujer Muerta to capture thirty-six bottles.

"So tell me about the tunnel," said Queesal.

"There's precious little I can tell you. The project is cloaked in secrecy. Officially, they're three weeks behind."

Queesal nodded. "I've read your reports. You have suggested that the whole thing would have collapsed without the Moroccan loan."

"So one gathers." Did Queesal's rank permit him to read these reports?

"Does the King really believe the tunnel will make it easier for him to join the EC?"

"He argues that Morocco is closer to Europe than is Britain and therefore has a stronger claim to membership."

"He's got to be out of his tree."

"That you'll have to take up with Rabat."

There was a knock and Asunción said, "Your car's here."

256

But Queesal was not giving up. "What reactions have there been here to the strings he attached?"

"Abyla Independiente isn't best pleased. Nor are the contractors. But the Moroccans are delighted, naturally."

"Will it be ready on time?"

"Impossible to find out," said Wavery. "But the date is a date they obviously believe in."

A taxi drove them to the residence. "This really is what I'm here for," said Queesal, waiting for Wavery to pay. "More than the sub-heads." He stepped off the pavement to allow Genia Ortiz to pass by. She turned back for another look at the corner of Calle Astray. Her face made no secret of her thoughts as she scrutinised the Consul General and his friend.

Queesal's attention lingered on the work-site opposite while Wavery unlocked the door. Wavery shielded the lock from Queesal's view. "I must warn you, George, the decorations are still to be finalised."

Queesal absorbed the rickety scaffolding. He stepped inside.

"Do you want to go upstairs? I've put you in the Royal Suite."

Queesal gazed about him. He delivered Wavery a quick smile. "Actually, Tom, if you don't mind, I think I'd better get on with this."

At eight o'clock, Queesal took himself upstairs and there was the sound of running water.

Half an hour later he joined Wavery in the dining room, at the other end of a long mahogany table.

Halima removed the earthenware cone from Queesal's plate. She wore a new white uniform and a pair of smart black shoes.

"Lamb tagine," she murmured, relishing the words.

The Foreign Office Inspector being Wavery's first guest, Halima had made an effort to reach the market early. Her effort had been rewarded. The butcher blessed the meat as he always blessed the first purchase of the morning and suspending the joint by its little scarlet gender he whispered how he had reserved this male for her – which much relieved Halima because she knew those like Señora Criado in the queue behind would have to make do with female joints, tasting stringently of lentiscus roots.

"I'm not sure if I ought to eat this," said Queesal eventually. He polished his lips with a napkin, first the top lip, then the lower lip. He was reflecting on Wilbow's fate in Luxembourg.

"She won't have used an aluminium pan?"

Wavery said, "I had them all recycled."

Queesal cleared his throat. He looked unhappily at the wine in his glass. It had not travelled superbly the thousands of miles from Lima to Abyla via Tilbury.

"More?" said Wavery, beginning to enjoy himself. Queesal's hand descended flatly to the rim. Wavery refreshed his own glass. He could taste the year on the label. They had just arrived in Lima. He could taste the *garua*.

He said, "I can't decide if I should serve it at the reception." But Queesal had not heard him, or else he was refusing the bait.

Halima cleared away the plates. "I don't suppose you have such a thing as a melon," said Queesal.

For the remainder of the meal the two men talked vaguely about the past. Talk of the office, of Lima.

"HE went rather to pieces after his geese flew away," said Queesal. "You'd catch him pulling at his beard and staring at the wall. When you asked what the matter was he'd explain he'd heard voices in the garden threatening to dispose of him in a variety of horrible ways."

"And Deirdre . . . ?"

"You know," Queesal went on, "when I came to leave Lima instead of feeling glad to leave that effing place, I felt sorry."

"I know what you mean."

"Despite my promotion." Queesal surveyed Wavery down the length of the table and gave his host a sad smile. The wine, bitter though it was, had fortified his belief that Wavery was one of those who hadn't come up to scratch. Earmarked once for Paris, then Lisbon, here he was ending his days in Abyla. Disgrace had made his colleague powerless. It revealed Wavery for what Queesal had always known him to be: a chinless wonder

258

from Oxbridge passing through the Foreign Office on his way from womb to tomb.

"Cullis sends his regards," he said.

"Oh, yes. How is Cullis?"

"He says to remind you the Queen doesn't like garnish and her husband won't sleep with a duvet."

"Right."

"He's chirpy at the moment. He's won a cruise for two in a limerick competition."

"Cullis? Writing limericks?"

But Queesal's attention was on the wall. "Nice painting. Who is it?"

"As a matter of fact, it's a landscape."

"One of Penny's?"

"That's right," said Wavery. He was surprised at Queesal's failure to recognise the artist for whom, to employ his own words, he had always a soft spot.

"How is Penny?"

"Fine. I think." Wavery had called on Christmas Day after the Queen's Speech. He was intending to tell her the story of his passport. She had picked up the telephone, laughing.

"Oh, it's you."

"Why are you laughing?"

"I'm trying to put up a cabinet in the kitchen." But her laugh had nothing to do with a cabinet. In it Wavery heard what he had never given her.

"Sorry to hear about that," said Queesal.

Wavery felt a powerful urge to say something new, but he said, "Probably for the best."

"Was it, as it were, that young woman we met at Rita's?"

Wavery nodded. Had Queesal expected to find her ensconced?

"I was getting on rather well with her," Queesal remembered. "Clarissa something."

"Catharine." Just when things were becoming really dire. Just when he needed a signal, she had written to say she was coming. It didn't matter that July was six months away.

259

"I always had a soft spot for Penny."

"She liked you too." Both of them wanted desperately to matter to people. "How's Shirley?"

"Fine, fine. She's now living in Miami."

"With Salvador?"

"I think so."

"From the Potato Institute?"

A tremor ran through the house. On the table a cheese knife rotated. Queesal jerked upright. "What the hell is that?" he asked, his eyes on the ceiling.

"They're digging a marshalling chamber," explained Wavery. Asunción had registered his complaint the day before, after which the tunnel foreman had made a point of calling on him personally. The Consul General was assured absolutely no damage at all would result to his house.

Wavery rang for coffee. "It's only Nescafé. Do you mind?" But Queesal was looking at the wall. He was surveying the strange unpainted moulding on the dining-room ceiling. "You really expect the Queen to stay here, Tom?"

"There's no problem at all," said Wavery. "We have six months."

Queesal prepared himself with a mouthful of Tacama. The truth was a sharp instrument and it should be wielded only when necessary. He was about to wield it now.

"Being brutal, Tom," he said, "this house is a disgrace. I'll have to tell London how things stand."

"It will be ready," Wavery repeated.

"No, Tom. It's pathetic – and I mean pathetic in the nicest possible way. All the same." He hoisted his eyes to the wires worming the air where a chandelier should have hung. "Jesus, Tom. Even a blind man could have done better."

Wavery poured himself another glass. His smile went skimming down the long length of the table. "Sometimes, George, blind men are hard to find."

Queesal was not listening. He appeared to have something in his eye.

"What's wrong?" asked Wavery.

"Something in this house is giving me an allergy."

"Could it be the air conditioning?" said Wavery, unable at that moment to recall whether in fact Pas de Problème had installed it.

"Do you have cats?" asked Queesal, his eyes half-closed. He made a hasty grab at his wine glass. At the taste he spluttered. He unscrewed his face. "Jesus, Tom. Where in Abyla can one get a decent drink?"

3

They walked without speaking along the Marina Española, Wavery leading the way. Ten yards from the telephone kiosk they heard an English voice. Silkleigh was talking. "I think that's disgusting. What did he say? Oh, he tried to blame you? So what did you tell him? You should have said, 'Because he can't stand your guts, sunshine.'"

"In here," said Wavery. He ordered two brandies. "Large ones, Mohamed."

"Not that I should," said Queesal. He took in the bull's head, the straw hat, the endless reflections of Mohamed scratching his crotch.

"Is there nowhere else?"

"They all shut by nine."

"All the same," said Queesal, pulling a trollish face.

Opposite, three ibis rocked up and down the television screen. The pictures were taken through a wide-angled lens from a boat. Two birds were filmed on a ledge, touching each other with the tips of their long red bills. They swayed from one foot to the other. Another half rose from her nest, beating her wings. She threw back her head-feathers and uttered a raucous croak.

"What appalling creatures," said Queesal. His eyes washed over Ghanem the Mute, Don Ramon the grocer and the bellboy, Gallo, strumming his guitar.

"And these people, you know them?"

"I do as a matter of fact," said Wavery.

"Really, it's too bad." The lights bent the shadow of Queesal's spectacles along his cheek. He was sniffing.

"Come now, make room," came a voice and Silkleigh appeared the other side of Queesal. He looked the two Englishmen up and down. "Who's been rattling your cages?"

"George Queesal, Joseph Silkleigh," said Wavery. The lights dimmed in the café as the two men shook hands. Wavery mouthed, "Foreign Office."

"Pleased to meet you, Sir George."

On stage Rosita stepped forward. Her eyes were closed, but small convulsions disturbed their lids. She folded her arms, elevating them. *"Cabelo branco é saudade da mocidade perdida,"* she began. Her voice rolled through the café. *"As vezes ñao é a idade, são os desgostos da vida."*

Queesal coughed. "Oughtn't to have left the bathroom," he said.

"Here. Drink that," said Silkleigh, passing Queesal his glass. "Drowns out the sound."

Willing to try anything which might accomplish what Silkleigh promised, the Foreign Office Inspector lowered his lips into a glass of Satan's Whiskers.

Silkleigh wriggled off his stool and came between Wavery and Queesal.

"So who's the ippety-oy with the bad breath?"

"He's from London. He's come to see how I'm getting on."

"How are you getting on?"

"I don't think," said Wavery, "that he's very happy."

"Silly fish," said Silkleigh, who was very happy. He wanted Wavery to be as happy as he was. He owed his felicity to the woman in the tinted car. "Who shall be nameless but who calls herself Cochabamba."

Silkleigh had invited her to see *Persadilla en Elm Street 5*. Even now the memory filled him with a lurid expression. He thought of her mahogany whispers, the hollow in her ankles like the base of a young tree, her breasts yearning against a white angora jersey that reached not quite to her waist, unlike her hair, but afforded him a glimpse of a thin dark wedge of flesh almost as enticing to him as her wrist.

"I tell you, old soul," he whispered, "she's *eine kleine* piece of *nacht muziko*. She's the juice. One of the friendliest girls you've ever seen. A smile that curls itself around her face and says, I've got a thousand secrets and I'm not going to tell you one of them." A finger tugged at his right eyelid. "The woman. Is. Beautiful."

She came originally from Excellency's neck of the woods. Bolivia. Probably she was the only one who might have seen Periclito fight a bull! Her father had emigrated from Tetuan after independence. She now worked for a hotel chain in Rabat. Her company wished to build an international hotel in Abyla. She was here on a preliminary tour of inspection.

"She's interested in my water purifiers," said Silkleigh. "*Extremely* interested, old soul." There was talk of a contract for the entire chain. Her interest extended to his boat. She loved diving too!

"Does she know how you feel?"

"Oh yes, I think so," said Silkleigh. "Not wishing to play it up, I told her she was sensational."

"What did she say?"

"She said she's thinking about it." But it was perfectly plain what she felt. "Her eyes are like traffic lights saying, Go, go go!" He twiddled the tip of an imaginary moustache. "I tell you, Mr Wavery. She. Is. A. Trip. In her embrace boys become old men –"

"In my experience," Queesal's voice interrupted them, "when a woman says she's thinking about it, she's thought."

The mirrors blurred as the doors swung open and Emilio's dog came in tugging behind him Captain Panteco and Dolores. The librarian retrieved her hand and stood moodily in the entrance. She knew how sexy she looked when she looked like this, but she was not feeling sexy. Panteco's superior, thank goodness, had summoned him to Madrid. Since the New Year, the policeman had become intolerable. Tonight he had hooted for five minutes outside her flat before bellowing at the window, "Dolores, come *on*!" And what had happened? In her hurry, she had squeezed into a pair of shoes too small for her.

She leaned on a pillar and with the toe of one shoe eased the other off by the heel. Severely she examined the big toe poking through the hole in her Charmed Life stocking. She wiggled it and thought of Dionisio Porcil, who had stumbled into her outside the library as she bent down to retrieve some books from the pavement, books borrowed by Senator Zamora ten months before which she had retrieved from him. Porcil had helped her into the library.

"Are you here tomorrow?"

She nodded.

"Good," said Porcil. A girl like that got her books carried.

And why not? thought Dolores. If you could read several books at the same time, why shouldn't you enjoy men simultaneously. She was sick of Panteco. Every time they went to bed it was like a walk in an enemy's field.

"I'm sure he's a coprophile," she told Rosita in the chemist's where she bought her breast-firming cream. If he was a Spaniard like Ernesto he'd put it in from the front, not the back. "He is difficult to make come. It is boring, boring, boring. He is like a theatre that never ends." And Rosita had sat through it for two years! Porcil at least was rich. He also listened, or pretended to.

"See a table, Dolores?"

She glanced at the policeman as if he was one suspicious pimple. Captain Panteco ignored her. His eyes went marching through a regiment composed of his dim images to the stage where Rosita was singing. He could not see a free table.

"It'll have to be the bar."

At the bar, Silkleigh and Queesal were talking in low voices.

"I was in contact with *Encounter*."

"Really?"

"Superficial contact."

Wavery listened to Rosita. "I want you more than life and if it wasn't a sin I'd want you more than God."

"I was at boarding school twelve years. Jesuit priests. Very strict," came Silkleigh's voice.

When next Wavery looked round, Silkleigh was explaining a schism in the Esperanto movement. A small group of Central Europeans wished to bring back the Latin preposition.

"Inevitable, isn't it! But Christianity had schisms at the same stage of its development."

Queesal nodded. He removed his spectacles, sniffing.

"Have some more of this."

Queesal accepted Silkleigh's glass. "I really shouldn't."

"Mohamed! Three *kleine trinki*!"

Rosita completed her *fado*. Silkleigh clapped. Someone called, "*Flamenco!*"

"The language of the future," Silkleigh was saying.

Queesal repeated, "*Al ni en Britujo makas leonoj?*"

"That's it. 'We do not have lions in Britain.' It's that easy."

Wavery tossed a glance over Queesal's shoulder and Silkleigh caught it. "Go away. We're talking high politics."

Queesal loosened his rotarian tie.

Silkleigh said, "A good diplomat, isn't he?"

"He is a good diplomat."

Presently Wavery heard the sounds of Silkleigh's laugh. "A house that has yet to be built? Let's think. That would be *domo konstruota*. One of Esperanto's subtle beauties, old soul. *Konstruota* means literally 'to be built in the future'. Adjectives may come before or after a noun, but stylistically in this case the post-position is preferable."

"Another drink?" said Wavery.

"Mr Wavery, sir. Thank you!"

"All right," said Queesal. He managed a twisted smile.

Silkleigh leaned forward, touching Queesal on the arm. "*Mi estas skribonta libro de mi vivo.*"

"I wanted to write," hiccupped Queesal.

Silkleigh confided him a glance. "Just one *problemo* . . ."

Queesal said, "If you've waited that long, don't start."

"*A Shadow in Love with the Sun* . . . *Crossing the Straits* . . . *The Mirrors of the Café Ulises* . . . *Fishing by Night* . . ."

"All wrong."

"*Word of Mouth* . . . *The Passions of the Strong* . . . *Snowfights in the Dark* . . ."

"Wrong, wrong."

"*The Dust We Play In* . . . *A Man Passing Through* . . . *The Leavers and the Left* . . ."

"Wrong from the start."

"*Wrong from the Start*!" Silkleigh tore open his empty cigarette packet.

"Another drink," said Queesal, confronted by the intent stare of the barman through a glass he was drying. "On the rocks," he slurred.

Rosita sang another song, about Lisbon.

"She's a darling," Queesal was saying. His voice was louder now. "I think so. I love her. Isn't she a darling?" Queesal turned to Wavery. "Isn't she the most wonderful woman? Don't you think so?"

Wavery said, "Who are you talking about?"

"Penny."

"Yes," agreed Wavery.

"Anyway. Go on," said Silkleigh.

Rosita finished. Gallo laid his guitar flat upon the stage and she clapped him. Then she bowed, her large hurt eyes avoiding the bar. In the torturing silence Silkleigh jumped from his chair, his boots squeaking, and clapped his hands above his head. The curtain enfolded Rosita and he sat down. He felt something beating against his leg. It was Toribio's tail. He looked about and he saw Dolores resting her elbows on the counter next to Queesal.

"Dolores!"

She was immersing herself in the mirrors. "Hello, Silkleigh."

"You stay pretty now. Where's lover boy?"

The librarian nodded to a spot behind Silkleigh. Unable to whistle, Panteco was barking at Toribio. Failing to attract the dog's attention, he stomped over to Dolores. His right hand sought a purchase on her hip as if to demonstrate his lordship over her, but her eyes slammed at him their independence.

"Now, Toribio, go over there," said Silkleigh. "Don't be a bore."

Dolores cast her gaze at Queesal, beside her. Glumly, he noticed her perfect breasts. There was a flashed ankle in her smile. He didn't have good in bed written on his face, she thought. But nor did Panteco.

Still not letting her go, the policeman had taken up position next to Silkleigh. His restless eyes fastened on the diver. Tomorrow Panteco would be travelling to Madrid with his chief, summoned to report on El Callado. His options were running out.

"What do we tell Madrid, Panteco? Who do you think he is?"

Who indeed? "*Jefe*, to be honest, I'm having trouble with Who." Lacking a Who, Panteco had been concentrating on What.

"What the fuck you on about?" said his chief.

Panteco explained. The Ford Maclaren had slipped its berth. There was a rumour that El Callado was waiting for a valuable consignment. Panteco's informant in El Hadu thought the consignment might be heading in from the Canaries. But Panteco was suspicious. He had an idea.

"*Jefe*, perhaps El Callado's boat is a blind. Perhaps it's a dumb boat."

"How dumb, Panteco?"

"Perhaps it's carrying not drugs at all, but illegal immigrants?"

Panteco badly needed a success. Apart from Mohamed the tobacco-smuggler, he had arrested no one in the past month save a boatload of Moroccans convinced they had landed in a different continent entirely. He found them on the beach, six gleeful Mohameds in their mid-twenties. They had been cramped in a hold and were straightening their arms and legs. He almost felt sorry for them, exercising like that, stretching away the stiffness, laughing. He stood over the leader, a small man with a barrel chest, dressed in a dirty orange T-shirt. "So,

Mohamed," he said, "What's up?" But Panteco knew what was up. Mohamed had boarded with his friends at Cap Spartel. They'd been bobbed round the sea for few hours, then unloaded here. They'd come up the sand, throwing handfuls of it into the air, the free sand of Europe. Because that's where they thought they had landed, somewhere near Barcelona, not horror of fucking horrors, in Abyla.

"You have reached Europe, Mohamed, in a manner of speaking. But not quite."

"But we have permits. Look!" They clamoured round him, unfolding papers bought for a year's salary.

"The papers are false, Mohamed."

He had dropped them at the border.

"Anyway, it's an idea, *jefe*. El Callado could be diversifying."

"I see Madrid decorating you for this, Panteco."

There was no other progress to report. Not with El Callado. Not with Sandra the Rapist who had affixed herself to the chairman of the antimony works in the gardens of the Republica Argentina, before vanishing into the shrubbery. Not even with the boat of Panteco's friend, Emilio, who before he died had promised to take him mackerel fishing.

He cleared his throat, meaning to speak kindly. "You haven't found Emilio's boat?"

"No," said Silkleigh. "Spookily enough. What about you?"

"It's not a competition, Silkleigh," said Panteco. "But naturally, you will tell us."

"Naturally, Captain. You're my friend."

"George Queesal," said Queesal, holding out a hand to Dolores. His eyes sprawled over the librarian, fumbling with her blouse.

At that moment Mohamed switched on the lights and Rosita could be seen walking between the tables. She held Gallo's guitar in her arms. She offered it to the drinkers. The money they put inside would go to the fisherman's family.

"Rose-beef!" cried Silkleigh, swivelling. He pursed his fingers and kissed their tips and opened the purse and sent his kiss across the room.

Rosita was about to walk away when Wavery raised his hand. She hesitated, as if she had never intended to come near the bar. She chewed the inside of her cheek, before approaching the crowd there. Wavery posted his notes between the strings.

"Thank you. I was three years in Lisbon."

"Rose-beef!" Silkleigh seized hold of her. He hugged her to him, brushing her cheeks with his own. "Don't go too close," he whispered, "but I want you to meet Lord Queesal, from Londono."

Rosita, ignoring him, stood apart. She addressed Captain Panteco. "Hello, Lustrino."

Silkleigh said, "I've been telling him about my book!"

Wearisomely, Rosita turned and she looked at Silkleigh in a distant way, as if what he said and indeed everything about him was to her a matter of epic indifference.

"First lay the egg, Silkleigh, then cackle."

Chapter Eleven

I

QUEESAL COMPLETED HIS report with military efficiency. Any hope Wavery might have entertained of sympathetic treatment dissolved soon after breakfast with the discovery of a flood traced to a blocked drain beneath the laundry room.

In the light of Inspector Queesal's recommendations, London despatched a telex at the beginning of February seeking clarification. It was felt necessary to remind Wavery that the residence had to be in a state of complete readiness by 1 July, one month prior to the Royal Visit. This was an imperative. The PUS would understand no excuse. The telex was signed by the acting Head of Department. Wavery wondered what had happened to Pulleyblank.

Wavery had become accustomed to such telexes. One of the problems posed by looking at the world in the manner of a reasonable Anglo-Saxon was the difficulty of persuading London you had not gone native. Wavery reacted by delivering his severest reprimand yet to Pas de Problème, to the effect normal incompetence could sometimes be mistaken for obstruction, after which he dictated a telegram assuring London he had conducted useful talks with the contractors and each side now had arrived at a clear appreciation of the other's position.

To OED he confirmed the safe arrival of the Daimler, parked on the pavement outside the Consulate.

Asunción noticed that he enjoyed driving home.

On a bitterly cold day in February Sir Derek Cullis entertained the head of the Intelligence Service to luncheon at his club.

"I've a problem, Max." The other man took a simple pleasure in Sir Derek's discomfort. It was rare the PUS admitted to a chink in his Service and he ordered a savoury.

"When you say Wavery in Abyla is not up to snuff – correct me if I'm wrong, Derek, but you chose him yourself."

"I tell you we were all very pleased when Wavery got the job," Sir Derek said. "He used to be one of our bright young stars." He stopped. Max, too, had been on the Appointments Board.

"Well then?" Max waited, amused. He had been one of Cullis' bright young stars himself.

Cullis pushed away his plate. "His eye's not on the ball. He's in love, Max."

"Are we still talking about Catharine Riding?"

"What do you mean 'still'?"

"I never know, Derek. You diplomats . . ."

Cullis ignored him, releasing one of his chill Scottish sighs. "Since you know everything, how *is* Mrs Riding?"

"Interesting you should ask that. She was seen, only very recently, in a travel agency."

"Don't tell me, booking her holiday in North Africa."

"I think we may assume so."

"You go up, Max. I'll settle this."

"White or black?"

"Black, no sugar," said the Permanent Under Secretary.

The other man walked to the library on the first floor. From a Portuguese waitress, he accepted two cups, dropping into his own a single saccharine tablet. He looked for seats and managed without spilling the coffee to overtake a bishop on his way to the sofa.

Sir Derek squeezed onto the sofa beside him. They sat in silence looking at the greying sky. Cyclical becoming westerly, escalating to gale force eight, reckoned the Permanent Under Secretary.

After a while he said, "You've heard the PM's latest angle on the tunnel?"

"The Trojan Horse theory?"

"You are up to date, Max," he said grudgingly. It unnerved him that his protégé enjoyed direct access to the Prime Minister. It was something he had learned to live with. There would have been mayhem if they hadn't got on. "It's irritating the PM should be so interested."

"Do you share his belief?"

"That we could be overwhelmed by illegal immigrants? If they chose to be difficult, who knows what the Berbers would do."

"Is there anyone who knows what they're up to?"

"Unfortunately, Worsnop in Rabat has had to take early retirement. We haven't chosen a successor."

"So Wavery in Abyla is your nearest man?"

"You see, Max, he's the one we have to rely on."

"Could you recall him?'

"Six months before the Royal Visit? Too embarrassing. No, I badly want someone who knows the place inside out. When the tunnel is up and running we'll need to monitor the Berbers. I need your help, Max."

Max's gaze returned through the empty trees. "I wonder who our agent is down there."

After a professional relationship extending ten years, the PUS was never certain how much Max knew, how much he pretended not to know.

"I'll find out," promised the man on the sofa next to him.

"If you would, Max."

"By the way, I clean forgot. Aren't congratulations in order? A dickybird told me of your prize."

Flights of duck passed through the dust, carrying spring on their creaking wings. Monte Hacho became yellow with broom and oranges settled on the trees along Calle Camoes.

For the first time since his arrival in December, Genia Ortiz noticed a change in her neighbour's routine. Now there was activity on his roof terrace. Before Christmas the Consul General had been in the habit of sitting at his round metal table, surrounded by a pile of books. Since then his routine seemed filled with a new resourcefulness. He read less, but with greater concentration. He had also taken to filling out page after page of foolscap. Genia Ortiz, watering her flowers and straining to get a better look, did not believe he was engaged in Foreign Office work. From what she remembered of Consul Cazes in the Hotel Zamora, he had not spent hours with his head in his hands, ripping up pages and writing out what must have been fair copies. Señor Wavery was either engaged in a book or a passionate correspondence.

The second change concerned the state of her neighbour's terrace.

Until he received Catharine's letter, the deterioration of Wavery's spirit had been plotted by his inattention to his surroundings. Since then his attitude had changed. He was never going back to Sintra, that much he knew, but he could measure the progress of the days which separated him from Catharine by transforming the terrace outside his bedroom.

To this end, Wavery had enlisted the help of Marie Amaral who was able to procure most of the plants he wanted from her Dutchman. He bought some tubs and painted them white, planting them with a special cistus which grew only on the tip of Cape St Vincent. He constructed a trellis against the low wall dividing his terrace from Genia Ortiz' balcony and on the trellis he trailed a clematis and a trumpet vine.

"How nice to see a trumpet vine again," called Genia Ortiz, although she would have preferred it pink not orange. It amused her the way Wavery diligently cleaned each leaf. After five years she no longer noticed the spoil dust coating the leaves of her flowers. Dry and sticky, it was something she had learned to live with, like the noise of the muck lorries, the mud on the roads, the interference on her television set.

"Might I ask, what it is that you're writing?"

"It's nothing really, Señora Ortiz. Just some things I've been meaning to catch up with."

Yes, but what things? If they were letters, he never seemed to send them.

The heat continued without let. A warm February carried the devil in its belly, warned Halima at the ironing board.

Halima's warning had been provoked by a number of fresh appearances from Sandra the Rapist. ABYLA LIVES IN TERROR! was the headline following her attack in rapid succession on two *ratas* and the chairman of the telephone exchange, to each of whom she had presented a bunch of flowers. "Venus Flower Trap" added a sub-editor, a reference to Sandra's seemingly inexhaustible supply of bouquets.

One afternoon at the end of February, Wavery's housekeeper telephoned the Consulate. The gist of her call was enough for Wavery to return home at once.

"Señor, señor, they've gone!"

"Who have?"

"Pas de Problème and Plaisir des Yeux!"

At the bottom of the stairs Wavery collided with Silkleigh. The diver crouched over the metal postboxes. He held a large bunch of pale pink roses. When he saw Wavery, he hid the flowers behind his back.

"*Ambasadoro*! What are you doing here?" he asked.

"I work here. What are you doing?"

"I'm going to a party," said Silkleigh.

"At two-thirty?"

"I'm early."

Wavery hurried on and climbed into the Daimler. Already as he drove onto Calle Camoes the implications of Halima's message were usurping in his mind the issue of whether or not, after their visit to the nesting site of the baldheaded ibis, the

Queen and Prince Philip should be advised to attend the bullfight.

Halima waited for Wavery downstairs. Half an hour ago, she had heard a noise upstairs and the sound of running feet. When she investigated she found both workmen in the Royal Suite. They pushed past her. She asked where they were going, what was that noise, who was that other person and what was she going to tell Señor Wavery? But they ignored her.

Wavery made a rapid tour of the house. The desertion of his workmen compelled him to see the residence as Queesal must have seen it: the unpainted exterior, the hall still awaiting the glazed tiles which Pas de Problème claimed to have ordered from a factory near Tetuan; the colour with which his foreman had chosen to break the white of every room, including the Royal Suite where Plaisir des Yeux, tripping on a wire between the boards, had plunged his left foot through the floor.

An hour later, at three-forty, Captain Panteco arrived. Moodily, he took details, but he could not concentrate on Wavery's problem. His mind remained on the beach below La Mujer Muerta, floppy with a shoal of grouper fish. The fish had been stunned by something. They had the dead-fish gaze of the Tercio's addicts, the look of people who had seen everything, done everything.

It was the look on his chief's face when Panteco showed him what he had found.

"The dope's coming up from somewhere,"

"Very interesting," said his boss. He returned the fish to Panteco by its stiff tail. But Madrid, as Panteco would recollect from their visit, were ambitious for arrests. "Don't shit higher than your arse, Panteco," he said, forbidding him to chase any more red herrings. If Panteco did not envisage a future camouflaging dog kennels, he might prefer next time to bring him El Callado, or one of El Callado's men – or, failing that, Sandra the Rapist. He understood from the hospital that the chairman of the telephone exchange had spent a comfortable night.

The chief waved a piece of paper in Panteco's fever-spotted face.

"Or even, Panteco, if you can't manage Sandra, what about finding the Consul General's workmen."

Captain Panteco disliked Señor Wavery's countrymen – his grandfather claimed the bullets extracted from the Tercio corpses had been English – but he promised Wavery he would search for the two men. Plaisir des Yeux he didn't know. Pas de Problème – he was another matter. He shouldn't be working on the residence at all. "He should be in Las Rosales. Locked up." But Pas de Problème had found an old man to confess to his crime.

"So it was you?"

"Yes, monsieur."

Beneath the burnous, the man had smiled and two shiny black dates dropped onto the dunes of his face. His smile conveyed to Panteco not the smallest trace of humour.

"I am the one you want." He had brown teeth, like the cardboard seats in Plaza de los Reyes, and carried a bag with a broken zip.

"So, Mohamed, how come then I caught Abdul Hadi with the Winstons?"

"I am the one you want. I was in the water, monsieur. You didn't see me." The dates teased Panteco. Everything teased him. This Arab, his boss, Joseph Silkleigh, but most of all Dolores whose eyes never responded to him, who fell asleep when they made love and in whose handbag he had found a copy of *The History of the European Monetary System*, which, since she wasn't a known economist, he considered puzzling.

He nodded. "So how come I caught Abdul Hadi with the fucking Winstons?"

"You didn't see me, monsieur. I was in the water. I am the one you want."

"Mohamed –" He was caught in the fist of his impotent rage.

"You didn't see me."

"No, Mohamed, you're right." What did it matter? They were only American cigarettes. More important to Panteco at this

276

moment was Rosita. Last night she had told him at dinner, "I'm leaving, Lustrino. I'm going to South America. To stay with Periclito."

"For – for how long?"

"Until the bullfight."

4

After the policeman left, Wavery sat for half an hour staring at the hole in the ceiling.

"Listening to your hair grow?"

Wavery contemplated the enigma of Silkleigh's T-shirt. "How did you get in?"

"The door, *ambasadoro*. The door." Silkleigh entered the banqueting room. "So this is where the General spent the time on his front." He spoke in an effeminate way and then half marched, half minced to the mantelpiece where he posed. "You could give a darling party here."

"That is the intention," said Wavery.

Uninvited, Silkleigh sat down on a packing case, shiny boots on a chair. His T-shirt was laundered and the arms of a red jersey hugged his neck. The room became generous with aftershave.

Wavery said, "I thought you had a party."

Ignoring him, Silkleigh jerked a thumb over his shoulder. "Nice car outside."

"It's only here till August."

"I might beg to borrow it."

"Beg away."

Silkleigh became serious. "Now don't be like that. I went to your office. I spoke to Asunción. She was upset. She told me what's happened . . ." His words flagged. "I thought I could help."

Wavery sat unyielding. "What happened to your party?"

Silkleigh, inspecting the toes of his boots, said, "I wish you wouldn't go on about that." There had been no party. A surprise visit, that was all. "Lust, pure and simple." Cochabamba had rented the flat below the Consulate, but Silkleigh's appearance had not thrilled her as he hoped. "She fell asleep on the sofa as I was telling her a story. When I said I'd better go she said 'Yes' and sprang to life."

"You told me in her arms boys became old men."

"She's given me this to be going on with." Silkleigh tapped the Rolex on his wrist. But if Wavery must know, Silkleigh's expectations of the Bolivian race had so far outrun their performance. After a courtship lasting two months, Cochabamba's ecstasy appeared to be measured in kisses alone.

"Put it this way, you're invited to a grand house, but you're not allowed in through the front door. You're invited in through the kitchen. You smell all sorts of marvellous smells. You steady yourself. You roll up your sleeves – and then you're offered two olives and a peanut. Can you believe it! I want to spend my life with that woman, but I shouldn't think she'd let me share her taxi."

To tell the truth, he had been in this state once before. Then he had been suffering from oxygen poisoning. He had been diving too deep, to below three hundred feet. He had fallen into catatonic shock and his system had gone nuts. Everything muscular had started working to its utmost ability. "I could crush a block of wood as if it were a matchbox. I could snap a bar." Luckily, it had been only a mild case of poisoning. "If it had gone on longer," he said, "my muscles would have been torn from the bone."

And now this young woman from Bolivia was having the same effect. "She hurts my head, old soul."

Wavery had set eyes on Cochabamba once, in the stairwell of the Consulate building. A dark-faced girl struggled backwards up the staircase, dragging an aluminium cylinder between long, thin legs. The cylinder had cracked two tiles on the lower steps. Both pretended not to notice. Wavery carried the cylinder to her door. Her eyes were moth's wings, fluttering thanks. Installed in his office, he realised he had failed to notice the wrist which had first stoked Silkleigh's imagination.

"She's scandalously beautiful," said Silkleigh with an expression so solemn he might really have been in pain. He had taken her diving off Monte Hacho, near the military beach. They hadn't been allowed to land, of course, but they had swum near the shore. Cochabamba had never seen anything so lovely, so unspoiled. Not an advertisement. Nothing. As God had planned it.

He had shown her a monk seal and a puffer fish, the *scosophilis intenis* which swam up from the west coast of Africa and lived off coral heads and she had become almost as excited as Silkleigh at the prospect of finding Emilio's boat.

"She's also good for business." Her hotel chain had yesterday ordered one hundred and twenty water-purification systems.

"She's the apple of my eye," said Silkleigh. "'The apples of the daughters of the evening star.' Isn't that so?"

"Senator Zamora says they were oranges," said Wavery.

"That's by the by," said Silkleigh. "To tell you the truth, today was not the day for showing myself in all my glory." He drew up a sleeve and caressed his left arm where he had been stung by a sea wasp. The amethyst mark ran from wrist to elbow like a whiplash. "I've put some ointment on, which I hope bloody *soulages* the *douleur*, but it hurts like a bitch. Like sticking your finger in a socket." Gingerly, he pulled down the sleeve. "Of course, the best thing with a sting from the sea is urine. Get your friends to pee on you."

For the first time he appeared to notice the hole in the ceiling. "Fuck a duck," he whistled, abandoning his packing case. He stood staring. "And how long may I ask does Majesty have the pleasure of staying with you?"

"Just one night," said Wavery. She might stay a second, depending on whether or not she attended the bullfight. But he wasn't going to vouchsafe that to Silkleigh.

Wavery followed him out into the hallway. "I'm not surprised," Silkleigh was saying over his shoulder. "They're the most dishonest people and that's that. The more you give, the more they swallow." He pulled a face at himself in the mirror. He inclined his head, stirring his bald patch with a finger, his eyes angled upwards.

"I like that," he said. He had noticed Penny's portrait in the mirror. He walked up to it. "The missus?"

"It is by her."

"Does she do a lot of painting?"

"It's her thing, really," said Wavery.

"Sisyphus, I suppose."

"Yes," said Wavery, disconcerted.

" 'It is necessary to imagine Sisyphus happy' ", murmured Silkleigh. "Camus said that." Silkleigh's thumb jerked over his shoulder, up the stairs. "Mind if I . . . ?"

Wavery led him into the Royal Suite and Silkleigh kneeled by the hole in the floor. He gazed down to where they had been sitting, then drew back his eyes into the bedroom. "And all this for one night —" He stepped over the hole, to the window. He shook the brass handle. "Window not open?" he said. The frames had been freshly painted and thick coats of gloss had cemented them together. "Good view of the *maro*." He pressed his nose to the glass and waved at Genia Ortiz below. Startled by the rattling, she looked up. While she could not be positive, the face at the balcony window did not seem to belong to Wavery's *bonne à tout faire*.

Downstairs, the telephone rang. It stopped as soon as Wavery reached the hall. He returned to the Royal Suite, but it was empty. He found Silkleigh on the terrace. The diver had walked through his bedroom. He was watching Ham stroll over a towel on the wall, in her mouth a large grasshopper. He tried to remove it, but she leaped over his hand and darted up into the tree.

"Ever eaten grasshopper?" he asked Wavery. "Tastes like chicken." He indicated the tubs and the trellis. "I say," he said admiringly, "you *have* been busy."

Silkleigh unclipped the pencil from his T-shirt. He produced a packet of Winstons from his trouser pocket, tapped out the last cigarette which he lit and tore the empty carton open and flattened it on his knee. "Bottom line. No messing. When's the place got to be ready?"

Wavery hesitated. But there was no need for caution. The information was unclassified. "Four months," he told him.

"That's too bad." He tapped his nose and a sly expression entered his face. "On the other hand nobody knows his builders like Silkleigh. Bottom line. No messing. How much *dinero* do you have?"

Wavery revealed his budget and Silkleigh emitted another whistle. He looked at the figure he had written down. He said, "That's meaner than a hotel towel. And I suppose you initial the eggs in your fridge?"

"We do run a tight ship," conceded Wavery.

Silkleigh stood up. "Wait here," he said with authority. "Just you wait here, Mr Wavery. I'm going to sort this out."

Silkleigh sat down on Wavery's bed, taking the telephone in his lap and dialled a number. He reread the cigarette packet and tore it into little pieces which he dropped into the reed basket next to the bedside table. As he waited for someone to answer, his eyes roved over the rock plant, the message pad, the cinnamon scarf.

"Barney? It's Joe," said Silkleigh. He spoke rapidly, in a businesslike voice, squeezing the phone between cheek and shoulder and writing. "No, Barney. Not like yesterday. Like last month. We can sort out the details later."

"Well?" said Wavery.

"In the blink of a star," said Silkleigh. "I haven't pratted around here all these years for nothing."

"But that amount will cover it?"

"Absolutely!" Silkleigh tapped his nose again. Nobody knew his builders like Joseph Silkleigh.

"You wouldn't object if I discussed this first with Asunción?" said Wavery.

"You do that, old soul."

"But how can I thank you?"

"Don't think about it. Queen and country," said Silkleigh rising from the bed. "That's nice." From the table he picked up the scarf. He was looking for a label when Wavery removed the scarf from him.

"The other woman?" Silkleigh said gently.

Wavery blushed. Queesal must have told Silkleigh in the Café Ulises. He turned away, looking for somewhere to put the scarf. It embarrassed him to have been discovered like this, in his own bedroom. He felt exposed and sentimental, and now he must be grateful.

"I know how you feel," said Silkleigh, going out onto the terrace.

But Wavery was not listening. He had felt a movement in the air ahead of him, like a flag but invisible. She was there on the terrace. The low white wall was the Moorish castle and the city lay below. She whirled the scarf in her hands, wrapping Lisbon about her neck. They were walking after lunch, during which she had shown him the photographs in her purse. Two girls on a patio, their fingers pointing at the lens. Adam, lying on his back, one of the girls on his chest. The four of them on a sofa, not knowing whether the camera had clicked.

"I can't compete," he said, weighing the air with his palms.

"It's not a competition," Catharine said.

July was five months away.

"Have you seen Rosita?" Silkleigh's voice came from the terrace, where he stood rubbing his sting with his pencil.

"No."

"I'm not speaking to her."

"I'm sorry to hear that."

"I got really angry with her last night." She was having dinner with that irrepressible mediocrity Panteco.

"He's called Lustrino," she told him ever so sweetly – bitch!

"Your Lustrino is so physically revolting, I find it hard even to have a drink with him. You were with him once and it didn't work. Why again?"

"It's better to be quarrelsome than lonesome, Silkleigh."

"But he made you unhappy!"

"So long, Silkleigh." Rosita had returned to the policeman's table, and Silkleigh was left at the bar with Mohamed, who was as nervous as a dog on a boat, because that morning Silkleigh had clipped him on the ear for staring into Cochabamba's eyes.

"So I looked at Panteco, who, bear in mind, is an aberration, and – I tell you no lie – I felt sorry for him. I thought, You poor eunuch."

"Perhaps they were only having dinner," said Wavery. He waved to Genia Ortiz whose face had appeared suddenly at her window.

"She could have told me," complained Silkleigh. "Really, she needs to marry a football star who will fall down on his hands and knees and say 'Thank you' every time she fries an egg. Still, what am I worrying about? If the full moon loves you, does it matter if a few tiny stars decline?"

There were a number of books on the table beneath the tree. Silkleigh picked one up. "Camoes," he read aloud. "Famous name, famous name, but never read him. Any good?" He leafed backwards through the pages. "How old was he when he wrote it? I always like to know how old they are. Gives me hope." The book, a Spanish translation from the Portuguese, did not include biographical information. "Ever read Hemingway? Now, when I read Hemingway, my toes expand. He was a crackpot, of course. And not good at sex, which was why he wrote short sentences. But a writer needs a crack in his pot. Something for the dirt to gather in. This Camoes, did he have a crack in his pot?"

"I rather think he did," said Wavery.

Silkleigh replaced the volume and picked up another. "*A Concise History of Abyla* by Teodoro Zamora. I say, lucky you. It's immensely out of print." Without opening it he cast the book back on the table. "Hey, *kara mia*, what's this?" He had noticed a neat stack of pages. "Are you writing too?"

"Some papers I'm working on," said Wavery. He gathered up the pages, removing them from Silkleigh's view.

"Oh, yes?"

"About the house mainly."

"You know," said Silkleigh self-indulgently. "My mind is like this house. Full of empty rooms that have never been used except for storing flippers. That's why I want to write this book. To fill them up." A title had occurred to him as clearly as a title ever would. For this he had to thank the Queesal chappie. "I've been accused many times of reading too much into nothing, but your friend from the Inspectorate planted a veritable seed, old soul. I'm thinking of calling it *On the Rocks*."

From the branches came a disgusting, contented crunch.

"That's not a bad title," said Wavery.

5

"Hotel Zamora, four o'clock, 3–6 July."

Five words and some numbers, but they had altered Wavery's life as thoroughly as Silkleigh's workmen would transform the residence. (Led by a snappish foreman from Gibraltar, they were moving through the house room by room, but with admirable discretion.)

Wavery referred to Catharine's letter several times a day. Wherever he went, he kept it on him, folded inside its envelope. Each time he read the words he could extract a different interpretation. "Sit three men down in a room, tell them a story and they'll leave that room with three separate versions." That's what he'd been taught as a young entrant. It was the same with Catharine's letter. Was she coming only for the weekend? Or to plan the rest of their lives? Might she never come at all?

No verb even. But it had the effect of freeing Wavery from a situation that had begun to suffocate him so powerfully he did sometimes wonder if he would survive to witness the Royal Visit. Until the moment of Catharine's letter, he had believed his life was finished. In Abyla he had not been able to think of Thomas Wavery and remain sane. At the bar of the Café Ulises, he had suspended himself in others' lives so as to avoid concentrating on his own reflection. He now had a rest of his life.

Planting a garden was one way he prepared himself. Writing, he discovered, was another. Catharine had sent him a letter. He wrote one in turn. Since his appointment, he had drawn on all that his training and upbringing had taught him to suppress. Guided by Silkleigh and Senator Zamora he had steeped himself in Abyla, locking out the past. At his table on the terrace Wavery wrote down page after page to retrieve it. But he was writing something he had no intention of sending. Not since a brief period as a young diplomat had Wavery felt imbued with such a genuine sense of mission, nor such lucidity. Then, when he had been flying high, his energies focused exclusively on the sky above. He had avoided the landscape beneath him. Now at the age of fifty-eight he was looking down. If there was to be any virtue at all in these pages, he had to embrace the earth. He thought: I must force myself to see everything as it was.

March came, and April. La Mujer Muerta lay shimmering in the heat. The figs had not ripened on her forehead, and her dry flanks pronounced the death of the land. In the heat, men waited to harvest what the frost had spared and the wind not carried away.

On Monte Hacho the heat burned away the nasturtiums and sorrel, sparing only the pines. On moonless nights a pair of baldheaded ibis could be observed on their courtship flights. Every day the birds left their nests to forage. One morning at the Abyla Swimming Club, Wavery saw a rapid blue shadow on the water and an ibis dipped its beak in the surface. In the middle of April another was disturbed rootling in the dustbins at the Hotel Zamora.

The incident merited a small mention in *El Faro*. In Abyla, the "Stymphalian birds", as Senator Zamora called them, had been forgotten as Emilio's boat had been forgotten and it was the Straits Tunnel which once more dominated conversation.

Work on the tunnel was said to be on schedule. The confirmatory signal of the rock-boring machine could be heard through the night, and each night the churning rose a fraction in volume. For so long had this noise been part of the landscape, people no longer thought what it concealed was worth discussing. But what had been hidden below ground was shortly to emerge. In the Café Ulises, in the Club de Pensiones, in the streets and in the squares and on the roofs where children played hopscotch with pieces of brick, there was talk of little else but what would happen in August when the sovereigns of Britain, Spain and Morocco converged on Abyla, and Gibraltar and Abyla became International Zones; when Abyla became indisputably *el puerto de Africa*, the EC's exit to the continent, the Hong Kong as well as the pearl of the Mediterranean.

So ran the advertisements on television and in *El Faro* and on posters skirting the plinth below Leopoldo Zamora. Posters which also announced the timetable of celebrations, these culminating in a spectacular *feria de toros* at which Abylans could see performing for the first time their very own matador, Periclito Merimée Amaral – otherwise billed as The Earthquake.

Under the dust Abyla stirred to meet this fate. The scaffolding was removed from the Casa de Gobierno and Santa Maria de Africa. Fitted with gala uniforms, the conscripts now marched along the Marina Española with purpose. There was water in the fountain in the Plaza de los Reyes.

And in the Plaza de Africa, smoking a cigar and fitted artfully into a new white suit, Governor Menendez presided over rehearsals of the ceremony at which as her earthly plenipotentiary he would remove the cane from the Virgin's arms and present it on a red cushion to his sovereign, who would offer it in turn to the British Queen, the Moroccan King and a delegate as yet unspecified from Brussels where details of the International Zone awaited ratification.

There had been protests. Abyla Independiente marched through the centre of the city in a spiritless *manifestación* and a small bomb exploded opposite the Fosu de San Felipe, injuring an ice-cream seller. There the matter ended.

In the same week screams were heard on the harbour front where Sandra the Rapist was discovered by Captain Panteco affixed to the Italian Consul General. She was returned to the asylum in Calle Silvestre, resuming her place in the painting class beside Emilio's mother.

"I see a Medal of Africa in this, Panteco," his chief said to

286

Panteco, who had gone to watch the fishing boats come in. "Plus citation."

Cooped up in the ibis city, the diplomatic community grew steadily. Across the pool Wavery recognised the hirsute shoulders of Gabriel Volta, Sandra's ultimate victim. They had served together in Phnom Penh and there was excitement in his greeting. His last post had been Mogadishu where he was said to have been apprehended sending good-luck telegrams to all four sides in the civil war. Volta had taken a suite in the Hotel Zamora while looking for accommodation. Although shaken by his experience on the quayside he considered himself otherwise fortunate. The hotel was accepting no further bookings until the autumn.

Their conversation ran out beside the pool with Wavery's promise of an invitation to his reception in August.

"Perhaps that's what he's writing out – his guest list," thought Genia Ortiz.

The impending celebrations divided Abyla. Those who had not been invited to the opening ceremony, which included a reserved seat at the temporary bullring near the docks, made plans to spend the period abroad. Others such as Genia Ortiz, who had angled so assiduously to extract their invitation from the Governor's Chief of Protocol, spent a tremendous amount of time telling people what a bore it was and really they hadn't decided yet if they would attend.

Or was he writing to Silkleigh?

Soon it was Ramadan.

In El Hadu and the mountains beyond they fasted from sun-up to sun-down, at night celebrating with silk soup the month in which the Prophet had received his divine revelation.

The Playa Benitez in Abyla filled every afternoon with sun-bathers.

In the privacy of the Abyla Swimming Club, the owner of the enclave's most celebrated Eyes, climbed from the pool, slipped a finger under her costume and stretched the material back over the contours of her capacious bottom. The Governor's wife had grown fat as thin, sparrow-like women sometimes do in their fifties and her tastes had kept pace with her girth. She was bored. She liked drama. She liked fuss, but she found none of it in Abyla.

Beatrice Menendez lay down on her lilo and opened *Life Is Worth Living* by Monsignor Fulton Sheen in its Spanish edition. She dreamed of the men she had known. Periclito. A small Englishman. And lately, Lieutenant Casares.

She imagined Lieutenant Casares at her side. "Higher up, no, higher," she told him as he pounded a sturdy anthem on her back and rubbed an itch from her skin. But the itch remained. She floated her eyes, for so long unrecognised in Abyla Television's competition, over the pool. Lieutenant Casares was nowhere in sight: he was marching in front of her husband at another of the Governor's rehearsals.

Did the Governor have an equivalent list? She didn't much care. Her husband could not take a spoon to his mouth without it irritating her. When he ate his branflakes at breakfast she wanted to strangle him. She was bored by his proximity, by his fetish for white, by his hypertrophied ego. Irritated above all by the ferret ambition. It would genuinely surprise her if he could manage the time for an affair.

This morning there were only two people in the Abyla Swimming Club: the man whose job it was to skim the surface of dust and the British Consul General.

Up and down he swam as he swam every morning. To the Governor's wife a man's character revealed itself in his movements. Without his glasses, with his pinkish-grey skin and silvery hair, the man in the pool looked to Beatrice Menendez like a very correct and charming fish.

She doubted his intimacy with the passions that rent her body, but in the mornings she would greet him warmly. There were few good reasons to remain in Abyla: one of them Lieutenant Casares; another was the prospect of curtseying to Señor Wavery's Queen.

Wavery completed another length. Whenever he swam towards La Mujer Muerta and saw the blurred outline of a woman on her back he thought of Catharine. He was famished for her.

He wanted to be the person he had become when he was with her, who he might be again in July. Each time he swam towards La Mujer Muerta he was swimming a few yards more towards that possibility.

Each time he swam away from the mountain he wondered if their intimacy could be recreated. "Am I looking forward to something I know will never happen?"

Wavery's days had passed – like the lengths of this pool – into weeks. Only Asunción knew the extent of his distraction. Every day she heard his fingers marking time on the desk, his chair squeaking back, his tread across the floor to the window where she would find him looking out at the roof of the Club de Pensiones, or fanning his chin with an invitation he had asked her to refuse. So he waited, the progress of the weeks measured by the vine on his trellis and the pile of pages on his table and the state of his residence. So the weeks crawled by into months until it was the eve of her arrival.

6

It was the end of Ramadan and El Hadu was tetchy with fasting. On this particular evening, Wavery waited for Marie Amaral to bring him a consigment of tuberoses. She was supposed to deliver them at six. By seven-thirty there was no sign of her. She must have forgotten, he decided. He was upstairs, packing for the coming weekend, when the doorbell rang.

"Madame Amaral!"

"I'm sorry. I was lost." She was as white as a shirt.

"Lost? In Abyla?" He took the box from her arms.

"I could get lost on a straight road. I was in church. Then I took a walk."

"Is anything wrong?"

"It's Periclito," she said.

As she was preparing to come to the residence, a girl came running from the shoe shop. "Come quickly! It's Rosita. She's on the phone. There's been an accident." Her stepdaughter

289

was calling from Peru, a town called Huanta. The accident involved her son, the Earthquake, his stomach punctured by some Andean bull.

"Huanta," said Wavery. "Yes, I know Huanta."

Periclito had been a matador there. He had to travel thirty-six hours by bus to find such a town. But he wished to impress Rosita, his sister whom he had not seen for three years. The horns had passed in and out of his stomach wall so that for a few seconds he held his insides in his hands, like the coloured ribbons of his mother's bows. "They missed my balls like so," he told Marie Amaral on the telephone from his hospital bed. He was trying to sound jocose. They had told him not to laugh if he aspired to eat cassoulet again. "It was nearly my sweetbreads they served in the Royal Box!"

So she laughed for him, not knowing anything about Huanta, not knowing it was a village at the boot-end of tobacco road where every street was renamed Avenida Sal Si Puedes. But guessing.

He was too fat. He ate too much. All he ever did for exercise was make cassoulet. "And love!" He had no more technique than an ox cart. He relied, he said, on *intuition* – the same intuition that told him when a dish was ready for the table, when a knee was ripe to touch. The same intuition which had punctured his stomach so that forever after he would be compelled to carry two scars, the shape of close-set eyes, to the left of his bellybutton.

"Maman, it's not that I'm afraid of." More ominous in Periclito's eyes than his lack of technique or his failure of intuition at Huanta: he was shaping up to be a matador who couldn't kill. And the *feria* was less than two months away.

Shaping up indeed! snorted Marie Amaral's silence.

"What you are afraid of overtakes you, son."

And she was afraid for him. Oh, Periclito. You idiot. You beautiful idiot, she thought. My son with whom I cannot exchange a single intelligent sentence.

"Periclito, do you have a girlfriend to look after you?"

"Rosita's here with me. And I have a girlfriend. I'm not holy.

290

That's my place – if it exists," and she saw him stabbing a finger through the hospital floor. "You'd like her mother. She's Venezuelan. Lots of cats."

"I hate cats."

The line faded and when it came back he was laughing. Five thousand miles away she heard her son's illicit laugh. "Her husband came home while we were upstairs. She made me lie under the bed. He'd come home with a fever. Go home and go to bed, said the doctor. So he went straight to bed. I had to lie there all afternoon, all night until – Mother? Are you there?"

"Thank God, he's alive, that's all," Marie Amaral told herself that evening as she bundled up the hill from Santa Maria de Africa, not knowing where she was going, still thinking of the home-grown prayer she had said for her son – she who in thirty years had never attended Mass.

She was confused and upset. Because of his accident she had turned to a God she didn't much believe in, a God who inspired in her a feeling of intense irritation whenever she bothered to think of him and for whom she reserved the ungainly anger timid women have when they lose their temper.

The Bible was a book written by men, she once informed old Padre Ruiz. And she knew men. David's God had failed him. Why should He help her?

But this evening she had prayed and – this was the odd thing – as she prayed, there had come into her mind an extraordinary image, a figure she recognised as Tromso Ortiz. She had seen the director only from the back, with a worn carpet of hair as if the leg of a heavy chair had been removed. He was telling the cameraman what to do. He was appealing for quiet.

"But is your son all right?" asked Wavery.

"He'll be fine, I'm sure. He's tougher than any ox, he says."

"Please. Stay for a drink. Or I could offer you tea?"

She smiled at him. It was funny, there had been times when, reading her texts, she could have cried for the gentle reassurance of an Englishman.

"Some English tea?"

He led her through the residence, to the terrace. "I'll put the kettle on," he said. He was alone in the house, Halima having asked to leave early. She wanted to visit the market on her way to the mosque. Tomorrow her family would feast the end of Ramadan.

Wavery returned moments later with a tray and two cushions. "Here. Put that under you." Because of the dust, he explained, he never left the cushions outside. He sat down on the hard metal chair. Out of habit he patted the side of the teapot. It was standard issue, made of green porcelain.

"I'm afraid it's nothing like yours," he said.

"I like your dove tree. It is a dove tree, isn't it?"

"Take your pick," said Wavery. "A dove tree, a ghost tree, a handkerchief tree, a *davidia involucrata* . . ."

She moved away. All afternoon, things she didn't want to remember had kept coming back.

"The General must have planted it," he said. "It turns out the roots were blocking the drains."

"And that? I didn't bring you that – or did I?" She pointed at a yellowish green plant covered by the upturned base of a plastic lemonade bottle.

"From Peru," said Wavery, proudly. "I managed to smuggle some seeds."

She bit her lip. Peru, where Periclito was. Stabbing bulls in the Andes. Picking up girls on benches. Bewitching them with his cassoulet. His life one long and melancholy debauchery, strewn with the carcasses – picked, licked and gnawed to the bone – of women who still cared for him, of the animals which had fallen to his terrible pleasure.

"My God, things have come along," she said, raising her arms. "You've changed the house out of all recognition."

"Nothing to do with me," said Wavery. "The person I have to thank is Silkleigh."

Marie Amaral winced. "Ha! Silkleigh."

"Why do you say that?"

She shook her head at him. The Consul General was a childless man, but he was able to excite childish emotions in her. "I'm sorry. It does not matter."

Wavery agreed, "Silkleigh can be excruciating, but he's no more than a harmless British eccentric."

This was more than Marie Amaral could swallow. She looked at Wavery in a long cold stare. "Please do not pull your wool over my eyes, señor. You know what Silkleigh is. You know perfectly well what Silkleigh is."

"But, madame, what are you talking about? What do you know about Silkleigh?"

"I know all about Silkleigh. In the same way Silkleigh knows all about me."

We forge our own shadows. That's what Marie Amaral had come to learn, and one of hers was the English diver. He was a constant reminder of how she came to fetch up on these shores. For three decades he had dogged her, from the day she had screamed him out of her door in Oran and into the Rue Balzac. Less than two months later she was looking at his face in a newspaper. The man who claimed to be David's friend was a wanted man. He had been arrested at Joy's Grill half a block from Oran's main police station. He had put on weight since she had seen him. He was accused of selling arms to the OAS. He had escaped custody through a guardroom window while awaiting interrogation. "This man is dangerous," read the caption.

"When I arrive in Abyla who is the first person I see?" said Marie Amaral. "Your harmless friend."

"He was a gunrunner?" said Wavery, astonished. "For those fascists?"

"He must have told you."

"No, madame, he's never talked about you."

"Not about his friend Major Merimée?"

"Not at all."

"He hasn't told you I am an illegal immigrant." After all, a diplomat was a diplomat. Silkleigh might have traded his knowledge of her illegality for some favour.

"No. No. No."

Marie Amaral nodded to herself. "He may be a spy and a shit and a gunrunner. He may have done all those things in my husband's country. Neverthless, I esteem him for his discretion."

Wavery, pouring the tea, said, "How do you take it?"

But she was sobbing. Periclito's accident. The General's tree. The Consul General's teapot. Silkleigh. It was too much. She had not wept since Oran. And now some little breeze at the wrong moment had dissolved her proud shell. She was shaken by the fact she had exposed Silkleigh. Also impressed, she had to admit, by the discovery that he had revealed nothing.

"Marie, Marie!" said Wavery and he came towards her as if he was David about to lift her in his arms. That evening Wavery became the second person Marie Amaral told about Major Merimée.

The Frenchman dragged her from the window, out of the light. He was nervous. He tried to whistle. He whistled "Strasbourg, Strasbourg, You Lovely, Lovely Town" as he closed the door of her room. She wanted to tell him to stop whistling but terror silenced her. Major Merimée unbuttoned his shirt. The buttons were white except for one which must have come off and been replaced with a yellow button. The thread was sticking out. His touch was delicate. His palms had been torn by razor blades, hidden in the pockets of Arabs he had searched.

She told Wavery, "I wanted to meet a Frenchman and the first Frenchman I met raped me." She remembered only the smell in the room. It was a familiar smell. She had smelled it issuing from small restaurants on the Rue Narbonne, and once at a barbecue beneath her father's lemon trees. Afterwards Merimée's confidence returned. He did not appear concerned that the car outside might be identified, or the body it contained. It was as if he knew no one would come knocking. He crossed an arm behind his dyed head and talked. About St-Cyr. Vietnam. Oran. He had been responsible for the bomb which blew Colonel X through his ceiling. He would like to do the same to his president. De Gaulle was a Jew. A drunk. A traitor. "I'd make him swallow his medals. One after the other," he said, and then he hit her across the face. Her nose began to bleed.

294

Some drops of blood fell on his stomach. He picked her skirt from the floor and wiped them off.

"Here," he said, screwing her skirt into a tight bundle and giving it to her. She thanked him.

At last he left. It was with relief she found Rosita sleeping.

"They killed the wrong man," she told Wavery. "They raped the wrong woman. When they found out what they had done, they were too ashamed to confront me. So they used Silkleigh. They used him to buy me off . . ."

"But what on earth was Silkleigh . . . ?"

There was a movement on the adjoining balcony. Genia Ortiz was opening her windows. "I think it might be better if we went inside," said Wavery.

Later he walked her home. She lived near the Tercio Museum on Paseo Colon. He held her arm and she talked as if she had no power to stop.

She didn't know what had happened to Major Merimée. Pardoned, perhaps. Running a pharmacy somewhere in Périgord, where he chucked the chins of village children. Or guillotined at Barberousse after living for a fortnight on sardines and spaghetti. She didn't know and she didn't care.

But it was a relief to speak about it. Abylans didn't have the faintest clue. You didn't know where to begin. And why upset people? Once she had visited a psychologist. She had wanted to discuss her son. All she could face talking about were indigenous trees.

"I didn't want him. I tried to abort him. Normally you want your child to be like you, to repeat something in you. But not with Periclito."

They had arrived at the entrance of her apartment.

"Will you come in?" she asked.

"I have to finish packing," said Wavery. "Tomorrow I'm going to Africa. But promise me, Marie, you will come back whenever you like, as often as you like."

She opened the glass door into the block. "I am safe here, aren't I, señor? They won't find out, they won't deport me?"

295

"They won't find out."

Wavery waited until the lift cage protected her. Once more someone had read too much into his silence, mistaking it for authority. Once more someone had told him their life's sorrows. Privately, was she upset he hadn't come in? He knew enough about human nature to know you didn't necessarily embrace the first weeping French widow you met. Yet after what Marie Amaral had said about Silkleigh, what did he know about human nature? He had been so certain he knew the kind of man Silkleigh was, and he had been proved wrong. What further misconceptions was he capable of?

But it wasn't the time to be thinking of that. Not now. Tomorrow, after an abyss of nine months, he was meeting Catharine Riding.

6

At three-thirty on the following day Britain's Consul General to Abyla prepared to leave the Consulate for the short walk to the Hotel Zamora. He had reserved a hotel in Chauen for his weekend and was not planning to return to Abyla until Monday.

He had worked through the lunch hour.

In the morning he had telexed his acting Head of Department, informing him that bar the installation of a flagpole, expected any day from Gibraltar, the redecoration of the Abyla residence was complete. He had also drafted, and then, by God, sent a telegram of pure vitriol to his brother-in-law who had written about certain rumours to reach him concerning the state of readiness at the Abyla end. Wavery had taken the sincerest pleasure in instructing Air Vice-Marshal Sir Lawrence Tredwell to mind his own business.

Although he wore no tie, he was carefully dressed. Waking that morning before the alarm and disarming it, he had spent a while choosing which shirt he would wear, which jacket, which trousers. The green tweed jacket was new, fitted for him by a Fulham tailor in under two weeks. "You can wear the bottom button undone," the man had said. "In fact I advise you to do so."

He rose from the desk, feeling in his pockets for the keys of the Daimler. It was three thirty-five and she was arriving at four.

"Ah, *ambasadoro*. Is this a good moment?"

"To be honest, Silkleigh, no, it is not."

"I won't keep you long. I just need *eine kleine* cheque off you," said Silkleigh. "I've got to go to Gib to collect one or two artefacts and I thought I would pay your hungry workers. Then Cochabamba and I plan to za-za up the coast for a couple of days. I've reached a rather excitable stage with the girl."

He handed Wavery his invoice. It was the sum agreed on the terrace four months before. Wavery wrote out a cheque.

"Are you sure that covers everything?"

"Absolutely, old soul," said Silkleigh, opening his notebook. He folded the cheque between the pages.

Despite what he had learned last night from Marie Amaral, Wavery said, "I'm very grateful." Until Silkleigh had come to his rescue the man had been steadily driving him insane. But his workmen had been first-rate and there had not been a single harassment from London since their arrival.

"You know Silkleigh," said Silkleigh. "Anything for Queen and country."

Wavery was seasoned to the diver's banter. "How's the book?" he asked. He could afford to be generous for a few minutes more. Silkleigh had frequently swum into Wavery's thoughts as he sat writing on the terrace. He had wished to avoid Silkleigh's example, casting out stories he would never use, stories like fish, throwing fish that were too little back into the water, swimming away from the page which might describe his life, forever in search of one more shiny, slippery, rainbow-finned excuse. The whole point of Catharine's letter, Wavery understood on his terrace, was that it gave him no excuse.

"I've begun," said Silkleigh.

"The same title?" asked Wavery.

"Covers so many things, *On the Rocks*," said Silkleigh. Love.

Ships. The Pillars of Hercules. He was calling Chapter Two "A Croupier in Haiti".

"Well, I think that's all," said Wavery, now anxious to leave. "Isn't it?"

But Silkleigh stood there. "I saw you walking Marie Amaral home last night, *ambasadoro*. Is that going well, then?"

In his life before Catharine, Wavery might have ignored such a question. Fired by her imminent arrival, he sat back. He said, "Tell me something, Silkleigh. You claim to be the possessor of archives in this place. You claim to know everything. Tell me about Marie Amaral. You've told me about everyone else in Abyla, but not about her. You've never talked about her, or her son. What about them?"

"You mean Periclito?"

"That's right."

"The bullfighter?"

"And his mother. Go on, tell me."

Silkleigh looked more uncomfortable than Wavery had seen him. "Truth is, old soul, there you've got me. I don't know much about Periclito. Or his mother."

Wavery said, "That's not what I've heard, Silkleigh. Marie Amaral tells me she knew you in Algeria."

"Algeria?" said Silkleigh, his expression changing.

Wavery leaned forward. "What the bloody hell were you doing standing behind those French fascists?"

"It's not what you think, Mr Wavery." Silkleigh's barside manner had vanished. "Technically, I was working alongside the French government. I was supposed to infiltrate the OAS bastards."

"And then you came here, to Franco's Spain."

"Well, I do less and less. Anyway, it was a surveillance job. I didn't kick anyone in the stomach."

"What do you mean by that?"

All of a sudden Silkleigh had the steadfast air of a man who is pretending he hasn't seen an acquaintance in the street. He looked for a place to moor his eyes. He settled on Wavery's swimming trunks.

"Chapter Nine," he began. "In which Joseph Silkleigh, author, reveals to Thomas Wavery, the painful and hideous truth of Marie Amaral and in so doing reveals the hideous truth about himself, a confession indeed with far-reaching consequences for Thomas Wavery, whose mind is more preoccupied with the coming weekend."

"What *are* you talking about?"

"Listen, old soul . . . I'll have to come clean."

"Clean?" said Wavery. "Clean about what?"

For a second Silkleigh the author did not seem aware of how to continue. "The fact is, *ambasadoro*, you do one job. I do another."

"What job?" But even as Wavery asked the question, its dreadful answer was taking shape in his mind. "Silkleigh? What job?"

"I had a message from my people. They said to keep an eye on you."

Wavery looked at him, absorbing the implications of what Silkleigh was saying. He shook his head. He was stunned. Good God Almighty. This was the man he'd been patronising for months. He had made a complete drawing of Silkleigh's life and got him one hundred per cent wrong. The man he had hired as his foreman was in all probability a senior employee in his own organisation. He felt an explosion of rage. He sprang up. This was Queesal's doing!

"You bastard. You fucking bastard, Silkleigh. That's a most disgusting game to play. Why didn't you come clean before?"

Silkleigh went on. "*Kara mia*, you've been slightly out of earshot of the old *on dit*. They think you're unreliable. They thought there was the strong likelihood you might go off your rocker. The fact is they wanted me to put your house in order for this Royal Visit."

"So Pas de Problème and Plaisir des Yeux . . ."

"I found them jobs on the tunnel. If I hadn't told those sweeties to fuck off they'd have seen in the millennium."

Wavery's rage was no sooner expressed than it expired. A year ago, this revelation might have devastated him. Not today.

Not now. Silkleigh had offended a pride Wavery no longer took in his profession. Wavery had been reacting with the last vestiges of a Foreign Office man. But he was no longer such a creature. Since leaving Lima he had come to learn a truth fiercer even than pride. When a heart is utterly engaged nothing else matters.

Silkleigh said, "I can see your poor old mind going ooh-ah, *ambasadoro*. All I've been doing is standing around at second slip."

He was speaking to an empty room. Hearing a bell, Wavery had looked at his watch and surged from the Consulate as if one of Don Ponciano's champion bulls was after him.

7

The silver Daimler scattered the weeded gravel outside the Hotel Zamora and sped out of the Plaza de Africa towards the Moroccan border. Captain Panteco, standing on the red battlement of the fortress of San Felipe, did not see the car pass beneath. A part of his mind was on El Callado: he was on the brink of an arrest. He was concentrating, too, on the Arab who would fire the cannon. Too many times he had relied on Santa Maria's bell.

Another minute.

Panteco waited for the sun to lower itself over the escarpments of La Mujer Muerta. The light that gilded the cactus and haloed the backs of the dust-coloured sheep burnished his face. It was time. It was the end of Ramadan.

"OK, Mohamed," he said, and threw his cigarette lighter to the boy. The young Arab approached the loaded cannon. It hunched on a rotting wooden frame, one side more rotten than the other so that the massive bronze nose tilted at an angle between the ramparts. The barrel, corroded and green, was aimed at the sun. He rested a hand on the lifting handle, a dolphin with fins of acanthus, and applied Panteco's cigarette lighter.

There was a loud boom! and the sun died and fireworks raced

through the dusk above the roofs in El Hadu, twisting like sprats, frothing the night with red and gold and diverting the eyes of her children from the yard where Halima was slitting the throat of a lamb to feast the end of thirty days fasting, to feast a white spine of moon.

A horse shuddered at the firecrackers. Someone blew notes through a flute carved from a water pipe. A dog licked blood from the earth. The blood dripped from the suspended lamb, its carcass skinned and gleaming but for a small black head.

PART FOUR

Chapter Twelve

I

THREE DAYS LATER, on Monday evening, Wavery thrust himself through the tunnellers on Marina Española. It was the end of the afternoon shift and the yellow millipede was making its way home towards El Hadu. Among the *ratas* Wavery caught sight of Pas de Problème, who tried to hide his face.

Wavery pushed his way to the tail and walked in long strides beside the Playa Benitez, towards the mirador from where he hoped to watch the ferry carrying Catharine to Algeciras. Beyond the cemetery, the road rose steeply. The evening smelled of pine trees. The only movement was the smooth white drift of gulls against Monte Hacho. He reached the mirador, Abyla's highest point. An old man smoked kif against the hermitage wall. On the wall above his turban, graffiti told of couples who had contemplated the same view of Europe. He saw Wavery and spat into the bushes. A grey mast rose from a flowerbed glittering with empty beer cans. There was a cement wreath and a slab impressed by two small footprints. The heels were General Franco's, who, after praying to the Virgin of Africa, had directed his convoy across the Straits. This was the southern Pillar of Hercules.

There was a mist in the channel, and Catharine's ferry seemed to be borne away on it. Some time elapsed before Wavery admitted to himself he no longer saw the smoke from its funnel. The sun had set and the beam from the lighthouse parried the dusk. Near to shore, a lamp glinted on trails of coloured paper which groupers would mistake for sprats. From the south-east there was a light breeze. It was aromatic with hemp and carried the unmistakable cry of an ibis, nesting out of sight behind the fort.

A blankness assailed Wavery. He felt dead. He covered his face with his hands and knew himself to be alive only by the warm breath on his skin. The tears made an uncomfortable, ticklish path down his cheeks, lodging awkwardly on his upper lip before descending faster.

"Catharine!" he shouted.

Against the hermitage wall, the old man shifted on his bag. He removed the kif pipe from his mouth and opened his eyes.

"Catharine!"

The man grunted, as if telling Wavery to be quiet. He spat again into the bushes.

2

"Where were you?" Queesal sounded livid. He had been appointed Wavery's Head of Department.

"I was in Africa," said Wavery.

"I know. I tried your hotel."

"I changed my name."

"You did what?"

"For anonymity."

"What name?"

"Riding."

"You –" There was incredulity in the voice. Some automatic instinct for self-preservation stopped Wavery from replacing the receiver.

He said, "So you don't care what the Berbers are thinking?"

"That, Thomas, is precisely why we were trying to contact you. The PUS is, frankly, anxious."

"Why?"

"He's received an intelligence report about the tunnel. Con-

306

trary to what you are telling us, there's a suspicion it won't be ready by August."

"I'm sorry to hear that," said Wavery, as if the matter no longer directly concerned him.

"The Foreign Secretary shares his anxiety and so, I gather, does the Prime Minister, and, I might tell you, so do I. There's a belief growing PDQ that if we can't extract certain guarantees from your end, we might have to find an excuse to call the whole thing off. At least for the time being."

A telephone sounded in the background. "It would help if I had your unequivocal assurance . . . Hang on," he said. "Hello? Oh, Sir Derek. Yes. One moment. Tom? I've got to go."

Asunción opened the window. "Aren't you hot in here?" she said.

"I suppose so."

But his secretary wasn't thinking of the heat. She was thinking, Whatever happened in Chauen? Another man had returned from Africa. His eyes were hammocked with tiredness and his mouth was folded up and misery invaded his voice.

Before his weekend in the mountains, on the occasions when he was distracted, Asunción had felt able to tell him so. She would tell Wavery he needed to get out more, see more people, go to the cinema: it wasn't enough to make do with her father's books. You only had to look at her father, who had withdrawn into his murex shell on the third floor where he sat day and night, typing into the computer. His shape before the screen was so inert she had become worried. Soon, if they turned him over, she warned Clotilda, they would find a catalogue number.

Before, when she told these things to Señor Wavery, he would make jokes about saucepans. But that was then. Since Africa, he had passed beyond the saucepan stage. There was in his face an indelible pain. It was a look she recognised well. It reminded Asunción of Clotilda's face when Almestor, her first serious boyfriend, had left for Fez with Mariano, the photographer-monk. It was her own dishevelled face on the night when she lay in bed with Tromso, his ears cold on her chest, and found herself saying simply: "It's over, isn't it?" Most of all it was her father's face in the weeks after her mother died. When she came to her beastly death her mother's concern was for Teodoro, that he would cope, and he had not.

But when she asked the Consul General if there was anything the matter, Wavery had said, "Asunción, I can't talk about it, not now."

The truth was he had become a stranger to himself. He was lost and in this state he had grabbed at the one characteristic of his former self he remembered with confidence. What had happened between himself and Catharine in Africa he didn't want to believe, and therefore it wasn't true.

"Where were we?" he asked. When Queesal telephoned, they had been checking the guest list for the reception to be held at the residence.

Wavery looked down the list. The supreme head of the Nigerian Military Council had replied. So had the chairman of the telephone exchange and Señor Lavandier, manager of the antimony works.

"We've had three enquiries from British residents in Tangier," said Asunción. "They want to know why they haven't been invited." London had been unrelenting about numbers.

"And there's Volta," said Wavery, recalling the Italian Consul General.

Asunción added his name. "Another call from Genia Ortiz . . ."

Wavery said, "Let her come."

She said, "That makes two hundred exactly."

"No one vital we've left out?"

She thought not.

"I'll take it home. Meanwhile we'd better answer these," said Wavery. He reread the top letter on the mound. "To the Chairman of the World Wildlife Fund," he said and he dictated his assurance that the military authorities had been left in no doubt of HRH's express wish to dispense with a motorcycle escort, or anything that might risk disturbing the ibis, especially now that a chick had hatched.

"To your father," he said and he dictated a regret that Her

Majesty would be unable to accept the President's invitation to the bullfight, but would instead be represented by her Consul General.

"To the Chief of Protocol," he said. To the last he conveyed his pleasure to learn that in honour of the forthcoming Royal Visit and at some stage during her stay in Abyla, most likely in the privacy of his residence, Her Majesty would be graciously pleased to appoint Thomas Wavery a Knight Commander of the Royal Victorian Order.

Sir Thomas Wavery. He tried out the words on himself, but took no pleasure at the thought.

"Keep that under your hat," he added, looking at Asunción over his spectacles. "Is that it?"

"There's a letter marked personal."

Wavery accepted the envelope, addressed in Penny's handwriting. It contained a photograph of a house and an invitation to the private view of her exhibition. A message on the back said, "I know you can't come." But she was crossing her fingers for the Royal Visit.

The photograph was of a modest house of autumnal stone, a single oak twisting above the gabled roof. Penny stood on the chequer-mown lawn with her wind-cheatered back to Wavery.

He turned over the house. "Hornbeams, near Poole". His hands pushed themselves under his spectacles.

Asunción stood up. She addressed the magnified knuckles. "I've asked for the wine to be delivered tomorrow."

The hands fell away.

"I think I might go home now."

3

It was Halima's afternoon off. Wavery walked his body up the stairs, into the kitchen where Silkleigh sat on the table, boots on chair.

"How was Africa?"

309

"Fine," said Wavery. "Just fine."

Silkleigh tugged at his right eye. "True love," he said. "Dangerous ground. Not to be occupied by a novice." But he wasn't interested in Wavery's weekend in Africa. He was high on himself, so pleased with his achievement of the day before that he had forgotten all about his autobiography, about Rosita, about the undeniable advantages of the international language by means of which the world would become one great family circle. Emilio's boat had been found. "And you'll never guess who I discovered inside!"

Silkleigh rattled on ceaselessly and Wavery was content to listen.

He had been diving with Cochabamba between La Mujer Muerta and Punta Benzú when he saw the familiar shape of a ballast stone on the discoloured sand. He saw another stone beyond, and beyond that another, where Emilio had ripped out the bottom of his boat as he beat the sinking craft to windward. Silkleigh followed the trail to an ochre hull which lay on a reef among the wrecks of a Spanish wine-carrier and a seventy-four-gun English frigate, sunk in 1796.

"The sea proves whatever it does, it repeats," Silkleigh told Cochabamba.

A skeleton floated upright in the engine room. The body had been prevented from getting away by the *palangre* line. The rope entangled his ankles and was orange with blob buoys.

"Cochabamba knew who it was, sure enough. Even without his face." El Callado had been on Emilio's boat that day, having boarded at Las Palmas with his cargo. The cocaine was in the blob buoys. "It wasn't all fish that came to Emilio's net," observed Silkleigh. But that's how the fisherman had paid for his boat. El Callado was preparing to drop the *palangre* line when the *Grau* carved through the fog.

"There was one thing Cochabamba didn't know," went on Silkleigh, half addressing himself. He was exultant. "She didn't know that I knew all along."

The girl was the first assignment in years to excite him. He had been here a lifetime, doing odd jobs for the British, Interpol

– but not the French. They asked him once but he said no, not after Algeria.

"Frankly, when Cochabamba arrived, I couldn't give a fish's tit about any of them." But he could see what Cochabamba was up to. There was no question of him being at the dictate of her wrist. He had seen it all, all very distinctly, from the moment in their first conversation when he said, "Will you come out to sea? Tomorrow? Diving?" Because Cochabamba's principal interest consisted not in hotels, nor in water-purification systems, still less in dining somewhere with Silkleigh tête-à-tête which was why she could never make tomorrow night, and it was always can-I-wait-and-see about next week. Then, who knows? But if he happened to be taking his boat out diving, that was another matter. Cochabamba would always come diving. Then she would kiss him, liberating his tongue with hers if only for a brief second. "Can I come?" she'd say. "My *kleine belulino*. Of course, give me your hand, sit there," and they'd head out to sea and he would feel a sort of thwarted contentment.

He never touched her, not beyond putting a few munches on her. He might like to have spent any number of nights inside her underpants, but no, that wasn't on. "Sad to relate, it was the old Jesuit training. The more you conquer, the more there is to conquer. That's what they taught me about crumpet, old soul."

Wavery rubbed his neck. He was glad to concentrate on anything that would divert his mind from his weekend in Africa.

"But, Marie, what do you do when you want to forget?" he had asked, as he walked her home.

"I do what I've always done. I stare at something so strongly, it becomes something else. If I stare at something strongly enough, I can usually leave myself behind."

Wavery stared hard at Silkleigh and here in the residence kitchen he began at long last to see the Englishman for what he really was. A most successful provider of truths and disguises. An observer, leading other people down the garden path while absorbing any number of insults along the way. His cover had been sea-going, but it had become a passion too. Some people

311

spent whole lifetimes looking for a cover in order to disguise what they didn't do with their lives. Silkleigh had met his passion by way of his cover. Out of doors he was the fantasist. He flicked haloes at stones on the sand. He passed his torch over deep-sea creatures. He imagined their stories. But when he returned home and bolted the door behind him, he was a very good agent. A better agent, on paper, than Wavery ever was a diplomat.

With Cochabamba, Silkleigh had again been deceiving the deceiver.

Wavery asked, "Where is Cochabamba now?"

Silkleigh waved his Rolexed wrist in a gesture of farewell. With a trace of regret he said, "She won't be coming back."

Wavery walked over to the sink. He found a glass on the draining board and filled it with water.

Silkleigh removed his feet from the chair and stood up. "You still haven't told me about Africa."

Wavery drank. There was no doubt, since Silkleigh had installed his system under the sink, the water tasted fresher.

Silkleigh said, "I must say I've always found Chauen very overrated. There's one hotel and nothing else."

Wavery refilled his glass and drank again.

"Eye does not see, heart does not suffer," continued Silkleigh. "Perhaps you could change sex, like a cuckoo wrasse." When still Wavery had uttered no word Silkleigh said softly, "I'll go now, *kara mia*. I've got to arrange some security for this jamboree of yours. But before I go – if I could have your concentration for just two minutes – let me show you what I did today," and guiding Wavery into the Royal Suite, pungent with new chintz, he led him to the window.

"There. Look."

Wavery followed the direction of his finger. Bolted to the curving green ironwork of the balcony and rising like a gigantic bull's pizzle into the evening above the tattered palms on the Marina Española, above the tunnel mouth, above the cranes and the fishing boats and the camp-fire lights of Europe, he saw a lean, varnished pole at the top of which flapped the Union Jack.

"Up the flag!" said Silkleigh. "Which reminds me, what do you think of *Wavery's Last Post?*"

"But I thought you'd –"

A shudder ran through the house and Wavery had the sensation of something disintegrating in the vitals of the building, as if a structure had fainted.

4

Genia Ortiz felt the earth buckling in her sleep. She had retired to bed for a siesta and lay with her white hair in a net and her cheeks carefully not touching the pillow. She made up her face once a week, on Sundays before Mass. Otherwise she slept in her make-up, her face preserved beneath one of those masks distributed to first-class passengers on transatlantic flights. She had never yet travelled on an aeroplane, still less first class. The mask was a gift from Tromso.

Her baton lay beside her on the sheet, to stab out the eyes of intruders. On the right-hand side of the bed, where Ernesto had slept, *El Faro* was open at the arts page on which in large red circles she had ringed three literals.

Often, before his banishment to the guest room, Ernesto would be woken by his wife calling "Daddy! Daddy! We're stuck on a sand bank." Tonight her face was calm. A dictionary at her side, she had written to the Mayor of Balnasharki, informing him of her arrival at the end of August. She had been able to pay for her passage with the compensation owing to her by the Straits Tunnel consortium for aural abuse. On the day after the tunnel opened she would travel through it to Gibraltar where she would take her berth aboard the cruise-liner *Hummingbird* which would transport her as far as the Crimea. From there she would board a train to Kiev. Soon she would be repacking the green trunk under her bed. Soon she would be in Balnasharki again.

Since Christmas Genia Ortiz had existed in a state of pathological expectation. To those few who knew her intimately, it seemed something miraculous might be occurring.

"Is it me?" Senator Zamora asked Asunción. "Or is her squint disappearing?"

On her window cushion in the Calle Zamora she swallowed in vodka gulps the latest progress of the tunnel. To her collection of photographs on the cushion, she had added her boat ticket to Odessa, a new passport (her Nansen passport having been rejected by the travel agent), and three polaroids sent by the Mayor of Balnasharki.

In his most recent letter, the Mayor explained that the house and stables had been used to quarter twenty-four families. What looked like small flying buttresses were outside latrines. Señora Ortiz would find the central structure unaltered – although the cupola had been reconstructed with roof tiles, not copper plate. If she wished to reclaim from the council the lake and the east side of the park where it adjoined the town, he would do his utmost to assist her.

This was the fourth such letter she had received from the Mayor, a former theatre director. Each time he grew more expansive. "How well I know your family home!" he had informed her in a reply to her first letter. He had received his ideology schooling in the ballroom. Once a month he had sat beneath the finial-capped cupola while a man gave a lecture about communism's role in the modern world. "Everybody slept, including the communists. We looked at the dome. We looked at the lawn outside. We looked at the lake. Everwhere but at the lecturer. It was a comic dream."

He welcomed the end of that dream in a footnote to his next letter.

The difference between communism and capitalism had not been a difference between systems, he explained, but between nature and anti-nature. Capitalism was cruel, but normal. "The sin of communism is that it is abnormal. You cannot imagine, Evgenia Nikolaevna, how many of my generation became alcoholics, complaining, feeling miserable, day after day. A huge part of the population drank itself unconscious. Most of them divorced at least once. It became such a run-down country. Everyone, including my predecessor, had moments when they

314

wanted to leave. None of us found the energy. There was a universal lethargy."

She detected a note of apprehension in his latest communication. "I was thirty-four years in the theatre and for thirty-four years my theatre was sold out. Our problem in a totalitarian régime was too much culture. People wept when they saw Chekhov. They needed him. Now they are free, they don't need him any more. I'm very depressed, Evgenia Nikolaevna. We haven't had jokes since the communists have gone. I tell you very cynically, the bad have come back and they think themselves better than anyone else because they happen to have acquired the manners of a Viennese concierge. People here assumed that BMWs would come with democracy. Quite a lot did, but quite a lot were driven by those who steered the previous régime." He asked her forgiveness for writing so self-indulgently and at such length, but he wished to prepare her for what she might find. The longest journey was to return, he warned. "In the Ukraine today, perhaps there is no such thing as a return."

"What do you think, skunk?" Genia Ortiz had addressed a coloured photograph of Ernesto taken one week before his death. He was leaning on the balcony, making as if to hurl himself off. He was humming Bartók.

As well you might, she told him. His rehabilitation had been slow to establish itself. In fifteen years this was Ernesto's first time out of the green trunk. It had coincided with the arrival of her ticket.

She heard his hum. Lately she had dreamed of him, making him less stout, paring away the daddy-longlegs that fluttered from his nostrils, straightening his teeth, adding more broken-wired hair. In her dream a reconciliation had taken place in the Plaza de los Reyes. She wanted to make herself beautiful for him, but her curlers had short-circuited. She had bought a pair of sunglasses, to hide the disconcerting angle of her gaze, and because she worried she would break into tears. In the event, it was Ernesto who burst into tears.

"Do you still have bones in your heart?" he asked, seeing the unmelting snow of her expression. "Didn't you get the flowers?"

"What flowers, Ernesto?"

He had asked Marie Amaral to send gypsophila and jasmine, but the message must have reached her stall too late. The flowers had not arrived.

"My halfness," he hummed.

"Skunk." Senator Zamora was right. He was all tone, no content.

She sought another photograph of him, wearing a Moravian hat. In this one, he had an irritating expression. He misled in his photographs, as elsewhere. In life he wasn't as facetious as he seemed here, posing with one arm around the artist Alphonse Mucha and the other about the neck of a terrified Tahitian model who had once sat for Gauguin.

Would his eyes have widened so approvingly at the dress Marie Amaral was making for Genia Ortiz? What would he have thought of his widow's journey home? Would she have permitted him to share her berth on the *Hummingbird*? A gum-pink slipper circled the air. In her excitement she thought of their *nuits folles*. Too impatient to suck, she munched on a vita-min pill and looked away, to the balcony where she had heard him humming.

At the sight of her pelargoniums, Genia Ortiz was reminded to ask Marie Amaral to cover the plants with plastic, so the sparrows wouldn't peck at them in her absence. She would have asked the Consul General, but she had not set eyes on Wavery for several days. While she welcomed the sight of his lovely garden, she had become more than a fraction irritated with her English neighbour. The way he sat himself at that table, evening after evening. He was boring. He never entertained. Ever! And now that his house was ready he had sealed himself away inside.

Last Monday, worried that she had not yet received her invi-tation to the reception at the British residence, she had tele-phoned Wavery at home. She pretended she was trying to reach Asunción, but had muddled the numbers.

"Oh! Señor Wavery, that's not you? I hope I have not dis-turbed your writing." But since she had him on the line, would he perhaps care to come to a little dinner party she was giving

316

on Saturday. It wasn't smart. Nothing here ever was. But he would know them all.

"I suppose you might almost call it *une soirée d'adieu*. There'll be Senator Zamora and his daughters. Madame Amaral, the flower seller. The Governor and his wife. So I think you'll have some fun. At least *we* don't have to respect this fasting."

She waited for him to respond with his own invitation.

"That's kind of you, Señora Ortiz, but I'd better say no. I'm hoping to be in Africa this weekend."

"Africa?" repeated Genia Ortiz, uncertain whether she had heard correctly.

No. Señor Wavery had not turned out to be the asset to Abylan social life she once anticipated.

And now it was late afternoon and she slept and her husband floated beside her, sharing her glucose memories. Together they heard the bell ring through the water, not the cathedral bell ringing for Mass, but the bell her mother rang every evening before tossing bread at the lake. Her body lifted from the deep. It had taken her more than seventy years to rise this far. She rose evenly towards the surface. Her back shattered the water and the lake rippled into oily patches of colour. She was opening her mouth to feed when she saw a figure on the hard-frozen bank. He was bending down. His gloves were scraping the ground and there were figures on either side of him. Some carried torches over their heads, the flames falling orange on the snow. Others were pointing at the water, pointing guns. Colonel Slava! she thought. She saw the snowball in his hand as a terrible noise churned the air.

Senator Zamora arrived within moments and five minutes later, Asunción.

"It's all right, Genia," said Senator Zamora as she lolled her head now on one shoulder, now on another, her face pale as tissue. He too had felt troubled fins breaking the earth as he worked at his computer.

She said, one hand searching her breast, "Pablo's right. I'm getting very old, Teodoro."

317

"Nonsense, Genia."

"What do you mean 'nonsense'? Dr Alvaro said I should think of a hip operation. I have to look up words in a dictionary. I have to get up in the night the whole time."

Zamora realised he had not extended the appropriate sympathy. "But look at you! Even now you look wonderful."

He was dressed in bituminous grey. Nothing could persuade him to remove the colour of his depression. He felt as humourless as destiny. For two weeks he had burned in his poisoned cardigan, the shade of the fatigued sky above his city. Abyla, the design of its houses, the abrupt humps of its promontory, was as much a part of him as his fingertips. The idea that it was to be his no more had meshed together his eyebrows into one inseparable strand of bushy hair.

"Is it true, Teodoro, that you've resigned?"

Senator Zamora took his place beside her. His face was derelict, his eyes sunken. He had resigned, yes, this afternoon at ten past four, shortly after the decision was made to replace Leopoldo Zamora's clock with an electrically operated system manufactured in Zurich. He had been sitting on a bench when his hat blew off and a Benelux official, crossing the square and thinking Zamora must be a tourist down on his luck, threw in a coin. The Senator was required to look for no further sign that his political life had ended. There was nothing more for him to do. He had tried for five years to obstruct the tunnel, but he was no politician. Men who spoke with their heritage in mind made bloody awful politicians. He would remain as a councillor on the Corporación Muncipal until August. He would discharge his duties as President of the Bullfight. After that he would find fulfilment in the bosom of his family, and Menendez whose face was now stamped on posters with the effigy of a baldheaded ibis as a sign that under his historic governorship he had not only emulated the epic engineering feats of Tamburlaine and Xerxes, but managed to keep Abyla "nature friendly" in the process, could kiss the jellyfish.

"They spelled your name wrong," Genia Ortiz said feebly. She wrinkled her nose. Over the linseed on his breath, she sniffed something else. Another minute passed before she realised it was his cardigan.

When Señora Criado suggested she might wash his cardigan Senator Zamora had declined. Besieged by the Moors, Abyla's first governor had worn the same suit of chain mail for sixteen years. Two weeks was nothing. Nothing! On this evening it reeked not of Zamora, but of another of his cook's fiascos. Mournfully, the portraits looked at him as he passed. On the landing there was such dense smog he could see nothing except the feet of his monarch thrust into the air. Coughing, he found the door to his study, but it was Clotilda's bedroom he burst into, interrupting his youngest daughter in the course of a telephone conversation. She was wearing a man's cable knit jersey and there was joy on her face.

He closed the door, gesturing for her to continue the conversation. Far from delighting Senator Zamora, the sight of Clotilda's happiness had unsettled him. There was definitely someone in his daughter's life. He knew this much from the lavish applications of Tromso's make-up, from the time she came home at night, from the time she spent on the telephone. But after six months he was no closer to knowing this person's identity.

When he asked, "Clotilda, is there no one special you wish to bring home to dinner?" she merely became shy.

When he said, "That's a nice jersey, darling," she agreed.

When for her birthday he left outside Clotilda's bedroom a bunch of thirty orchids she had for a moment mistaken their provenance. For the first time in several years, dimples decorated her cheeks.

Who was it she hid in her dimples? Was he a fantasy, like one of those medieval rabbits in her room? Was he a married man? Or a woman? Dear God, was it a repetition of last time? Senator Zamora didn't believe he had the stamina at this moment for another interior decorator, but he supposed anything was more tolerable than the alternative, a prospect which had haunted him since Christmas, and which he didn't have the courage to voice even to Asunción.

319

Senator Zamora was concerned about his daughter and he was heartily sick of politics. Singly he might have coped with these tribulations. But what had added noodles of worry to his brow and made his eyebrows stiff and twisted like a ginseng root, was the matter of Pablo's computer.

This afternoon he had tiptoed through the smoke to the playroom on the third floor. There was only one dignity, he told himself, settling at the keyboard. There weren't two. He was rejoining his people, the bedouin of the sea. Together they would lose themselves in the fabulous mackerel sauces of Carteia. He switched on the computer, he inserted a disc, and calling up his much ignored file on Baal-Rosh, Lord of the Promontory, he faced a blank screen.

In the flickering monitor, through wisps of smoke, he saw the library burning at Carthage. He saw the quinologist's boat sinking in the Bay of Mexico. He heard Virgil's instruction to burn *The Aeneid.*

Senator Zamora removed the disc. He turned off the computer. He turned it on again. He inserted the disc. Nothing! Frantically, he rose from the table to rouse Pablo. But Pablo was in Madrid, visiting his father.

In the nursery, Senator Zamora felt the oblivion of his life's work. His face drained of all erudition. He was considering whether to pitch the computer and all his files into the Calle Zamora when he had felt the rumble in the earth.

"You poor thing," he repeated and he held Genia Ortiz' hand, patterned with spots like a carp's belly. He would go this minute to the work-site. He would speak to the foreman. He would demand to know what had happened.

5

Marie Amaral also felt the tremor in the earth. It travelled up Calle Camoes from the Marina Española, passed beneath the stall where she was sewing the last of the buttons onto Genia Ortiz' dress, and shivered the surface of the fountain.

She sat down hard on a bucket and concentrated on the poster taped to the inside of her door. She read her son's name and looked at the painting of a bull's head. But she felt the tunnel slithering towards her through the earth.

Every time she felt the drilling-machine her heart squeezed back upon itself. It sent out soundless squeals of fear and the tunnel heard. She sensed its vibrations everywhere, in the meek interior of her flowerstall, in her bedroom, in her kitchen where she always kept the radio switched on. Once, during a power cut, she caught herself whistling a tune to hide the noise. She hadn't known the tune. She was wondering where she might have heard it when she realised with a stab of horror she was whistling "Strasbourg, Strasbourg, You Lovely, Lovely Town".

Her nights were torn from the tunnel. She tried to sleep but her dreams were violated by black shapes in laughing silhouette copulating against an orange glow. There was no longer an irritating god to protect her. David's god was in the death-ditch. He floundered there with the prawn heads, the clam shells, the pork gristle, the yellowy sediment flushed by Captain Panteco from the sides of his latrine, the Governor's nail clippings, Señora Menendez' dental floss, red-ringed copies of *El Faro*, flower heads, foetuses, all flowing in a dank tide through the tunnel in which the powers of David's Gehenna seemed united.

Since dissolving into tears on Wavery's terrace four days before, Marie Amaral had worked hard on Genia Ortiz' dress. "Oh, madame! That's going to be marvellous," said the conductor's widow, holding it against her chest. "Now, you'll let me pay you properly." They stood side by side, admiring the dress in the mirror. She was surprised Genia Ortiz didn't notice her seamstress' expressionless face.

She had accompanied Senator Zamora to the cemetery on the headland. After removing his anorak, which Minerva had never liked, and laying seventy-two iris on his wife's headstone he pointed out the empty plot next to it, covered with red sallow. "Hideous aren't they, but I will get the sun." When the sun came out, why didn't he see she cast no shadow?

The shadow she cast was inside her.

Blankly, she told the Dutchman of her requirements for the first week of August. "That'll fill the lorry," he said. "What's it for? Tania's wedding?" Tania, he had to remind her, was the nun in *The Strong Tend to Leave*.

"No," she said, "we're having a bullfight."

She spoke again to Periclito from the telephone in Rosita's shoe shop. After a weekend in bed, he had discharged himself from hospital.

"How's your stomach?"

"I'm not walking gorgeously, but I will be. I will be."

"How's Rosita?"

"My nightingale! My singing Hesperides! She's well, I think," he said. "Although I'm not certain Peru is mature enough for *fado*."

"Is she –"

But Periclito did not wish to speak about his nightingale. He had one thing only on his mind. The *alternativa*! He had thought of nothing else since Christmas. But nothing.

"Who am I fighting with, Maman?" She could forget that unfortunate episode at Huanta. In the past season he had fought with Raul Medniola, Gitanello de America and on a tedious and mediocre afternoon in Tumbes with José Antonio Canetero.

"Wait, Periclito. Wait. Let me get my spectacles." She leaned forward, beckoning Rosita's assistant to open the door so she could read the names printed on the poster.

"From Algeciras, Rafael Lara, 'Larita de Algeciras'. From Cadiz, your sponsor, Antonio Troyano, 'Troyanito'. I'm not sure I know him."

"He's *exceedingly* well known, Maman –"

"And from Abyla, Periclito Merimée Amaral. 'El Terremoto'."

"'The Earthquake'!" He savoured his sobriquet. "You wait, mother. You wait. Only two weeks now."

They both waited, he for his mother to say something, Marie Amaral because she didn't know what he wanted her to say.

"Bye, Maman," said Periclito at last.

322

"What were you saying?" She heard the echoing click at the end of the world. "Bye, Periclito."

And now, sitting on her upturned seat, Marie Amaral thought, Perhaps it wasn't the tunnel after all. Perhaps that's what it was – an earthquake. She looked into the square, not daring to move in case she released the noise trapped beneath her bucket. Oh, Marie Amaral, why did you come here? she asked, feeling the billowing mushroom of her fear. Here of all places?

But her question expected no answer. Thirty-one years ago, she had been left with few alternatives.

One by one the French left Oran. Everyone slept on the quay, waiting for boats. They slept on their suitcases. They learned not to say, "I can't believe this is happening."

Marie Amaral remained. She didn't want to go to France. Or even to Portugal, where David's sister lived. (She had sent Rosita back. She could no longer keep the child.) She didn't want anything more to do with Europe. With Rosita and her baby, she moved out of her house in the Rue Balzac, into a fourth floor walk-up behind the casbah. The other occupants had deserted the block, except for some young men two floors below. They were whispered by the concierge to be OAS, but she ignored the woman, who soon left.

She had lived there two months when those in the flat beneath opened fire on crowds celebrating Independence.

Moments after the young Arab had shot the mirror, three FLN soldiers appeared. They found Marie Amaral wrapping Periclito's head with a towel. Zohra, the maid, had fled and Rosita sat crying in a corner. One soldier collected Silkleigh's money, scattered among glass on the stone floor; another searched the rooms. They drove her in a truck to an austere building near the port. The tarpaulin was torn and everywhere she could see white, green and red flags.

The building was crowded with women and children, and a doctor dashed between rooms. One of the soldiers found a fresh bandage for Periclito's head and gave Rosita a bar of chocolate, making her a paper dart with the wrapper

Marie Amaral was led into a bare room, brightly lit. There was a man holding a camera to his shoulder and another who twisted her head towards it.

"Look there," he told her.

She would be seen that night on the televised news. She was described as the daughter of a *gros colon*, no different from the other fascists sharing her building, who had fired into the peaceful crowd. The only difference was, she lived.

They taunted her. "Why didn't you follow the others, madame? Why don't you go to France?" But they were puzzled. After three days they released her. She signed a paper, agreeing her two children had been well treated by the new authorities. However, she would not be permitted to live in her flat. Her flat had been appropriated for relatives of the victims. She must seek accommodation elsewhere. A hotel was suggested.

Marie Amaral bundled her children and belongings to the one hotel she knew. She spent a fortnight in the Saint-Sulpice, in a small room overlooking the kitchens, hating it. In Oran under the French when she walked down the street she had met others' eyes. She was made to feel as if she existed. Now, after Independence, no one looked at her, not even the hotel waiters. She didn't exist except in the names that were called after her. So she avoided looking at people. If she looked at them it was dangerous. But after a fortnight she did want someone to look at her, to confirm she was alive.

One day she sat in the hotel garden, feeding Periclito. The garden had become an untidy slope of long grass and mud. There were no slats in the benches and she balanced on the frame. She wanted to hear the blackbirds again, but the blackbirds had disappeared. She wanted to weep. She bit her lip. She said, "Don't, Marie Amaral. If you see yourself as a victim, you will excuse yourself anything." She put a hand inside her blouse and when she produced an orange Rosita thought she was plucking out her breast. She peeled the orange and began sharing it with the children.

Then from somewhere, as if a bird had stayed behind after all and was hearing her thoughts, there came a hesitant whistle.

A blackbird! Excited, she looked about. A blackbird! A blackbird! But where? Behind her, Rosita retrieved her paper dart and hurtled towards her.

"There's someone in the grass."

A man stood up. He removed four fingers from his mouth and she recognised David's friend, Hacine the poet. He spoke, but there was something wrong with his mouth. His mouth was an ugly split in his face. With difficulty she caught the words. He said, "They caught me drinking." They had caught him in the garden, behind that tree, drinking from his Rosé Marsala. He touched what might have been a smile. They had cut off his lips, but he could still whistle, still imitate the birds. The soldiers may have eaten them, but they could not prevent him crouching in the long grass. In the evenings he whistled for courting couples. "They don't know! They never guess!" Excitement danced on tiptoe over his eyes. He didn't see the slatless benches, nor the stumps where the trees had been taken for firewood. He saw branches trembling with lovesong in the days of the French occupation.

A tongue peeped at his mouth. He wet his cracked, hideous lips. "Listen."

"Marie! Madame Amaral!"

There was shouting in the square. A man was running from Calle Camoes, where the orange trees were hung with lanterns. He was running towards her. Marie Amaral put down Genia Ortiz' dress and rose from her bucket and was ambushed by the sight of Dr Teodoro Zamora de Avellaneda Mancheño y Centurión.

Marie Amaral did not remember people in abstract, just as she could not remember yellow in abstract. She remembered them in images, in precise, improbable moments. She would never forget the moment on this evening in July when she saw Senator Zamora running towards her.

He was a man who when he walked normally, walked with a loping, graceful stride. He wasn't a man who should be skipping. But he came towards her, skipping.

"Marie!" he called, his face animated by such radiant energy she barely recognised the opposition politician of recent months.

"Marie!"

He seized her about the waist, clasped her to him, kissed her rapturously on one cheek, then another, stroked the hair she had so carefully brushed back, saying, "Marie . . ."

"Teodoro," she murmured. He tried to lift her up but her weight was too much.

"Marie, what news I have for you. What news!"

"What news, Teodoro?" She hitched down his collar and brushed some dandruff from his shoulder.

He gave her a fortune-teller's wink.

"Senator Zamora . . ." Julio Berlaguer, *El Faro*'s cub reporter, had finally caught up with him. Breathlessly, he held out a microphone. "Senator, can you comment on Captain Panteco's speculation that it is the work of the Basques?"

"Later, Julio, later. I have to see Menendez." And Senator Zamora planted a final kiss on Marie Amaral's forehead, before pirouetting across the square towards the Casa del Gobierno with Berlaguer beside him.

6

Ninety feet under the ground, Pas de Problème had been dreaming of Madrid when he felt a jolt. He raised his head. His body was tired. He felt numb from sitting too long in this seat, envious of the colleague who had made it to the other side. Yesterday he had received a postcard from Plaisir des Yeux, of the Prado.

There was another jolt and his machine lunged forward. He heard its famished whine, but instead of earth it bored air. Surprised, he removed the thrust and reversed. He was not drilling under the sea but inland, into the promontory. The direction he was facing, with his back to Europe, in his opinion diminished the likelihood he had met a team advancing from across the Straits. His opinion, admittedly, was not expert. Recruited to work in the spoil lagoon, Pas de Problème had

326

graduated to replacing the teeth on hand-drills. A four-day induction course had led him to where he sat now – at the controls of a rock-boring machine.

He surveyed the bank of VDUs. The laser guidance system told him he had not mistaken the angle of his attack. He climbed from his seat and squeezed between the blades of the drill head.

The passage ahead was silent and dark. He smelled a rancid smell. He called out nervously. "*Allo? Bonsoir, messieurs?*"

He shone his torch to the side of the shaft. Water oozed from the limestone fissures and the soil between had changed colour. He scooped up a handful of the loosened earth and winnowed it. A hard object remained in his glove. It was the fragment of a pot. Panicked, he directed his light at the tunnel face and breath was punched out of him. He dropped the torch and jerked down to retrieve it, but slipped. His body covered the light and the soil entered his mouth. He spat into the darkness, turning from side to side, digging the torch from under him, at the same time stretching out his arms. One hand grabbed air, the other something slippery, disgusting. He moaned to his feet, cannoning backwards into the drill head. The blades dislodged his helmet as he squeezed through. Alerted by the sounds, the Spanish foreman moved to the cabin window. He saw a monster stumble from the earth. Of its face, only the eyes were visible. It staggered forward to the glass, holding out its stiff hands, moaning.

7

"Well," said Menendez, when he heard the news. He stroked the side of his face.

"They refuse to violate sacred ground!" said Senator Zamora, who had read out the law preserving ancient monuments and structures.

"Well, well."

"It could be Lebtit or Exilissa, or even Auza."

The Governor's expression did not change until he swallowed

and then the muscles on his cheeks and forehead came out in relief. He sank back in his chair, hairy hand on white jacket.

"Well, well, well."

Minutes later, Senator Zamora gyrated through the security gate. He moved through the dense assembly of *ratas*, scattering men to the right and left of him.

"Stop!" He stood on the steps of a spoil lorry. He stood seven thousand five hundred and fifty-nine metres tall. "Stop!" he shouted, waving his hat. He held aloft the order for a cessation of all activity while a preliminary excavation was conducted into what in his critical opinion constituted the single most important burial ground in North Africa since Father Delattre's excavation of the necropolis at Carthage.

"It's signed by the Governor!" With those words, Senator Zamora disappeared underground.

8

"What's a tophet?" asked Queesal next morning, sniffing. The news that all the Moroccan workers were refusing to work, coming as it did ten days before the Royal Visit, had reactivated his condition.

"A place of sacrifice," said Wavery. He decided now was not the time to mention its proximity to the residence.

"Humans?" asked Queesal, his tone evoking the circumstances in which he might approve of tophets.

"Animals too."

"I see heads rolling here, Tom. Unless certain things are sorted out PDQ."

"The Governor is adamant this stoppage is a temporary affair."

Something else puzzled Wavery's new Head of Department. "Forgetting, for a moment, the Moroccans. This tophet, from what you say – it's not in the main tunnel."

"They were intending to seal the rock-boring machine there."

"You mean . . . *it's still under the sea*?"

So Senator Zamora was able to tell Asunción. The main shaft was complete, but not yet the service tunnel.

"They reckon on another week."

In London Queesal was silent. He said, "I'll work on a document to preserve the ambiguities of our response. The PUS is going through the programme with the Foreign Secretary tomorrow. It is my feeling the smallest thing at this stage could rock the whole boat. The smallest thing, Thomas."

"The Governor has promised a statement tonight."

"I expect you to ring me immediately."

9

After a night spent underground, Senator Zamora, son of Abyla's most famous son and indefatigable lord of the headland, was not altogether himself.

At lunchtime he stole into the kitchen to clasp his ecstatic cook around her middle. "Whose bread I eat, their song I sing," he crooned, massagingly.

"Señora Criado, what wonderful things are you proposing to gorge us with tonight? Pablo! Money for ice creams? Have your hair cut as well! Clotilda, more of this soup? No, don't get married. A ridiculous institution. Asunción! My turtle-dove! Of course, I'll come to the Consul General's party. Tromso? Dear boy, how are you? We missed you at Christmas. Delighted. Anything to help. I don't know if it would make a *great* film . . ."

In the afternoon *El Faro* had printed a special edition in colour. Senator Zamora was photographed standing on the basaltic cobblestones which paved one of three access shafts to a network of pit tombs submerged by the Lisbon earthquake of 1755.

On the tarpaulin at his feet were samples of initial finds. While his professional colleagues might find precipitate the speed with which he had brought these items to the world's attention, he asked their indulgence. It was necessary to demonstrate beyond doubt the need for an immediate halt to the tunnel before Abyla's heritage was destroyed.

Abdul Hadi, the tunnel-operator, had bored into a chapel consecrated to Baal-Rosh. The exhibits came mostly from this chapel: an ostrich egg with facial markings, some aromatic rushes, a piece of red segamum bark for dysentery and a votive statuette of a veiled lyre-player fashioned in pink granite.

The most impressive object was a marble sarcophagus with a gabled lid. Carved into the marble was the figure of a man, surrounded by birds, animals and fish. Senator Zamora himself could make not head nor tail of the cursive script. But if the text was dedicated to a god, the iconography would suggest Melcart, prince of navigation, dyes and patron of the tophet. Whatever it was, this discovery provided the elusive evidence pre-historians had been waiting for. "This will fill the void in our Punic understanding, a gap which has contributed to the nebulous hypotheses of so many interpreters, notably (and regrettably) from the Peninsula."

The interview extended for three pages during which comparisons were made with Renan at Byblos and Quagliati at Scoglio del Tonno. The Peoples of the Sea, Senator Zamora told *El Faro*, took their ideas from many sources. "And these they felt as free as the *levante* to reinterpret." This explained the thronging intricacies of their art, the outbreak of animal and plant carvings, the abundance of bird and fish imagery.

In their *horror vacui* they omitted nothing. No symbol of faith. No example of daily life. Nothing!

The front page also devoted space to an interview with Governor Menendez. Photographed over three columns, his face in relief not unlike that of the funerary mask discovered by Senator Zamora on the second level, Menendez emphasised the pride he had taken in this discovery. "This is a historic day for Abyla and for Abylans everywhere." As everyone knew, the Phoenicians were a magnificent, much misunderstood race. He confirmed he would be making a statement to the chamber at six-thirty in the evening.

The horizon above La Mujer Muerta darkened with streaks of antimony and in the afternoon it rained. Outside the Governor's palace, the telegraph wires sparked because of a bad connection. Menendez, distracted, watched the sparks from his bedroom and the rain flowing onto the road, like fat on tin foil, hissing. He scratched the back of his square neck.

From her bed, propped on not-quite sun-tanned elbows, Beatrice Menendez, inspiration for Abyla Television's "Whose Eyes?" competition, surveyed her naked husband and thought: all you ever do with that is water the lawn. He thought: she is only ever happy when something is wrong. That's why she is on such good form. She is wreathed in smiles because she recognises the symptoms of disaster.

She closed her book and turned her unclaimed eyes on him. "What are you going to say?" The truth was she didn't greatly care, either about her husband or about his tunnel. His fingers stopped their scratching. They tugged at his gold chain, imprinting a red line in the backfold of his neck. They descended over his face, where his shaving line spread like a grey paste, to his chest. They became wild horses on the plain such as he had simulated in his days at Radio Salamanca. He said, "I wonder what people in the past thought of this weather. Would it have been worse for them?"

His wife said, "I suppose they accepted it. As we do."

He nodded. Then he said, "What do you think people in the past would have thought of this rain? It would have been worse for them, I imagine."

She nodded. "I suppose they would have accepted it."

He nodded. "That's the truth. Don't you think? It would have been worse for people in the past." And he guided his belly into the bathroom.

Untended for so long, Beatrice Menendez launched a pugnacious look at her husband's back and collapsed onto the pillows. Soon her gaze had tangled in the blades of the overhead fan and went into a slow and lazy reverse returning her to the never-to-be-repeated afternoon when Lieutenant Casares had shyly sought her cheeks to say goodbye, señora, thanks for the tea, it was a lovely – and found his mouth fastened to a pair of skatelips that sucked him upstairs, along a corridor, through two cedarwood doors and puffed him onto a bedspread of pink corrugated cotton where, gaspingly, without words, without explanation, with her skirt still flustering her waist, she made him remind her of what it meant, O God, O sweet, incorrigible God, to be a woman again.

"Gentlemen, Deputies, Ministers of the Chamber . . .". Under the loose nozzle of the shower, the Governor rehearsed his speech.

The thought of Lieutenant Casares led Beatrice Menendez inevitably to think of another who had made the same pilgrimage to this bed. Gratifying as her experience with the Lieutenant had been, it in no way eclipsed her memory of Periclito.

She had been thinking recently a good deal about Periclito. They had seen something of each other when she first arrived in Abyla. Aware of this, her husband had tried to be kind, which she found irritating. And now Periclito was coming back . . .

"Please believe that I . . ."

In the bathroom, the Governor was still expressing himself to death. He was unsuited by temperament to the admission of failure, that was the problem. And to judge from the look on his face, suggesting he had mislaid a vital expression, he had been staring at it with some intensity since yesterday evening.

". . . it is with enormous regret that I announce to the chamber my decision to postpone the opening of the tunnel by a further year."

Another year! She had only stayed this long in Abyla to meet the British Queen.

Beatrice Menendez propped herself on her elbows. "Darling," she called tenderly into the steam. "That doesn't mean they'll have to cancel the bullfight?"

In the Café Ulises, they were watching the Governor's speech live on television. Unnoticed, Captain Panteco marched up to Silkleigh at the bar. The policeman was accompanied by the fisherman's dog. He gripped an axe. "Unless you like hospital food, Silkleigh, you're coming with me."

Silkleigh held up his hands. "Relax, Panteco. If someone's an arsehole, that's what they are. Period."

"Shh," said Dionisio Porcil, the banker, and, mopping his forehead, he turned back to the screen.

The policeman drove through the deserted wet streets to the Consulate building. As they climbed to the first floor, Panteco said, "It might interest you to know I've been watching you day and night for the last fortnight."

"So?"

Panteco made a supreme effort to continue. "It might interest you to know it isn't you."

"I say, old thing, that *is* good news," said Silkleigh.

"But that girl you're going out with in your boat, Silkleigh." Excitement brightened Panteco's eyes. His tongue roamed un-inhibited over his lips. He raised his axe. "I have a funny feeling she is not all she claims to be."

An avalanche of snow, that's what Panteco hoped to find as he splintered apart the door. That's what he hoped he'd found when he saw the boxes carefully stacked one above the other to the ceiling. Hundreds of them! One box was enough to merit a *Medalla de la Ciudad* – and citation. He stumbled through the boxes, sending them tumbling. Impatiently, he tore at the grey sealing tape. He drew out an object contained in a plastic bag.

"What's this, Silkleigh?" He turned to the diver, sitting on a box, with Toribio licking his face.

On a label fastened to the bag were written in clear print the words THROTTING & WHITTLE – WATER SYSTEMS. SIMPLY THE BEST.

"Something's cropped up," explained Sir Derek Cullis. He would not blind his superior with mere details, but it was clear that Max's man had done his job. "We're going to have to postpone the Royal Visit."

The Foreign Secretary heard him out. "Frankly, Derek, I'm relieved." In another year there would be a new government. "As I'm sure the Prime Minister will be."

The two men walked together down the corridor. "I'll tell him tomorrow – and we'd better let the Palace know," said the Foreign Secretary. He would reallocate the time to review a batch of crime books for the *Telegraph*. "Tredwell will be disappointed. But that's for the military to cope with. Who's our eyes and ears in Abyla?"

Cullis told him.

"Thomas Wavery. Do I know him?"

"Very unlikely, Foreign Secretary."

"Where was he before?"

"Peru."

"Ah, yes." The Foreign Secretary nodded. "Didn't Winnie the Pooh come from Peru?"

"I believe that was Paddington Bear, sir."

"That's who it was." He tapped his head. "There's no question, Derek. The old memory is not what it used to be." They had reached the top of the staircase. "Going to the Danes?" The new Ambassador was giving a reception.

"I've got to pack. Hilda and I –"

But the Foreign Secretary had remembered. "Good Lord, Derek, did I never congratulate you?" Not for the first time, he reflected on the unexpected light which pulsed beneath the dour bushel of his colleague. Cullis in print was unlike the Cullis he knew, dramatically unlike. The prize-winning verse returned to the Foreign Secretary as they walked down the stairs, in the soporific Scots lilt of a shipping-forecast.

My Hilda though simply divine
Is shy both of men and of wine
But with Dornoch Vine's label
She's simply unable
To think of the English for "Nein!"

A voice trilled up the staircase. As always when he heard that voice, the Foreign Secretary experienced a terrible foreboding. Somewhere in the world, he thought, a catastrophe is about to happen. His hand found the grey marble bannister. "I wonder who she wants this time?"

They both listened.

"Telephone for Mr Queesal. Telephone for Mr Queesal."

"Funny," said Cullis. "He was here a moment ago."

Again came the voice and this time concern was expressed there. "He says he's calling from Africa . . ."

PART FIVE

PART FIVE

Chapter Thirteen

I

THE SKY WAS a bowl of Fezzine blue. It was the day of the Virgin, the day for which Abylans had waited five years and their promontory – once more to have been reunited with Europe – since the beginning of history. The day which was to have celebrated the Straits Tunnel opening.

The new bell of Santa Maria de Africa joined the band of the Third Africa Regiment. On her custard-coloured bier, the permanent Mayoress of Abyla inched out of the dark interior into the butterfly sunlight. She was supported by members of the regiment, concealed by the ornate frame of her bier except for their white spats. The spats shuffled to a halt at the top of the steps while Lieutenant Casares whispered directions through the shoulder-borne tracery of wood. Hesitantly, magnificently, a quivering barque, the Virgin of Africa was launched on the square. She was dressed in black. She sat on a dense bed of red and white carnations, her left hand gripping an olive cane at the level of her breast. Called upon to relinquish the symbol of her power, the Virgin had not failed her city.

By the world at large, Abyla had been left alone. Before yielding her freedom, the wayward daughter was to have thrown an unprecedented party, to be attended by Kings and Queens (as well as an actress from *The Strong Tend to Leave*). No one wished to visit a city where such a party had been cancelled.

At least, that is how matters were perceived on the Peninsula. Abyla felt otherwise. This was still her day, the fiesta of her

patroness and possibly the last such fiesta. If there was to be no
tunnel opening today for the populace gawping at the Virgin as
she jelly-wobbled along the Marina Española, at least there
remained the sensational *corrida de toros*. There remained the
prospect of Periclito.

2

"I hope he fights well, for his mother's sake," Halima told
Wavery, who stood drinking a glass of water at the sink. The
señor Consul General had interrupted her in the kitchen as she
was consulting a card from the concertina folder. This was to
have been the evening of his reception. Despite its cancellation,
she wanted to treat her master to a special meal. But she was
worried for him. When she had seen two hens looking into each
other's eyes she had known Emilio would die. And this morning,
in a courtyard in El Hadu, she had observed the same omen.

"Yes," said Wavery vaguely. He filled another glass and went
upstairs.

"I've put your shirt on the bed, señor," she called after him.

Halima wanted to believe that Señor Wavery was depressed
about the tunnel. But it had nothing to do with the tunnel. This
depression her master had caught the other side of La Mujer
Muerte. She didn't know what had happened in those mountains, but he had returned from Africa with a different mouth.
His eyes were different too. The glasses magnified the ripples
of flesh beneath, as if his eyes had been thrown with force
against his face.

Since the weekend of his visit to Chauen he had become a
statue of himself. He had not once been swimming. He never
noticed Ham's horse-shoe of fur against his leg. He stayed in
his bedroom with a huge pile of paper on his lap. These were
the pages he had written on the terrace. But Halima never saw
him writing anything. Nor did he read as he used to. Instead
he sat on a cane chair by the open window, picking up each
page and passing his eyes over it with an expression of such

blankness that Halima was reminded of Ghanem of the Mute, on the occasion she had to collect her husband from the Café Ulises (after Berahu had decided to taste for himself whatever it was the Nazarenes made such a fuss about).

Last night she had tried to galvanise her master from the chair. "Come here, señor, come here. Look!" She led him to the tree on the terrace. In twenty years this was the first time she had seen it in flower. She held back the branches for him to see. The white, veined oval broadened under the leaves. "The tree is dreaming."

Briefly Wavery stared at the handkerchief, before hitching his eyes over Senator Zamora's roof. His mouth was silent, but it told Halima he was trying to find the world smaller than a star.

3

The Earthquake was back. Quite as fat and very red, one leg trailing slightly behind the other, no room between his mouth and nose for the black moustache that trembled with wine drops. Periclito, the gourmet who bridled if you asked whether his famous cassoulet was tinned, whose heart never failed to bounce like a hare at the sight of a blond head, such as the once-blond head of Señora Criado, the cook, who whenever she thought of their nights together thought of a double-door falling upon her with the key still in its lock. Periclito, the lover of two hundred and eighty-nine such women, who walked stiffly off the ferry wearing a surgical corset. Periclito, the blue-jowled, fast-talking, tender-hearted and passionately immoral owner of the Café Ulises. Periclito Merimée Amaral, the bullfighter who had travelled the world as fourth, third and very occasionally as second fiddle to the matadors of Bogotà, Lima and Caracas was back in Abyla.

"A name to watch," declared the review *Olé y Olé* (No.14), including him in a list of twenty-one talented unknowns.

*　　*　　*

341

The day had begun brilliantly. There was a clear brow on La Mujer Muerte while across the Straits Genia Ortiz could see the limestone ridge of Gibraltar. The surrounding sea was calm. It was one of those flat seas over which Silkleigh, waiting on the quay to greet Rosita, boasted he could see yesterday leaving and tomorrow arrive. But Berahu the dustman smelt wind as he transported the last truckload of sand from the Playa Benitez to the temporary bullring on Canoñero Dato. By mid-afternoon, a breeze ruffled the posters announcing TOROS EN ABYLA! It cooled the crowds taking their places, dressed in clothes they had ordered, pleated, taken in, for a different occasion. It carried the sounds of the small band playing beneath the Royal Box on what had been intended as the regiment's final appearance before disbandment.

"They're playing Ernesto's tune!" thought Genia Ortiz, entering the bullring in her bunting. She moved towards her seat, tapping the backs of chairs to the tempo of "On the Promontory".

"Look! There she *is*. Do look."

"What does she think she looks like? The Virgin?"

"Whatever it is, she doesn't."

Squarely rigged in the yellow and blue colours of Free Ukraine, Genia Ortiz glided forwards.

Inside the Royal Box, Teodoro Zamora was delivering a severe lecture to his grandson. He had only very recently forgiven Pablo for the trick he confessed to playing with a rogue disc, which for several days persuaded Zamora he had destroyed his entire life's work at the press of a computer button. And now the boy was misbehaving again, to judge from the words he admitted to writing in the telephone kiosk outside the Café Ulises. The message itself was bad enough, but after it the boy had added his grandmother's telephone number. So far one call only had resulted. Never in her life, not in any of her conversations with the General and not once in more than fifty years of marriage to Ernesto, did Genia Ortiz believe she had heard a suggestion so repellent.

"Wherever did you learn such words –"

"Look, there *is* Age!"

Senator Zamora, empurpled in Tyrian colours, observed Genia Ortiz' progress. He was pleased after all he had offered her one of the seats reserved for the absentee monarchs. Even though her suitcase was packed, her Motherland was calling and tomorrow she was to join the *Hummingbird* at Gibraltar, she had looked forward to this day. "Thank you, Teodoro," she said, accepting his invitation to replace the British Queen who had said no. "I would like that very much."

Senator Zamora, President of the *Corrida* and possessing supreme power over the ring, had arrived earlier with his grandson in order to explain to him something of the background to the afternoon's spectacle. He had taken the boy behind the *barricada* and onto the ramp overlooking Don Ponciano's seven bulls. But his explanation was mechanical, distracted.

His mind remained underground. While Zamora continued to enjoy the sanction of history, his initial euphoria had been tempered by certain aspects of his discovery. The remains were not as extensive as he had thought. The site was probably not after all the Lebtit of the Arabs. It was not Tarshish nor Auza, nor even Hecatomyplus. Possibly, it belonged to the burial ground of a middle-ranking Phoenician settlement. Beyond the chapel dedicated to Melcart and the objects photographed on the tarpaulin, he had subsequently found little except a number of cinerary urns.

Three of these urns contained the ashes and bones of animals. Zamora was preoccupied by the discovery of a fourth urn. This held the remains of something which disturbed him very much indeed.

In the thesis for which the University of Oran had awarded Zamora his doctorate, he had paddled with a single mind against conventional wisdom. He dismissed as Herodotean hyperbole the one aspect of the entire literature he could never bring himself to believe in: the image of mothers coming forward with their children, implacable, forbidden to shed a tear, their faces twisted in gladness as they offered the blood of their sons and daughters as a libation to Melcart, the Phoenician Hercules.

Such remains, where they existed, he argued, belonged to unfortunate individuals who had died of natural causes.

He wrote then, "Those who believe in Flaubert's graphic fictions are guilty of anti-Carthaginian propaganda . . ." But all the signs of the Abyla burial ground proved him wrong. In the tophet below the Marina Española he had found the bones of a young woman; also those of an older man. He judged the two of them had been immolated alive. The vacuum conditions in the chamber had preserved the skeletons so perfectly their immolation might have taken place yesterday.

The evidence had sobered Zamora's faith. It detracted from the pleasure he might once have taken in this morning's letter from the Peninsula, urging him to resubmit his thesis. What was a thesis but three hundred and eighty-two pieces of paper if it could not begin to understand how Hercules had failed his Phoenicians?

What had happened to make them sacrifice not a lamb but a girl? What unspeakable dread? What oppressive deities, what dark ocean gods had demanded this appalling piety? Zamora could not guess. Experience, like Señora Criado's pies, had to be broken down and digested. He was still puzzled, for instance, how it was that when that fool of a policeman had dropped the funerary mask, it had not cracked as he would have expected, but bounced.

"Look! There's Daddy."

"Oh, yes." Politely for his grandson, Zamora leaned forward. Below, against the blood-red barricade, Tromso was filming the matadors, picadors and bandilleros. He had grouped them one behind the other as in a school photograph. Over their heads a sound-recordist brandished a long pole on which slithered an object resembling a grey seaslug. Another man used a circular reflector of white cloth to throw light on their faces.

"Why is Daddy filming *them*, Grandpapa?"

"For his documentary, child," said Senator Zamora, explaining how the subjects of his thesis – and now Tromso's documentary – had introduced bullfighting into North Africa, the Moors taking it with them into Spain.

"Remember that footprint we saw at Cap Spartel?" In Phoenician legend, Hercules fought at the edge of the wilderness with a bull-headed monster and was killed.

"Will Periclito be killed?"

The President tapped his foot to this familiar tune. What *was* this music? he wondered, unable for the moment to place it. Whatever the tune, it was strikingly unoriginal.

"Not if he fights well – "

He leaped to his feet. "Clotilda!" His youngest daughter had paused at the low gate into the box. She was scanning the crowd for someone. When she heard his call she looked round, at the same time jerking back her head. Senator Zamora saw a wasp had become entangled in one of her pigtails. He hurried to her and lifted up her long corn hair. "There," he said. "Gone."

Relieved, she hooped her hands around his neck. She rubbed a kiss onto both of his cheeks. "Thank you, Father," she said.

Asunción followed two steps behind. She wore a pale blue skirt, a spotless white blouse and a red silk jacket that reached her knees. She smiled down at her husband in the bullring. Afterwards, Tromso had invited them all to dinner at the Café Ulises.

"Don't close the gate! Your mother-in-law's behind." He waved. "Madame Amaral!"

4

Wavery waved back, until he realised the President did not intend his salutation for him.

"Señor Wavery," nodded Marie Amaral, taking her place beside him. She had not spoken to the Consul General since the evening on his terrace. A finger admonished him. "Who has ignored me?" she said, rocking herself comfortable on two foam cushions.

"The mother of the matador." Wavery resumed his place. "I am honoured."

"I was so emotional," she said. "I am sorry. I never told you how grateful I was."

"Not at all, Marie." But there was no resonance in his voice, just as there had been none when he had greeted Dolores, or ten minutes earlier Joseph Silkleigh.

Silkleigh asked anxiously if Wavery had seen Rosita. He had not.

"She may have stood at the back of the queue when God was handing out noses, old soul, but I simply can't get her out of my mind."

"Your first bullfight?" asked Marie Amaral, too excited to appreciate anything but her own happiness. She indicated the ring. She could see Tromso's bald patch. He was directing the cameraman. He was appealing for quiet, like David's God in her dreams. Last night she had woken again, laughing.

"No," said Wavery. "But it isn't quite my cup of tea."

Marie Amaral understood his Anglo-Saxon revulsion. It was the same revulsion she had felt when her father first introduced her to the ring in Oran. At the age of seven, she wished nothing so much as to vomit into her mother's black satin lap.

More and more as she grew older, Marie Amaral detested cruelty to animals. She hated the men lying patiently in wait for green turtles on the military beach at Monte Hacho. She hated the boys on La Mujer Muerta who inserted feathers through the beak-holes of butcherbirds and tied their legs with string and waved them at passing cars like kites. And most of all she hated that part of herself which attracted her on this breezy afternoon to the *corrida de toros* and the spectacle of her corseted son, short, fat and out of breath, unable to run but (she hoped) nimble with his sword, whose swordplay she would find it somewhere in her heart to admire because whatever the distance between them, a distance which from childhood he had filled with women, bulls and cassoulet, he was her son.

This afternoon, despite her reservations, she looked young, relaxed. In the morning a palmist had read her fortune, saying that if she squeezed it tight into a fist he would promise to tell

346

her how many children she had and whether she was leading a double life.

"Like that?"

He pronounced her very honest, very human and able to separate her head from her heart.

"And how many children?" she wanted to know.

He counted the lines. "Two."

On a cushion next to her Wavery remembered, "I think my first fight must have been in Lisbon."

"Pshaw!" exclaimed Marie Amaral. "That's not bullfighting. The animal is led through the whole process – and not killed! But killed in a butcher's shop. Very frivolous," she said, "For a fighting bull not to fight to the death is not to fulfil his life."

In the Royal Box Genia Ortiz was making a favourable comparison with Kiev's Horse-Racing Society.

She leaned forward, enjoying the sight of her son and his camera-crew, enjoying the sun flashing on the brass as the Tercio band rested their instruments. There had not been a *corrida* in Abyla for twenty years. Every seat was occupied.

Asunción wiped away the lipstick on her father's cheeks, left there by her younger sister.

"Where are my other handkerchiefs? Clotilda? Pablo, give those to me! For God's sake, Asunción, control your son."

An official tapped his watch. It was time! President Zamora gestured he knew this perfectly well. He waved the white square of silk. A trumpet sounded and a door opened in the makeshift stadium and a black bull trotted into the ring.

Periclito's first bull was the third of the afternoon. He took the *alternativa* from "El Troyanito" in the presence of Rafael Lara. He limped into the centre of the bullring, waving at the crowd who answered him with a murmur of the flowers they held back, but intended later to hurl at him. Troyanito waited, sweating, as the bare-headed *matador de novillos* hobbled towards him. They shook hands, and Troyanito gave to the Earthquake his

347

red-serge cape and the sword with which ten minutes before he had despatched the second bull.

Periclito saluted President Zamora and Zamora responded by dipping his white handkerchief against the side of the Royal Box.

Sitting beside Wavery, Marie Amaral repeated to herself the prayer she had uttered on hands and knees before the Virgin of Africa.

A trumpet sounded.

Afterwards, it would be said that Periclito's elevation to *matador de toros* was assisted by the fact that his own stiff movements were reflected in the bull from Don Ponciano's prestigious stable. In any event, he acquitted himself well enough, and although the crowd considered the moment not yet right to bestow on him their bouquets they called for the President to award Periclito the foot of his bull.

"Pata! Pata!" they called. It was an Abylan tradition, the foot, and President Zamora responded with another silk flutter.

Marie Amaral breathed out. Periclito waved to his mother and she waved back. She could relax. This was the first time she – or indeed any of them – had seen the Earthquake fight. Her son, her mirror-wounded son, had survived. It was a good bull which accepted the death a bullfighter gave him. She squeezed Wavery's arm. She had remembered everything her father said at that first fight in Oran. She wanted to explain.

What they had just witnessed was not a confrontation between a spherical matador and a vital animal. No. It was a meeting between Man and his own Animality. The bull incarnated our most profound apprehensions about ourselves, the transgressions we do not dare perform from fear or desire.

"This animality must be conquered," she told Wavery. "But it must be conquered aesthetically and harmoniously. It must be suppressed, not punished. It must be treated with courage, style, sympathy, force – all the conditions that make us fight for life."

"Is that right?"

"It's bad if the animality invades you, señor, but if you treat it well it's very creative. It's one of the most important things a man can have."

In that moment Marie Amaral observed Wavery's features. Had he lived, she realised, David would have been the same age. But his face, his face, she thought. It exhaled an intolerable sadness as of a portrait rubbed out with turpentine. Surely the bullfight could not have upset him so much? Had he listened to anything she had said? What was it that blighted him?

Flustered, she went on. "I can see you find this a lot of nonsense, that you might find it disgusting. But if you are too literal, you can find everything disgusting. On the other hand, if behind the person in the bathroom you see another dimension, then – ah, then life becomes a religious ceremony."

"I suppose so," said Wavery.

And suddenly it was more important than anything she convinced him, that she show her gratitude.

" Señor," she began. There was concentration in her face. "It has taken me sixty years to realise something I should have known at twenty. Good and evil are not wheat and chaff. You cannot separate them. The only way you become a human being is when you do something you shouldn't do. Like Adam and Eve. When Adam and Eve were ready to say 'No!' to God, they were ready to be normal. They were ready to recognise evil in themselves. Like a child when he says his first lie," she said, thinking of Periclito.

She remembered her English texts, all those Elizabethan tragedies she had read and never taught. They came from Señor Wavery's country. "Your Hamlet didn't want to kill – and why not? Because maybe that was his major desire. Maybe he wanted to kill too much. But there comes a moment when to do something good, you must do something bad, and not to do this is the most destructive of all. If Hamlet had killed Polonius earlier . . . Ah, if he had killed Polonius earlier, señor, not just literature would be different."

*   *   *

The shadow seeped over the sand. The buzzards balanced overhead. Two more bulls pounded into the ring and died in the shade. The trumpet called, and it was time for Periclito's second bull, the last bull of the day.

An enormous cheer greeted Periclito's re-entry into the ring. This time he paraded with a covered head. He circled the ring until he stood on the sand below Marie Amaral. He removed his frizzy woollen hat. He dedicated this bull to his mother, he said, touching his chest with his fingers and bowing. With an extravagant flourish he lobbed the hat towards her. The hat spun through the air where a gust of wind diverted it onto Wavery's lap. Marie Amaral accepted the tribute from the Consul General and directed to her son a little embarrassed bow of the head. He rotated on his heels and swaggered across the sand, to lure away his animality from the bandilleros.

A front foot scraped the ground, heeling the furrowed sand over his black flanks. Urine dribbled from his tasselled penis, darkening the sand. Three white spears quivered in his back. Suddenly he charged the barricade. He leaped, his head and front feet lurching over the rudimentary wall.

"Menendez!" someone shouted. The crowd laughed, necks craning to look for a white suit in the shade, where Menendez sat between his wife and the Bishop of Cadiz. Yesterday he had announced his resignation as Governor. He was returning to the Peninsula.

"*Musica! Musica!*" they called and the band struck up "On the Promontory".

Marie Amaral shook her head. "This is a bad bull." He didn't want to fight. He didn't want to meet his destiny. He wanted to go back. A bull that wanted to go back was dangerous. You never knew his perversion. He might wish to attack Periclito instead of his red and yellow cape. If he looked for his body to destroy it, that was a perverted intention.

A strong wind made this perversion more likely. It tugged at Periclito's cape, blowing sand in his eye.

"*Agua! Agua!*" He walked to the side of the ring, passing his cape to Mohamed who plunged the hem into a bucket of water.

350

Periclito passed over his sword and Mohamed wiped it with a dishcloth. Across the ring, the bull slithered down the barricade and onto its feet. Periclito turned. He limped forward, dragging his wet cape in the sand. The wind fanned the remains of his hair. The bull eyed him. Periclito stamped his foot. One of the spears fell from the animal's flank. The bull looked at the spear on the ground, scarlet-tipped with his blood. The crowd muttered, breathing with the breath of the bull. Periclito insinuated his crotch into the animal's line of vision. He took another step, drawing a poppy-red sword from his cape. He stood on the tips of his toes and prepared to jab the sword between the horns, into the neck. He lunged. The sword bounced out. The crowd booed.

Periclito retrieved his sword slowly. He stalked off after the bull. He lunged again, but he was too far away and again the sword fell out and again the crowd booed, but louder.

"*Aviso!*"

Senator Zamora looked at the bullring clock. Ten minutes had passed. "Pablo, the handkerchief. That's it. Come on, child, give it here!"

He fluttered the first warning.

Tightly encased in his silver lamé suit, his cheeks warted with sweat, Periclito shambled across the sand to where the bull was trying a second time to scale the *barricada*. Once more, to the audible crack of bone, his inglorious sword bounced to the sand. Once more, he was assailed by jeers.

In the Royal Box Genia Ortiz was telling Asunción how well she remembered, during the final fight, the sight of the General tucking into the first bull's sweetmeats.

"But he wasn't relying on Periclito," she said.

Senator Zamora meanwhile was hoping there would no repetition of the incident in the old ring when the sword had jerked out of the tossing muscle and javelined with awful force into Don Ramon's grandfather, sitting in the third row.

"*Aviso!*"

Three more minutes had passed. President Zamora found his purple-red handkerchief, smeared with Clotilda's lipstick.

He shook the handkerchief at Periclito. There remained to him two minutes only in which to complete his third act.

What a disaster! What a wretched disaster! The Earthquake had hoped to dazzle Abyla. Instead, he was shaming the city – and Tromso was recording his shame on film! He flushed until his cheeks were the same hue as the yoke of blood around the animal's neck.

"Fuera!" cried the crowd. Away with this matador who could not kill! Bullfighter? they shouted. Bullshitter!

Periclito advanced on tiptoe as if making his way barefoot through glass. He raised the sword for his fifth thrust. Sitting behind Wavery, Señora Criado squeezed her face in her hands and said, "I daren't look, I daren't look." Periclito plunged, and this time the blade took root in the flesh. The bull moved back against the *barricada*, his bollocks rising up and down, his tongue curving up and out, stretched in a taut arc, the breaths coming shorter and shorter until with blood snorting from his nostrils he collapsed among the foam cushions and oranges and wine bottles that had been thrown in protest at really this most dismal performance by Abyla's very own Periclito Merimée Amaral.

The crowd sought President Zamora's handkerchief, but inside the Royal Box confusion reigned. Rising to the occasion and meaning to hurl her programme into the ring as an indication of her extreme disapproval, Genia Ortiz had thrown instead her husband's baton.

"He wasn't ready to meet his destiny," observed Marie Amaral as men in blue overalls tethered the carcass to a horse and trotted it away.

The crowd stirred to their feet. Many held to their chests the flowers they had withheld all afternoon. They shook their heads, disappointed, as a voice came over the loudspeaker. Marie Amaral stiffened at the voice. Her son was speaking.

"I fought badly," said the Earthquake. The volume was turned up. "I fought badly," he repeated. "So I give you a seventh bull. I give it as a present to Abyla."

There was a buzzing of approval. People sat down again. The

seats were hard. They had thrown away their cushions, but it didn't matter.

A man yelled at Genia Ortiz, peering over the side of the enclosure. "Sit down!" he yelled. "Donkey meat is not transparent!"

Wavery retrieved his spectacles from his breast pocket. He said, "A seventh bull? Does this happen often?"

Marie Amaral admitted: "It doesn't happen very often. He has to pay for the animal himself. But to give a bull is not a special thing," she said bravely. "A special thing is to have a special afternoon."

Down in the ring, a door opened. A roan-coloured beast trotted into the shade, the steam rising from his angry hump, his head. In the middle of the sand he paused. Unhurriedly, he turned. He waited for the picadors.

This was one of Geryon's oxen, thought Zamora.

"Ah, this is a bull," said Marie Amaral, watching him slam into the horse and withdraw his horns, webbed with the animal's guts.

Soon it was the third act.

Periclito removed the hat returned to him by his mother. He placed it on the sand. He stood erect, inhaling the air perfumed with blood and his mother's withheld flowers. He hobbled forward.

The whole ring went absolutely silent.

In the centre of the ring, an ear twitched.

5

In the silence the new bell stuck four. It was four o'clock.

Alone of the crowd, Wavery raised his eyes from the ring. He had been upset by the previous spectacle. The taut tongue of the bull as the animal swayed backwards in a diminishing sway found repeated in him an unpostponable agony. Instead of Periclito and the seventh bull, Wavery saw the miraculous crag of La Mujer Muerta, the goddess who had loved against her father's wishes and been turned by him into stone.

Nothing could be drier than her slopes, nothing. Beyond her peak, Wavery felt the intense, saturated, throbbing of Africa as he had felt it on an afternoon two weeks before, sitting in the Daimler beside Catharine.

Chapter Fourteen

WHEN THEY WERE not at school, or lobbing oranges at one another from slings in El Hadu, Halima's three children, all sons under the age of ten, stood on La Mujer Muerta a mile from the border spading parabolas of sand off the tarmac which the *poniente* had spread in small dunes like the hieroglyphic bumps on Captain Panteco's face. Whenever a car drove by, they held out their hands and waved their spades. The spades were fashioned from flattened cans, forked into pine branches. To Norredine, the youngest, fell the task of shovelling back the sand each evening before they returned to El Hadu. On a busy day they might collect fifty or sixty dirhams from grateful tourists.

On this late afternoon, a splendid silver-grey saloon drew to a halt beside them. Its driver wound down his window and gave Norredine five dirhams.

"*Merci, monsieur* . . ." He cocked his head. ". . . *mademoiselle.*" Too late, he gestured for the others to come quickly with their examples of purple crystal, their butcher-birds.

With the sun blazing on its windscreen, Abyla's one and only Daimler accelerated into Africa.

Catharine laughed. "It was worth coming all this way, just to be called *mademoiselle.*"

Then she said, "Are we . . . ? Still?"

"Yes," he said. He thought: Only through hearing their voice can you truly appreciate a person. But at this moment her presence was as hard to endure as her absence had been. He placed his hand on her leg, gripping it hard. She took his hand between hers, kissing it, opening its fingers, pressing them to her lips.

He sensed her inspection, her immaculate smile. "Tell me you love me," she said.

"I love you."

"Tell me again."

Again, he told her. "I didn't know if you'd come."

"I didn't know if you'd received the letter." She touched the side of his face. "You're greyer," she said. "But slimmer."

"Lots of swimming," he said. "And no parties."

"We're on the same time span again," she said. "Every time I thought of you, you were one hour behind."

He swivelled a glance at her. He was monstrously happy. "Can one be closer than this?"

She kissed his fingertips. She anointed him with her smile. "I don't want this day to end," she said.

At the end, when in a concerned voice Catharine said, "Darling, where *are* you going to retire to?", Wavery would be incapable of summoning up a single nugget of gaiety. Neither then nor at any time earlier had he been able to form the idea for himself. Her question would be a silencing force, hard as the African light. As soon as he heard it he knew he had never properly adjusted to the idea he would be alone. That Penny would not be with him. Nor Catharine. But neither had he asked himself why it was that Catharine might have changed her mind about seeing him again.

The truth was, Wavery's imagination failed him beyond the three days he had planned in Chauen. In that respect Penny was right. "Women see the whole picture. Men see it obsessively, piece by piece." Catharine's visit to Abyla, the possibility of which had occupied his mind for six months, was a piece of this picture. Since the day he received her letter, it happened also to be the only piece.

If pressed to say what he felt as he drove her through the mountains where Lieutenant Zamora had warred against the shadows and Zamora shot his pig, Wavery would most likely have borrowed a phrase of Silkleigh's: "There's no future tense in Arabic, *kara mia*. Unlike the language of the future!"

They reached Chauen at seven, the dry hills yielding the town at the last possible moment. A crown of houses and minarets balanced white and blinding on a rocky brow above a river. The hotel lay on the far rim. Asunción had booked a double room in his name.

Catharine blushed. "Could we change it to mine? In case he rings." The manager scored out Wavery's name. Dutifully, he entered the names written in Catharine's passport. "It's the Riding that matters," she said, and to Wavery, simply, "I'm sorry." He ordered drinks on the terrace. It overlooked the town occupied by Lieutenant Zamora in 1921, but Wavery did not see the stone bridge or the women washing clothes or the mule raising a dripping nose from the river. For nine months he had experienced the pain of not being able to share a view with Catharine. Now there was a whole continent to explore, he could look only at her.

At eight she took the room key. "I'll just make that call." Twenty minutes later she came back and kissed the top of Wavery's head. Her breath was warm on his neck.

She said, "And your other reality. How is she?"

"We're more or less divorced," he said.

She drew up a chair. "Oh, Tom, no," she whispered. "But that's dreadful." She looked away. Darkness was cooling the valley. On the riverbank a woman loaded the mule with wet clothes. From the water came a sound of frogs. The dusk smelt of cumin.

"It would have happened anyway."

She looked back, bowing her body over folded arms. "I didn't realise. I presumed she was in London, or –" She was shaken.

He touched her arm. He said, "Did you ever get my message?"

"What message?"

357

"Never mind, it's not important." Her husband must have failed to pass it on.

"What message, darling?"

"It doesn't matter. It's just that once I called you."

"But when?"

"When I heard about my appointment."

"No one told me this!"

"It was a moment of weakness."

She stared back at him. "So it wasn't me who broke our promise?"

"No. It wasn't you."

She went on, speaking quickly, "I read it in the paper. Adam kept it for me. I couldn't understand. I thought, what's happened? Why isn't he going to Lisbon – like he told me? Where is this place – Abyla? And I looked on the map and I felt . . . I felt it was such a terrible shame."

"Please," said Wavery. "Don't be silly."

"It's stupid," she said in the same rapid voice. "I don't know why, but I felt guilty and no matter how often I told myself, no, it could be nothing to do with me, I was not to blame, this feeling grew and grew. Then one day it became too much. I couldn't bear to feel it a moment longer. I was hugging my daughters and it was you I was touching, and – and that's when I wrote."

"Catharine, I'm glad you did," said Wavery.

They ate an early dinner. Afterwards they went upstairs. He undressed. She came up behind him. He felt her breasts against his back, then lower down her hair.

"Lie on top of me," she said. "I want to feel your weight."

Afterwards, her back curved into him, she talked. "I remember leaving you at the airport and collapsing on my bed and Adam saying 'Good weekend?' and my falling into a deep sleep and finding your grey hairs on my jacket when I woke. I'd been frightened of embarrassing you with my feelings, of embarrassing myself."

He held her hands.

She went on, "I went through all the photographs of myself

as a child, just to see if there was any trace of that look you talked about on Rita's terrace, the one that you said gusted through you. I couldn't see it."

"I love you," he said.

She said, "I never stopped thinking of you. Once or twice I was talking to someone and I had to stop because suddenly I have had this clear image of your face as we made love that night. I was worried I'd become glass, that everyone could see through me, see what I was thinking."

"I love you." He wished he could have been the first man to use those words. They were all he could say, and each time he said them they became more inadequate.

She withdrew her hand. Drawing a long breath, she said: "We know, don't we, that this is all we have? We have a pack of cards, that's all. We can play them how we like, but there are only so many cards and the pack is going to run out. We know that, don't we?"

"Yes," said Wavery. "That's right," and he kept from his voice what he could not keep from his mind. The reason she had broken her promise, the reason she was here in Africa – did it have to do with her problem? Or was it to solve his?

She slept and for a while he watched her sleep-ironed face. He slept tangled with her and he woke with her face at his shoulder, disturbed by the muezzin.

In the morning, he stood before the mirror, shaving. She came into the bathroom and he kissed her, leaving foam on her cheek. "It's been so long since I spent time with someone I didn't know," she said. She looked at his face in the mirrror, blurred by the steam. "I was dreading the little things. You wearing pyjamas, or a vest. Or I'd hear you say, 'Is it all right if I use your toothpaste?'"

They had Saturday and on Saturday night it happened as it had happened before in Lisbon. She was above him, her hair falling across his face, her body rising and falling with his, when suddenly he felt a shiver in her wings. Her head jerked sideways into the hollow of her arm. Her expression changed and she stared at him. Another person raised her face. She arched back in a convulsion. A tearing sound came from her throat as if something was ripping inside.

"No!"

It was the excoriating, primal cry of a terrified child. "No! No! NO!" She struggled to free herself, tearing against some hook in her flesh. She hurtled away from him, her arms flailing, her hands hiding her face. She ran from the bed and burrowed into the corner of the room where she wrapped her arms around her knees, coughing out her fear in short, hoarse moans, repeating, "Don't make me, no, please don't, please, don't."

In the next room someone pounded on the wall.

He gathered her in his arms and she held onto him, weeping. She said, "Tom, I have to tell you something . . ." He stroked the hair from her face. He pulled her back from the abrupt edge. "Look at me," he said. "It's me."

Her eyes looked at him. They were filled with waves breaking. "I have to tell you . . ."

But she was speaking to herself in a thin, frightened voice. Her pain carried him down. It was an anchor dragging at the root of her being. It was as if she was responding to some immeasurable damage, so deep it might never be found – and if found the more damaging it would be. He caressed her face, her arms. He was in uncharted, boiling waters. This was an experience for which nothing in his life, nothing in his books, had prepared him. He said, "I love you."

She pummelled her knees with her fists. "Don't you see? Don't you see? I'm worried your love will turn into something as strong against me, and I don't want it to."

"It won't. How can it?" He stilled her face with his hands. "Tell me, Catharine. I want to hear."

But she shook free her head. "I can't," she said in her locked-away voice. And with the trust of a lost animal, she allowed him to carry her to bed.

Not once on Sunday did she allude to what had passed between them. All day she was bright and loving. In the morning they explored the town again and in the afternoon they walked to an abandoned mosque where olive-pickers stood on ladders and flexed back the branches, their heads lost in leaves.

That night he approached her again, and she welcomed him. She undressed. She lay down, looking at him, holding his face between her hands as he moved in and out until it was not a part of his body moving inside her, but his whole being, when suddenly her eyes disappeared and there was a mouth screaming in terror again, and hands punching at him, beating his face, pushing him away.

She sprang away from him, collapsing against the wall.

"Tell me," he begged. "You must tell me."

She was vomiting her breath on the floor. He went to her and she held up her hands, sobbing. There was a knock at the door, but he didn't answer. He picked her up under the arms. "Catharine, tell me."

She shook her head. He had never seen such pain before. The colour had left, as though a bandage was falling away. Instead of a young woman of thirty-four, she had the bark cheeks of an old woman.

"No!"

The terror in her eyes appalled him. It was the terror of one of Penny's creatures. Catharine had met something in him which frightened her off, but what was it? In the outstretched silence, she looked at him. Her very being was pressed to her eyes, beating in silence against them, calling for help, sliding away.

"Come on." He guided her back to bed.

"I'm frightened," she said in a voice not much louder than a breath. "There's nowhere left to go."

He caressed her to sleep. At some point he woke. His arms were empty. She lay fully dressed on the floor. She allowed him to take off her shirt, her skirt. She stretched out under the sheet, her legs together, her back slanted from him. At last she spoke, and it was a hiss.

"When I wasn't with you, I annihilated you. I thought of reasons to destroy you."

"Why do that?"

"Oh, Tom, you don't understand. Feelings like these don't

disappear. You have to kill them, stamp on them, murder them."
Her words lacerated him. She wanted him to feel her pain, the
pain he had caused her to feel by loving him as she did. She
spoke over her shoulder. "Don't you see? I want to kill it. I want
to stop this unending lie."

Wavery sat up. "Catharine, you have to tell me." Everything
she was saying was making it impossible not to tell him. "Please,
can't I help you unlock this? Let me tell you over and over again
the only thing I can tell, what I told you last night. I love you."

She turned on her back. She had crossed some threshold of
pain and her breath was slower. "Thomas?" She twisted her
head. She had to say the words twice before he heard. "Hold
me." He did so and she began speaking, her voice separated
from her body as falteringly she revealed the wound that ran in
tree-rings to her core.

So it was that in the early hours of Monday morning Wavery
learned of the demons unearthed by their love. He had only
become conscious of Catharine at the moment he rescued her
from Queesal, but in fact she had been aware of him earlier
in the evening. Such an ordinary thing had triggered the attraction she felt for him, something ridiculous, nothing more than
the black paint mark from Penny's easel on Wavery's trouser
leg. Catharine had seen it across the room. Everyone in that
room had been so smart, so important, so sensitive to how
smart and important they were, but here was this man with
a dark disfiguring patch on his leg, and unaware of it. People
need to show they are successful, yet it is vulnerability which
draws love.

But it was more than that. The patch of blackness mesmerised
her. Ever since childhood she had felt the same colour louring
over an unexplored part of herself. And when they talked, she
felt at once that she could tell him about herself. Under his
protection she had felt able to start scissoring away at the vast
edge of her forgetfulness.

"In Lima, yes, I felt something. I didn't know what it was."

She found out what it was two months later, in Lisbon. That
night in her hotel room when Wavery had tied on the carnival

mask, he was blotting out her face with another mask, a military mask.

Catharine? The door knob turned.

There had been a birthday party for her sister. Suddenly she saw a table with bright coloured toys and she ran up to the table. Her movement caught his eye. He was talking to someone else's father. He placed his hand on her head. She had Chinese hair. He liked its texture. He ran his hand through it, feeling the hair. She was four. From the other rooms, children came running. She watched, unable to move, as they took the toys. Eventually, he let go of her hair. She threw herself at the table. There was one present left, the small metal model of a tank. She gave it to her sister.

The door opened. Catharine?

Her father's voice, the voice of a military man, a war hero, pleading.

"Catharine."

His fingers in her hair, the fingers which had urged men into battle and squeezed triggers and fastened about throats until his own men had to hold him back panting. His hands, enormous like a god, descending from her head. Smelling of cigarettes, like her toys, her hair. His massive fingers wettened by his tongue. His breath coming louder, smelling of peppermint because he had brushed his teeth.

"Catharine."

The stairs she would climb when her mother was away. The bed she occupied. The flesh she made swell in her mouth. The stickiness she felt on her face, could smell in her matted hair. The woollen balaclava that smothered her face so all she could see were the polished caps of his brogues. The father she loved at all other times because he was sweet and funny; whom she missed with an untranslatable longing when he died, having buried within herself everything that passed between them at the age of four and five and six and seven, until suddenly in her eighth year, when her mother took her daughters away to live in another house, his demands ceased.

Her lips trembled. She explained herself so badly. This happened before she could articulate. Her first language was this. This touch, this pain, this pain mixed with love, this intimate terror. "For thirty years I didn't remember, I didn't remember. It had faded to blank, gone underground, been thrust into the pit." Until the moment in Lisbon when through the mask she had seen Wavery and screamed. Because what she saw was not Thomas, but another man and what she felt was herself under him, his hands over her mouth, his body pressing down on hers, the massive nose between his legs between her legs, reaching up to her throat, her father whom she loved, shushing her, saying nothing had happened, her father whom she hated as she would hate Wavery because they were the same, indissoluble, and there was nothing that could ever in her mind separate Wavery's face from his. Whenever he touched her she would scream.

"I tried to deny it, Tom. I tried to tell myself this had never taken place. We were a good family. 'No, it's never happened,' I've said over and over. It's just me, inventing. But it's not an invention. It happened, and each time I think of it I need a day to recover."

"How could he?"

"Don't judge, Tom."

"It's a great art, not to sit in judgment."

"Tom . . ."

"I don't think I have it."

He lay away from her. He faced the window, the mountain skyline. He knew of no vocabulary with which to respond, and he knew there was something awful still to come. He turned back, holding her to him. "We'll slay those demons," he managed.

"You can't imagine. You can't imagine, Tom."

In Lima, when he had come towards her on Rita's patio, she had reached a turning point. It had stirred in her mind before and she realised it was there to be confronted. She could have slipped back into the mould of her pretence and buried her demon so deep she might have completed her life without disturbing it again. But circumstances had taken control. Wavery had protected her in precisely the way she should have been protected by her father, instead of the reverse. He'd protected her from humiliation. He had done the very thing her father hadn't done, and in return she had loved Wavery with the kind of love that demands absolute honesty.

"Does your husband know?"

"No. No. He doesn't know. He wants to adore me." Only Wavery knew. Her mother was dead and her father had blown his brains out in his seventy-second year.

She was weeping again, the tears falling stronger this time. "That's all I've done. From the beginning, that's all I've done. Smile and say yes, yes, he's wonderful, isn't he?" Sustaining the myth of her father, the great war hero. The myth of her husband, the brilliant businessman. Her own myth.

"Where's *my* reality, Tom?"

Her suffering annihilated him. Her head was hidden in her hair as she rocked from side to side. "I've never been a virgin, Tom. I never felt a virgin until I met you."

All the time he had known Catharine, this is what she had been struggling to solve. He felt numb. This is what had frightened her so much in Lisbon when the mask blotted him out, leaving him high and dry. She had needed his help, not his love. She had wanted him as a very other father figure, and what had happened? He had failed her on every count.

His numbness spread. He felt a different person. She stirred against him and he ceased to be Thomas Wavery. He was a father holding the child he'd never had. He was the war hero, wanting to staunch his mutilated spirit with her innocence. He didn't mean to hurt her. He sought her unquestioning love, that was all. He wanted her to return him to his own childhood, to a landscape uncratered by warfare.

Her fingers reached behind him, probing, digging, causing pain. The pain chimed with a feeling he had that was unbearable. She turned away, at the same time pressing herself to him. He responded, and together they went forward into the dark, mephitic earth. A cry dried on his lips. He thought: this is how death tasted.

In the morning she said, "Something terrible happened last night, didn't it?"

"I know."

"And it's worse than that."

He heard the fatality in her voice.

"I can't – I can't remind you of him. Don't tell me that."

"No, Tom, no, no . . . But I can't help it, there's something there. Can't you see, it's the same territory?".

"Every time I come near, you will scream?"

"I don't know, I don't know. I don't understand."

All she understood was that something inexpressible had been exhumed by her love for him. And pulling up her love to see what was growing, she had found this atrocious thing clinging to the roots, devouring them.

"It's no one's fault, Tom." But her eyes were empty.

There had been tighter security than usual in the port. He showed his diplomatic card. They walked onto the ferry. She clung to his arm and he returned the grip. He supported her up the gangway, coming to terms with the certain knowledge of why she must leave, why she must leave now.

She said, "We could have made a life together, couldn't we?"

He nodded. "Our garden in Sintra."

"Yes, yes, our garden in Sintra and everything, Tom. Everything else."

"Darling, I want –"

"Yes, darling, and I'll always want it too." The fog-horn blasted twice.

He pulled her to him. His hands sought her face and he held it, searching her eyes. "Catharine, I –"

He wanted to say, I'll help you, my darling. I'll do anything to help you. But no words came. He was part of the beast that had to be slain.

She saw his face and she said, "Last night I sought a companion to go up those stairs. An impossible wish. I've got to go up alone, haven't I? As I did all those years ago. Which is as it should be." She fetched a meagre smile, but her words were irrevocable.

The horn blasted again.

He said, "We won't see each other again."

"I don't think so. I love you, Tom. You do know that. I won't leave you feeling I haven't said anything?"

He could not speak and she lay her head against his, just as she had in Lisbon at the time of their first kiss. She moved away to let him walk down the gangway. He waved twice. She waved back, a quick rub of the hand. Then she turned, and then he knew that this time she would never come back.

Chapter Fifteen

IT WAS OVER. "Come," said Marie Amaral as they walked together along the Marina Española. She took Wavery's arm. "You must come and celebrate."

"If you don't mind, Marie."

"Nonsense," she said, and she led him under the awning into her son's café. "Tonight, you celebrate with us."

Several weeks had passed since Wavery's last visit to the café. He was surprised how sparkling clean it was. Mohamed's preparations to receive the eternally awaited owner had commenced a month before, but only gathered momentum during the week. He had wiped the dirt from the mirrors, polished the glass over Lieutenant Zamora's portrait, removed a spider from the nostrils of the Andean bull over the bar, waxed the stage where the General had three times won the Miss Dainty Ankles competition, beaten the red and gold curtain on which Ulysses drank to forget Calypso, replaced the dead light bulbs and taken a call from the owner at Lima airport. He assured Periclito everything was fine, that the whole town was indeed impatient to see him distinguish himself at the *"sensacional corrida de toros"*, that seats were passing hands at black market prices, that Señora Criado was very well, and the tunnel – how was the tunnel? Probably not very well, Mohamed had said, ducking his head but unable to see under the awning.

And now Mohamed waited to welcome his master.

Behind the bar, he was excited. He had left the bullring early, to be here well in advance of Periclito – and what had happened? At the exit Mohamed had walked into the Governor, followed

368

a step behind by his wife. As soon as he looked at Beatrice Menendez, Mohamed knew his search was at an end. At last, he had found Her. All year he had grabbed the shoulders of vexed or bewildered strangers to ask if they were "the Eyes". In this way he had addressed himself to the wife of a Canadian geminologist; a New Age traveller from Dijon who had been abandoned by her boyfriend on Playa Benitez; an albino ethnographer whose parents, yeomen farmers from Urcos, had brought her up since childhood wearing a canary-yellow wig; and someone who turned out not to be a girl at all but Mallorca's third greatest popstar.

But there was no time now to savour his victory. Here, coming through the doors, was Periclito! Here was the *triunfador de la feria*! He sat on the bar-counter, his white shirt rolled to the elbows, his fat little legs squeezed into matador's breeches, ordering Mohamed to serve free drinks to everyone.

Soon the café was warm with the herd-breath of drinkers. They were toasting Periclito's sacred *cojones*. They were raising their glasses to the matador, to the gory roan head above him, to the matadors and roan heads they saw in every spotless mirror.

The whole head!

President Zamora had responded to the crowd. He had rewarded the Earthquake not with the tail, not with an ear – but the whole head! He did not know if he had been correct, but who had ever seen such a blizzard of handkerchiefs?

Periclito lay one arm along Señora Criado's shoulder while with his other he stroked the tanned back of his stepsister, Rosita. He raised his hand from the cook's shoulder. Caution crept into his face. Let them not be carried away. Much had also depended on the bull. He raised his glass to the pillar where the bull's head had been suspended below that of Lieutenant Zamora. Two wires of blood dried on the bright glass beneath the neck flap. What a wind-drinker, eh!

They toasted the wind-drinker and on behalf of the animal Periclito accepted their toast. He wiped his mouth, beaming. But how well he himself had performed. His limp had vanished before those horns. Where his paunch had been, there was a hollow. The horns had respected him. They had torn away a tassel. Look! He lifted a leg. But five minutes later – five minutes, Criado! – where were those horns?

"The hollow of my hand!"

He rotated on the counter and reached behind. In his hand he held a gold-knobbed cane.

"So that's where it is!" exclaimed Genia Ortiz, at that moment entering the café accompanied by others from the Royal Box.

For the seventh bull Periclito had used Ernesto's baton as a *palillo* from which to hang his cape. He flexed it now as a sword. He beckoned Rosita. "Put your feet together, my darling!" He poised, the baton above her, while his left hand searched for a napkin. He had performed the *mariposa*, the butterfly, on the bull's nose! The bull had been no less astonished than his sister. "I landed the butterfly like this, and softly, softly I sang to him until the moment came when I did that." The baton descended down the length of her spine. It was approaching the waist-band of her dress when Genia Ortiz seized it.

"Thank you very much," said the conductor's widow.

Señora Criado asked, "What did you sing, Periclito?"

Periclito faced his sister. "Rosita! I sang one of your songs!" There was more applause, if less enthusiastic than before. He hugged her to him. "One of your *fados*, Rosita. Imagine! The bull was bewitched. Bewitched!"

"They should name a dish after you."

"A cassoulet," said Señora Criado.

A cassoulet! Periclito threw up his arms. He had almost forgotten. He propelled himself from the counter in the direction of the kitchen.

Wavery accepted a glass from Mohamed's tray.

Through the herd he saw Rosita, her head leaning back on a familiar shirt. Wavery looked again and caught Silkleigh's eye.

"*Ambasadoro!*"

On the diver's chest Virgil was still the frog boy.

370

"Tonight was to have been his party," Silkleigh told Rosita sadly. "In his new house."

"How are you, Silkleigh?" asked Wavery. He had not spoken to him in a fortnight.

Silkleigh released his grip on Rosita. He slipped from his stool. With great formality he shook Wavery's hand. "I am in what people with limited vocabularies would call a propitiatory mood."

"Have you been away?"

"I thought it best to absent me awhile. My people wanted a report. You know the score, old soul. First-hand, no nonsense, eyeball to eyeball."

Mohamed approached bearing a tray. Wavery took another drink. He asked, "What happened to Panteco?"

Silkleigh, placing a thumb and a finger on either side of his nose, converted a smile into a scowl. "Chippy bugger's been sent to Rabat." He darted his eyes at Rosita, speaking to a worried Zamora. She was telling him, "But I saw her just now – with Asunción."

"To look for Cochabamba, old soul," whispered Silkleigh, and he tugged at his eye.

As soon as she heard the name, Rosita's eyes became mutinous. She tried to move away, but Silkleigh threw an arm about her neck.

"*Nada* in the larder. Honestly. All mink and no knickers. Not like my *kleine* . . ." Silkleigh bent his mouth to her ear.

"*Don't* use that word." Her eyes dilated in anger. "It's too special."

"That's why I used it," said Silkleigh. With his lips he brushed her cheeks with a touch as light as spray. "Darling Rosita. *Si kantas plej bele*. What you feel about someone when they're not with you is the correct –"

"How's the book?" asked Wavery.

"Yes," said Rosita, withdrawing. "How *is* the book, Silkleigh?"

Silkleigh glanced up. "Actually," he said, smoothing down his T-shirt, "I'm glad you asked." He looked around, but he could not avoid himself. "The thing is, when I thought more about it, the title, I'm not saying it was bad, not at all, but . . . well, it simply wasn't *right*."

"Silkleigh!" Periclito appeared before them. He held two dishes in each hand. "Eat some cassoulet."

Out of the glare of the coloured lights, Zamora occupied Ghanem's chair beneath the television set. Two tables had been joined together and he sat at the head.

He had taken off his cardigan and was talking to Asunción, who held Tromso's hand under the table, about Pablo.

"*Querida*," he was saying, "if you let him do what he wants, he'll have no one to blame but himself – and that can create enormous problems afterwards." To himself he thought, Could it really be in ten years time that Asunción and Tromso will be sitting on a sofa saying to the young man between them, "So you want to be a hairdresser?"

"Cassoulet!" Periclito arrived with more plates. He set them down and turned off the television.

"Hey!" said Tromso.

"Talk to your wife, Tromso." Periclito, chucking Asunción under the chin, kissed her full on the mouth. An olive pip distilled on his lips. He spat it into the ashtray and drew back two chairs.

"Mohamed!" He pointed to those in the room who lacked a full glass. "Maman!" he called on his way to the kitchen. "Rosita!"

Periclito's sister had removed her gold braid belt, her black top. She wore only a dark slip and a girdle of red silk, folded twice about her hips. A long amber necklace bounced against her bare stomach as she moved in small steps onto the stage. In the coloured lights her face was expressionless.

Gallo followed behind. When she half turned to indicate his chair, the lights glinted on something shiny in her hand.

David's teapot! thought Marie Amaral and her heart pounded so fast against her chest she could not breathe.

"Rosita!" called Periclito, careering from the kitchen with

two more steaming dishes. Still he could not see his stepsister. He had seen her talking to Silkleigh, but the diver stood alone. Periclito was scanning the tables around the pillar when he heard the sound. His head jerked towards the television set he had turned off a moment before. "Tromso!" he was about to bellow. But it wasn't the television. It came from behind him, from the stage. He spun round, a plate of hot cassoulet in each hand.

Until that moment, no one else was alert to the commotion. Several of those nearest the stage, when they heard Gallo's portentous guitar chords, lowered their heads and groaned. But the café was too noisy, too crowded for those in the middle of the room to know what was going on.

It can still be nipped in the bud, thought Periclito, lurching forward. "Rosita. . . .." She sipped from her glass, then placed it on the floor beside the teapot. She cleared her throat, nodding to Gallo. She had eyes for no one. With a stamp of her foot she stepped into the red and blue light.

"*Não peças demais à vida*," she began.

It was not until near the end of the first verse that she caught the café's ear. Her voice began low, finding its balance, finger-tipping its way through talk of Periclito's performance, between the back-slaps and the toasts and the sound of Pablo's knife against the beer bottle.

"Pom, pom, pom," said Silkleigh to himself at the bar, something furrowing his brow.

This is ridiculous, thought Periclito, desperate. He saw his victory snatched away, all because of his stepsister's crucifying disregard for harmony.

"Quite out of this world," Zamora was saying, rhapsodising over his cassoulet.

And now the voice breasted its way into the open, struggling to free itself of everything it had been taught by the conductor, so that Zamora hesitated over his fork and Periclito forgot the hot plates in his hands and Pablo looked up from the beer label he was mutilating and Asunción wrested her gaze from Tromso and Marie Amaral felt the same profound shudder as Genia

Ortiz, whose first protective instinct was to grip her white stick, and together they all looked towards the stage where a small woman, growing less nervous by the second, was singing *fado*.

It was unlike anything anyone had heard. It was no longer the voice of Rosita Amaral, Ernesto's student. It poured out raw, like blood, as if announcing itself for the first time, unadorned, honest. It was a voice smelted by despair. It sang of shipwrecked sailors and a dead bull, but to all who heard it, the voice seemed to understand the exact measure of their own pain, reaching into the most locked-away parts of themselves, insisting they forget what only minutes before they had been saying, thinking, drinking, eating – and listen, because in the perfect expression of her pain there was affirmation too.

She stepped down from the stage, her necklace swinging in a wild improvised dance. "But Rosita . . ." Periclito tried to whisper as she passed him, his chins descending in silent lips to his throat. She revolved to face her brother, dancing her way backwards through the silent tables to the bar.

"Rosita," whispered Silkleigh, prodding Mohamed in the back with his glass to stand aside and let him see. Mohamed, misjudging the mood, stumbled forward and squatted behind her in the narrowing space. His hands made circles, outlining her bottom, mimicking the motions of her stomach, until Silkleigh kicked him out of the way.

The song was over. In the silence, Silkleigh found his voice. "Bravo! Bravo! Rosita!" Soon everyone in the café was chanting. They tapped the floor in an accelerating rhythm of feet, shouting "Ro-si-ta! Ro-si-ta! Ro-si-ta!"

She danced through the last of the chairs to the bar where Silkleigh and Wavery were standing. Slowly, she turned to face the two men. Wavery could smell the sweat on her breast.

"That. Was. Magic," said Silkleigh.

Under the television set, Periclito set down his steaming plates, howling.

The drink was working its extravagant effect on Wavery. Magic. Love. They had nothing to do with knowledge, he reminded himself at the bar. They were illusions. Just as his career had been an illusion. Just as Abyla was an illusion, and all the people in this café who lived on top of each other, not knowing about each other, only Silkleigh knowing, Silkleigh the mirror, piecing together the shards of their lives, holding up the result, catching the multi-coloured lights and shadows, saying "Hey! That's you, isn't it, *kara mia*? What do you think?"

Wavery drank again. The alcohol encouraged him to think of Catharine and he felt panic. The certainty of life without her was intolerable, as unendurable as life in the diplomatic service. There was nothing left he wished to serve.

Wavery looked up and in the mirrors he saw Lieutenant Zamora. The soldier advanced towards him and retreated. Everywhere Wavery looked he was there. And again there. Hand inside his jacket. Feet on the carpet. The Hero of Africa. The Death-Betrothed. Receding, advancing. His head under a lopsided halo. Severed from his body. Painted by Sandra the Rapist. Painted by Emilio's mother. Painted by Penny.

"I have to go," he said. But no one was listening.

"Maman," said Periclito. "I must get rid of these mirrors,"

"Where is Clotilda?" Zamora was asking anxiously. Through the crowd he had seen Silkleigh. The diver couldn't possibly be his daughter's lover, not the way he was holding Rosita. But if it wasn't Silkleigh, who was it? He called out, "Has anybody seen Clotilda?"

In the residence Halima was waiting for Wavery.

She opened the oven and drew out a tray, basting the duck according to Penny's instructions on the white card. She also scattered onto it a few drops of orange flower water. Her *maaz-ahr* was known to cure everything from anger to hysteria. Before she went home she always took care to leave a bowl in his bedroom. So far it had not been able to soothe her master's face.

The water hissed into steam.

Where was he?

*   *   *

375

Unobserved, Wavery left the Café Ulises. Outside, the sky over Abyla had reddened with the Lieutenant's blood and the sea become green with his laurels. Wavery crossed the Marina Española. The breeze had burrowed away somewhere and all that harnessed him to earth was the sound of the surf crashing on Playa Benitez.

Inside the kiosk the telephone began ringing. Without thinking, Wavery opened the door. The interior had been recently painted, although there was some fresher grafitti. He picked up the receiver.

"Hello?"

It was a strange voice, from a long way away. A woman's voice. Asking for Periclito in Spanish.

"One minute, I'll get him – Hello?" But the line went dead. He waited to see if she would ring again. He had waited like this for two weeks, waiting for a call he knew would not come. He had forbidden himself to leave the residence. On the few occasions anyone telephoned, he made it clear that he needed the line to be cleared. At the same time he felt a contradictory emotion. If ever Catharine did telephone, he wished passionately to deny her his presence. His only power was his absence. He had become absent even to himself. Depression had overtaken him so completely that on meeting his reflections in the Café Ulises just now, he had been shocked to discover he was a material thing.

The one person eager to speak with him had been Queesal. "I am sorry it's been called off," said the man who could not cry. "To be honest, Tom, I think it's for the best. It gives us time to prepare things properly." But in view of recent events, it had been decided to recall Wavery to London. The decision had been taken at the highest level. "They're promoting you," said Queesal, who had never sounded so reasonable. "I'm afraid it means you'll have to forfeit your knighthood, but the PUS is talking about a CMG." Wavery would in due course receive the official notification, but it was Queesal's pleasure to inform him he had been appointed a Sensitivity Officer.

"Sir Derek's on holiday at the moment," said Queesal, whose

report to the PUS had concluded with a recommendation that Thomas Wavery should never serve abroad again. "But he was especially keen I passed on to you his personal congratulations."

In the kiosk, Wavery listened to the surf, waiting for the woman to call again. His hand reached out and then drew back. He knew what could happen if he touched that telephone, what number he would ring. How many times in the last fortnight had he nearly completed her number, had he been prevented from doing so because he foresaw the outcome?

He found five coins and dialled a number.

"Penny?"

"Tom."

"How are the tortoises?"

"Are you all right?"

"I rang to congratulate you." The announcement of her marriage had arrived that morning.

"Oh, Tom, that's very sweet of you."

"Aren't you thrilled?"

"Don't be silly, you know I'm thrilled."

"And Patrick?"

"I don't know if he's thrilled."

Wavery overheard, "Darling, of course I'm thrilled."

"I'll pass you over to Patrick."

"Tom, hello."

"We've never met, or not for a long time."

"I was just telling Penny I was thrilled."

"Tom." It was Penny again. "It's me again. I'm sorry about –" But the pips interrupted her. Wavery said, "Hang on."

He fed in another coin. "Penny. Penny?" There was a click into silence. He put down the receiver. He had three more coins. He dialled again and a machine answered. "We are unable to connect you. Please try later."

Wavery replaced the receiver and opened the kiosk door. A few yards away a white Renault was parked against the pavement, its engine running. Only one headlight was working. A young woman sat in the passenger seat. Her face was bowed, screened by a waterfall of fair hair. He could see that she was crying. The driver was attempting to embrace her when he became aware of Wavery. In the sudden lights of a lorry passing, Wavery recognised the white suit, the gold neck-chain and the agitated face of Abyla's departing Governor. The girl raised her head. It was Senator Zamora's younger daughter, Clotilda.

Wavery gave an awkward salute. Menendez waved back. The car drove away.

Inside the kiosk the telephone was ringing. Wavery walked along the esplanade to escape the sound. He went on walking until he no longer heard it. There was only the faint tap-tap-tapping of windows in Calle Silvestre and the sound of the surf on Playa Benitez. He was a long way past his residence.

He stepped onto the beach.

At the end of the beach, under Monte Hacho's military cliff, the turtle lay panting. She had found her virgin sand. She had laid her eggs. But the strain showed on her face. She moved her head from side to side, scraping the sand from tumorous growths beneath her eyes. She was preparing to make her cumbersome return to the sea, but her stomach ached from the exertions of the last hour, from the nylon fishing line she had eaten, from the oil she had swallowed, which made it difficult to dive.

She sensed a movement on the shore. Her heart pounded against the eggs protected by her mossy, imperfect carapace. She jerked her head above the little ridge she had built for herself.

Nothing. The shushing of the waves. The call of a gull in the cliff. The calm-again sea.

Suddenly. A beat on the sand, not her heart. A pair of legs, two arms, a hand.

The hand grasped her shell at its bitten edge, turning her upside down, twisting her neck, so that all she could see was the sky and a face as vacant as the sky.

The scuffle on the shore had frightened the ibis. The birds cowered on their ledge, lifting their long red bills and shaking their wings. The noise woke the chick. He straightened into the wind and tottered on his little webbed feet towards his parents. In the gloom the elder birds saw a goshawk eating something on the sand and for a moment they relaxed. But now they heard another, louder, noise. They tensed in their nests, feathers erect and quivering on their hind-ruffs, their necks stretched out, immobile.

Below them, Ghanem the Mute stiffened too. He pressed his stomach to the sand beside the olive carcass, his sack of eggs. He watched the shoreline, alert. On the beach there stood a man, possibly a sentry.

Wavery had come to a low barbed-wire fence. He climbed over it, catching his trousers on the wire. He inspected the tear, and sat down on the sand, cursing. The sand on this side was scored with the tiny white tracks of crab shells where the night herons had regurgitated their pellets. It was otherwise crisp and clean and unpitted by footprints.

Wavery peered tipsily at the sea. The drink had created in his mind a Chauen bazaar of images. As the last of the sun's rays died away to the left beyond La Mujer Muerta, he experienced a curious sensation. It seemed to Wavery that from the moment he had stepped over the wire he had come to inhabit one of Penny's paintings. She had picked an orange blob-buoy from a tree outside the Consulate and rolled it between the folds of Zamora's newest cardigan. But she didn't know what to call it. She didn't know how to go on. It's one of those paintings she turns upside down, he thought, as he took off his shoes, then his socks.

He rolled up the torn trouser legs and pushed himself to his feet. In the Straits there was the pulse of a fisherman's carbide lamp. Beyond were the embers of Gibraltar. A large cruise ship was sailing towards the harbour, its lights pricking the bay at neat intervals.

Europe, thought Wavery. Where Catharine was. Catharine, who had had to give up the one thing that might have redeemed her life.

The herring gulls called her name. "Catharine, Catharine."

379

He thought, She has been liberated by her cries in the night. Now they are out, in the fresh air, she is free. But where do I go?

The wind breathed over the canvas, arousing the waves, flaking the paint.

"Catharine, Catharine."

He heard her calling him and Wavery, holding his shoes, shouted back. "Catharine!"

His voice was amplified by the cliff behind. His shout reached the birds crouching on their ledge. Alarmed, the ibis rose. They flew from their nests in short, bat-like flaps, their bodies against the wind. Then, free-falling in an arcing swoop they passed straight over Wavery's head. They had nowhere to go. They had flown to the edge of the world and now they headed out over the water, low and hunched and chasing their shadows with fast, squeaking wings.

The waves tumbled to catch them. One wave, larger than the rest, tossed itself at the birds. The ibis climbed abruptly to avoid it, quickening their beat, but the wave had divided them. They lost height and clambered back into the air. Two flew onwards, skimming the Straits towards the cruise ship, calling *"kay, kay, kay."* Four veered west, into the guttering sunset.

Wavery saw the flash of their wings in the dark like fleeting ghosts. Quickly, he undressed. He had been swimming for the past ten years, twenty lengths a morning. He must have more than measured the distance of the Straits. He was a fit, healthy man.

He was naked when he stood up. He felt the wind on his stomach.

The gulls called him.

Inside the Café Ulises they had finished their toasts to Periclito. They were drinking to Genia Ortiz on the eve of her return to the Motherland. Now that both son and baton had been restored she decided she was after all enjoying herself. She was happy to see Tromso, who had not changed at all, not to judge from the exasperation on Asunción's face. But what about Balnasharki? Would her family home resonate with emptiness?

So she sat, cold and a little tired and a little fretful about the journey.

Marie Amaral had not noticed the cold until now. She was squeezed between Zamora and her son. For the first time she had been able to enjoy a moment of calm with Periclito.

"Just look how fat you are."

He laughed, nuzzling his nose against her ear, and she knew what he was thinking. This afternoon in the ring he had met his reflection at last.

"How's your love life, *mon chéri*?"

"The bed is too small a theatre, Maman," he said, blowing on his scalded hands. "My love life? It's pathetic."

She could not help her impatience. "Periclito, that's true of everybody. What happened to the woman with the sick husband?"

"I had to leave her, Maman. She had six Siamese cats. It wasn't something a gentleman could bear."

"Periclito, there's someone I want you to meet." She looked about. But she could not see the Consul General.

"Later, Maman, later," said Periclito, slipping from his chair. First he must see to the pudding.

Across the table Silkleigh was telling Rosita, "I've been thinking." He pushed the hair from her ears. "A great book is a great evil . . ." Her eyes nibbled at him. Her serene face said, I'm happy. It's so lovely to be happy. She said, "You're full of swamp gas, Silkleigh." He tickled her stomach. She seized his hand. She fanned out the fingers. Tonight, thought Marie Amaral, she would become gold under their touch.

But how cold it was suddenly. Marie Amaral slipped the cardigan from the back of Teodoro's chair over her shoulders. Zamora was saying something and she came into the shelter of his voice. No one understood as he did this tongue of rock, despite its lack of space, its lack of tenderness. This magic teapot into which everything was stirred and out of which everything poured anew.

Zamora turned to her. Periclito's stew had caused him to forget all about Clotilda. "Isn't this cassoulet delicious, Marie?"

he said. It had to be better even than the mackerel sauce of Carteia! "Isn't this absolutely delicious!" He looked her directly in the eye. There was chicory on his breath.

Marie Amaral heard the violent flap of the awning outside. She bent her head to look. She saw a surly sky, waves bucking and birds heading west. She murmured, no longer thinking of the British Consul General, "It's the black wind, Teodoro."

Out of nowhere, as if uncurling from deep within the earth, the *levante* had returned.

The black wind nosed the streets, a lost animal clattering the lids of the garbage bins in the Calle Zamora, puffing at the palms in Plaza de Los Reyes and denuding each tree as if it were an ageing chrysanthemum in one of Marie Amaral's buckets. Unimpeded, it galloped along the Marina Española, scuffing its hooves on the sea.

Down on the beach, the waves broke about Wavery's knees, stroking him into the sea. He dipped his fingers in the surf. The water was warm. It gloved his fingers in a bluish-gold glow. He stepped forward and the waves caressed his stomach. He pushed out, swimming in a restrained breast-stroke. His breathing was regular. The glow settled on his chest. He kicked out. With every movement, the phosphorescence grew brighter, until it would have been bright enough to read by. Soon his arms were turtle-shelled with colour. An aureole shone about his face.

"Catharine!" called the gulls. He heard their urgent cry. He was swimming towards her. She was only fourteen miles away.

A wave removed his glasses.